Shadows o

(The man who refused to die)

Sequel to Edge of the Rainbow

a novel by Maria Bojanitz

This book is dedicated to the memory of my mother Edna, my father Alfred.

I thank my close friends for their interest, encouragement, and patience in waiting for this book to emerge.

I am grateful to Alfred Neugebauer, of the Hanswille family of Neubeckum, who made various documentary enquiries on my behalf. Furthermore, I am grateful to them for accommodating me during several visits, enabling me to explore places of personal and historic interest.

Part 3 Onward to England

CHARACTERS

The Ztoanjib Family (several of whom feature in Edge of the Rainbow)

Alfred: central character.

Stefan: Alfred's father.

Mathilda: Alfred's sister.

Joanna and Fritz: Alfred's sibling twins.

Kate, Tobias, Freddie: Alfred's Sister, brother-in-law, and baby nephew.

Stephanie: Alfred's sister.

Extended Family:

Berni: Cousin to Alfred's deceased mother Marija.

Helga and Trudi: Berni's daughters.

Bernhart Nurville: Great uncle to Alfred and his siblings.

Annalisa Nurville: Great aunt to Alfred and his siblings.

Ida: Stephan's Housekeeper and later wife.

Sylvia: Ida's daughter.

Milorad: Stephanie's fiancé and later husband.

Lenka: Alfred's Aunt.

Mentioned family members: Aaron, Thomas, Wilhelm, another Wilhelm, Manfred.

Benedictine Trappist Monks:

Father Spyridon: Abbot.

Father Benedict: A monk who works closely with the abbot.

Brother Ivan: A monk.

Brother Misha: Novitiate.

Brother Andre: Novitiate.

Brother Philip: Novitiate

Brother Alfred: Novitiate and central character.

Various unnamed monks.

Brother Martyn: Deceased blind monk.

Other religious characters:

Mother Superior: Red Cross worker.

Sister Monica: Red Cross worker.

Missionary net- work:

Father Franz Augustus: Leader of the missionary team.

Alfred: Missionary former novice monk and central character.

Mr Robert Rundmann: Mission House master.

Eilish Rundmann: Wife of Robert Rundmann, in-house mission helper.

Sergi Rundmann: Mr Rundmann's nephew.

Mr Jaager: Electrical shop manager.

Manfred: Young mission worker.

Werne: Young mission worker.

Mrs Tiveresky: Link missionary, helping victims in transit.

Mr and Mrs Roensky: Safe house providers for victims in transit.

German residents of Belgrade:

Cecil Nettlebaum: German Jew.

Herr Stromitz: Head man at The German Embassy in Belgrade.

Gisella Schein: Herr Stromitz's secretary.

Other characters of Lubljiana and Belgrade:

Mrs Nijinsky: Landlady.

Mrs Hand: Landlady.

Mr and Mrs Alexandra Paverosky: Guest house residents.

Isobel and Anna: Guest house residents.

Leonard and Lauretta Moniuszko: A married couple.

Omer Moniuszko: Their ill son (who has five younger siblings).

Paulo: Restaurant manager at the Grand Hotel.

Cynthia: Chamber maid at the Hotel

Garth: Hotel worker

Catholic Priest: Of a church in Ljubljana.

Hotel Staff: Bell Boy, door man, young waiter.

Police sergeant: and police officers.

Sergeant Gora: Night sergeant.

Marco, Sylvester, Gora: Police Officers.

Red- Cross workers and their mortuary attendant.

 An un-named general: cooperating with The Red Cross.

Passport officers

German Characters:

Cadet recruits

Erika Stein: Alfred's long-standing friend and fiancé.

Marta and Matthias: Erika's parents.

Peter: Stefan's friends.

Amelia: Peter's wife.

Mentioned characters: Peter, and Amelia's baby daughter-Klarissa, woman -farmer in Graz region.

American Soldiers:

Sergeant: An American Jew,

Jones (American soldier)

Two unnamed black American soldiers: Whose bravery and Christian compassion is known only to God and to the descendants of the protagonist, who have been given life because of their tremendous act of love.

French Characters:

Injured young woman: Patient, on a Red Cross plane.

Dr Pettiff: French Doctor.

Mrs Angelique Prunier: His loyal housekeeper.

French based receptionist of German army base.

Army medics

French Mademoiselles: Young women of Cherbourg.

Characters in Poland:

Polish Jews: Starving Ghost like figures in and around the shells of buildings.

Hospital -ward sister and various doctors including a Nazi sympathiser.

Various patients: including Alfred and a traumatised air pilot.

German residents of Beckum and Neubeckum:

Morag Bertenhause: Captive victim of the Nazi officers.

Susie Swarz: Captive victim of Nazi officers.

David Reichmann: Musical student.

Millie Weiss: Student

Baron Weiss and Lady Weiss: Parents of Millie.

Cyril Weissenbaum: Student.

Matthias Müller: Student.

Billy Braun: Student.

Sarah Klein: Orphaned child of Neubeckum.

Wilhemn Klein and his wife: Bomb victims.

Sarah's siblings: Heinz, Freda, Gretchen, Emile,Wolfgang: Bomb victims.

A warden: War time person officiating after bombing raids.

. Sarah's **friends:** Anne Marie and her mother Frau Kemmner.

Victims: Of air raid bombing on an air raid shelter.

Survivor: Elderly guardian to a boy.

Holocaust victims: Samantha, Elijah, boy with small head, girl with withered arm.
A compassionate Nazi officer, and others.

Gretchen: Compassionate woman within the 'Joy Division' establishment.

Mentioned character: Alfred's former infant teacher Frau Breitenbach

German Officers and others of authority

Captain Schnell: Riding Instructor.

Captain Scharfmann: Nazi Officer.

Sergeant Minden: Officer in WW2.

Sergeant Bauermann: Officer in WW2

Sergeant Trapp: Officer from Schwarzenberg.

Sergeant Korff: Aachen based officer.

Dr Heike: Nazi Doctor.

Colonel Trapp: An officer of the Cologne regiment.

Waldmann: Officer and sadist in the 'Joy Division'.

Large unnamed officer: Frequenter of the same establishment.

Gretchen: Secret victim supporter within the same establishment.

German officials: Heydrich, unnamed Colonel at Court Martial, General Schleiben, General Hennreck.
Dimitric (Red army officer)

German soldiers:

Rupert Reich: Neubeckum resident and war time recruit.

Helmut Werner, Edward, Werner, Lofty, Larry, Harold, Tobias: Cadets at Aachen.

Martyn Schmidt: Soldier of the Cologne regiment.

Georgo: Train driver in Russia.

Leonard Weiss: Soldier in Alfred's sub group.

Max, Paul: Companions of Alfred in war torn regions.

Prisoners of War:

Klauss Larsman, Emile Schwartz,Martyn Feldmann, Paul Stuckmann, Proffesor Stephan Schmidt, Max, Paul, Arno, Emile, Hans, Hermann,Karl, Doctor Joseph Knash, Fritz, Kurt Schmidt, Josef, Booby, Heinrich,Manfred.

Scottish Characters

Commander Mc Bride: In charge of the Prisoner of war camp in Scotland.

Deacon Mc Angus: A minister of the prisoner of war church (Kirk)

Amy Mc Farlane: A musician for the church (Kirk).

English Characters:

Ellen: Alfred's fiancé and later wife.

George: Ellen's father.

Daisy Hornsworthy: Ellen's aunt.

Harriett: Ellen's sister.

Bertram: Ellen's brother.

June: His wife.

Missionary Doctor.

Hilda: Ellen's friend.

Mary: Ellen's aunt.

Maude: Ellen's aunt.

Ivy Swift, Albert Swift and their daughters Susan (aged 10) and Rachel a little older: villagers of Steerton.

Dave: Steerton child.

Reverend Hywell: Steerton Parish Priest.

Miss Elsie Frances: Ellen's friend.

Short man: Of Steerton church choir.

Marcia: Farmhouse assistant.

Farmer- Farringdon.

John: His four-year-old son.

Tamsin: Land girl.

Gerald: Farmhand.

Jo: Old man of the village.

Joe: Ellen's boss and best man.

Alice: his wife.

Colonel Sharp (Sharpy): Reverend Hywell's friend.

Wedding Guests:

Best man Joe and wife Alice, bridesmaid Susan Swift and her parents.

Wedding host: Aunt Daisy Hornsworthy.

Other relatives: Hariett, Mary and Phyllis Perry, Percy, and Flo, Will and his daughter Linda, Emilia and George, Maude, Nel and family, Maurice, wife Colleen, and baby daughter Bernice.

Friends: Elsie, Annie, Nada, Joyce. The Pittman's,,Mr Eves,Mr Piccin Ewue, Mr and Mrs Redfern, Mr, and Mrs Mirrosh, Mr Thomas. Reverend and Mrs Hywell.

Many passing characters feature as do animals, many of whom who are to be highly regarded for their loyalty, love and suffering within humankind's war fields.

"There were once five and twenty tin soldiers; they were all brothers for they had been born of the one old tin spoon."

The hardy tin Soldier
Hans Christian Anderson

Sketch Map

Based on a true story, this sequel follows on from my first novel Edge of the Rainbow that began in Serbia. In this second novel the aftermath of The Great War briefly subsides. However, some individuals, whose memories and hearts refuse to heal, are set upon misplaced revenge. New unrest emerges and over the course of time, another world-war erupts.

Lives are cruelly disrupted and unbelievable inhumanity emerges: Fascism rises physically strong.

In poignant contrast, quietly without a murmur, God's work continues in the hearts of those who truly serve him. Selflessness is at war with selfishness.

As we move on through time and history, good and bad people are revealed within various organisations. Uniforms do not necessarily symbolise the hearts of those who wear them. A war of light and darkness runs parallel to physical war, created by misguided humans.

All that the human can sink to happens in this novel and all that the human can aspire to takes place. As the author, I am also a reader moved to tears and raised to laughter at various stages of the story.

It has been no quick process authoring this novel that recreates through several war-torn countries, the tremendous, impossible journey, of a great little man, a real-life character, whose racial background confused those who needed to apply a label of racial identification on every human within Germany and the lands they invaded. This novel embraces a story of a man of faith, who, against the odds-on numerous occasions, walked on the edge of death and who refused to die.

Part One

Journey from the Abbey

Chapter 1

The Abbey (1935)

Seated in a large leather chair, Father Spyridon, Abbot of Dienesperg Abbey, crossed his feet and wiggled his long toes. He relished the smooth, comfortable sandals expertly crafted by Brother Martin. The young man standing nearby observed the tall abbot's unruly lichen-textured white hair, a feature bringing him into biblical dimensions. Beneath his calm exterior a prophet like vitality radiated into the atmosphere. "Do sit down Alfred" he said, and opened his palm towards a carved chair. As the candidate, Alfred, sat down, he noticed the abbot's green-grey eyes home in on something beyond the ancient leaded window. Following the direction of his gaze he observed, out in the garden, two monks disputing some issue, rather than tend to flower beds. With discerning glance, the abbot commented, "It is their task is to complete the garden before vespers."

As he spoke, he leaned back into his chair; his casual posture helped Alfred's interview tension disperse. At a quick scan of the abbot's face, Alfred guessed he was in his mid-fifties. In Father Spyridon's return of a momentary glance Alfred felt the spiritual man's gift of discerning. What he did not realize, was that he also had the gift.

Turning his attention to the room he studied the detail of the surprisingly comfortable carved-chair he had been offered. He noted a questioning tone in the abbot's voice as he said, "You look surprised."

"I was thinking about this chair. I imagine the wood carver to have had the contours of the human form in mind. Even the doves, on the end of the arm rests, fit under the hands."

"It was carved out by one of the brothers, who a year ago left us for his final home. In this life he was blind."

"That's amazing; to his credit it's remarkably comfortable."

2

"He wanted to illustrate that forms and beings that appear uncomfortable can have a mystical capacity for offering strong support. Furthermore, the idea presents us with a perception of how things that appear smooth and comfortable can sometimes project hidden discomforts, far removed from the centrality of God."

"Through his hands, the monk reveals a great insight for seeing both spiritually and physically," Alfred replied.

Close by, several large, dust free books, lined the otherwise dusty book-case. Amongst the books Alfred noticed three Bibles, one Cyrillic, one German and the other, Latin. Above the book case was a large framed impressive picture of Christ on the cross. Not the dead Christ but Christ in his par-eschatological state; as the crowned king, the great high priest, departing from the cross. The more Alfred looked at it, the more he perceived it to be a prophetic icon, a resurrection perspective of the crucifixion.

Quietly observing, Father Spyridon asked, "This morning you mentioned a photograph and message from your brother Witold in July of 1929?"

"Yes, it was redirected from Neubeckum."

"May I ask what your brother wrote?"

"Yes, it was 'Remember the French Foreign Legion, these are my comrades. Six months later we received news he had been killed by a stray bullet in a Moroccan desert."

Following a prayerful pause Father Spyridon replied, "It was good you heard from him. He had not forgotten you as you had thought. He seems to use the word 'remember' in a prophetic sense. Do you agree?"

Astounded that the abbot had noticed the word prophetic Alfred asked himself '*Is he a mind reader*?' At this stage he was unaware how his spirituality was being tested.

"Now that you mention it, I think it does. Our Lord used the word 'remember' at the last supper when he was about to die. Witold was a tolerant and compassionate brother who knew he was risking his life by joining the legion."

"He remains your brother. Death is but a small divide, but it was sad he was only eighteen."

In steady tone he added, "This is the moment to conclude our meeting today. We will continue at the same time next week."

3

"Thank you, Father."

***

As Alfred walked along the courtyard, a monk coming alongside said, "Alfred I am Brother Benedict. I will show you the room you have been allocated."

"Thank you, brother."

Alfred followed him under ancient arches and across a lawn. The building they were entering was recent, having been built in the late nineteenth century.

Halfway along a white washed corridor, Brother Benedict took a key from his habit pocket. As the monk unlocked the door, Alfred observed his small room with a crucifix hung on a nail above a narrow bed. Habitually he bowed his head to the suffering Christ conveyed in the carved image. A white tie belt had been placed on the rough-weave bed cover. Tidily arranged on the bedside table was a Bible, prayer book and honey-combed, wax candle, set in a wooden candlestick. Recitative like, Brother Benedict chanted, "Supper will be at seven, giving you time to change into your habit before you come to the chapel."

With penetrating glance, he emphasised, "You will hear the chapel bell five minutes before evening prayer. Three other novices, recognisable by their hoodless habits, will be present."

"Thank you, brother," Alfred replied as the monk departed.

***

As he looked out onto allotments backing onto a stretch of woodland, he noticed the same two brothers he had observed near the abbot's room. The stance of the over-weight, muscular monk dominated; the other, slight in stature, youthful, dutifully listened. At a second glance the monks had gone.

Distractedly he flicked through the pages of the Bible, and randomly stopped at the virgin's song in St Luke's Gospel. *Magnificat anima mea Dominus; et exaultavit spiritus meus in deo Salvatore meo,quia respexit humilita tern ancilae suse!* he read aloud, and mentally translated it into his own Serb- Croat language:

My soul doth magnify the Lord and my spirit hath rejoiced in Christ my saviour, for he hath regarded the lowliness of his handmaiden.

4

He imagined Mary's perplexity and joy as she conceived the son of God by means of a spiritual happening. In a personal whisper, as if aiming to make thoughts materialize, he said, "It was a miracle whereby the spiritual body expressed its supremacy by uniting in divine love and by manifesting that love in the conception of a unique and divine human form. Such love can break through the laws of nature. We imagine our physical body to be our real body but St Paul tells us that our heavenly body is the true body. That pure body should govern our mortal state. We should not be governed by worldly passions, on the other hand the letters of St Paul were written before the gospels, and I wonder if St Luke tries to incorporate Paul's concept of the spiritual body into the context of the conception and birth of Christ, but I dare not say so. Perhaps it truly did happen as written. Do such thoughts belong here in this place?"

***

The following week Father Spyridon, seated in his arm chair, scratched his well-defined nose. He looked out the window where the Brothers Misha and Ivan should have been working. As on the previous occasion some heated debate was in progress. Drawing in the invisible telescope of mental observation, the abbot's mind returned to the room. With a trace of compassion he said, "Following on from your discussion with Brother Benedict a few days ago, does your spine continue to trouble you?"

"A little, and as you can see, I am shorter than I should be" Alfred explained.

As the abbot retorted "Not conspicuously so" he noted a flame of hope ignite in Alfred's eyes.

"Thank you, Father."

"Are there any problems?"

"A few; my ribs could do with more space, and when I am under pressure I can black out. Doctors believe it due to the spinal injury being close to the spinal cord."

In fatherly tone the abbot replied, "Well my son, now it is you who is only eighteen, but there's time for the healing hand of God to work in your earthly life. How did you and your family manage when you arrived in Belgrade? You must have felt the loss of your mother deeply."

5

"Yes, we were stunned. For a long time, nothing seemed real. My father was shocked to discover how things had changed. He learned that two years prior to my mother's death, his mother had died. We children were sad because we had hoped to get to know her. I am told that my Uncle Thomas had by then become Lord Mayor of Belgrade, or at least somewhere in that region. Uncle Aaron, who is still at the farm, was by now married, and had a family. Father said something about having once again walked through the annals of time. I do not know why he said that."

"Didn't you say your mother mentioned your father having lost his memory during the Balkan war?" the Abbot quietly added.

"Yes, that is what he referred to. It would have been ideal to have stayed on the farm. Uncle Aaron offered, but father did not want to go there, I do not know his reason, it could have been pride. We moved to a house in Belgrade."

"Pride or memory?" questioned Father Spyridon.

"It's hard to know. From time to time, my father had a problem with drink. Before we left Germany, Mathilda was being cared for at an orphanage. In Belgrade, my father might not have been able to keep her, had not his housekeeper declared they were unofficially living as man and wife."

"You haven't mentioned Mathilda before."

"She was born a month or two before my mother died and was placed in an orphanage for a while. My father had difficulty retrieving her. The German authorities wanted her to remain there. It was Father Augustus who rescued her. She was about six months old when we left Germany."

"Father Augustus eh, well he has told me all about that narrow escape with a baby under his cloak, and she is your sister. Well, well, well."

"So, there's strong possibility your father had a housekeeper for you and your sibling's sakes, rather than his own?" Father Spyridon challenged.

"You are probably right, especially as she was registered as my sister's guardian rather than her step mother."

"In that case she would have been registered as a housekeeper rather than as a common law wife." Alfred looked perplexed.

6

"An unmarried woman living as a wife in the worldly sense; however, whereas she had time for your sisters she never had time for you?"

"That is true. She preferred the company of girls and I was thirteen by then."

"And you found it hard to accept your loss of early childhood years with long stays in hospital? You felt she sought to take the place of your mother?"

"Looking back that's a strong possibility."

Impressed with Alfred's capacity to listen, Father Spyridon decided the time ripe for prizing open the depths.

"How did you feel when you realized your father and the housekeeper were becoming close?" the abbot asked.

"I think they have become closer over the years, but I do not think my father's likely to re- marry. He loved my mother too much. All these disruptions and changes happened about the time I was seriously ill with rheumatic fever. I was fifteen, and the doctor had dismissed me as attention seeking. I was dying, and I managed to stagger some three kilometres to the hospital where I collapsed in the doorway. For quite some time I remained at the hospital as a patient. By the time I returned home my father and his house keeper may have been living as spouses, I do not know. She was kind and helped me through convalescence. As a widow with a daughter, she treated my sisters Mathilda and Stephanie as additional daughters. Over the course of time, I felt like an intruder, I cannot explain why."

"Tell me the name of the housekeeper who took on a maternal role?"

As Alfred replied "Ida" he realised the abbot's aim to direct him into thinking about the person behind the role.

"And these changes at home led to your getting in touch with Father Augustus?" he said.

"After leaving Germany as a boy, I had often corresponded with him, and he always replied. It felt as if a miracle had happened when he came to Belgrade to do mission work. I began to spend less time at home and more time at the mission. At first my reasons were mixed."

Father Spyridon appreciated Alfred's honesty; a quality he considered as essential foundation for the development of integrity.

"Yes, I see" he said.

"Long before I had contacted Father Augustus, I had sensed a growing relationship between my father and Ida. By the time I was sixteen I spent most evenings helping Father Augustus in his mission."

"Ah, that must have been the half hour chime; I think we must finish now, I've a meeting shortly. At the same time next week, you can tell me about your missionary work?"

"Yes Father."

Chapter 2

Spiritual Searching

The following week, Father Spyridon and Alfred prayed in silence before discussion commenced:

"Now where were we, ah yes, Father Augustus mentioned the several tasks you had in the mission."

"Yes, I helped with the games he organized, and I went out onto the streets to let children and adolescents know about us. Our evening events helped prevent them becoming involved with unsavoury characters and getting into trouble. Father Augustus showed me how to run cine films that followed the activities."

"Ah, the evening films of the holy land and the life of our Lord."

"Yes, that is right. He has a wonderful collection."

The abbot paused before adding, "It must be at least three years ago. He is a very prayer centred priest."

"Yes, that's true."

"We were fortunate to have Father Augustus stay here when he first arrived from Germany" he informed.

The abbot considered how a reference from him would not have been written casually. He knew that his work among the German community and their associates in Serbia to be outstanding. Augustus was a missionary priest who, whilst leaving no stone unturned, kept the running of the mission straightforward and simple, always with Christian values at heart.

Ruminating over the meeting he'd had three weeks ago, with several venerable gentlemen, Father Spyridon remained pleased they had asked his opinion. Positive reply had sealed the unanimous agreement that the priest be decorated with the title of 'Honorary Constitutional Council member of the diocese of Ljubljana.'

Returning to the present he quietly asked, "After you decided to leave home did you ever visit your family?"

"Yes, quite often- mainly because I wanted to see my sisters."

"Of course, if you are accepted into monastic living you would not be encouraged to visit your relatives. Never forget we are Benedictine–Trappist, and your home would be your prayer life. It would mean holding in prayer your father, his companion, your sisters, your brother and all who have passed over the great divide. Your father, it appears, is a man who has had much to bear."

He paused to reflect, and as Alfred's puzzled expression relaxed, continued to say, "You may be interested in how well I was acquainted with Father Grünberger of Futog. He thought highly of your father."

He noticed the questioning look in Alfred's eyes.

"Father Grünberger went to his final home about five years ago. Among stories of his ministry, he mentioned the discussions he'd had with a young man of good insight who found direction into the Catholic faith. Your father, at that time not a great deal older than you, had some sound ideas. I'm told he possessed a profound spirituality. It was his misfortune to find himself amidst complex situations that did not end when he left Serbia for Germany."

"My mother explained some of it but it was hard to understand. I was only eight or nine years old."

"And you had only known Germany. You must remove any trace of resentment and pain about your father's second relationship. It might not be a physical relationship but a simple solution to bringing up your sisters."

Defensively Alfred replied "No one can replace my mother."

"I doubt Ida replaces her in your father's heart and mind, but she eases the pain of loss and loneliness. You must reflect upon whether you are truly called to monastic life or whether--"

Realising the implication, Alfred had not forgotten his initial encounter and continued in awareness of the abbot's capacity to investigate the depths of his soul that he as a novice could not comprehend. He was about to define it as the gift of discernment when the abbot commented, "I note your priest does not account

10

for most part of last year. Where were you? What were you doing during that time?"

"Father Augustus suggested that as a test of faith and calling I live independently for a time. I went to Lipica for a while and then on to Ljubljana where I knew he would be extending his mission work the following year."

Perceiving how the jigsaw pieces fitted together Father Spyridon enquired, "What made you choose Lipica?"

"Father Augustus had suggested that as a test of faith and calling, I follow something of great personal interest. I am fascinated by horses, and as you know the Lipica stud farm that breeds the world- famous white Lipizzaner horses, used in the Spanish riding school in Vienna, is situated there. At the stud farm I learned a great deal about working with and managing the incredibly special horses."

A smile played around the Abbot's thin lips as he said, "I wonder why these horses attracted you? Do you think you were motivated by the Austrian connection?"

"Yes, in part, but even though my mother was Austro Hungarian, her lineage was Jewish. These noble creatures reminded me of my freedom."

"Oh! Tell me why."

"When I was in hospital as a small child, I could hear horses outside, and in my mind, they carried me to freedom."

"I understand" the abbot empathised.

"The Austrian background is interesting. One imagines the forerunners of these horses going to the Archduke's court in Vienna."

"Or to his own capital of Graz" the abbot added.

"Yes. In a sense these creatures bring history to life."

"Then what was the decisive factor for leaving?"

"It came to me one day as I was riding. An inner feeling took the form of a sentence-

'It is the wings of prayer that provide true freedom.' Prayer creates the substance of angel's wings. Through prayer we're visited by the holy realms of heaven."

The abbot quietly admired the small glimpses of God's profundity within Alfred's developing insights.

"What work did you do in Lipica?"

11

"When my money ran out, I took on casual work, including work as a stable hand at the riding school."

"Wasn't it a bit of a come down?"

"Not entirely, I continued to receive unofficial training from a trainer who had become a friend. I was only there three months and by that time Father Augustus was in Ljubljana. So, I moved there, found lodgings, and managed to get work as a waiter in the Grand." "Ah yes, the English have an equivalent called the Ritz. What did you regard as the most crucial element of that work?"

"I was interested in people. Snippets of conversation prompted my return to mission work on a deeper level. People had many problems, all out of perspective it seemed."

"What impressed you most in Ljubljana?"

Firstly, there were outstanding churches. I often visited the Ursuline church with its massive columns and pointed arches."

"Ah yes, a baroque building: very ornate."

"Yes, and in the early morning I often prayed at the seventeenth century Franciscan church. I was drawn by its simplicity."

"Were there other things that drew your attention?"

"Yes, I liked people's colourful clothes that matched their cheerful personalities."

"Did you learn anything from this?" asked the abbot whilst wondering if the candidate saw with the eyes of the heart.

"Well, my soul felt uplifted by the magnificent architecture of the city and the beauty of the surrounding countryside. I learned how the world around us influences our inner life. God spoke the message of how we need spiritually minded people to carry God's beauty into the dark places of the world."

Quietly the abbot wondered whether Alfred's work should continue in mission rather than within contemplative life of monastic living.

"Do you think God's beauty, present but unseen was already there before us, during Christ's suffering, and throughout the resurrection and beyond?" asked the abbot.

"Yes, I do; from the source of prayer, beauty and light enlightens dark places."

"And that's something we learn through our deepening life of prayer and meditation" the abbot concluded. With a welcoming smile he got up, walked across the room, and held open the door.

Chapter 3

The Monks

In the woods, after much cajoling Brother Ivan managed to persuade Brother Misha to give in to his inclinations. Ivan, the dominant of the two, making first move, kissed him with a lingering kiss that only lovers' exchange. "How do you feel?" he asked the younger monk.

"Confused- about my feelings-"

Having completed a spell of fasting Ivan's suppressed desires burned fiercely. Brusquely he asked "Misha would you like to lie in my bed with me?" Absorbing the direct and ambiguously powerful look in Ivan's eye the young monk enquired, "What do you mean?" Pushing aside feelings of vulnerability, that made his stomach queasy and his knees weak, he gradually awoke to his meaning. In a dilemma, for Ivan was his closest friend, he remained rooted to the spot.

For a moment, battling with desire, Ivan walked away. Conscience argued with daily prayers he had engaged in. He considered how he had frequently broken his vow of celibacy in a manner regarded as an extremely evil act. Worse still, he knew he was not in love with Misha. His desire persuaded him that it did not really matter because most people could not believe or comprehend that men could fall in love with men. Fleetingly he empathised with God who was not believed in by a vast number of humans. Thoughts of the Almighty stimulated conscience that he knew to be a receptor for the voice of God.

The voice of conscience, without argument or judgement formed a sentence, *'If you truly loved Misha, as he loves you, you will leave him alone.'* He reflected on the past when, for the unspoken purpose of ridding himself of worldly temptation, he had entered monastic life. Then it had gone wrong, he had succumbed to a relationship with a seasonal worker. Two years later he had had a similar relationship with a young stonemason working at the monastery. Somehow, he had kept his secret from the monks but liaisons had fired strong sexual desires. Pausing from his thoughts, he listened for a moment to God's unconditional creative gift of the luscious melodies of songbirds. He noticed a wealth of textured plants within the woodland and asked himself if he had allowed his prayer life to become choked with weeds of corruption. Somewhere deep within he wrangled with the ambivalence of who he truly was, within the centre of that so called corruption.

Often during daily office prayers, his thoughts fleetingly drifted towards God. Having recently read a passage in Luke's Gospel he wondered if he had he left the room of his soul unguarded. Had seven devils of lust stronger than the initial temptation entered? Then dismissing the idea, he returned to Misha and whilst he kissed him repeatedly, ignored the scream of conscience, *"Why?"*

Noticing tears running down Misha's face Ivan recognised his inner disturbance about the direction of his inclinations.

"Do you think someone might be watching?" Misha anxiously enquired.

To his own ears Ivan's tone was thick with seduction as he replied, "There's no one here except us."

Meanwhile, across the woodland, Alfred's silent prayers, merged with the prayers of other monks, flowing from the abbey into the world. For a moment the disobedient monks felt the touch of the crucified Christ and fleetingly Brother Ivan inwardly glimpsed Misha unhindered, gentle, and compassionate in his service and devotion to God.

"Are you alright with our arrangement Misha?" he asked.

"What else can we do? It must be secret. I long for your company and I cannot imagine life without you. Besides you are good in shouldering most of the physical work we do."

A subconscious question loomed large in Brother Ivan's mind, *'Have I manipulated him and abused his love. Have I honed in whilst the nails were being hammered?'*

"But you are in your twenties and I am in my forties. I seem to have led you away from our saviour. I cannot change, I try but I cannot."

15

"I know it is wrong, but I have always felt I was a girl and now I am a woman trapped in a man's body. When I pray, I feel our blessed virgin's tears, I hear God telling me you do not love me; that I represent your younger self, the one you have lost. But I live in hope that you will love me for myself and that we never will be parted. God reminds me that I should remain celibate in his service. Yet you have drawn me to you in a way that must be unnatural because St Paul tells us it is wrong."

"Yes, but he was a Roman citizen. It was Roman practice to let centurions and various officers of rank teach young men methods of love making. There were no virgin minded bridegrooms in that society. St Paul's statement did not go beyond that situation into later societies. I wonder if some of us have been created different."

"Isn't God's creation meant to be perfect?"

"No, God is the perfection within an imperfect world."

"I understand what you are saying, but even so, I fear I am hurting God. I cannot break away, unless you help me, unless you want me to break away."

"I can't," said Ivan.

After swamping Misha with more kisses, he harshly pointed out, "There's no record of Christ ever having said that men should not be lovers."

For a moment they heard the rustle of leaves and wondered if someone was lingering. Then as the toll of the bell summoned, they quickly ran to the chapel for vespers.

At the abbey church, during the evening prayers, they sat some distance apart. Even so, at the end of the service, Brother Ivan reddened as he became aware of the abbot's scrutinising gaze. Ivan's aim to quickly leave, after a period of meditation, was foiled. The Abbot beckoned him and said, "I would like to see you in my study during supper."

Subdued, Ivan replied, "Yes Father." Nine monks and three novices later, Misha passed the abbot.

"May I see you after supper? I shall be in my study," said the abbot.

With an element of surprise Misha answered, "Yes Father."

***

The following week Ivan left the abbey. Father Spyridon and Father Benedict kept silent about reasons for his dismissal. The abbot was uneasy and sad regarding the monk's denial and lack of remorse. Confession and repentance were words he would have liked to have heard. It grieved him immensely that such direction had not occurred to Ivan.

***

Following periods of prayer and deep discussion the abbot recognised in Misha's tearful and heart-felt confession a genuine cry for forgiveness. He therefore arranged a second meeting with Father Benedict and two other senior monks present. After much searching and discussion, the brothers unanimously agreed that Misha should remain at the abbey. The abbot disclosed how a village girl, intent on gathering blueberries, had inadvertently trespassed into the woods.

"She had witnessed all that was said and took place. In her distress she had accidently ran into the monastery grounds. Father Benedict brought her to me" he explained.

Distraught, Misha replied, "I'm sorry Father."

The Abbot continued, "Rumours about Brother Ivan have circulated in the past. We dismissed them, especially as the tales were linked to villagers rather than the brothers.

Father Benedict is to be your spiritual director. You are further required to have a period of discussion and prayer with me every day, until such time you become single minded, confident, and strong in spirit, mind, and body."

The postulants knew nothing of these events. Alfred enjoyed working and praying alongside other monks in training. He appreciated being able to engage in simple discussion within the context of their rule of life.

***

There was something special about dawn's light breaking in upon the shadowy world during early- morning vigils. In the moment when shafts of light shone through the stained-glass windows, to cast shades of rose and blue upon the praying monks, love existed as an entity. That pinnacle of time pointed towards late morning, when the sacraments would be received as a visible sign of Christ's body and blood, given as a selfless sacrifice, to heal the world and bring about salvation and promise of eternal life. Through the vibrant power of Christ's Eucharist, Alfred realized and felt in his heart he was receiving an element far beyond the earthly quality of bread and wine.

On this blustery morning they moved on to a large discussion room where minds focussed on the design and wonder of the creation. They whole heartedly agreed that the working relationship of the world, the stars, the moon, and the sun, were too well thought out, and interdependent to have happened by chance. Alfred bravely made the suggestion "Perhaps the Genesis seven days creation story might represent seven billion years, made up of the ice age and other ages that have evolved in what would seem one day to our omnipotent God."

***

During evenings, following a daily discipline of working in silence, they were invited to share their insights with Father Spyridon and Father Benedict. Often this occurred within context of learning practical skills such as cheese- making, bee- keeping leather craft, wood- turning. Training sometimes included unpleasant, rigorous menial tasks. Today it fell upon Alfred to tackle the unenviable task of emptying the cesspit. Disregarding his churning stomach, a sense of achievement unfolded as strongly as that experienced in Lipica, when he had mastered advanced riding skills.

Father Benedict's prime objective was to awaken the deep resources of their soul. Sometimes, within less structured situations, he encouraged his wards to engage in creative tasks. Brother Philip added the last two pieces of pottery to his mosaic of his chosen topic from the book of Exodus, of Moses and the burning bush. Sensing Brother Benedict close by he looked up.

"What have you learned in spiritual terms from this magnificent project?" the monk enquired.

"That from a state of brokenness something new and meaningful can be created."

The abbot, having that moment entered the room, thoughtfully commented. "You have portrayed something old in a new way. Your Moses is very youthful and the flames of your burning bush are like the tongues of fire at Pentecost. You have revealed a hidden prophecy that I had not seen before I looked at your mosaic" he said.

18

Alfred quietly listened, and when the abbot was gone, he looked at the work of the novice seated beside him. Brother Andre had combined his own skills along with those of his fellow monks and produced a bound book of poems copied in beautiful calligraphy.

"May I read the poems?" said Alfred.

"Yes, please do."

Later Alfred enquired, "Would you mind if I copied this poem of particular interest?"

"Do borrow it and take as long as you need."

As Alfred copied the poem, he visualised Father Spyridon intent as he gazed at the first light of dawn stream through the window. He wondered if the abbot had authored the poem.

MONASTERY WINDOW
Through this monastery church
In a kaleidoscope of colour
Dawn's light brightly shines.
She brings to notice jewels in leaded glass
Portraying leafy emeralds on ancient branches
of smooth satin birch,
Reminding mortals of Revelation's eternal city

Dawn's light looks deeper to the central orb
Dancing upon the windowsill
Where new creations stream from
Glass created by past craftsmen.
Yes, from those ancient devotions,
New colours filled with the voice of God,
Project into this time and beckon new saints.

This light looks deeper into deepest deep
And rejoices in prayerful listening hearts
That through grace, receive-
Selfless love, and holiest light.
Within this monastery church
In a kaleidoscope of colour
Dawn's light brightly shines.

When Alfred had read the poem, he thought of St John's gospel and a passage describing Christ as the light of the world.

Putting down his ink pen he eagerly returned to his chosen task of basket making. Occasionally his grandfather-Wilhelm had made baskets. Hardly could he remember what his grandfather looked like, although he well recalled his he enthusiasm. He remembered him say '*My father was the expert but I know enough to show you the basics. After that it's up to you to develop the skill.*'

Wilhelm had established method, '*When, you have your starting cross, just like the cross in church, and you have inserted your long fine and bending willow sticks for the frame, just keep weaving in and out. When you come to the end turn down the ends and weave them in. Baskets need a nice smooth top. You can even make a lid by making another cross and ensuring you keep the willow frame flat throughout. You'll need a bunch of five or six fine willow sticks and some fine binder. Bind it closely.*'

He was about to finish a marginally lop-sided basket; a reminder of the one he had given Great Aunt Annalisa. He recalled her proudly using the basket for shopping. Later, when the handle had come loose, she used the basket for clothes pegs. A spiritual message was evolving in Alfred's mind and heart when Father Benedict asked, "What has the Holy Spirit said to you Alfred?

"He tells me that we need a basket of prayer to contain all the spiritual riches of God's love. It seems to me that without the prayer basket, lives can easily become empty and meaningless."

"Very profound, do you think what you now perceive may be the Holy Spirit's continuing of something you have recently heard?" Father Benedict quietly replied.

"Yes, Wednesday's reading; how baby Moses would have sunk into the river had his basket not been sealed. Perhaps the bitumen represents fore-thought and love. Were it not for his mother's love and response to God by using bitumen, he would not have been saved, and the whole history of the Jewish and Christian faith would have been altered. Her response to God, her one small act was significant in God's eyes, as it allowed his plan for people of the Jewish faith to move forward in faith, and into the generation that saw Christ come into the world.

"It also symbolises a situation of suffering that alters meaning, and direction, when placed in God's hands. It can lead to a deepening of faith. You are listening to God and that is the start of doing well in God's scheme of things."

Chapter 4

Lenten Journey

Eleven months had passed since Alfred entered the abbey. Currently the novices were nearing the end of a strict and challenging Lenten period of discipline. Repentant Brother Misha, leading study groups, was under unannounced observation. Gradually, over the weeks his profound perception unfolded. His imagination proved to be the vehicle through which he was able to convey his interpretation of the dramatic Biblical accounts that had led to the terrible crucifixion.

In mind and spirit Alfred felt he was on the hill of Calvary empathising with Christ as he suffered extreme physical and psychological pain as the result of wilful cruelty. In a metaphorical sense, here at the cross, Alfred comprehended the experience of nails effectively hammered in by the jeers of the crowd. He also felt connected to the experience of many who were healed, forgiven, and blessed by the crucified Messiah. Within his soul he realised the reality of the all and beyond time event. A voice in his heart cried, *'Your despair will turn to joy, Christ's healing goes beyond the grave for all who were and are and will be, and into life eternal.'*

From early dawn to dusk, frail, white haired monks, born in the early eighteen forties, led prayer groups. Particularly at dawn Alfred sensed the healing power of prayer emanate into dark, troubled places of the world. Long before the monks entered, Father Spyridon prayed alone in the chapel. Often in spirit he knelt alongside Ivan in his dark prison cell. Today a spiritual connection felt so prevalent, he knew Ivan to be responding at soul deep level. Meanwhile, in his cell thirty kilometres away, Ivan closed his eyes in prayer. Gradually, as if by transfusion, he experienced an empowerment of spirit. The picture in his heart was clear- of Christ's blood flowing from the crucifix on the wall into the veins of his soul. 'Is it that same Holy Spirit singing Panis Angelicus within me?' he wondered. He knew for certain this experience was of the heavenly bread, the nature of Christ, a living truth awakening within his heart.

He deduced his sexual orientation to have been the real reason for imprisonment. It was likely that a villager's false allegation of theft had been rooted in the source of the girl having seen them in the wood. The tide of his spirit, turning in this timeless moment, urged him forward, towards the possibility of complete service to Christ. In the light of Christ, compassion awakened within him, for the men he had not loved but used. He thought of the women he'd envied and saw that he had not been the selfless person God intended him to be. As he reflected on how he had used what he was in a selfish manner, shame overwhelmed him. Faced with the love of Christ, he instantly realized that he had not valued himself. As the moments unfolded, he saw how his coercive control of others was rooted in his own sense of worthlessness. He had deliberately manipulated situations to prevent his intended victims forming natural friendships with others. In causing them misery by disguising his methods beneath a veil of platitudes, he had secured their dependence upon him. Now he knew that he had been a man full of fear. In this time of turning to Christ he was for the first time seeing beyond the darkness he'd wilfully perpetuated. His inner voice seemed to resound around the cell '*I did not realize how worthless I felt under all the bravado. What right had I to enter monastic life? I am ashamed of how I have acted. Father Spyridon was righteous to have dismissed me. He knew I was the controller. I resented his control but it is a different sort of control. His control was simply to push me into a situation of self-examination in the light of our saviour.*' With a long sigh of relief, he handed that self-love over to the arms of the man of special conscience, Jesus Christ. For a moment, full of greater depth and breadth than the kiss of betrayal, he let himself fuse with the reality of God's love. That fusion was freeing him from confusion. From the seed of prayer, flowers of empathy were growing faster than weeds that had filled the room of his soul. One day he would go out, live simply in the hope of finding a lifelong companion. Quietly he prayed, "*Lord, if you send me a companion and we, on equal terms, think about relating physically, I promise it will evolve only because of contemplative prayer-and the voice of your love. If no consent is heard deep within me, lead me, and the human companion you may send to me, into deeper fulfilment in following the path, dear saviour, you have set out before us. Amen."*

During the fourth week of lent Alfred's heart pounded loudly as Father Benedict declared, "Your next test of faith will be to sleep in coffins for the remainder of lent. My hope is that by prayer you will overcome all worldly fears."

Alfred faced his worst nightmare. During the first night he retracted into his tenth year, and in the early hours of morning awoke gasping for air. His dream world had been full of images of his mother lying in the coffin. "Did she hear the stones tumble down on the lid?" he murmured upon awaking.

The following night, trembling like a leaf in the wind, sweating profusely, he eventually fell into a sleep full of grotesque dreams about Christ's agony. Next moment he was looking at his mother's body in a state of decay. Finally, as dawn shone through the tiny window, he wondered if he was imagining the voice of prayer in the form of a girl in a distant land. Did he really hear a voice calling, *'Come away from monastic life; I need you here?'* When he woke, he heard his own mutterings, "If I leave it will be my own decision. Besides, my childhood friend Erika is the only girl close to my heart."

Two days later and on successive days he went to the chapel at dawn. On the fourth day he noticed the abbot praying there. *'Perhaps he's been here every day in his hidden area'* he thought. Taking care to not make a sound he crept into his seat to meditate. Later when he quietly slid out of the pew, he came across the abbot standing there, with a questioning look in his eyes. Prompted by something beyond himself Alfred enquired, "Father Spyridon may I have discussion with you?"

"Yes, it will have to be after the week end. Would Tuesday morning at eleven be suitable?"

"Yes, thank you Father."

On Tuesday morning at eleven, Alfred sat in the carved chair and listened as the abbot asked with spiritual authority, "Would you like to tell me what's on your mind and heart?"

24

Providing explanation Alfred said, "Until now I felt I was meant to live my life here, but a change of direction is happening."

Momentarily the abbot's eyes filled with disappointment but instantly conveyed understanding.

"In what way is that?" he replied.

"Increasingly I've been thinking about mission work and how I might continue on a deeper level."

"Is that the only reason?"

"No, I have been unable to enter the final discipline of lent. I can see its purpose but I was reminded of my mother's death. In contrast to her death, in the light of dawn, I am reminded of her life, vitality, and how she cared for others. Within the context of that discipline, I could not get beyond my experience of loss and into the death and resurrection of our Lord. I am too close to people to distance myself from them. I understand death and resurrection through physically helping those who need resurrecting from demanding situations. That is not to say I do not understand the contemplative life. I have and do experience the supreme importance of prayer and reflection."

"If you truly have listened to God and sense his sending you out into the world you are right to have come to me. I have seen a few novitiates close their ears to God, rather than change direction. Inevitably they have come to regret it later. The world will be a richer place for your presence. You have learned a great deal, and are unaware how your spirituality has deepened during the time you have been here. Through the Lenten discipline and journey, you have found your true calling and direction. When you first came here, I wondered if God might be calling you to ministry in mission.

"I picked up on those thoughts."

"Yes, you can be intuitive. Always remember that like those of us who live within the abbey, the only true protection in life is closeness with God, and unending discourse and communion with him. Listening is the greatest gift, the foundation for all the fruits of the spirit. You have zest and energy and a great love of people. Use your gifts wisely. I shall always pray for you during my time here, and in eternal realms.

"Thank you, Father. I will remember in my heart and prayers, all who serve here."

Expounding, the abbot replied, "Let us pray together. I shall pray the words Simeon prayed as he received the infant Jesus before carrying out religious circumcision according to Jewish custom. Through the life of Jesus, it was revealed that the physical ritual was not important. What was important was that people's hearts be kept clean and free from the infection of dark thoughts and actions. Let us pray as Simeon did, we will turn to Luke's Gospel chapter 2 and read his final prayer: Lord, now let thy servant depart, in peace according to thy word, for mine eyes have seen thy salvation which Thou hast prepared before the face of all people to be a light to lighten the Gentiles and to be the salvation of Thy people Israel."

***

Noticing how Alfred retired to his room each evening rather than continue the Lenten discipline, fellow postulants guessed he bore a change of direction in mind.

A week later, after grace preceding supper, Father Spyridon declared, "I wish to bring a few matters to your attention. Firstly, a young man recovering from tuberculosis is to stay here on retreat for a period of at least two months."

The abbot proceeded to set out general instructions for a programme for the youth, of rest, prayer, and healing that was to begin with early mass.

With a tinge of regret he conveyed, "I also wish you to know that our brother Alfred has come to a profound realisation that monastic life is not God's ultimate calling for him. By his actions, words and by how he loves God, I see how his time here will remain an important part of his journey into the wider world, where, assuredly, on a deeper level, he intends to continue mission work."

With a twinkle in his eye he added, "There is one final matter. He may come to regret having mentioning riding skills. It will surprise him to learn that he will be leaving on horseback. The father of the young man has a cart but no horse. Alfred, you can begin your mission by ensuring our faithful dappled friend arrives safely at the residence on the outskirts of Belgrade." Laughter rippling through the hall made Alfred chuckled. As laughter died, and the Abbot requested a brief period of silence; they instantly complied. "Alfred, we offer you our love and good blessings" Father Spyridon concluded.

Two days later, not long after Alfred retired to his room, there was a knock at the door. He opened it. Andre, standing there, warmly said, "Alfred, I'd like you to have this bound copy of poems I have collected." Realising that his brother in Christ had spent many hours copying up, in finest calligraphy, the collection of religious and spiritual poems by monks past and present, Alfred was moved by his kindness. Grasping Andre's hand he answered, "Andre, I cannot thank you enough. This collection is superb. I shall not forget any of you brothers, and wherever I go, I shall always remember you."

Next morning, with fatherly tenderness, Father Spyridon advised Alfred about his future and on practical level, provided him with sufficient funds for a fortnight's living and travel. From that point things quickly moved on. Already they were coming to the end of the lavender path. "Up you go," said the abbot. Whilst mounting the popular and well-loved short legged dappled mare, Alfred noted her tendency to toss her head from side to side. Quickly he settled into the saddle. During the moments the monks gathered round, he saw in their expressions a unanimous reluctance to see him leave.

As Alfred rode on, he turned and smiled, regardless of his emotions. The monk's faces conveyed good will and affection an image he resolved to always carry within his heart. Without warning, the horse with a toss of her head, shot off. However, as soon as possible Alfred pulled the reigns. As the mare submitted to his expertise Alfred knew she had gathered there was to be no gaming. As laughter died and Alfred turned to give a quick wave, he absorbed the brothers' changed expressions. *They were impressed* he thought as then he rode onward across dancing shadows beneath whispering trees.

Chapter 5

Mission of Mercy

With the abbey no longer in sight, Alfred had some misgivings about having left like- minded brothers of the community. *'What should I do after this journey is finished? It would not feel right going home so soon; I will return to Ljubljana, to 'The Grand.' Hopefully, they will have some work for me. Then I will try to contact Father Augustus. If I do things the other way round it would speak of failed self-sufficiency, wrong motives, and things I cannot put into words.'* Deep down he knew he had made a wise decision.

Sensing her rider wasn't concentrating, the dapple-grey mare trotted to level ground beside a stream. Her change of direction brought to Alfred's notices sunlight, dancing on the water surface. He appreciated the magnificence of lovely reflection of several kinds of trees. As he dismounted, the whisper of the breeze through over-head branches awakened the idea of the relationship of all trees to the misused tree of Calvary. Suddenly, for him they were living symbols of that one salvation day in the history of humankind, flowing down stream and onwards through the annals of time, deep into hearts and beyond, into the sea of eternal life.

As the horse dipped her dappled muzzle, into the dappled stream, rainbow sprays were created in the sunlight. Further downstream Alfred noticed how the tree tops met to form a transparent arch of silver edged greens, olive, lime, and moss green.

***

Later, when he arrived on his stead in the region of Belgrade, he was glad to not have to visit the city. Quickly he scanned the abbot's directions, *'When you approach Belgrade from the north you will come across The Magpie Guest House. Three kilometres*

*past the guest house is Fern-lake Lane. Go right, into Fern-lake
Lane, Mr Leonard Moniuszko lives in the third on the left.'*

Confidently he proceeded, but at the beginning of Fern-Lake
Road, hesitated.

Not a single house was in sight. Several kilometres further,
the horse's ears pricked at the sound of human voices. Through
a thick bushy hedge Alfred caught sight of a large house and
several cottages. In his mind he saw the abbot's eyes dance with
amusement and realized that during the course of his sermon he
had intentionally conveyed, *'You can never be certain you have
the exact picture a person has expressed in voice or written
word. Therefore, one needs to read the scriptures over and over.
That is the only way one begins to absorb some of the infinite
dimensions of God. We need to listen to God's prayers; it is
essential for our approach into prayer and theology. Everything
must be in balance like the yin and yen our Chinese brothers
portray.'*

Alfred's thoughts extemporised, *'Oh yes: in the heart of
winter summer is born. According to faith we know how through
sorrow and tribulation as well as through moments of joy we can
come to know more fully the profound depths of God's infinite
love.'*

***

A painted sign **Moniuszko; Mill Cottage** caught his eye.
Cautiously he rode along a rough side track, at the end of which,
excited screams of five children, running around tumble down
sheds, startled him. A window of the nearby house opened, a
tired motherly face looked out and yelled, "Quiet please, your
brother can't tolerate it." Suddenly she was aware of a visitor.

"I am sorry, I did not see you. Are you from the abbey?" said
the woman.

"Yes, I am" Alfred cheerily replied.

"I'll come and let you in." She closed the window and came
to the door.

"Father Spyridon mentioned he would send someone on
horseback. Do come in" she said.

He followed her indoors.

"I will wake my husband. He has a nap after our midday meal
and then works in the fields until dusk." She walked along the

hallway and called through the doorway of a room, "Leonardo, wake up, a young man from the abbey is here."

A mumble emerged and the woman replied, "Yes, he has the horse with him."

Returning to Alfred she asked, "Would you like to go to the sitting room? My husband won't be long. Can I offer you coffee and rolls, although the rolls have become hard and are no longer light and fluffy."

"Thank you, I prefer bread when it's crisp," Alfred replied.

More relaxed she smiled, and went to the kitchen. Alfred retreated to the sitting room and sat on a rickety wicker chair. A brief time later dark-haired Leonardo Moniuszko, about forty years of age, entered. His dialect was broad, his warm brown eyes friendly as he said, "Please don't get up." Stifling a yawn, he leaned over and with firm grip shook Alfred's hand. With a trace of anxiety he asked, "Would you very much mind telling my son Omer about the abbey? He has never been away from home, and is apprehensive about leaving. Partly due to illness he has nightmares about being shut away in his imaginary abbey for ever."

"I'll gladly put his mind at rest," said Alfred. He followed Leonardo along the hallway, into the youth's bedroom. As he walked towards him lying so ill in the bed, he had a keen sense of the abbot's seal of approval for mission. Omer's thin, pale face showed surprise.

"Good day to you. Were you expecting an old and wise monk" said Alfred jovially. Omer, liking the friendly manner of the young man from the abbey answered, "Yes, I wasn't anticipating anyone as young as you."

"I happen to be on my way to do God's work elsewhere. Monks vary in age from young to middle aged and elderly. God has a habit of calling people at any stage of life. I understand you are going to stay at the abbey for a while?"

"Yes, I am worried about it. Will it be old and gloomy and will I be locked in?"

"You've no need to worry, it is certainly not old and gloomy, and it is full of light. The monks are spiritually minded and kind hearted. The beauty and tranquillity of the place is beyond our understanding. No one is forced to stay there; most enjoy being there."

As he highlighted how peace within the soul perpetuates healing and recovery of mind and body, he did not miss a glimmer of interest light up Omer's tormented blue- grey eyes. Moments later, with a trace of a smile on his face he fell asleep.

"Well, we'd best be having coffee and rolls or I shall never hear the end of it," said Leonardo. Alfred followed him into the sitting room, and once again sat in the rickety chair. Mrs Moniuszko entered carrying a plate of rolls and butter that she placed on a small table. Following a quick exit, she re-entered with a round wooden tray containing a coffee pot and jug of milk.

"We're grateful for your help," said Leonardo.

"I'm glad to be doing God's work" Alfred replied.

When they had finished, Leonardo thanked Alfred for bringing the mare.

"She will be well fed and watered and we will make certain she gets some spells of rest during the journey. I shall set off early tomorrow morning with our son."

"That's a sensible plan."

"You'll manage everything, won't you Lauretta?"

"Yes, easily" his golden-haired wife replied.

Sensing some change, the mare pranced uneasily.

"She is a good mare, needs gentle, firm handling. Between the shafts she will be less frisky and she will soon realize she is homeward bound." Alfred pointed out.

"Thank you again. We so want Omer to make a full recovery. Thanks to you, he will have a chance to get better and I shall have time to give my other children my undivided attention."

Forestalling the next question Leonardo explained, "Thankfully Father Spyridon has arranged for someone to take me to the nearest railway station for my return journey, and neighbours have offered to collect me. Your best route to the city is along the footpath, and across those fields. The styles indicate the route. Eventually you will come to a long lane leading to houses and streets."

"Thank you, that sounds much easier than back tracking to the main road."

31

Half way across the field, Alfred turned to wave. He was glad to see the children feed the horse carrots. As if to say farewell the mare paused and for a long moment looked across the field.

Chapter 6

Connections

Having had a good night's sleep in a suitable room in a city guest house, Alfred made his way to the near-by railway station. A quick scan of the station timetable informed him that his train was due in a quarter hour. He would arrive in Ljubljana late afternoon, and would have time to search for accommodation.

A sudden hiss and the sound of weight on tracks preceded the train's arrival. Across the platform he veered right; a third-class carriage came to a halt in front of him.

"Bull's eye" he whispered.

He opened the door, and faced an ill clad woman struggling with her luggage and two infants. "Let me help" he said.

"Thank you" she shyly muttered.

One by one he took her three large bags, deposited them on the platform and helped her down. Having quickly contacted her two infants fearfully looking down at the track, he gently said, "It's alright." He lifted them down, and stood them in front of their mother.

"Thank you. You are truly kind." she emphasized.

***

In the compartment Alfred wished he had not sat down quite as quickly. Something hard was pressing against his left buttock. He rapidly got up and with a look of distaste picked up and wrapped in paper, a half-eaten lollipop. Stooping, he placed it under the seat and as he stood up noticed the bemused expression of an elderly man entering the carriage. Simultaneously, before sitting down, they exchanged smiles of amusement.

***

As the train gathered speed Alfred recalled Witold's expression, whilst relating a childhood experience of a larger-than-life woman boarding their carriage. He pictured his

33

mischievous brother splitting his adolescent sides with laughter as he said, '*Quite rightly Mother was cross but I was nearly peeing myself because I thought the woman was going to sit in our carriage and squash us*'.

Gradually carriages were filling. A large- boned middle-aged woman with black hair and dark eyes entered, and sat opposite. Out on the platform the guard slammed shut a few open doors, then taking position he waved his flag. On cue, with a loud toot, the train steamed out of the station.

***

As minarets, domes and the river junction of Belgrade disappeared Alfred thought of his family and Ida their home-keeper. Had not this present moment of time, seemed to belong to a different physical quantum he might have visited them. With thoughts drifting into earlier life in Germany, his imagination relived conversations of the past.

Whilst the elderly passenger fell asleep, the woman struck up conversation.

"You look as if you are thinking of home" she said.

"Yes, I am" Alfred replied.

Taking his reply to be an invitation, she talked in great length about her family; too late Alfred realized he was a captive audience.

Many kilometres later, along with the chuff, chuff, chuff of the train, the woman concluded her soliloquy with details of the ambitions of her various sons. The name of a minor station appeared causing her to suddenly gasp, "Oh, I have to get out soon."

As an after- thought she added, "What's your line of work?" Avoiding mention of the abbey Alfred replied, "I used to work at The Grand in Ljubljana."

"My word that is a good establishment: I stayed there many years ago on my honeymoon. They say it is as good as The Ritz. Oh, we are here. Goodbye."

"Goodbye" he answered.

Opening his eyes, the elderly man smiled as he said "Now you know why I nodded off."

Returning the smile Alfred simultaneously mulled over the name Ritz, new to his ears. Several towns and villages ended

34

with "I-T-Z." He began to wonder if the name of the Hotel had originated there. He recalled the names Chemnitz, Zwonitz, Gobnitz and Nurwirschitz. Just for a moment Paulo's voice with a rare utterance of praise came to mind, 'You have the makings of a first-class waiter.'

Bearing in mind how things might have changed, he decided to ask Paulo if he might be reinstated. Instinctively, synchronizing with the monastery prayer time he now prayed, and when the train slowed into its next station, he was deep in meditation. Abruptly the train stopped, and as Alfred looked out of the window, he refrained from averting his gaze from the eyes of a boy, about twelve years of age, and with a noticeable disability. Alfred smiled, and at the same time perceived the lad's appreciation of rare communication. For a moment the boy hesitated; then with tremendous effort and will power, he spasmodically teetered across the platform. Remembering his own childhood illness, Alfred empathised greatly. With a gentle lurch the train chugged forward. As the boy diminished into the distance, Alfred prayed, 'Lord Jesus, and Holy mother of Jesus bless that dear boy wherever he goes.' He imagined pouring holy oils upon the lad's head. *'Was he feeling lighter in spirit, he wondered.'*

***

Gliding through sunshine and showers, the train at last arrived in Ljubljana. Glad to be leaving the cramped compartment, Alfred strode along familiar city streets, until he arrived at his former lodgings. Firmly he rang the bell, and soon Mrs Nijinsky opened the door.

"Heavens above, Alfred, what are you doing here? Come in for tea and tell me."

"It's good to see you, and thank you, I'd love to" he replied. Except for her feet being more noticeably swollen, Mrs Nijinsky had not changed a great deal.

During afternoon tea, as she listened to Alfred's account, her blue grey eyes lit up with interest.

"You have made a wise decision Alfred. You are an active person with a great interest in people. I should hate to think of you remaining behind monastery walls for the rest of your life."

"It was an abbey. It was a good life that suited me in many ways but it was not what God wanted, and that is the only reason I left. It was part of a greater calling that life will unfold."

"Well, that is beyond me I am afraid. Now I expect you will need lodgings again?"

"Well yes, but I did not come for that reason alone. I came to see you."

"I know that. That is why you had tea and cake. Now I'm afraid I am fully booked for at least a month but I am certain that a friend of mine, Mrs Hand, who lives at number twenty-seven, two streets away, would be able to help. She was apprehensive about having guests, but the arrangement has proved invaluable to her and her lodgers, all of whom I have recommended. Do not give away that I have told you this, simply say I sent you."

"I will, and thank you."

"Also, could you let her know I will call in to see her tomorrow?"

"Certainly, and thank you so much Mrs Nijinsky. What was the name of the street again?" "Twenty-seven, this'll do--"

"Sorry I didn't catch that. His words were lost as a car noisily rolled by and Mrs Nijinsky closed the door.

***

Later he deduced the street name was *Thistledown.* A second hurdle was the confusing numbering system. Time was wasted checking numbers. Hearing a door being opened, Alfred seized opportunity to ask a smartly dressed man, emerging from the house, "I wonder if you would you be so kind as to point me in the right direction for number twenty-seven?"

Without a word the man raised his umbrella, and pointed it in the direction of a house, set well back at the end of a long path.

"Thank you. I didn't realise the house belonged to this street."

Briskly Alfred walked along the street, and up an over-grown path, where he avoided treading on pretty dandelions, growing between flagstones. He pulled the string of the lopsided bell; it resounded crisp, and clear; he waited, no one answered. Again, he rang the bell. Squeakily the door was opened from within, and cautiously a flummoxed woman peered out.

"Good afternoon. Are you Mrs Hand?" Alfred enquired.

36

"Yes, and who are you?"

"Alfred Ztoanjib, I used to lodge with Mrs Nijinsky and have just returned to Ljubljana and called in on her. She suggested you might have a room to let?"

"I do, and I can help, but will need a few hours to get everything straight. Will you require a meal today?"

"Not today thank you but would it be convenient for me to leave my bags and return in about three hours? I wish to call on several acquaintances."

With a look of relief Mrs Hand readily took the bags.

"There is an envelope for you from Mrs Nijinsky. She mentioned visiting you tomorrow."

"That'll be nice," she replied, and took the envelope.

With her thick fingers she opened it and with much squinting read the note.

"I shall have your room ready by the time you return" she said.

"That's very kind, thank you."

Alfred went on his way to the main square and when he reached the location, noticed the open door of the Ursuline church. He went in, and remained there for an hour of devotion and prayer.

* * *

Later, upon entering the modern Grand Hotel, he hardly recognized his own image in the mirror at the far end of the entrance hall. His worn crumpled suite and old coat reminded him of Thomas Moore's discourse about counterfeit pleasure. *'What was Moore's point? -ah yes, nobility should regard the poor as kings of real worth, and materialists amongst the nobility should regard themselves as unworthy, because of their need to establish self- worth by the counterfeit means of wearing rich garments and jewels.'* The bell boy's voice cut in upon his thoughts. "Are you staying Sir? Can I take your coat sir?"

'Obviously an inexperienced, impartial, Utopian bell boy' thought Alfred.

He replied, "Yes, thank you, I would like to go in and order dinner."

In response to the dubious glance of a door attendant, Alfred took out his wallet and flicked through the wad of notes the

37

Abbot had provided. His thoughts turned to the profound mind of Thomas Moore, the author of Utopia, who would have used similar tactic in the presence of a personal servant of Henry the Eighth. Taking over the situation, the puffed-up peacock of a door attendant squeezed out his sentence, "Would you like to follow me Sirrrr?"

A quiet voice within Alfred's heart created thoughts, *'I'd like to answer.... Of course, I will not for there is only one I follow-- the true God of all creation. Oh yes, I will follow you to the table and I pray that you will look to things spiritual and that you will go to that special table that offers the one and only special bread of life'--- 'Ah Alfred, another of your silent sermons-Thank you for your constancy.'*

"Thank you" said Alfred to the departing door attendant. He hoped the cost of the meal would serve the aim he bore in mind. A young waiter approached to offer three samples of wine. Drawing out the process of tasting, Alfred replied, "If you don't mind, I'd prefer the Chatteau D'ave." There was a stutter in the waiter's voice as he replied, "Excuse me a moment sir. I will enquire."

***

A little later, reluctantly, he emerged with the Chatteau D'ave. "I'm sorry for the delay, I had difficulty finding it. The Chatteau D'ave is a special wine reserved for the king's nephew, but as it happens, he dined here last night. For that reason alone, we can offer a half bottle."

"Well, if it's good enough for the king's nephew it should be good enough for me" said Alfred with a wry smile.

"Would Sir like to order?" the waiter asked.

"I will not have a starter. I will have duck with orange and apple sauce and with slow- cooked vegetables in garlic butter please."

***

The meal was worth the waiting, and the wine he'd always longed to taste proved rich and warm to the palate. Later, when he'd almost finished his meal, a passing group of people entering the dining area, stared coldly. He was thankful to see them head for a reserved table at the far end of the room. No sooner had he

38

put down his utensils than a waiter approached to ask him his choice of desert.

"I'd like caramel junket please?"

"I'm afraid we only have the items on the menu sir."

Well might I have a word with the manager or his assistant?"

"I-I- I will see what I can do-do- do- do sir" the young man stammered.

Feeling guilty about using him as a means for contacting Paulo, Alfred thanked him. As anticipated Paulo dramatically flung open the double doors and strode across the restaurant area. Thinking how ill-mannered the guest was, to be hiding behind the menu, he asked, "Good evening, Sir. How may I help?"

The hands holding the menu looked familiar. Who was this guest who knew some of their secrets he wondered? The voice, strangely quiet and drawn out, had a familiar ring, "If possible, I would very much like to work here."

"Why is that sir? Does sir have a problem with the bill?"

"No, Sir doesn't have a problem."

As Alfred placed the menu on the table, he watched Paulo's public facade dissolve. "Alfred, Alfred, you wicked-it is so good to see you. Do you really want to come back, and work?"

"I do, if possible, if there is a vacancy."

"As it happens you have come at the right time. Good weather's bringing many foreign-visitors. When would you be able to start?"

"If you are happy to have me, I could, if convenient, come on Thursday. It would give me time to sort things out. Here is the money for my meal, keep the change."

"Thank you. Yes, Thursday will be suitable. I'll see you at seven fifteen sharp, in time for the guests' eight thirty breakfast."

"I'll be here and I look forward to seeing you."

Chapter 7

Open Doors

Early morning Alfred opened the ancient door of the Catholic Church. As he entered the building the priest, athletic, tall, aged about thirty-five, sorting vestments, looked up.

"Good morning, can I be of help?" he asked.

Looking into the priest's lively brown eyes, Alfred quietly said "I am sorry to trouble you. I wonder if you are acquainted with Father Augustus? He works here in Ljubljana?"

"Yes, that is correct, I do know him. Why do you ask?"

"I'm hoping to get in touch because I once helped him in his mission work in Belgrade."

"I can give you, his address. Do you have pencil and paper?"

"Yes."

Alfred scribbled down the address the priest dictated.

"I'm interested in the Belgrade Mission- do tell me a little about your experience there."

Briefly Alfred told him about the aims of the mission and the activities he had been involved in. "Most interesting, our church community will do all we can to offer prayer support and the occasional donation" he said.

"Thank you, Father, I wish you every blessing."

***

A brief time later at Father Augustus' residence, Alfred knocked the familiar 'rat a tat' on the black door. From within, the lock turned, the door opened and Father Augustus peered out. Seeing Alfred, he enthusiastically said, "Alfred, how good to see you. Do come in."

Whilst following him along the corridor Alfred noted an uncharacteristic meticulous tidiness. Momentarily whilst tripping over a suitcase, Father Augusts' voice oscillated.

"I am glad you called. Father Spyridon mentioned you were in the area; I didn't know your address. Having trained a local curate, to take over mission work in this area, I am returning to Belgrade, today as it happens." Disappointed, Alfred replied, "I thought someone had taken over the Belgrade mission."

"They did, but he is a lay worker and a priest's work is essential, especially with all that is happening. I have received information about Belgrade- Germans facing an overload of bureaucratic and social difficulties. Come, sit down, and tell me some of your news over a cup of coffee."

He left the room and when he returned with coffee, apologetically said, "I'm afraid it'll have to be black, there's no milk."

"That is fine. Thank you. I am glad to have made contact."

"I cannot believe the change in you. You are a young man, no longer the adolescent."

"Yes, I don't know where time's gone."

"You are still young. I was forty-seven when I first came to Belgrade."

"That was 1932, wasn't it? I was fifteen."

"Yes, that's right, and you were getting over rheumatic fever."

"I miss mission and hope to return to it."

"Father Spyridon mentioned as much. I can tell you that current demands meet with your calling. It will involve risks that will deepen or break any mission worker's commitment. It would be good to have you with me, particularly as it comes with Father Spyridon's recommendation and blessing. You will need to build up finance from employed work if you are to join us in our under-cover- mission work. Will you get work at The Grand again?"

"I have contacted Paulo and I will be making a start on Thursday. I had hoped to find you here and-"

"And see if I was doing mission work here?"

"Yes."

"Well, God's plan will evolve as it is meant to. At least we have made contact."

***

Following Father Augustus' departure, Alfred, eager to engage in mission, knew he would have to apply himself in hotel-work. Gradually he settled into his lodging, where Mrs Hand's friendly manner and punctual nutritious meals, provided guests with a sense of stability. In a fleeting period, a family atmosphere filled the household. In this environment Alfred was aware how his spiritual growth had evolved within life at the abbey. His spiritual core was ready for fusion with the challenge of future mission during this time of social-political unrest.

At the hotel Alfred's unflagging enthusiasm pleased Paulo immensely. The following month, during an afternoon break, Paulo beckoned to say, "Alfred I've enough work as assistant manager without having to be head waiter. I would like to offer you that position."

As Alfred got up from his seat he enthused, "Thank you, I gladly accept." Then, looking Paulo in the eye, he shook his hand. "Let's join the others and tell them our news" said the restaurant manager.

As Paulo addressed staff members, he noted, except for Cynthia, their unanimous approval. Why she looked so downcast remained a mystery. Whereas everyone's attention focussed on Alfred, Cynthia's violet eyes were void of expression. Dismissing her lack of interest Paulo assumed she'd rather be looking at fashion magazine.

***

During the evening, the young woman crept downstairs to talk with sullen Garth, who had not long arrived for duty. "Alfred's been offered the job of head waiter. Someone said he has worked here in the past, and has been reconnected to where he left off" she murmured. Garth, tall with the look a heavy drinker, gratingly replied "I do not accept that policy. If a person leaves, they should start again. I have been here longer than him, longer than everyone in fact."

"Yes, but they say he left for a call of faith."

"The church should keep to its own affairs. The sooner it's stamped out and the state in control, the better."

***

Soon news circulated that German political parties were striving to dominate certain areas. Knowing he held the metaphorical cards; Garth began a quest of subtle innuendoes. Initially it baffled Alfred but gradually Garth's attitude became

42

transparent. Falling back on training Alfred wrangled with the daily practise of encompassing Garth in prayer. Even so, as time progressed, the persistent grind of unmerited prejudice squeezed in on Alfred's prayer space to a point of suffocation. During a coffee break, glowering Garth, staring hard at Alfred, markedly rolled the 'R's' and spat out the 'T's' as he forcefully said, "I hear that a German official called Heydrich, has formed a Reichssicherheits-hauptampt."

Sweetly, violet eyed Cynthia asked "What in heaven's name is that?" Seizing the opportunity, she had provided, Garth, with a hard stare in Alfred's direction, replied "The RSHA is a network directing and controlling wherever it can. Who knows how far it reaches? For all we know we might end up with one of its members in control here."

***

A few weeks later, during a similar break, Garth waving a folded newspaper, tauntingly asked, "Would anyone like to read this?"

"Why?" said several voices.

"It is about the German annexation of Austria. The Germans have a way of pushing their way in and taking over."

***

When Alfred apologetically declined his meal back at his lodging Mrs Hand enquired in a motherly fashion "What's wrong Alfred? You have not been yourself for weeks?"

"I've such a headache, I think I will go for a walk. I hope you will not mind."

"Well, no, but make certain you come straight back if you're feeling unwell."

"I will and thank you."

The cool air of the March evening served as refreshing contrast to the heat of the restaurant. Alfred's steps took him across the main square, into the Franciscan church, where the peace and tranquillity of the high vaulted atmosphere enveloped mind and soul. Eventually he heard the deep thoughts of his heart, *'There are situations in life we need to walk away from. It is only by walking away that one begins to see.'* Later, when, with clearer head, he returned to his lodging, he once more apologized for having missed the meal. After retiring early, a

43

passage from the biblical book of Isaiah came to mind, '*How beautiful are the feet of those that preach the gospel of peace-Go to the mission- Yes Lord. I have some financial backing now and our priest will know I haven't gone there because I don't know where else to go. He will know that I go there because you have sent me.*' With these thoughts in mind, he slept easier.

***

Next morning, having made his way to The Grand, he mentally practised what he might say to Paulo. However, as it happened, Paulo, during the day, became aware of Alfred's distracted manner.

With sadness in his eyes, he realized what was happening and commented, "You've decided to leave haven't you?"

"Oh Paulo, you read me like a book, you have the gift of discernment you know. I feel that with all the adverse news about Germany rather than the Nazi party, people will regard me as German, and over the course of time it would cause you and your staff immense problems."

"Isn't that a case of giving in to fear?"

"No, I sincerely do not think so. In a sense Garth is playing a part in God's plan, making me see my true direction. Garth's needling brings to the fore a growing problem of racial division within the community. It is there I am needed."

"Oh!"

"Before things escalate someone has to go to the mission, and work within the community. Father Augustus has sent me a news cutting."

With a puzzled look Paulo scratched his head but soon, understanding Alfred's intentions, he patiently said, "Go on I am listening."

"In order to do that, I need a reference. Will you give me one?"

"Of course, do you have work there in mind?"

"Yes, the advert is for seller of vacuum cleaners close to the Belgrade mission. Here look." Taking a crumpled bit of newspaper from his pocket he handed it to Paulo.

44

"Such work, out–and-about, would provide excellent cover for mission work. There are many innocent German people in trouble" Alfred explained.

"Should I mention your mission work?"

"No, that is strictly confidential. I would not let the company know of my role in mission or of problems Belgrade Germans are facing."

"I'll do the reference this evening, but Alfred it is such a low paid and ordinary job, do you really want to throw away a promising career?"

"I am sorry Paulo. Three years ago, I would have accepted what you are saying but monastic living has taught me deeper listening. Besides, on another level, my father has written to say he would like to see me."

Defeated, Paulo, with a wane smile, managed to go about his duties. Feeling sad about opting out of Paulo's plans Alfred prayed for him, and for all who worked at the hotel.

***

A week later, on his final day, of which staff members were not yet aware, it was with mixed emotions he made his way to The Grand. Unknown to him, Paulo, to avert suspicion, had arranged a staff gathering on Garth's, day- off. Five minutes before a planned extended break, Paulo ensured Alfred was present. As the break came near its usual finish time, Paulo picked up a wooden mallet and banged it three times on the table. Chatter ceased and everyone listened as he succinctly and eloquently explained, that much to the Grand's loss, Alfred was leaving, to be near his family in Belgrade. Alfred noted expressions of regret, acceptance, and good will on the faces of staff members. Someone whispered, "There would have been trouble from Garth if he'd been here today."

"Well thank goodness he's not here" someone loudly replied. Making mental note, Paulo decided he would dismiss Garth if any member of staff became a victim of his prejudice. He suspected trouble existed between him, a married man with children, and the unaware chamber- maid. She was looking full in the abdomen and all he could do was watch and wait.

When farewells were over, staff members dispersed to their duties.

"Paulo, I left my clean work uniform in my locker. I'll get it for you, and there are a few personal things in the locker" Alfred explained.

When he returned, and handed Paulo the outfit and locker key, his expression was quizzical.

"Paulo, you know that young waiter I teased the first evening?"

"Yes."

"Well, if he can withstand that during his initial week, he must have great potential."

A spark ignited within Paulo's mind; he wondered if the young waiter might fit his dream for The Grand. He turned to say *Darn it, man, you have managerial eyes* but Alfred had gone.

Chapter 8

Belgrade

Alfred's possessions fitted into one bag, making travel easy. There was only one occupant in the compartment he chose to sit in. Hungrily he took from his crumpled brown paper- bag one of Mrs Nijinsky's buns. As he bit into the bun, he recalled how pleased she'd been to have him call before leaving. At the end of the street, wondering if he would see her again, he'd turned and waved. Miss Hand too had generously provided cheese sandwiches.

As the buildings of Ljubljana rolled by, he considered how contemplative life at the abbey had enabled him to view things through the eyes of faith. He had come realize Miss Hand's strength of character, a person possessing maternal qualities of compassion and empathy. Her caring attitude helped people feel at ease and alert to their own potential. Through homely skills she had embraced her guests as family members.

He checked his jacket pocket, thankfully his wallet containing a thousand krona was safe. The money would help him through his transition. For a moment closing his eyes, he let imagination take him forward into mission. Soon sniffs, coughs and the occasional half whispered 'Ahhhh' distracted him.

"Are you alright?" he asked the very elderly gentleman. "Are you alright?" he asked again.

This time, by chance, the man, now looking in his direction, replied in oscillating voice, "I think you're trying to talk to me. I am stone deaf and I cannot lip read very well."

In apologetic gesture Alfred opened out his hands. Then, opening the paper bag, he offered the old chap a bun.

"Well, I'll be darned. Thank you," said the oscillating voice.
***
The buildings of Ljubljana had been left behind. Now, as the train slipped through villages and countryside, a cart losing its

load near a river loomed into view and disappeared. Alfred's thoughts wandered to the forthcoming interview that would not have been possible without Paulo's cooperation. Thankfully, he hadn't held him to the full term of his contract. Whatever the outcome of the interview, he planned to stay with his family one night only. He did not want them to think he planned to stay long term.

For a moment, as the train rolled into Belgrade, the waters of the river lapped turquoise and indigo against a wall of granite. Then it was gone from sight, and the platform came into view.

'Is it them?' Alfred wondered.

As he opened the compartment door, his sister Stephanie, no longer an awkward fifteen-year-old, but an elegant long-limbed woman, sauntered towards him. As she drew close, he noticed the sparkle of hazel in her brown eyes. The sheen of her dark hair gave the impression she had brushed it a thousand times. He noticed the style, with its mid parting that emphasized her wide eyes, and curved mouth. Ida and Stefan, a short distance behind, looked relaxed in each other's company. A noticeable light of welcome shone in their eyes. In turn he hugged them, and was glad to find his father free of the stale odour of alcohol. *The fruits of prayer and care* he thought. Ida looked happier, "I have my fourteen-year-old daughter Sylvia living with us permanently" she said.

"I look forward to meeting her. She is about the age I was when you first came to father's house" Alfred replied.

"Yes, I remember."

As they walked along the platform, Stephanie said, "I have some news too. I have a gentleman- friend."

"What's his name?" Alfred guardedly enquired.

"Milorad, he's tall and, well, a little older than me."

"It's a lot to take in. I look forward to meeting him."

With a trace of concern Ida said, "He's twelve years older."

"And a divorcee with children" Stefan added.

"He was divorced a long time ago, before he met me. His children are older than Sylvia and his wife set up with someone else when he was away in the army. You agreed it was not his fault Papa, and told me you approve."

"Yes, he is likeable and he obviously loves you. The fact that he and his brother are royalists is admirable. Do you know, Alfred, they had places of honour at the wedding of Prince Paul and Princess Olga?"

Stephanie continued, "Milorad said the Duke and Duchess of York came over from England for the occasion, but Milorad's first wife soon made it clear she was no royalist. I think, even then, she must have been influenced by her admirer."

"I am incredibly pleased for you Stephanie. It all sounds good, but you must not build up dreams until you know more about him, and more importantly, know for certain that you are in love with each other" Alfred advised.

Because he had sounded rather monastic, Stephanie folded her hands in feigned prayer.

"Yes Alfred" she solemnly answered.

Cheekily he smiled, feeling well pleased she was still his teasing younger sister.

When they were drinking coffee after their meal, Stefan announced, "I have some important news."

"Oh, what's that?"

"Three weeks ago, Ida and I were married."

"I guessed as much. You looked so relaxed in each other's company. I am extremely glad for you, congratulations."

"Thank you and Ida knows I shall never forget your mother. Anyway, what work will Father Augustus require of you? It will not affect your job, if you get it, will it?"

"No father, not at all, most of my mission work will be during the evenings. In his letter Father Augustus mentioned problems several Belgrade German- families are facing. The situation's getting worse."

Ida revealed, "Despite living here all her life and her late father being Serbian, Sylvia's been bullied at school."

With adolescent bashfulness Sylvia looked through a strand of fair hair at the guest.

Cuttingly, Stephan emphasised, "With all these pockets of unrest I hope history won't be repeated."

"What, you mean another great war?" Alfred questioned.

Silence gave answer.

As Ida passed Alfred a second cup of coffee, he saw her in a new light. He knew he had harboured unrealised adolescent indignation about her entry into the family. All in a few hours he had become highly aware of her thoughtfulness. It thoroughly pleased him how unafraid she was to mention his mother.

"Alfred, tell us about the Abbey and Ljubljana" Stephanie insisted.

With the occasional gasp and comment, they listened intently with noticeable interest.

As he finished his account, his father was quick to point out, "you are your happiest when you are amongst people. Prayer is important, but you are a sociable person rather than a contemplative."

'For once he might be right' Alfred thought and admitted he felt pleased about it. In the same instance he was aware of the early influence of Father Augustus at St Joseph's, and the later episode of losing his mother. The latter had drawn him towards and away from the contemplative life--*'Yet it's not away, it's within and a part of me for ever-even into eternity'* he thought.

"Alfred, won't you stay for at least a few nights?" Ida asked.

"It seems pointless getting lodgings until you know the outcome of your interview" Stephan added, in blunt but practical tone.

"Oh, do stay" Stephanie pleaded. Sylvia smiled coyly.

Relenting, he replied, "Unanimously you have persuaded me."

***

By Thursday, feeling rested, he left the house, dressed in a smart outfit Ida had pressed.

"Good luck son" said Stefan in a manner offering apology for past failings.

Alfred's smart suite served as an irritating reminder of the impending interview. Already he longed to change into his old comfortable clothes.

With light heart he walked to Elbe Street where he easily located the open doorway of the 'Jugoslavische AEG Elektricitats-Aktein- Gesellschaft' that he worked out to be a stockholding office, and shop for electrical goods. Cautiously he entered, and gradually his eyes adjusted to the dingy, dusty

50

salesroom. As if on guard, ten vacuum cleaners stood in a corner of the room. Various electrical goods were displayed on various tables. In response to the sound of a squeaky door hinge Alfred looked across the room to where a pale, over-weight, bald-headed man, emerged through the doorway of a small office. As he walked towards Alfred, he asked, "Can I help?"

"I am looking for Mr Jaager" Alfred replied.

"That's me. You must be Mr Ztoanjib. Not a Jugoslav name surely?" the man replied as, with the use of a large handkerchief, he mopped his brow.

"Yes, it is, although we settled in Germany when I was a child and the name was Germanized slightly."

"Oh well. Do come into my office. There are two chairs."

In the cramped office, Alfred soon realized Mr Jaager was not well educated. Therefore, he answered his questions precisely and clearly. He could see that simplicity and clarity pleased the store manager.

Eventually the prospective employer asked, "Finally, how you would you deal with an awkward customer?"

"It would very much depend upon the context. If I was selling at a hotel I might find out when a difficult member of staff had his day off. As for householders they are sometimes lonely and can invent reasons to get a sales person to call again. One should always attempt to make a sale by encouragement rather than argument. One needs to balance understanding of people, with business skills."

"I've asked a lot of questions, are there any you would like to ask?"

"Yes, the name on the door indicates you are a stockholdings society?"

"That's why this office exists but I also deal with sale of electrical goods."

"Oh, I see. That was all I wondered about."

"Rightly so young man, the job is yours if you would like it."

"Thank you, yes I would."

"Fine, I will show you how to service the demonstration model. In fact, that part is easy. The hardest part is coming back here to take it to anyone genuinely interested. How will you transport it?"

"Well, I can make a trolley and obtain a water proof cover."

"I meant to include that question in the interview. As it happens, we already have something like that. Follow me and I will show you."

"Wouldn't it be best to take the demonstration model as a matter of course?"

"Well if you've the stamina. The last chap couldn't manage it."

"I am sure I could. This district is quite flat."

By now Alfred was in front of the demonstration model on its trolley." Do you mind if I make an adjustment?"

Taking cue from the quick nod of Mr Jaager's head, Alfred turned the vacuum cleaner around so that the handle no longer protruded at an oblique angle. He proceeded to steer the trolley a few circles.

"You see, when the balance is right there's no problem."

"Very good!"

***

Later, Stefan, relieved to learn that his son was employed, went upstairs to tell Ida. She in turn came down to congratulate him.

"Thank you. Have you seen Stephanie?" Alfred enquired.

"She's outside."

Alfred went into the garden where he found his sister seated on a bench reading her First Aid book. Suddenly aware of his presence, she looked up. "How did it go?" she chirpily asked.

"I got the job."

Briefly her face fell and Alfred knew it was because she did not want him to move into lodgings.

Overcoming disappointment his sister positively commented, "It'll mean you can do real work for the mission."

"Yes, but keep that to yourself. The way things are going, the authorities would regard our work as counter-productive to their political aims."

"I understand. I expect that's what happened before Christ's trials and crucifixion."

Amazed Alfred laughed, "I doubt there's comparison."

"If you go into lodgings, you will come and see us, won't you?"

"Of course, is that Ida calling?"

"Yes, sounds as if supper's ready."

"I'm glad father decided to marry Ida" Alfred affirmed.

"Me to" she replied.

***

Between courses Alfred talked about his experience at the Grand. He spoke well of Paulo. Recalling his own friend and their journey up the Danube in the little blue boat many years ago, Stephan asked, "Do you remember my friend Peter?"

"Yes, we went there a few times when I was recovering from rheumatic fever."

"Well, they have a five-year-old daughter."

With an involuntary snort Ida added, "Yes poor Amelia thought she was getting too matronly too soon."

"That's wonderful news, I mean about the child. What is her name?" Alfred enthused. "Klarissa, and yes Peter did know about our little Klara who died."

Suppressing the painful memory of his deceased child, Stefan continued, on a practical note, "I recall his cousins having rooms to let near the town centre. Would you like me to call on Peter tomorrow and make enquiries?"

"Sounds a good idea, thanks; I'd much rather get accommodation through a contact if possible."

"I suppose that works both ways."

***

Next day the letter box cover flipped. Stephanie picked up the crumpled sheet of paper, read the untidy script and called, "It says, everything's fine, and Alfred can move in on Tuesday."

After smoothing out the paper she went into the sitting room and placed the note on the mantelpiece. She began to wonder what her brother's mission work, extending well into the evenings, would involve. Later, whilst preparing tea, her thoughts turned to her father and step- mother and what they might have bought today at the market. However, the luxury of trivial thoughts was short lived. Her main concern was Milorad, she hoped he was safe, and bitterly resented the need for armies and war. His words 'I'm sure time apart will strengthen our bond' conflicted with her emotion. Her heart informed her she could not happily live without him.

53

Later, the sound of her father and step- mother entering the house helped her focus on here and now.

"There's a note for you, on the mantelpiece Papa" she called.

"Thank you" he replied and went to read it.

With optimistic tone he enthused, "Oh that is good- Peter's cousin can provide accommodation. I see you have made a lovely tea Stephanie; I am famished."

Ida added, "Thank you Stephanie, my feet are killing me, I shall be glad to sit down."

***

The following Tuesday Alfred, thankful for a light, airy bedroom, had a splendid view of the river. Stephanie, who'd insisted upon helping him, had brought with her several reminders of home. He noticed her expression of delight as she arranged a bouquet of pink and white flowers in an oversized blue vase.

With arranging this and that and changing arrangements to what had first been decided, the afternoon passed. All too soon the clock chimed six.

"It can't be that time, can it? Best go home now."

"Yes, you'd better make a move. Ida will have your meal ready by half past. Thanks for your help, Stephanie, see you at the weekend. I'll let you know how I get on. Do not worry about Milorad. Everything will be fine." He accompanied her downstairs and watched her, in her powder blue dress, skim down the street.

***

An hour later someone rang a hand bell. With three other guests Alfred went down to the dining room where Peter's cousins, Anna, and Isobel, were waiting. A few days ago, when, with his father, he had met them, they had emphasised he would be staying on equal terms to other guests. 'I believe in equality and wouldn't accept an alternative' had been his positive reply.

Chapter 9

Journey of Faith

During the first week with the electrical firm Alfred successfully sold vacuum cleaners to several large establishments and six wealthy families within his sales circuit. Today, a Saturday, was free. Taking Father Augusts' advice, he followed the river bank to the mission hall but found the door locked and windows boarded. Around the back of the wooden building, every access was locked and boarded. Male voices, and the sound of footsteps swishing through long grass, drew his attention. *Would the owners of the voices ask him what he was doing?* "Hello Alfred, how are you?" said each young man in turn. "We thought you'd left Belgrade for good" the shorter man added. Alfred's puzzled expression dispersed when he realized they were adult versions of the thirteen-year-old boys he had formerly instructed. His smile was keen as he retorted, "Well lads, I mean men; it is good to see you. Yes, I did leave a few years ago but as you see I have returned."

"Yes, we heard."

"I am meant to be starting today. Tell me, what has happened? Things were not like this a week ago. I have not seen Father Augustus around."

In a mature voice the taller of the two quietly explained, "Father Augustus explained that because the authorities disapprove of the mission, it now takes place in a private house. He asked us to look out for you." "Thankfully, you're here and we can take you there" said the shorter of the two.

"Thank you, Manfred, isn't it?" Alfred replied.

"Yes, and he's-"

"Werne"

"Yes."

As he cautiously walked behind them, he wondered if his parents had been as apprehensive when they had moved to

Germany. The group of three left the river bank and walked along a narrow track that led to a quiet road. Half way along the road Manfred whispered "That is the house opposite. We will leave you now."

"Thanks Manfred, thanks Werner. See you soon I hope."

He crossed the road, walked up the stone drive leading to a large 1820's house, and pulled the bell rope. The broad, short legged man opening the door, reminded him of a toy man he had once owned. It had been impossible to knock the toy over. He remembered its painted grin and how, for quite some time, it had rolled from side to side before bobbing upright. Suppressing his sense of humour in the presence of this flesh and blood man wearing a dour look, Alfred brightly said, "Good morning. I'm looking for Father Augustus."

"There's no one here of that name" the man replied.

Inside the house a familiar voice resounded, "I recognise that voice. Alfred come in, do come in." With a barely noticeable sigh the tense man relaxed and with pleasanter countenance said, "Would you please come this way."

Alfred went in and gladly spent several hours discussing with Father Augustus the changing work of the mission. Increasingly, mission was extending beyond helping displaced families, into the realm of complex political tangles. Such were the grim harvest of official control and restrictions.

"The great increase in social problems echo on a much wider scale than you experienced at The Grand," said the priest.

"Men like Garth are stirring things up?"

"Yes, we must reverse the situation, by adding wholesome ingredients, if we are to counteract matters." Inspired by their conversation Alfred was fully alert and enthusiastic about using his sales-man image as a mission work cover. The combination worked, especially as he was willing to put in a great deal of time. Record sales had provided him with comprehensive insight into the escalating change of attitudes towards Germans. Sometimes he made late calls to German households, where he heard distressing stories of individuals being taken away for brutal interrogations. Without disclosing his mission, he regularly reported back to Father Augustus. Through such information the priest diligently supported families, and kept unrest at bay. Only a few people, working closely with Father Augustus, knew of the Christian work. The community accepted Alfred as an excellent salesman and good listener. Three months or more, everything went well, and many people were reunited with their families. Some were helped back to health following brutal interrogations. A few, for their own safety were smuggled into Germany through a route known to Father Augustus alone.

***

At the guest house, during supper one evening, a senior resident, Mrs Paverosky, looked up, and with a mischievous twinkle in her eye prompted, "Alfred, I have had a marvellous idea. You are fluent enough in German. Why don't you try selling vacuum cleaners to the German Embassy? I am convinced you would be successful."

A few guests teased, "Yes go on, we dare you."

Annoyed about his diminished status as centre of his wife's attention, Mr Paverosky snapped, "Alexandra Pass the wine-and a glass-and a napkin."

As Alfred conversed with fellow house guests, he decided he would try the embassy, not so much as a dare, but for the purpose of mission. He had often passed the foreboding establishment, and wondered if it were unrealistic to imagine that his role in mission could be the start of bridge- building across the social divide.

***

On Monday morning, when he went to collect the demonstration model, Mr Jaager was not around. Without anyone to question him Alfred headed for the embassy.

At the location, he went to the tradesman's entrance at the back of the building and pressed the well -worn bell button. Would anyone respond to its feeble sound? Hope rose with the light tap of footsteps descending the stairs. The door opened, a young lady with hostile green eyes, and head of unruly ginger curls, peered out. Forestalling being sent away, Alfred quickly said in German, "Many establishments have benefited from vacuum cleaners. They are efficient."

Noticing her waning interest, he casually added how, by using vacuum cleaners, companies were saving money as well as time. In Saxony accent she replied "Well if the vacuum cleaner is as

57

efficient as you say, Herr Stromitz might be interested. Wait here; I will ask him if he'd like to see you."

Glad to have re-captured her interest, Alfred listened to her footsteps ascending the flight of stairs.

***

Nervously she knocked on the door. "Come in" said Herr Stromitz in a clipped voice. Succinctly, Gisela Schein explained about the vacuum cleaners, how other establishments were making use of them. She could see that the need for fewer cleaners was of interest to her employer. With a suggestive look in his eye he said, "You have persuaded me, send him up."

He watched her curve around the door way. With a sigh he imagined intimate scenes with her, and blissful escape from daily scathing remarks from his wife.

A short while later, Gisela's footsteps returned, followed by slower steps and the bump of the vacuum cleaner being dragged or wheeled upstairs. As the salesman entered, Herr Stromitz, scrutinising, challenged, "So you speak German?"

"Yes, I was born in Neubeckum, and lived there until I was eleven."

"My home town is Münster, not far from there."

Step one 'identifying with the potential customer' had been achieved.

"I'd like to ask your secretary to tip out the contents of the ashtray onto the carpet."

"Pardon?" said Gisela.

"Oh, I see! Proceed," Herr Stromitz affirmed with a chuckle, and watched his secretary empty the ash onto the carpet.

With looks of curiosity they watched the visitor plug in the vacuum cleaner, switch it on, and in a matter of seconds use it to suck up ash.

"You see no trace left" Alfred declared with a smile.

"Goot,goot,goot; I will have six models."

"Do you mean you wish to buy six models?"

Yes, yes. Ten kroner each you said, didn't you?"

"Deliver them in the morning and I will pay you sixty kroner."

"Thank you, Aufwiedersehen" Alfred replied.

58

Regardless of having to pull the demonstration model, Alfred ran back to the shop because he knew there were only seven vacuum cleaners in stock. A short distance from the shop, he looked on with dismay, as a hefty man struggled to pull a vacuum cleaner through the doorway. As the man passed Alfred, he said, "I could do with one of those trolleys."

Avoiding conversation Alfred smiled briefly and quickly entered the shop. "Please don't sell any more" he gasped.

"In Heaven's name why not?" Mr Jaager replied.

"I've an order for six and need to deliver them tomorrow."

"Well done. I knew you had it in you."

"There'll be commission on top of your wages for that number of sales in one week." "Really, thank you, I didn't realize."

"Who's made such a generous order?"

"Well, actually, um, the person in charge at the German Embassy!"

"God's truth, you've a nerve, but that is what selling's about. However, in this instance I advise that when you have your money you don't ever go there again."

"I'll take your advice."

"Good and I should have warned you. You –young- people don't really know what is going on."

***

Next day Alfred made three trips to the embassy. Each time taking with him, two vacuum cleaners, precariously balanced on the trolley, which caused the trolley wheels clatter.

"I'm sorry about the noise" he said to an old man emerging through a door-way.

"It doesn't bother me. Do I detect a German accent?"

"I spent some of my childhood in Germany" Alfred explained.

"My name's Cecil, I'm German- Jew," said the man.

"Like me you are a mixture, Alfred's my name. I would best be going now as I must make several trips to this establishment."

During the day Cecil mulled over "several trips," and eventually convinced himself that assuredly, the vacuum

59

cleaners contained secret documents. "He must be a spy" he muttered. By late afternoon, hoping to prove his worth as a good citizen of Belgrade, he visited the police station.

Seated at his desk, the sergeant agonised over several unresolved pockets of unrest, for which his superiors needed concrete evidence. At the appearance of the irritating bent backed regular visitor, he sighed loudly.

"What is it now Mr Nettlebaum?" he snapped. Initially, half listening to old man's prattling, he became suddenly alert at mention of the German Embassy.

"He might be a spy. He comes from Germany. Pointedly the elderly resident conveyed, "He's not a real Slav; hasn't lived here all his life, as I have."

Grasping the glimmer of hope for resolution, the sergeant positively replied "Thank you. We will investigate."

With a self- satisfied look on his face, Nettlebaum departed.

***

Next day, due in part to Mrs Paverosky's insistence the previous evening, they would have a supper time celebratory toast, Alfred had a head ache. He pictured the house guest raise her glass and in light- hearted tone say, 'Let's raise a toast to Alfred's success in selling vacuum cleaners to the German Embassy.'

Somehow, he got through the busy day ahead, and planned to have a relaxing, quiet evening. However, during late afternoon, at the end of Bendall Street, someone with an aggressive voice grabbed him and pushed him to the ground. Something hard, someone's knee by the feel of it, pressed into the small of his back. Two new male voices were on scene. Large hands wrenched his head to one side and into the pavement. In a quick glance he identified them as police officers. An officer grabbed his wrists, handcuffs closed tight on his skin. In seconds, his hands felt numb, but before he could object someone hauled him to his feet.

"What's happening?" he asked.

"No questions; keep walking. We are taking you to the station" said the second officer.

***

60

At the station the sergeant, at his desk, ignored the bewildered look on the suspects face.

"You're Alfred Ztoanjib?" he asked in automated tone.

"Yes, I am."

"Take him to the cells. Get the truth out of him," said the sergeant.

Of the three officers, the heftier police officer forced him down stone stairs into a large cell. When he unlocked the handcuffs Alfred's relief was brief, for the man said "Remove your jacket." Rifling through Alfred's pockets he found the wallet containing savings of a thousand kroner. The second policeman, medium and muscular in stature, grabbed Alfred's wrists and forced his arms to the front, and clipped on the handcuffs. Through gritted teeth Alfred managed to say "What's this about?"

A clenched fist hit him across the jaw.

"Just answer the questions."

Almost passing out, Alfred heard the sergeant's voice echo strangely down the stairs,

"The night duty sergeant has just arrived. He says you can work a bit longer if you need to."

Smirking, the first police officer answered, "Thank you sergeant, we'll do our best to get some information."

"Don't be too long."

With a brief apologetic glance in Alfred's direction a third police officer, nudged by the first, replied, "No sergeant."

"And don't go overdoing it" said the sergeant's voice from above the steps.

With mock obedience they simultaneously replied, "No sergeant."

Alfred watched the hefty policeman's eyes move in the direction of the slighter officer who removed truncheons hanging on wall hooks. Alfred noticed how he masked a reluctance to hand over the offensive weapon.

"Now that the hard of hearing, night sergeant is on duty, we'll try again. Answer yes or no or short replies.... Are you German?"

"Yes- born there."

The bully nodded to his assistant, immediately a truncheon repeatedly struck Alfred across the back of his legs, almost flooring him.

"Did you go to the German Embassy yesterday?"

"Yes."

"Why?"

"I went to sell vacuum cleaners."

Vice like, the policeman's grip tightened around Alfred's throat. Menacingly the interrogator spat out his words, "We don't like lies."

Forcefully the accomplice struck Alfred across his cheek and nose, narrowly missing his eyes. In softer tone the persecutor snapped, "Turn around." As the accomplice unlocked the handcuffs Alfred wondered if he might be released.

"Place your hands against the wall," said the accomplice.

"Tell us about your work as a spy" his voice continued, less dictatorial.

"Tell us, tell us whispered the prime instigator close to Alfred's ear.

He picked up the remaining truncheon and energetically reigned blows on the prisoner's back. Alfred felt his spine burn like fire from its core, and as an antidote he willed himself to focus on Christ and the beatings he had endured. In his heart and mind, he repeated over and again "Adoramus te Christe, benedicimus tibi, quia per cruem tuam redemisti mundum-Christ I adore you, blessed one, redeemer."

"Are you a spy?

"No."

"What did you do before you sold vacuum cleaners?"

"I was a waiter in Ljubljana."

He felt the agonizing blow of a truncheon across his ear. Through a thick fog someone asked,

"Why did you come here?"

"To be near my family"

"What did you do before you were a waiter?" Truncheons smashed against each hip.

"I was a postulant" Alfred answered with a grimace.

"You were a what?"

"A novice- monk."

Amidst the sound of their insane laughter, they continued with their beatings. Unable to see clearly, Alfred clung tightly to Christ's words on the cross, *'Forgive them; they know not what they do.'* A crescendo of laughter echoed and the words *they put on him the purple robe* swept across the rapid pump of his heart. Purple enveloped him and he was unaware of the police officers recoiling at the sight of his weird and fiendish fit.

The sound of his grinding teeth and the sight of his foaming mouth, unnerved the police officers. Leaving the prisoner inert on the cold stone floor they left the scene. Whilst turning the key in the lock the second policeman commented, "Let's hope he doesn't die before we get some information."

"Come let us get home. The night sergeant will not bother to come down here. You can clean the truncheons" he said to the third policeman. As the two bullies left, the slight policeman picked up the offending truncheons, washed them in a stone sink in an adjoining room, and placed them on a small table. He was about to leave, but turned back, opened the cell door, unlocked the hand cuffs, retrieved the prisoner's jacket, and covered him. He hoped some warmth would help the unfortunate man survive the night. As the young police officer locked the cell door and hung up the key he considered reporting matters to the night sergeant, but he knew that the consequences would be grave. He would be out-numbered and his witness would carry little or no weight.

***

The strike of four coming from the distant tower clock resounded through the purple- darkness. Little by little Alfred regained consciousness. Soon the monks would be praying, and he would be strengthened. Gradually as he fell into disturbed sleep, the words 'escape, escape' whispered through his soul.

Next morning the day sergeant arrived early.

"Good morning, Marco, anything to report from last night?" he enquired.

"Everything was quiet."

"Good."

"Sylvester, do you realize you're early?"

63

"Yes, I want to get on with my report. By chance I met up with one of my duty policemen, last night."

With wry humour he said, "With the way we're going we'll soon have to start writing our reports before an incident happens."

With a cough he added, "At least you're moving in the right direction. Do you need me to stay?"

"There's no need."

As soon as his colleague had gone, the day sergeant looked at the officer's brief report and picked up the telephone receiver. Punching out the syllables, he clarified, "Operator, could you put me through to the nearest monastery beyond Ljubljana?"

He tried two establishments. The second voice on the receiving end helpfully said, "Well, the only other place I can think of is the Catholic Abbey, about ten kilometres from Belgrade. It's your area code and their number is 312."

"Thank you for your help" the sergeant replied.

He dialled the number and relayed, "This is Sergeant Gora of Belgrade Police Station. I'm enquiring about the back- ground of a German by the name of Ztoanjib. He says he was a monk."

"Did he say that? He was a novice; his Christian name is Alfred."

"Can you tell me why he left the monastery; I mean Abbey?"

"He left of his own free will."

"Can you tell me his nationality?"

"During his childhood he lived in Germany. His parents were Serbian I believe. I hope nothing is amiss?"

"No, not at all, thank you for your assistance."

He slammed down the receiver, took a large key from the desk drawer, made his way across the room, and down the stone steps to the cells. Noticing Alfred's comatose body on the cell floor he furtively glanced around, picked up the recently washed truncheons from the small table and placed them in a room close to the cells. Something in the tone of the voice on the other end of the telephone line stirred his conscience. He unlocked the cell door, went in and bent over the prisoner. Thankful that he was breathing, he picked up his jacket, helped him to his feet and supported him in standing position.

"We have decided to release you. If you mention anything against us, we will have you back. Do you understand?"

Alfred nodded and winced as the police sergeant urged him forward and up the stairs. At the main door Alfred noticed his forcing down of compassion as abruptly, he said, "Go and don't let me see you here again."

Now aware that Alfred was about to collapse, he continued helping him along the street.

***

Away from the police station the sergeant's tone was inoffensive. Realising the man's anxiety, Alfred cooperated as best he could. Regardless of mental fog he guessed the officer was afraid of losing his job. He came across as one whose position in life conflicted with conscience. Alfred sensed reluctance to regard foreigners with contempt. This police sergeant knew that the prisoner had been wrongly arrested and persecuted. This man, taking risk, was operating within restricted context. This man was blessed.

In the fresh air of early morning, with no one about, the sergeant supported and pushed Alfred along the road. He helped him put on his jacket and deposited him on the baker's doorstep a fair distance from the police station. Through the fog of semi-conscious stupor, Alfred heard him say "Someone will see you when the shop is opened. Remember you answer nothing except to say that someone attacked you, and you do not know who."

***

The sergeant, on his way to the station, considered that if the worst happened, they would have to change their records. Suppressing emotion, he forced himself to justify his actions and to overlook the predicament brought about by the abominable cruelty of some officers. Mulling over the fact that Alfred had left the abbey of his own free will, he toyed with the idea that he might be a spy. His better nature fought for breath and he settled for compromise, he would have a word with his men about their heavy handedness. He knew for certain that two members of his police staff were gaining pleasure from interrogations. Their action was putting prisoners at risk and undermining the true authority of the police force.

65

First to pass the shop doorway; was a man of the road. He did not want to get involved. Close to two hours later, Father Augustus, returning from early house communion, happened to come that way.

'What is it?' he wondered, "Oh no-A person, a battered one at that!

Heavens- above- its Alfred. What has happened? Come let me help you. I will take you to the mission at Mr Rundmann's house."

A momentary moan of relief welled up in Alfred's throat; next moment he was comatose.

Later a woman's voice connected him with reality.

In undefinable accent she said, "Holy mother of God, who has done this terrible deed? His face is barely recognisable. Hopefully, his sight will not be affected. I will get a glass of water and a straw so that he can drink."

Vaguely, Alfred remembered someone bringing him here. The woman's voice continued, "With such a swollen mouth he will only be able to drink a little at a time. I will see it is often. Robert, I need linen cloth, bandages, iodine, and a bowl of warm water."

Her subsequent request indicated the presence of the two mission helpers, "Manfred could you see if there are any drinking straws?" After pausing for breath, she continued, saying,

"Werne, there's goat's milk in the larder. Can you get a pan and warm it on the stove? Poor Alfred, do not worry we will help you get better. Firstly, I need to wash you and your wounds. I will have to use iodine and it will sting a little I am afraid."

Slowly and painfully over the initial weeks he began to respond to the healing hands of the nurse. Because his swollen eyelids obscured his sight, it took him several moments to recognize his God sent nurse as Mr Rundmann's Irish wife, Eilish. At first, he had not identified her as the large, silent, heavy- handed woman he'd seen scouring pots. "Lord, forgive me my earlier misjudgement and thank you for sending such a kind and gentle nurse. Mind you I am glad I'm not a pot," he whispered.

Several weeks later, feeling stronger, he was able to relate all that had happened.

"Father Augustus, I need to contact my family and the people at the guest house."

With assurance the priest commented, "Your story confirms all we'd suspected. I informed people at the guest house that you are ill. I visited your family to let them know that the police may have misjudged your social standing. My reply to Stephanie's asking if things were related to mission work was, 'I don't think so, no one has spoken to me.' Your family are aware that you are in some secret house. They asked me to let you know they are thinking of you. Hopefully, everything has been thought of."

"Thank you, but I'm wondering if, for practical reasons, you might be able to contact them."

In a lilting voice Eilish interjected, "You are not to worry, Father has seen to everything. He has even collected your belongings from the guest house. He realised you would not want to go on paying for not being there."

When three days later, Alfred's eyes opened, the light was at first, painfully bright. However, as his eyes adjusted, he was profoundly thankful his sight had not become impaired.

On a sunny day, during the following week, he was able to sit in the garden. There he noticed on a bush of the fuchsia category, a small species of bees buzzing in and out of orange-tinged flowers. After a while, his attention was drawn to the pitch of their droning. It reminded him of something-

But what? Ah, I know, intoning; the pitched intoning of The Lord's Prayer-intoning is not man's invention it is a style of praise already existing in the natural world. It is a necessary part of prayer that helps everyone return to their natural place within God's presence.

Chapter 10

Escape

Father Augustus found his way to 'The Elektricno D fustro A.D.' As he looked around the doorway of Mr Jaager's office he sensed God at work in bringing Alfred to this place. For a moment he silently prayed, giving thanks for his mission workers, and the strangely miraculous arrangement that was proving their loyalty. Neither had disclosed to the other their mission role. From his list of Catholics with German connection, the priest had seen a positive factor in Mr Jaager's absence from church services. Of further advantage Mr Jaager never involved himself in religious or political debate. Viewing him as a fringe sympathiser, the authorities never questioned him. Because Father Augustus had never reproached him about his waning church attendance, friendship and loyalty had been secured. Only as the plight of Germans within the community worsened had the priest requested Mr Jaager's help with passports.

At first, when he light heartedly had said, "One of your official stamps could easily be mistaken for a passport stamp" Mr Jaager had not understood. He recalled looking the mission contact in the eye until he realised the implications.

On this September day, the return of his smile dissolved, as Augustus asked, "I would be grateful if you would sign and stamp Alfred's passport. Because of what happened to him I must urgently get him out of the country."

"But haven't there been enough risks? They are tightening the screws."

Deducing his meaning, Father Augustus reassuringly added, "I have adopted a new strategy and I doubt anyone will look at the passport. Trust me it is a precautionary measure."

Tempted to ask about the new strategy, Mr Jaager realised it best to not know.

"I really do not want to lose Alfred. He's a reliable worker."

"I know, and the fact he was brought up in Germany is a hindrance in this political climate. You do realize that had he not had contact with me there, he would not be doing mission work here."

"Ah, I see, so he's on board also. What happens if my work for you is discovered?"

"I have thought of that. If you are questioned you can explain that the ink pads and ink stamps have been stolen, and that your signature must have been forged."

"But what if an expert verifies the signature as genuine?"

"I will type up a letter on a private typewriter and ask Werner to forge your signature and keep it in our safe. Should a situation arise I'll use it as supporting evidence."

"I'm confused"

"It simply means that if they suspected us, the signature wouldn't be compatible with your signature on the passport."

"I'll comply but I'm not entirely comfortable" Mr Jaager replied.

Moderately appeased, he opened the dark navy cover of the passport. When he had found the appropriate pages, he signed one signature in red and the other in black. Whilst screwing up the lids of the ink bottles he explained "I've put the date of his arrival 6th July 1938 on one page in black, and today's date 20th September 1940 on the other page in red. It looks authentic. As he handed back the passport he commented, "Hopefully all will go to plan."

"I hope so. Remember God loves you for your part in our-his work. Even though you are unaware of your role, you are an instrument of peace. Your small contribution is helping save lives."

"I am glad you see me like that. My wife calls me an argumentative old sod, and I must admit I'm no saint."

"Saints do not happen over- night; they become recognised through the work of God within and beyond their earthly life."

With a new sense of self- worth Mr Jaager pointed out "I don't want to see anything happen to that honest, hard-working young man."

"Good. Then I'm certain you will not mind one more request."

"What's that?"

"Quickly write out a testimonial for him, in case he needs it."

"I have a supply of headed paper. What do I say to the authorities if they find the reference, I mean testimonial?"

"Just say he left of his own accord, and that's why he asked for a testimonial in person."

Mr Jaager went over to his desk and constructed in basic Serb-Croat, a testimonial about Alfred's loyal, hardworking, honest, and cooperative attitude.

"Father Augustus, I'm afraid the grammar isn't too special."

"Never mind that, it'll serve its purpose and he'll be able to apply for work wherever he goes."

***

Later, Father Franz Augustus gazed out of the window and watched the orange orb of sun sink behind the houses on the opposite river bank. He sat down, ran his fingers through his springy greying hair, and remained silent and still, watching and praying several hours. With all his heart he hoped Sergi would not meet with difficulties along his journey. As night fell, he headed for the mission, all the time handing over his concerns to prayer and the love of God. Gradually his thoughts came into rational focus. Sergi, Mr Rundmann's nephew, had, for the sake of the mission, established himself as a regular and familiar tradesman- farmer from beyond the far side of the city. God was assuring him of Sergi's valid excuse for visiting Belgrade.

At the mission house, Father Augustus went to the kitchen to get a hot drink. Hearing the doorbell ring in recognized pattern he stalled his task, opened the door and hastily ushered Sergi in.

With great relief he said, "I'm glad you have safely arrived. Is everything in order?"

"Yes. Your man can hide in the straw under the canvas. If he keeps silent no one will know he is there."

As Alfred entered the room, the lean fair haired young man stared.

"Alfred this is Mr Rundmann's nephew, Sergi."

70

Amazed that the lean, tall fair haired Sergi was related to the stocky, bald-headed Mr Rundmann, Alfred shook hands and thanked him twice over.

"You're in a better condition than I expected" said Sergi.

Enthusiastically Father Augustus added, "Well, a month has passed since I wrote to your parents. Thanks to your Aunt Eilish, Alfred's made excellent recovery. When your aunt and uncle are up and about you will have to visit."

"I suppose at this hour too many lights going on, rather than off, would arouse suspicion" Sergi replied.

"Exactly, now Alfred, I presume you have your passport, your testimonial and my letter?"

"Yes, I do."

"Good, now repeat the procedure."

"I'm to go through the end of the garden. When the train stops, a large lady, by the name of Mrs Tiveresky, will open the door of the third compartment."

"You've missed something."

"Oh yes, I must put on overalls before getting on the train."

"That is important. They are railway worker overalls."

"Now, what comes next?"

"I pretend to check the carriage door. The moment the signal man looks the other way to change the signals and track, I get in. I say nothing, quickly remove the overalls and give them to Mrs Tiveresky who will place them in her large bag. No one will question her, as her brother works on the railway. When she's seated, I crouch down behind her skirts."

"I hope she won't have eaten pickled onions the day before" Sergi teased.

Father Augustus pretended to not hear, Alfred coughed.

"Sorry, I forgot my manners" said Sergi.

***

Suddenly the mood changed, Alfred did not miss the look of concern in Father Augustus' blue eyes as he came over to hug him and bless him.

He opened the door and added, "God bless you too Sergi, and protect you from harm. Thankfully, by the sound of it, your horse has found the bucket of water."

Outside, in the night air, the horse, sensing imminent departure, quickly consumed the water in the bucket. No one was about, and quickly Alfred got into the cart, to hide under the straw. To ensure his passenger was well hidden Sergi rearranged the top layer, and deftly flung a canvas over the straw.

"Have you enough air?" he whispered.

"Yes, my head's near a gap between the planks."

"Good."

In the darkness they trundled towards the outskirts of Belgrade.

**

Later, in the heart of the countryside, the phosphorescent light of the full moon enhanced the beautiful wings and glowing eyes of moths, flitting in small clusters near the gap between the planks. A bat flew close and away again, involuntarily, and briefly, Sergi cried out.

Around two hours later, driver and passenger were silent. Finally, cold, scared and lonely Alfred sensed the horse take the weight of the cart as they rolled downhill and came to a halt.

"You can get out now" Sergi whispered.

**

As Alfred crept out, he noticed, beyond the gate, a short distance down the road, a large, moonlit country house with a long garden backing onto a railway track.

As planned, not a word was exchanged and Sergi, pretending to know nothing of a passenger, continued onward up the next hill, towards his own farmstead.

Hiding in the shadows, Alfred took in the spectre of bright-eyed moths darting through the busy night. As he walked along the front path, he noticed how the limestone walls of the house glistened brightly in the moonlight. Mythological in appearance, creeper eerily snaked up to the slate roof above the ledges of the highest windows. Thinking that someone was behind him he jumped, turned, and instantly realized how the light of the moon across a heap of rusting machinery had created the shadow. According to plan he went around the side of the house and tapped the mission rat a tat on the window. Two people seated in the room remained still. Several minutes later, without a word, one of them, a man, came over, opened the window and withdrew. As planned Alfred remained silent until the couple had left the room. A measured space of time later he clambered through the open window, shut it, and closed the curtains. He crept across the room, through a doorway and into an inner hallway.

Hearing a kind voice say "Hello, I'm Mrs Roensky, and glad you've arrived safely" he looked up. His host's compassionate face was surrounded by a mop of premature white hair. Her brown eyes were direct and welcoming.

"I'm very pleased and relieved to meet you," said Alfred.

"I expect you are cold and hungry; come have some hot soup before you retire. Well hidden, behind a stack of books in the attic, you will find a bed made up and ready."

"Thank you, you're very kind, and if someone saw me enter through the window it validates my status as intruder."

"Come, meet my husband" she said.

Along the corridor they went left into a small room where Mrs Roensky introduced him to her husband, a broad-shouldered man. With too firm a grip he shook Alfred's hand and from beneath a walrus moustache his strong voice boomed, "Well young man we will do our utmost to help you on your way. It's a dangerous time for everyone."

Ignoring the throb of his knuckles Alfred enquired, "Don't mind my asking but does your accent indicate you come from elsewhere?"

"I am Polish and my wife is of German origin. Three generations ago our families settled here. You could say we are 'in- between people.' We understand that things are not black and white. Of course, Serbian officials assume I would not help Germans, but, as my wife pointed out, it is The Nazi Party, not Germans, behind the invasion of Poland. I cannot envisage Serbian authorities taking the trouble to look back three generations where they would discover my wife's German ancestry. She empathises with people like us. Anyway, enough of that, it is well past midnight, you must be hungry, let us eat."

During the meal Mrs Roensky related how, during her fifteenth year, Father Augustus had helped her find her siblings who had been placed in orphanages.

"My husband was my brother's childhood friend. After we married, we decided to support the work of the mission."

"And Father Augustus saw potential in you and the location of your house?"

"Yes, he is amazing. He finds a solution to every problem."

"Assuredly he's a clear channel for God's work" Alfred replied.

***

Later, in the attic, Augustus's plan repeatedly ran through Alfred's mind and he could not sleep. From time to time, in the eaves, birds shuffled in their nests. Eventually, by imagining the birds settle for the night he also managed to settle and sleep.

***

All too soon it seemed, Mrs Roensky called "Breakfast's ready." Quickly Alfred got out of bed, washed, dressed, and on his way found the convenience where soap and clean hand towel had been left on a small table near the sink. He went into the dining room, where Mrs Roensky observing his anxious expression, assured, "Do not worry, God is with you. He will protect you."

"You are right. Thank you but do you mind if I don't have breakfast?"

"Just take some deep breaths. You need to eat well, because in addition to the journey being long, much of it will be spent in an awkward position for which you will need stamina."

"I know, but Mrs Tiveresky is a large woman with meters of clothing. I am to crouch only when she taps her umbrella as indication of someone coming."

"I have a group photo with her in it, here on the shelf. She is the fifth one along from the left, back row."

"Gosh, she is big, but looks kind."

"She is, and she's a good woman."

"Let's hope she has a compartment to herself" boomed Mr Roensky as he left the room to see to the pigs.

"Here are the overalls. According to Father Augustus' instructions I have shortened the arms and legs," said Mrs Roensky.

In process of finishing a second bread roll Alfred mumbled his thanks.

74

Whilst Mrs Roensky took crockery to the kitchen, Alfred slipped the overalls on. *'Thank goodness, they're a perfect fit'* he thought. For a moment he sat and discreetly prayed,

"Please protect me throughout this journey Lord, and protect others who have and those who will be travelling within Father Augustus' safety net. Dear God please see Father Augustus safely to Neubeckum, before matters become impossible. Bless my family members wherever they may be. Amen."

***

As anticipated, at five O'clock, the train that would remain stationary for a half hour was arriving. The rhythm along the track stirred up memories of the childhood railway incident following his mother's death. In this moment of time, he was crouching behind a different bush at the end of another garden. How he longed to run back to the people he'd just said his farewells to. Through the loud thud of his heart beat the words *'things mustn't go wrong'* repeatedly resounded. Fumbling in his pockets he wondered if he had lost his passport and papers. Eventually, much to his relief, he located them in another pocket.

The train arrived, ground to a halt, and through the gap of a partially opened door he saw Mrs Tiveresky, the woman in the Roensky's photo. He ran to the carriage and pretentiously checked the door. Thud, thud, thud— 'he *couldn't slam it again, could he? Would the signal man never look the other way?'* Alfred pretended to tie up a loose shoe lace.

'I'll have to check the door'--thud. Suddenly the signal man pulling various levers looked the other way. Mrs Tiveresky opened the door, Alfred jumped in, took off the overalls,

"Quick, give them to me I'll put them in my bag."

Mrs Tiveresky flopped into her seat. With no time for embarrassment Alfred crawled on the floor, and crouched behind the layers of her skirt.

Twenty-two minutes later the train steamed into motion. Throughout the long journey there were occasional stops. At one such station some Germans alighted, having been granted, at great expense, official passage of return. Unabashed, Mrs Tiveresky informed him, "They took one look at me and quickly retreated to another compartment."

Chapter 11

On the Train

Anxious and silent, Alfred lay down on the carriage floor.
"Quick, hide, ticket inspector's coming" Mrs Tiveresky whispered.

Rapidly reverting to crouching position behind the vast layers of her skirts, Alfred cast agonising back ache to the back of his mind. Already the ticket inspector was entering. *'Why in heaven's name is Mrs Tiveresky asking a string of unhurried, polite comments?'*

Shortly afterwards he surmised, that she needed to distract the inspector.

What Alfred could not see was how, after opening a window, the inspector unguardedly smiled at Mrs Tiveresky.

Unaware of Alfred's presence or his awareness of the man's enticing tone, the ticket inspector crooned, "We wouldn't want you getting too hot madam would we."

Having found excuse for a move in her direction, he flirtingly slid his foot under the hem of her long skirt. Having worked its way under the front hem, the foot continued to the back hem, and currently remained precariously close to Alfred's hand. As the shoe touched his finger tip he froze with fear.

To his relief, Mrs Tiveresky, avoiding mention that she was widowed, talked about her husband and his love of trains. Her words were to advantageous effect; the intrusive foot slid away, and with its partner took the inspector out of the carriage, and along the corridor.

"Phew, that was awkward. He looked very sheepish as he left. I suggest you come out, stretch your limbs, and lie straight for a while. In a few hours we will be going through Hungary."

As Alfred tentatively emerged, Mrs Tiveresky opened her bag. "Could you please put these overalls back under the seat

where no one will see them. My brother will collect them later"
she said.

"So that's how it's done" Alfred replied with a chuckle.

"What time do you think we'll arrive in Czechoslovakia?"

"Around nine, they will be checking passports. After that we
transfer to other trains where we will remain until around five
O'clock tomorrow morning."

"In a way I will be glad to have my passport checked, because
I will then be able to sit upright. I do not know if I will survive
many more hours of hiding."

"You will, because your life depends on it."

Later, ponderingly, Mrs Tiveresky commented, "I wonder
how the Czech people are coping under the
'Reichsprotectorate'."

"You mean the state protection. The meaning's ambivalent.
They certainly will not protect the Czechs or anyone else. I must
admit I feel uneasy about returning to Germany."

"It's a worry."

"You are right. Had I remained in Serbia I would have been
tortured and killed. They might have targeted my family."

"Oh, time to get in the queue. Do not forget, Father Augusts'
net- work is reliable."

"Yes, he learned that German officers checking passports
were trained to detect immediately, German origins. He assured
me they would be focussing on the first two pages of each
passport at this stage.

"I wish you all the very best, good luck."

"Thank you for your help. God bless you in your mission."

"I have to get out here too."

As they left the carriage Alfred's heart thumped loudly. Only
as he silently prayed on his way to the check point, did his pulse
steady. Following a few tense moments, the guard, without
checking the final pages, suddenly let him through. Appreciating
a few moments of freedom, he longingly looked up at the
beautiful wooded hillside. Mrs Tiveresky was catching up he
noticed. Moving his lips as little as possible, he quietly said,
"Thank you; you have altered the whole course of my life. I shall
always think of you as Saint Skirt."

By now they were beside the bus. As Mrs Tiveresky hauled herself up the bus steps, she suppressed a giggle. Alfred and several other passengers followed. The driver drove the bus a short distance around winding, narrow roads. Loudly someone mentioned how this interim means of transport prevented potential fugitives switching trains before the next check point. The driver stopped outside the Czechoslovakian station, from where the early morning train would transport them to their destinations.

"We'd best separate now. Eyes are everywhere" Mrs Tiveresky murmured.

Briefly, Alfred smiled and watched her walk to a front of train compartment destined for Berlin. When she was out of sight, he made his way to one of four compartments for western Germany at the rear. Three men, of similar age to him, were already seated. A voice over the speaker system informed that no one was allowed to use the platform toilet unless escorted by an official person. Because everyone was in the same predicament, the complaining platform officer had to work a half hour or more over time. When, at last, everyone was back in the carriages, doors were locked.

***

Early morning, at a time when many people were sleeping, they felt a jolt and heard a clunk as carriages moved and separated. Tracks clicked into position and soon, the engine pulling the Berlin section chugged out of the station, Alfred caught a glimpse of Mrs Tiveresky, who to all appearances did not notice him. Observing her nostalgic smile, he wondered if this might be her last journey home after visiting her Serbian brother.

Remaining passengers were permitted to use the platform toilet facilities after which Alfred gratefully sank into the comfort of a seat. He could have slept had not new travel companions entered. They were eager to include him in their conversation. Carefully limiting background details, he talked about his home town of Neubeckum.

"It's an awkward time to be away from one's own country. Have you been working away?" he enquired.

"Well yes in training. We are medical students, and we were placed in a hospital in Czechoslovakia. We were fortunate to have had some training under the medically well recognized son of famous Doctor Kalensky" said the young man with thick-lensed horn- rimmed glasses.

"It is a pity he was a Slav. The authorities made him leave" commented the student in the middle.

Noting disrespect in his clipped tone Alfred replied, "The name Kalensky rings a bell but I don't know why."

With a flash of his piercing blue eyes the student flippantly replied, "Well that goes to show he's not as important as our German specialists, particularly those of the Nazi party."

Controlling his expression Alfred remained silent. By now he had privately given each of them a nick name. Sensing some tension, the fattest of the three, Roly Poly, who had not said a word until now, endeavoured to change conversational direction. "We are needed in Germany. We will have to join the medical corps of the army and go wherever we are sent" he said.

"Whether we like it or not, we all must be involved in whatever's happening" horn- rimmed- glasses lamented.

"Surely it will end soon. It cannot go on" said Roly Poly.

Weasel features piped up, "Well, unlike you I shall take my uncle's advice and join the Nazi party. Prospects within the party are much better than in the army. I do not have to remain in the medical corps. The Nazi movement is a greater power than the army. My uncle says the Nazi party is beginning to own and control everything."

The plight of the medical student whose views were more to do with power than compassion both saddened and worried Alfred.

At Leipzig, the young men disembarked and as they walked across the platform they waved briefly. Now alone, Alfred had time to observe, especially with lengthy delays due to frequent security checks.

***

When at last the train drew into Beckum Station, he and a few others left the train and headed for another platform for the Neubeckum train. At 1.35 a.m. at Neubeckum Station, passports were checked a final time.

"This hasn't been stamped properly. What is 'The Electricno D Fustra A.D'?" 'Lord not at this stage' Alfred thought.

"It's the place where I worked."

"How did you manage to come through on this? This way please."

Stunned, Alfred found himself firmly escorted along the platform, into a small room where a duty officer checked papers. Smugly, the guard pointed out, "Some passport details do not appear to be in order sir."

Alfred tried to explain. "Be quiet until I have checked for myself," said the officer.

'If you are in trouble when you get to Beckum and Neubeckum make certain you hand over the letter' said Father Augustus' voice in Alfred's head.

"I forgot to include this Sir."

"I said silence!" said the officer, but none- the- less snatched the envelope addressed to The German Passport Officer. Glancing at the familiar style he quickly opened the envelope. As he read, his small bright eyes lit up with interest. Less formal he condescended to say, "We are aware of this priest's work. He does not know it, but he's a useful tool for our own cause. Where will you be staying?"

"At the home of Bernhart Nurville's in South-Wood Street."

"I will make a note of that. Someone from the regiment will call in a day or two to take details."

Part 2

Into Germany

Chapter 12

The other Side

In the cool night air Alfred felt alert as he walked the familiar route. When he arrived at South-Wood Street, a strange, eerie darkness seeped into the core of him. No solitary light shone from a window to cast a glimmer of hope into the darkness. As if in hiding, everything conveyed apology for having the breath of life. Along the familiar path Alfred's thoughts turned to the past and those who had who had walked there. In his inner vision he saw his mother Marija, his brother Witold, and other family members. Someone in the house, in response to his knock on the door, shuffled downstairs. Just a little, the door opened. His heart skipped when the door opened, and Great Uncle Bernhart, thankfully as sturdy as ever, sleepily stared out. Sole indicators of passing years were his head of white-hair and a more pronounced weather- lined face.

"Who the blazes can it be at this time of night?" he asked.

"It's me, Alfred. I'm back."

Gradually, Bernhart took in the adult version of the child who had left.

"Alfred, Alfred my boy, it's you, I can see it is you. Welcome; how did you get here?"

"Let me in and I'll tell you."

"Well hurry up, come on in."

"It was through Father Augustus' help" Alfred explained as they walked along the small entrance hall.

"Some time ago he wrote to us about the dreadful situation in Serbia, but we never expected you to turn up like some apparition." "I can assure you I'm completely physical, and extremely hungry. The journey was horrendously long and uncomfortable. Is that Aunt Annalisa coming down?"

"Yes! Annalisa Alfred's here, he's come back."

In her eagerness Annalisa tripped on the last stair. Even so, with a smile she glanced into her great nephew's eyes, and comprehended directness and honesty strong as ever.

"Alfred my dear child, I mean young man, this is hard to believe. It's wonderful to see you. Come let me hug you."

"Thanks Aunty......Ooh you're almost suffocating me."

"Sorry. Now come, have something to drink and eat: hot cocoa and a sandwich perhaps?"

Berni, emerging from the attic, now coming downstairs, distracted them.

"Hello Berni."

An inquisitive expression informed Alfred that he had not been recognized.

"How are the girls?" he asked.

Instantly in the picture, Berni replied, "Like you, pretty grown up; makes me feel old."

"Well, you don't look it, you've hardly changed," laughed Alfred.

"Come, sit down. What happened after we received your last letter? You mentioned you were about to leave the monastery?" Annalisa inquisitively asked.

Interjecting Bernhart commented "That can wait until morning, if you're not too tired perhaps you can tell us about your journey?"

Between sips of cocoa Alfred glanced at their ever-changing expressions of anticipation, surprise, anxiety, and laughter. Empathy flashed across their faces as they listened to the story of his remarkable journey.

Finally, through a stifled yawn his Great Uncle said, "That'll have to do until tomorrow." Soon, when Alfred was in bed in the upstairs spare room, he pulled up the eiderdown to his chin and instantly slept.

Next morning when they were finishing breakfast, Bernhart habitually leaned his elbows on the table. "Alfred, we can now catch up on the remaining adventures" he said. Noticing their enthusiasm, Alfred related all that had preceded his arrival here. The places he'd visited, people he'd come across and the situations encountered, drew their fascination. Gasps of surprize emerged when a commonplace train journey became an incredible risky adventure

"Remarkable, a miracle, God be praised that you've arrived in one piece" Annalisa affirmed.

"Appears to have turned out that way" he replied.

Averting further onslaught of questions, she asked Alfred if he would like more coffee and rolls.

"Yes please" he replied.

"Have you been in touch with Kate and the twins recently?"

Delaying biting into the crispy roll he said "I wrote to the twins via Kate, about the same time I last sent you a letter. Since then, letters have not got through and I never received reply."

"Well Kate and Tobias have an eighteen-month-old son, Freddie."

"Heavens above, you mean I'm an uncle?"

"Indeed, you are."

"Around the same time as each other, the twins were engaged to their sweethearts" Annalisa informed.

"Goodness, fancy that. After mother died, they did remarkably well to cope on their own, and remain employed in Germany. How's Gertrude by the way? I know they saw her as a second mother."

"She is doing well although she had similar symptoms to those of your mother. Fortunately, she made a doctor's appointment and subsequently had an operation.

Pushing aside painful memories he replied, "Well things always improve over the course of time and some people have to die before answers are found."

"I usually go to Beckum on the second Saturday of each month. Would you like to join me today and see your family?" Bernhart asked.

"Thank you, I'd love to."

"They will be surprised to see you. Johanna still works in the drapers. Fritz could not tolerate the cramped solicitor's office so, following in Witold's footsteps, he took as job in the market garden. He has done so well he is now sub manager. Because Alfred did not comment, Bernhart realized he was thinking of Witold.

"How's the 'Tobias Bakery'?"

"Good, except they get inconsistent orders from the Nazi party. Consequently, they must stay up half the night to get everything baked and ready. It is hard for them to see to Freddie's needs the following day. To make matters worse they only receive half the price they should."

Annalisa's tone was sympathetic as she replied, "That's difficult." She turned to her husband and asked, "Will you need the pony and trap Bernhart?" "Not at this stage; there are tighter controls now and they prefer people to travel by train. It enables them to keep close checks on everything."

***

It didn't take long for Alfred and his Great Uncle to walk to the railway station. As a familiar local character, Bernhart easily purchased two day- return tickets. As he came out of the ticket- office and onto the platform, he needed no reminder as to why the guard politely nodded. Forestalling any query, Bernhart walked over to him and said, "I would like to pay for Mr Ztoanjib's travel from Serbia to Neubeckum. You will have it in your record book."

"I don't need to look it up as it has been mentioned, thank you for your cooperation. I must comply with the regulations."

"I understand."

"I'll repay you one day" Alfred promised.

"I know, but do not worry about it. These are strange times."

A half an hour later they arrived at Beckum Station and from there they walked the kilometre to Kate and Tobias' home. Close to the house, they breathed in the tantalising smell of newly baked bread. Kate, standing at the window and holding her infant boy in her arms, momentarily disappeared to open the door.

"Uncle Bernhart, Alfred" she called and ran towards them. Whilst balancing Freddie on her hip, she somehow managed to hug Alfred and Bernhart.

"Kate, it has been a long time. It is good to see you and he seems to have taken to me," said Alfred.

Along with Bernhart he followed Kate into the small sitting room. For a moment nostalgia filled his heart as he listened to the slow tick of his mother's clock on the mantelpiece. He was reminded of childhood hours spent watching patterns in the coal fire flames. Various paintings hanging from the picture rail also served to take him back in spirit to their childhood home.

Taking in the spectre of his plump sister he said "You're looking well Kate; he's certainly full of life."

As she brushed back a strand of brown hair her blue eyes mischievously twinkled. "Here, do take Freddie from me" she said, and put her squirming bundle of a son onto her brother's short knees. The boy, immediately at ease, chuckled and grabbed his uncle's left ear.

"He is a strong little boy. Good you have named him Friederich, after our still- born brother. Our mother wanted us to never forget him. How's your husband? I look forward to meeting him one day."

"He is all right, not exactly a knight in shining armour, but determined to continue the family business. The biggest threat to our security is the war. There are few sales because we must ration the amount of bread sold to each household, so sales are poor. Nazi officers make huge orders that we must let them have cheaply. When that occurs, Tobias and his father must spend all night baking. I used to help, but it is too much for me with Freddie to look after."

Hearing cheerful voices, Bernhart went to investigate. It was Johanna and Fritz at the front door.

"Well hello Johanna, Fritz, we have a visitor," he said.

Johanna, first in, quickly walked along the hallway, and inquisitively looked around the doorway of the sitting room.

"Alfred, Alfred is it really you?" she said as she ran to her brother's side.

Being slight, she looked ever youthful, a fact made noticeable as she danced around him. Alfred knew she observed a brief twinge of envy in his eyes as her tall twin brother entered. Affirming his observation she whispered, "I'm glad the abbey hasn't made you too saintly."

Without words Fritz came over and grasped his brother's hand for a moment, during which they recognised their inherent characteristics.

***

As they drank their coffee, conversation escalated. Diplomatically Bernhart prompted, "Alfred, why don't you tell your sisters and brother the sequence of events?"

So, Alfred re-told his adventure, and his siblings listened with amusement and awe.

As exchange of news expired, Bernhart, with serious expression, emphatically stated, "If the army sergeant comes for your details Alfred, he will want you to enlist. You would best comply. Only six kilometres from here my nephew was minding his own business, walking up the road, after tending his father's cattle, when an SS officer on a motor cycle drove up to him. The man pointed a gun at his head and ordered him to enlist. The youth had little time to run in and tell his parents what had happened. He had to be ready to be picked up by truck within the hour."

"What in heaven's name is happening? Surely that was a one-off case of bullying?" Alfred queried with a ring of disbelief.

Horrified, he listened to Johanna explain, "Last week there was a party we were invited to, at the manor. Seventeen-year-olds Morag Bertenhause, and her friend Susie Schwartz, were doing a marvellous bit of acting, imitating the strutting march of the Nazis. They wore saucepans on their heads, and most of us were doing our best to hide our laughter. Shortly after a guest had asked to use the telephone, Nazi officers arrived. They arrested Morag and Susie.

Matthias Müller` who had accompanied Cyril Weissenbaum's rendition of Schubert's song, 'The Erlking,' narrowly avoided arrest because of some comment Susie had made to a Nazi. Everyone affirmed that the youth did not have anything to do with their act. Regardless of their unanimity, an officer struck him across the face with a leather whip, an act that affected his eye. The officers were very rough with the girls; Susie was crying as they marched them away, Morag defiantly held her head high. No one knows to where they have been taken." "Hopefully, it won't be the kind of thing I faced in Belgrade Police Station," Alfred interjected.

Not wanting his brother to steal the show Fritz interrupted.

"Believe it or not, the Nazi's wanted me to join their party. I replied that much as I liked some of their ideals, I was not happy about my friends being taken away. Then one of the Nazi's hit me across the face and at the same time snarled, "You have not mentioned Jew, but you meant Jew. No German must have Jewish friends. The Jews are enemies of all Germans."

"Well, we have Jewish roots," Alfred commented,

"I know, even though it was hushed up. We all had best keep quiet or they will be taking us away to some obscure place."

"Some close associates of the Führer say he had a Jewish teacher when he was a young boy. His teacher constantly criticized his artwork and frequently ripped up his paintings. Not only was this done in front of the child but with the whole class as witness. If the story's true, the boy would have suffered much taunting," said Kate.

Alfred thought back to the abbot's words during a sermon, *'Behind every extreme act is a very frightened child.'*

"I've never heard that Kate, but anyway, from then on, I kept quiet. I shall never be able to forget the look in Elijah's eyes when they dragged him away. It was as if he was saying *'What have I done to deserve this. Can you help me?'* The worse- part is, no one knows where they have been taken" Fritz expounded.

In a tone conveying senior wisdom Bernhart informed, "A friend of mine has a son who is concerned, even though he is a member of the Nazi party. Many honest Nazi's like him are worried about what they rightly comprehend as the escalation of corrupt attitudes. My friend's son told him that Himmler's working out some process of ridding Germany of unnecessary consumers. That is all that he could reveal."

"Surely, they don't mean 'get rid of' in the final sense?" Alfred suggested.

"It is propaganda, but all the same, odd things are happening and I am glad my baby is not handicapped. Some friends of ours had their fourteen-year-old daughter, Samantha, taken away by some Nazi's. She is a lovely girl but has downs syndrome. Also, the sanatorium for the mentally ill has been closed and all the patients removed to an unknown destination."

Optimistically, Alfred replied, "Probably to a safer area as there've been quite a number of bombings around here."

"Surely our rulers wouldn't deceive their own people, especially during wartime," Joanna commented with a questioning lilt.

"I hope not but we can't help but wonder," Fritz answered.

"It would be nice to hear that Samantha's safe. Her parents are inconsolable," Johanna conveyed.

Chapter 13

The Missing Ones

Faster than she could manage the men forced Samantha into the truck. Their smiles were not open and loving like Mamma and Papa's. Mamma had had a troubled look when she had said 'Do as they tell you Samantha.' Like Mamma, Papa had looked as if something inside was out of tune with how he had to behave. In the truck Samantha counted nine passengers in addition to herself. Cautiously she watched as a man in strange clothes came and sat beside her. His clothes were identical to those ones worn by the man starting up the engine. Her eyes smarted as she watched Mamma and Papa for as long as she could. Now the truck was taking them over the hill, and Mamma and Papa were no longer in sight. Gradually she came to realize that all passengers were slow, deformed, or both. Because the look in their eyes conveyed how they wanted to be loved, she smiled. Their happy response made her feel like a princess. The songs without words they sang with their eyes, told her she was at the top of their tree. She knew she was almost like one of the other people who were quick and clever, although many of them were never genuinely happy.

"Samantha thirsty" she said and tugged at the man's coat.

"Are you now, well I am afraid there is no more drinks for you. We must make room for perfect people."

She wondered where Mamma and Papa were, they always gave her a drink if she needed one. Again, she tugged his coat. His response was to slap her hard across the face. Somewhere beyond the smart of pain, as she rocked back and forth, he laughed. The boy sitting opposite, whose head was almost half normal size, made strange movements with his arm. Minutes passed before Samantha realised, he wanted to give her his apple. Feeling better she took it, and bit into it, a wonderful sweet bite made sweeter by kindness. The man noticed, snatched the apple, and threw it out of the truck. The boy with the poor head jerked uncontrollably. Smack, thud, the man who called himself soldier, hit him hard on his small head. Like small frightened animals, the others looked on. For a time, all was quiet, then the truck screeched to a dusty halt.

"Get out, quick, quick."

The princess understood, taking the boy's hand she helped him out of the truck. In comparable manner the others followed. Suddenly the lovely moment ended when the man called 'soldier' finished speaking to the driver. "Quickly, march ahead," he ordered.

Hindered by disability many stumbled; the soldier who had driven the truck kicked and forced them to catch up. Samantha wondered where they were going, to a shop perhaps; and they had to hurry before it closed.

"In you go, quick, quick," said the soldier.

As they entered the bare hall, faces clouded with disappointment. No sign of love here, everything empty, bare floorboards, whitewashed wooden walls, no windows to let in the light, except for a tiny one near the ceiling.

No sooner had the soldiers left the room, than two women, with taught, unsmiling faces, entered. Without a word they stripped each person, and left them, naked. Rocking back and forth, captives shivered and tried to hide their deformities. Samantha was about to tell them how frightened everyone felt, when the women rushed at her and pulled off the pretty dress Mamma had made. Because of the speed of it all her only defence was to bite one of the women on the arm. The second woman's response was to knock her to the ground and remove her undergarments. As soon as the women left the room, the two soldiers entered to imitate their naked victims. For several long moments cruel laughter resounded around the hall. Samantha watched a poor girl with a withered arm cower in a corner of the room. With no means of hiding the arm, the girl whined high pitch. Out of control, the sound of her prolonged distress would not cease. Samantha's move to comfort her drew the soldiers' attention. With secret smiles they lustfully eyed her body. One of them whispered to the other, "For a young girl she has a womanly body."

"Just imagine she has a beautiful face," the truck driver hissed.

***

"Come, we need you for an experiment" said first soldier. Whereas Samantha did not understand the word experiment, she understood the hate in their tone and the sinister quality of their expressions. As they dragged her, into a private room she fiercely but vainly tried to pull free. Inside the room the man who had driven the truck turned the key. 'Expe, expe' Samantha thought, 'Not like Mamma and Papa.'

The hand that had hit her friend with the small head pushed her to the ground. He held her whilst the driver took down his trousers and pants and lay on top of her. The man pressed his face on hers, she could not breathe. The attacker lunged up and down, and took his face away each time he lunged. She hurt inside and was about to scream when the other soldier put his hand across her mouth. 'Mamma, Papa' she screamed with her mind. The soldier with his hand over her mouth cheered, as the other lunged again. Then, as they changed positions, Samantha shook violently, and knew what to expect. As the second man lunged and grunted his victim experienced indescribable pain and grief. When at last the ordeal was finished, she tried to stand up, but felt faint, all the time, in distorted manner, hearing their continuing laughter. Eventually, as she regained consciousness, she saw the soldiers look into each other eyes and talk of more experiments, "-together-you- upper deck- me lower deck."

***

A siren sounded, and quickly she was pulled her to her feet and shoved into the bare hall where the handicapped victims were waiting. Moments later one of the women in charge came in and re- counted. Sharply she commented, "I counted nine last times, now there are ten. I am sure she was not here last time."

"You must have counted wrong, idiot" replied the driver in a high anxious tone.

"The commander is due any moment now," said the second soldier. Judging the mood of the woman, he submissively handed her some silver coins. With a sneer she hastily accepted. Seconds later a commander entered.

"Is everything in order?" he snapped in clipped- toned voice.

"Yes Sir."

"Go, quick, quick."

Along the rough track where Samantha and her companions were herded, other groups filtered in. Many people looked extremely thin and poorly. Samantha felt very unwell since the men had hurt her, she had difficulty walking. She was aware of streams of blood running down the inside of her thighs. Moments later, because she was thinking of others, and reaching out to take the hand of the weeping boy, she forgot her pain.

As the boy looked up into her unusual face and into her kind slanting eyes, he told her his name was Josef. He leaned against her as he walked, and in so doing felt less inclined to cry. A youth aged about fourteen or fifteen noticed.

"Hello, what's your name and where are you from?" he whispered.

"Samantha, I live with Mamma and Papa in Beckum."

"I am Elijah. I also come from Beckum; here take my hand."

As the three children filed into the cold chamber, a Nazi officer argued with his colleague," That boy there is Karl, my son Karl. I must get him out."

Elijah saw the man's companions restrain him. He heard the Nazi uncontrolled sobbing that broke into hysteria. Through the narrow slats he saw two officers' approach and frog march the conscience-stricken officer away. It was followed by a single shot, and Elijah knew that the boy Karl would never, in this life, see his father again-

***

As yellow fumes descended from the ceiling, the three children hugged each other. The more they gasped for breath, the less air they received. Amidst floundering crushing limbs of adults, they- oh so slowly, died.

The gas reached the little boy Emile last-

"When will it end, I am alone?"

For a while his muscles contorted in unimaginable cramps, and as every bone in his body cracked, he continued to look - finally, the officer who believed he was Karl came in through the wall, stretched out his hands and carried him upward into the light.

As man and child journeyed onward, bits of uniform fell off, into the dirt and decay-a thousand years below-until nothing, not even the memory of it remained. Just for a moment he saw a monument inscribed with words of acknowledgment for handicapped victims, their role of support to each other and their giving of unconditional love to their families and friends during their earthly life. Now Samantha and Elijah were in the ever present, and in fatherly manner, Karl's father gently put him down alongside them. Emile, turned smiled, and watched myriads of beings in bright garments guide his helper into some realm for adults. A voice like a thousand flutes called him and all children. They followed and entered a beautiful tunnel composed of rainbow colours. From this place a universal mother carried them across a river into a beautiful garden, where every flower was lovelier than those seen on earth. In song, light, scent and colour each petal and stamen emitted vibrant praise to the creator. The lady smiled and her flute like voice played on the surface of the river and streams, as she said, "You don't have to go any further until Mamma and Papa arrive."

They remembered only the beautiful things on earth, because here in the ever present, negativity, pain and all things that preyed upon good no longer existed. As Elijah looked at Samantha, he thought and felt with his whole being, how incredibly beautiful she was and he could not remember her being anything other than the perfect being she was in the ever present.

***

MILLIE'S BIRTHDAY

On the evening of Millie Weiss' twenty first birthday celeb ration, Susie had been arrested and transported to this large house. Why had the Nazis' brought her here? She wondered.

She stared out of the window at the ornamental lake serving to provide a momentary illusion of freedom. Next minute she was distracted by the sound of sobbing in a nearby room. Two weeks ago, she had cried in comparable manner in this room that had become her prison.

On the night of the party, with their slim figures, long legs, blue eyes, and fair hair she and Morag had almost passed for identical twins. *The only difference is Morag's single mindedness. If I were not such an obedient girl, I would be out of favour with my parents but free from this imprisonment, as Morag is likely to be by now. I do not know why they do not let me go home,* she thought.

***

In an atmosphere of anticipation, guests had arrived. Cyril Weissenbaum had sung a painful rendition of Schubert's Earl King accompanied by Matthias Müller, who had nearly seized up during the demanding accompaniment. Some famous people and dignitaries had been present, including Morag's second cousin, the famous pianist Paderewski. Susie had overheard him say, to Lady Weiss, 'One needs to keep the arms and hands relaxed if one is to maintain control of the constant rhythm, and convey the spirit of' Goethe's poem.'

'Sounds as if the Earl King's horse has five legs' Morag had whispered. Susie had suppressed a giggle. An outburst of clapping had saved the day, and giggles had been swallowed up in the noise. Cyril and Matthias had regarded the clapping as complimentary, rather than relief that the rendition had ended. Suddenly their host had announced 'Morag and Susie will now perform.'

***

Two days prior to the concert, not knowing what they would provide, they had gone to Beckum shops in search of props and ideas. There they had witnessed Nazi officers ceremoniously meet with dignitaries. The girls thought how ridiculous the officers' stiff legged march had looked. They had wondered at the men's expressionless faces. As if designed without flexible muscles, arms had been raised and voices had declared in automated manner, 'Heil Hitler.'

'Looks like a strange religion- as if 'Heil Hitler' is a parody of 'Hail Mary' Morag had whispered. When the ceremony finished and things returned to normal, the girls had continued shopping.

Back at Susie's house, Morag had had an idea. She had found a saucepan, placed it upside down on her head, and with eye liner had pencilled in a moustache just like Herr Hitler's, and had managed to perform a hilarious imitation of an officer, similar in stature to Hitler. Susie, with the help of a cushion up her jumper, and a larger saucepan on her head had managed to copy the inadequacies of a fat officer on parade.

Now, on the day of the concert, young people enthusiastically laughed at the parody. Adults wanted to laugh but dare not. Susie remembered Lady Weiss looking worried about the time a guest had asked to use the telephone. When their act was over, no space was given for applause. An accordion player instantly performed some light music, people chatted among themselves. Next, a hideous noise emitted from the accordion. Unitedly heads had turned and witnessed the arrival of a Nazi officer who had instantly pushed the instrumentalist over. 'Whose Zaucepans are these?' he had shouted whilst lightly tapping on the table.

Forgetting she wore a pencilled moustache Morag had remained silent and pale. The Nazi had come over to her and asked again, 'Whose Zauzpan's' are these?'

She had refrained from reply and his response had been to strike her hard across the face. In a small frightened voice Susie had called out, "They're ours."

In a trance she had watched the officer come over. He had pulled her head back by her hair and forced her to look at him.

'So, you enjoy making fun of officers, do you?' he had said.

'We meant no harm.'

'And what was your favourite concert item this evening?'

'I liked the accordion music best.'

'Ah the accordion, you squeeze it, like this, and it makes a noise,' he had tauntingly answered, whilst all the time watching Susie's pained expression. He had returned to Morag and asked in threatening and seductive tone 'And what is our favourite concert item?' With a trace of defiance, she had answered 'The Earl king'.

'Well, I shall remember to tell my colleagues. Now you both are to come with us.'

The second officer standing to the side of the room had come forward and grabbed Morag by the arm. She recalled his words directed to Millie's father, 'Our driver has left. We want the keys to the Mercedes. We wish to borrow the car and whoever owns it can have it back when we have won the war. Quick give me the keys, Heil Hitler.' Under scrutiny from the second officer Millie's father had reluctantly gone to a coat stand in the hall, and taken the keys from his pocket and handed them over. Susie imagined how he would have inwardly raged. Within different circumstance he would not have hesitated to have the thief arrested. Susie surmised how he would have felt as she and Morag had been marched away. With all his heart he must have wished he had not given the soldiers the key. Did he imagine how it might have been his own daughter being taken to an unknown destination?

Had he gone to their home that night to explain the events to their parents?

Susie dared not think about the grief her parents would have experienced.

***

Under pressure last week she had been forced to sign papers agreeing to become a mother for the perpetuation of the perfect race. This was to be her way of honouring the state, a demonstration that she was for the Nazis and their ideals.

'Morag was not far wrong with the Hail Mary parallel. Am I meant to offer myself as Mary offered herself to God? And what am I to think of that now, for God was Mary's father. It all seems a bit muddled.'

Although Morag had tried to explain, Susie, like Mary was not quite certain how babies were made. The unnatural tight voice of the officer echoed in her mind, 'You will have the best medical support, but you will not be able to keep any babies. You understand. They will belong to the party. As all that is imperfect is eliminated, you, and others, volunteers like yourself, will produce perfect children.'

She had not dared answer his insane logic. There had been no heart and soul in his words. Feeling as if she was being sucked into some impersonal war machine imposing its madness even upon the unborn, Susie, unable to speak, had silently nodded.

She was to be on a six-month programme with an officer. Already he had used her twice and she had to comply whenever he wanted. The first time he had shouted at her and when he had finished the painful process, had said 'It's not you I am angry with.'

There had been a moment of humanity in that sentence, and after he had left, she had heard him shout down the corridor, 'In

97

future I do not want to fuck a virgin. In future I want it easy. I do this for country not for self.'

She knew it was more to do with his pre- Nazi standards and principals that the war machine had not reached. She wondered about Morag, and whether she had returned home.

***

Morag faced the obese commanding officer. As he put his face close to hers, she smelled his fetid breath.

"Young woman you will learn to obey your superiors. This is your last chance to sign the document. If you refuse you will be placed in the Joy Division."

"Do you understand what that means?" he added.

"No, I don't and nothing can be worse than your proposal to use me to produce babies. I will not sign."

"Well, have it your own way. I believe you like fun and games."

He ordered the guard to take her away. With some arm twisting the guard forced her along the corridor, out along the path and into the back of a truck. Inside were two more officers and four girls about seventeen years of age. With timid eyes they looked at her, but even so their eyes lit up when she held her head high and defiantly pushed her chin forward.

The driver started the engine, with a jolt they were on their way to an unknown house. After a while they couldn't tell where they were, because the one window at the back of the truck had been whitewashed. Suddenly the truck stopped and they were ordered out, Morag managed to whisper to the girl beside her, "This is the sanatorium near Münster."

Except for the windows on the top floor, the remainder were boarded. In a quick skyward glance Morag observed a curtain move and a frightened face look down. Another quick glance enabled her to see someone inside the room come forward quickly to close the curtains.

"This is the officer's 'Joy Division' said the guard as he herded them upstairs. Morag found herself pushed into a room and the door locked behind her.

"Food has been left for you. Eat well, sleep well for tomorrow afternoon your first day of work begins," declared a guard outside the room.

As Morag looked around the surprisingly comfortable room in red velvet, she wondered what work she would have to do. She opened a door, and discovered a bath- room where she freshened herself with a good wash.

Being thus confined, she lost all sense of time. Next day, a woman came in to speak to her, much to her surprize Morag learned it was noon. The woman, features cheapened by colourful make up, was dressed in an alluring, low- cut violet coloured dress. Her appearance and manner conveyed a dichotomy of qualities.

"You'll have to dress in this love," she said, and handed Morag a red velvet robe. Morag noticed kindness in her tone and manner.

"You may be requested to dress in other garments from this bag. Just do whatever you are asked; it is better than being dead."

"What do you mean?"

Lamenting the appeal of Morag's widening beautiful blue eyes the woman answered,

"The Joy Division is a house of prostitution. I understand you are here as penance?"

Morag's lip quivered, and as she put her hands to her face her brave profile dissolved. She sobbed uncontrollably and felt the arms of the older woman around her shoulders, offering consolation. Through a haze of disbelief Morag listened to her hushed voice.

"Look at me-I was thirteen when I was forced into prostitution. I had to do it or die of starvation. I have survived and so can you; you must for your family and friends. The only weapon for survival here is to pretend you enjoy it more than they do; that really takes away their power. People like them must be pitied because they have not learned to know their true self, and because they do not know their true self, they do not relate well to others. They do not know how to govern in the different sense of selfless love. Therefore, they seek to govern others in a forced and unnatural manner. People can only truly govern if they have come to understand themselves, and that kind of governing is the sort of love that Christ conveyed."

Morag was both surprised and comforted to hear such profound thoughts emerge from such a woman. The mention of Christ reminded her of home.

"One day, all of this will be over" the woman assured.

Quietly she left.

***

An hour later the door opened briefly. "You are to remove your gown and put on the items in the bag. Do not argue or question, and be quick because your guest will arrive in five minutes" the guard ordered. He slammed shut the door.

When Morag opened the bag and took out an officer's hat, a shortened version of the Nazi jacket and a pair of long boots, she felt physically sick. She undressed and shivered in fear as she put on the garments, because her lower body was completely naked. Choking back tears she uttered aloud, "I ridiculed them in innocence and now they will ridicule me in a cruel and carnal manner."

As the key turned in the lock, she willed herself to concentrate on what the woman had said. As the door slowly opened, she covered her pubic hair with her hands. 'God help me, I'm only seventeen. Help me, please help me' she thought. Within her heart a gentle voice said *'they cannot touch you deep within your soul. I am with you; I will give you strength until it is all over.'*

She recognized the unwelcomed intruder as one of the Nazis who had dragged her from the party. His eagerness to arrest her came into focus as a leering grin swept across his face. 'What a bastard' she thought.

"Have you ever been with a man?" he asked.

"No" she whispered.

"Well, this afternoon I shall be kind. Remove your hands so that I can look at what I want to see. Now sit on that stool, good." Morag sighed.

"Do not do that, smile, that is better- now open your legs- wider-wider. I just want to look" he ordered.

He sucked in breath as if someone had stepped on his toes- Morag wished they had. "Now stretch your leg right out, further, further, that's right."

His piercing eyes burned until Morag's emotions were quenched by the words ringing in her mind *'pretend you enjoy it; it's your only weapon.'*

"Right, now stand up- let me feel what you have under your jacket."

Outwardly she smiled- inwardly she winced as he fondled her breasts. Her feelings crawled as he put his face against her breasts and proceeded to lick and suck them.

"Now bend over towards me, take off your jacket. Let your breasts hang down into my hands."

She felt him squeeze them as he uttered, "Good, good, ah, good."

"Now stand up straight, look into my eyes and tell me what you see."

Morag did not answer

"I'll tell you what I see, fun and excitement. You like fun and excitement, don't you?"

As he put his hand between her legs Morag's stomach churned and even more so as she felt him almost invade inside.

"Lie down on the bed" he commanded.

Outwardly she complied and dreaded the worst.

"You have done well. Tonight, I will teach you more. Tonight, will be real fun. Heil Hitler" he sharply relayed. He left, slamming the door behind him as he did so, Morag heard the key turn in the lock.

Late afternoon, the same woman brought tea and a sandwich that Morag refused.

"Look love, this could be your survival kit. If you are not up to what they want they would not hesitate to kill you," said the woman.

Realising the truth of her words Morag methodically ate the sandwich and drank tea, hardly noticing its unusual taste.

"I have mixed camomile tea with the ordinary tea- it'll help you relax a little. I suggest you drink some later, before Waldmann comes. I warn you he can be a nasty character at night. Make certain you comply."

Shortly before midnight, the guard opened open the door.

"Put on your robe, your officer will be here in ten minutes" he said.

101

When Waldman unlocked the door, and entered, the first thing he did was to force a kiss on her. She reeled at the smell of alcohol on his breath, and she nearly choked as he thrust his tongue down her throat. Billy Braun, during their last year at school, had told her about this sort of thing, but she had not believed him. She had spoken to Billy at the party and they had intended speaking again after the performance. After Waldmann ended his abusive kiss, he bent down to pick up something he had dropped. With terror, Morag realized it was a whip, she willed herself to refrain from recoiling in horror. She watched as he slowly unwound the whip. "Take everything off" he ordered. Suppressing sickening feelings, Morag fixed a smile on her face, and secretly reluctant, but outwardly compliant, hastily removed her clothing. All the time out of the corner of her eye she watched him, snake-like trace his thin lips with the end of his tongue.

"Now put on the boots and march across the room like we do."

She had marched five steps when suddenly, the whip lashed around her naked waist. In the corner of the room, cowering and shaking with fear, she wore a brave smile. Laughing loudly the officer urged, "Now dance, dance, keep dancing."

The crescendo of his laughter imposed as he shouted "Dance faster, faster, faster." As the whip lashed her buttocks she winced in pain. She could see his excitement as her breasts bobbed up and down. The faster he lashed, the faster she had to move to avoid the lashing whip. Only the words of the woman who understood helped her fix a smile that hid terror. Finally with a flick of his wrist, the despicable man lashed out, walked over and tied the whip around her. Holding the whip handle he walked away and pulled her towards him.

Whilst untying the whip, he snapped, "Place these two cushions of the floor."

He undressed, stood, pot- bellied, and forced her to look at his limp penis. Next, he lay on the cushions so that his pelvis was raised.

"You will notice here a button on the floor. It is always on when I am here. If I press it, they will come and without question shoot you. Do you understand?"

"Yes"

"Now face me. Sit on my knees and slide down my thighs towards me; more, more. That is right. Now for fun and games, eh?"

She was silent.

"Now pretend that, like the Erl King, you are riding a horse. As he hummed out the rhythm, something happened to the limp member.

"Come now, more, more, up down, up down. Go on, that is right."

Morag felt his penis rise firm as he held her to him as she descended. He pushed up inside so violently she cried out in pain.

"You dare come off, stay, and stay. Now more, more, up down, up down. Go on, ah, oh, oh" he moaned.

A warm wetness ran down her thighs. The Nazi's eyes closed with selfish pleasure and when he opened them, he ignored the tears streaming down his victim's face. When he let her get off him, he tipped her so that she could not avoid the problem of her breasts hanging close to his mouth. He licked the breasts, laughed, and moaned. In a state of shock, she hung on to the words '*Do what they want. Stay alive. One day it will be over.*'

For several weeks she was left alone until one evening another officer, a large man, came into the room. With his face close to hers she had to control the urge to retch as his sewer-like breath invaded her.

"I hear you are being exceptionally good. This week end I shall honour you with my presence. I want you to show me how extra good you can be" he said in a grating voice.

***

Four months later Morag opened her eyes for the first time and saw the kind woman beside her.

"O love, I thought we had lost you. Do not worry he never visits the same girl twice. One day someone will kill the evil bastard. England would not believe us if they were told the German officers do this to their own people. It's evil, organized evil under the state banner. One day it must be defeated. Good will win over evil. Until now I haven't told you, my name. I'd like us to be friends. Would you like that?" Morag nodded.

"My name's Gretchen. You can call me by my name, but not when they are around."

Now that they were loyal friends Morag felt a sense of relief, but at the same time the flood gates of all the sobs sloshing around in her heart broke free. With difficulty she related her story.

"He had a machine, like a small electric windmill. It beat my buttocks whilst he mercilessly raped me. The more he pushed the more I was pushed towards the machine and the more I was hurt from both angles, and the more he enjoyed it." Her sobbing continued ten minutes or more and finally, in a whisper, she conveyed "he said the look of pain in my eyes excited him. He squeezed my throat until I was almost unconscious and whilst I was in that state, he raped me several times."

"Come dry your eyes. He will not come again and I can assure you he is the worst of them."

A gentle voice whispered deep within her heart '*I am with you, within your soul.*' "I'm hanging on, I won't give in" said Morag as she reached out and clutched Gretchen's hand.

Chapter 14

Erika

During the dismal return journey from Beckum, as if of its own accord, a cloud of despair enshrouded them. Black out blinds down on all carriage windows made matters worse, and only by counting the number of stops were they able to determine which station they were at. "Tell me Uncle is Erika at the same address?" Alfred enquired.

Bernhart looked puzzled, quickly adjusting to the next generation he replied.

"Oh, you mean Erika Stein. Yes, she still lives with her parents. Why do you ask?"

"Well, each time I wrote to you and Aunt Annalisa, I also sent a letter to her."

"She never mentioned it, but I never talked about your letters to us either."

"Up to the time I went to the abbey I wrote to her. Quite some time before I escaped from Belgrade, Father Augustus said he had received a letter from her in which she expressed how upset she was that I had been accepted for monastic training. He had been so busy, that his intentions to reply to her were put aside. Then it was too late for letters to get through. Before I left Belgrade, he suggested that I try to contact her."

"Well, tomorrow's Sunday. I suggest you call on her after dinner. Her parents rarely go out and I expect you will find them at home."

***

As Alfred made his way to 8 O'clock mass next morning, a cold breeze was stirring. He was thankful for the reflective and peaceful essence of the service. He recalled praying deeply at the abbey where often in heart and mind he had felt an emotional bond with Erika. Yet, at the same time, a mystical inner vision, the whisper of a voice in a foreign land, had caused him to think, *'Perhaps one day we'll marry and live abroad -but then perhaps she's changed her ideas because she believes I'm living a monastic life.'*

"AMEN" the voice of the priest resounded. Suddenly aware of how thoughts had wandered, Alfred quietly walked to the altar to receive the sacrament.

***

Regardless of being busy with basket making in Aunt Annalisa's hallway, the morning passed slowly. In the kitchen, his aunt, by the sound of it, was beating a round of beef with a rolling pin. Later, when the smell of roast dinner filled the house, thoughts about the slaughtered animal quickly shifted.

Outside, familiar voices drew near. By the time Alfred packed away his willows and half made basket, everyone had gone indoors. He followed them to the sitting room and listened to their chatter about the priest's overtly zealous swing of the incense censor that had caused a ripple of excitement.

"Did you see the look of amazement on everyone's face?" Uncle Bernhart enthused.

"He accidentally let it go" said Berni. Trudi, unable to control her laughter, held her aching sides, and eked out "He accidentally let it go, and it, it, it s-s-s-sailed through the air, right along the aisle and landed beside—Lord-'n'- Lady s-s-s- Steinbeck."

"Yes, right along the aisle" Helga reiterated.

"Dinner's ready, after which you can tell me what the sermon was about" Aunt Annalisa loudly called.

Laughter subsided, everyone sat at the table, and Bernhart said the grace. Following an enthusiastic 'Amen' Annalisa raised her glass.

"This is especially for you Alfred. Welcome home. Soon they will need you, as they also will also need Bernie and his son in law. Those of us at home will have to do our duty. But today we'll pretend there's no war, and enjoy being family."

"To Alfred" they said, and with a neighbourly clink raised their wine glasses. Later when the meal was over, and chatter faded, Annalisa declined Alfred's offer of help.

"Helga can help me and you can go to Erika's."

Eagerly Alfred replied, "Thank you Aunt Annalisa."

106

As he walked down the road, he knew Annalisa was watching, and felt glad her maternal role, that had been essential for his survival, had remained strong.

***

When he reached the end of South-wood Street he turned right, and wound his way through two further streets. Delaying going to a third street, aptly named St Joseph's, he walked to the church yard, to his mother's grave. It was his first visit since the funeral many years ago. He found the grave well cared for. His thoughts felt exoteric as he stood near the grave, *'Oh Mutti, I love you--I love you. I am home Mutti; I am on my way to see Erika. You will remember her coming with us on picnics.'*

He recalled another September on his way to school, and how compassionate his mother had been when Erika fell and grazed her knees. Outside the school building, in conversation with the teacher, he had absorbed his mother's words 'Fraulein Breitenbach, she is such a pretty child, and more importantly she is kind too. The other day I found her rescuing snails from the road, putting them back into the hedge, so that no one would tread on them.'

A breeze whispering through the branches of a nearby horse chestnut tree that had been a sapling, on the dreadful day, reminded him of when he had last stood there. Once more his gaze returned to the grave. He thought of his sister Kate, who would have placed flowers in the sunken pot. He removed the dead flowers, and placed them on a compost heap on the edge of the graveyard. From the plentiful source of wild flowers surrounding the grave yard, he picked a cluster of pink, white and blue. He returned, and as he placed them in the rain filled pot, was reminded of the flowers of the field where he, his mother and his siblings had had their last picnic. Even now the memory of her voice echoed strong- *'It is not just a field. How many things can you see?'*

He whispered, "Oh Mutti, I see so much more than I used to. My journey of life is not away from you but towards you. May God bless you -always."

Tears of gratitude, sadness, and joy, streaming down his face fell onto the grave. In the precious moments he remained still, after which he quickly walked along St Joseph's Street and beyond.

The external, fairy tale appearance of Erika's family home was formed by a network of timber frame. Another feature of the fourteenth century cottage was a tiny doorway, and windows giving the impression that a family of small stature, from a long past era, may still be dwelling there. In spritely mood Alfred thought of jumping over the low fence, but instead cautiously opened the gate. In dignified manner, he walked along the short path. A hanging basket filled with colourful, overflowing autumnal plants was swinging and dripping with water. The door handle was wet, Alfred noticed. A strange sound caught his attention. *What is it?* A gradual glissando gave answer with a slow deep bass voice, in gradation transferring to baritone. Deducing that someone had been winding up the record player Alfred was quick to recognize the song from Schumann's song cycle of a poet's love, 'Dichter-Liebe.'

***

Eagerly he knocked on the door, and heard what must have been Mr Stein, say, "I wonder who that can be? It is unusual for anyone to call on Sunday."

His slow walk to the door affirmed his identity. His leg had been injured many years past. When the middle-aged man opened the door, he initially failed to recognize Alfred, who'd been a boy when last seen.

"Ah, I think it is Alfred, I recognize you from the photo Erika has tucked in the corner of her dressing table mirror" he said.

"Yes, I am Alfred, and very pleased to see you."

"What are you doing here? Come on in, and tell us. Marta, we have a visitor" he boomed.

The gramophone volume diminished as Mrs Stein came into the tiny hallway.

"Do you recognise this young man?" her husband asked.

"I can see who it is. What a lovely surprise Alfred. Erika's down the garden. She will be delighted to see you."

Alfred's smile conveyed enthusiasm.

"I'll fetch her. Why don't you and Matthias go into the sitting room?"

Alfred's gaze followed stout Mrs Stein down the back garden path and rested upon the slender girl emerging from behind blackberry bushes.

"Oh, mother why do you want me to come in now? Can't it wait? I have nearly finished."

"Oh, alright, if you insist" he heard her say.

He watched her place her basket on the ground and a handful of berries spilled onto the grass. Whilst she retrieved them, Mrs Stein forged ahead to usher him into the sitting room. Mr Stein, quickly finishing sorting out gramophone records, sat on the settee. By now, seated in an arm chair, Alfred watched Mrs Stein leave. A moment later she wheezily announced

"Go into the sitting room Erika, you have a visitor. I will sort out the coffee."

Erika's eyes, similar in shade to her fathers, lit up with joy to see Alfred seated in the armchair. As she pushed back her dishevelled brown black hair, and looked into her special friend's eyes, her smile was radiant.

"I don't believe it; I really don't believe it" she said with much delight. She walked towards Alfred, placed her hand on his shoulder to teasingly ask "You're not a ghost, are you?"

"Thankfully, I'm not."

As Mrs Stein entered, carrying a laden tray, she prompted "Now Alfred, you must tell us what you are doing here, and about life in Serbia. You will not be able to go back now, will you?"

"You're absolutely right- it's too dangerous to go there."

He outlined events until he arrived at a point of describing his extraordinary journey on the dapple-grey mare. "What happened next?" Erika enthused. Intermittently Mrs Stein topped up their coffee, and as Alfred continued, Mr Stein, at every pause irritatingly commented, "Well I never. Who would have believed it?"

Eventually, as Alfred concluded, he noticed how deeply moved Erika was, particularly concerning his terrible ordeal in the Belgrade police cell.

***

An hour later, the two young friends were walking together across town and through an unfamiliar area of woodland.

109

Eventually it linked up with the path to the meadow, where he and his siblings last had spent time with their mother.

As the couple chatted about games, picnics, and shared childhood memories he thought how uncanny it was for her to have unwittingly chosen this significant spot. A few moments of silence felt sacred, ending with the plaintive cry of a hawk overhead. Cautiously Alfred held Erika's hand, and there she let it remain as they continued walking.

Honing in on thoughts he had had after leaving the abbey he encouragingly said,

"Look Erika, look downstream at the distinct colours. How many shades of green do you see?"

"Goodness-well green, just green-no-I can see powder green, moss green, blue green, silver green and many others. Hey look there, a fish."

Briefly he glanced at a small fish darting into the shadows under a stone. When he looked up, his eyes met with Erika's and saw conveyed, a pure, simple love, full of hope. Spontaneously he squeezed her hand and held her in his gaze.

"Erika, I know what you must be thinking. It's difficult to understand the call to religious orders, you must wonder if I think you second best?"

"I don't know what I think."

"Well, the fact that I left, indicates that I was missing God's love within his people out in the world. In some ways you are equal to others, but in a personal way you are top of that list. Every time I prayed, I saw you in my mind and heart, and I wondered if God was telling me you were thinking of me. I wondered if you need me in your life? I need you and I certainly love you."

With a sigh of relief she whispered, "I love you too."

He looked deep into her eyes to convey the point, "These are uncertain times but when the time's right will you marry me?"

"Yes Alfred, I will. This has been my impossible dream for a long time, and now it is coming true."

As they held each other close she nervously kissed him on the cheek. Alfred breathed in her autumn smell of blackberries, grassy banks, and fern. From his pocket, he took out a small box, opened it, took out a delicate chain, and threaded it through a silver loop on a heart shaped locket.

"I had all my saving stolen in Belgrade but have managed to save enough to buy you this little locket. One day I'll buy you a ring, but for now will you accept this as a token of our engagement?"

"Oh yes Alfred, assuredly" she answered.

As he put the chain around her neck, she smiled to feel his warm finger slide the locket onto the chain. He secured the clasp, took her hand, drew her close and said, "It's my turn to kiss you now. His kiss lingered on her cheek a few seconds and caused her heart to warmly stir. Then as he lightly kissed her on the lips, her love for Alfred felt intensely awake. It was the best feeling she ever had had known.

Chapter 15

Aachen

Uninterrupted family life was fast disappearing. A truck with a heavy sounding engine drew up. Cautiously Annalisa peered out of the window. The vehicle was directly outside their house, her heart missed a beat. With a knot in the pit of her stomach she dumbly watched an army officer get out of the truck. Now he was coming up the path. Forestalling she rushed to the door, opened it, and said, "I expect you have come for Rupert Reich who received papers three days ago. He lives three doors up, this side of the street."

"Madam I am here to collect Herr Reich but I am also here to inform you that we require Alfred Ztoanjib for recruitment and training at Aachen. The situation is urgent, no longer are we sending out letters or telegrams. This is a list for him, of the things we required him to bring. I shall expect him at Neubeckum Station at six O'clock sharp on Wednesday morning."

Compliant Annalisa replied, "Yes Captain."

Noticing the sadness of her tone the officer took the edge of it by adding, "It's Sergeant." "My husband will give him a lift to the station" Annalisa said.

When the sergeant left, and Annalisa related the news to her family, she saw their worried expressions. Summing up the current mood of the community, Berni poignantly said, "The sunshine seems to have lost its sparkle and capacity to lift our spirits."

***

Next day, when Bernhart had absorbed the urgency of the situation, he briefly disclosed events of his own experience in the Great War of thirty years ago.

"Alfred, I took care to never to panic. That was the reason I safely came through" he emphatically concluded.

"The type of resilience you refer to touches upon the deeper spiritual peace I entered through meditation in the abbey, I shall do my best to follow your example Uncle" Alfred replied.

***

Too early on Wednesday morning the sound of clattering crockery and the chime of the grandfather clock woke Alfred. With a groan he turned over, but remembering it was Wednesday, he quickly got up, stripped the bed and folded the blankets. After a kit check he was off downstairs.

"Good morning" he said, as brightly as possible.

Uncle Bernhart seated opposite, looked glum. Annalisa was obviously tired and anxious.

"For the reason you said your farewells last night Alfred, I haven't disturbed the others."

"That's alright, I understand."

The husky voice of his Great Uncle offered reassurance, "Well dear boy, Aachen isn't very far and the officer mentioned you'll have a free week end at the end of every month."

"That's not much, seeing as the training lasts three months" Annalisa objected.

"But it'll break up the rigorous routine; they're not overtly sentimental" her husband retorted.

At twenty to six, with the intention of fetching his horse, Uncle Bernhart went outdoors but stopped in his tracks as an army truck sped up and came to an abrupt halt. The driver indicated he wanted him to go to his side, on the right of the truck. Bernhart responded and the driver wound down the window.

"Are you Herr Nurville?" he asked.

"Yes I am."

"A change of plan: because we have more recruits than expected I can use every seat and take them in the truck. It will save you having to drive your car to the station."

"Oh, I do not drive a car. I drive a horse and cart" Bernhart replied.

The officer got out and walked around the truck. Annalisa, having come outdoors at that moment, wondered at the wry smile on the officer's face.

Ready with his kit bag on his shoulder, Alfred appeared.

113

"Right lad, you pass inspection. Quickly, get in the back."

"Yes Sir."

"You mean 'Yes Sergeant'"

"Yes Sergeant" he replied.

Before jumping in, Alfred briefly grasped an arm each of his Great Aunt and Uncle.

***

Inside the truck a man of similar height smiled briefly. A young man opposite appeared to be day dreaming. The direction of his gaze, Alfred noticed, was towards the emerging sunrise. Another recruit, noticeably nervous by his repetitive habit of drawing in his lower lip, introduced himself as Helmut. Alfred sensed he had no disillusion about what might lie ahead.

Several streets later the truck came to a halt. A second officer got in and sat beside the driver. When seated he turned his head and quickly scanned the recruits. Not missing his snide expression, Alfred made mental note to be on guard.

***

He recalled a debate 'I quite agree' Father Spyridon had said 'You must trust that God given perception about another person's inner self, but it must be matched with an understanding, of their background. Furthermore, it is wise to listen to the reaction and advice of others who you know to be close to the heart of God.' Alfred's thoughts moved on to thinking about Brother Misha- *Why am I thinking of Misha? Ah I know, he once talked about Aachen, the cathedral City with its holy and healing springs, a place of pilgrimage.* Alfred wished he was going to Aachen on a pilgrimage rather than being made to train for war. The conflict with unbreakable vows pulled strongly at his heart.

Oh God help me. Help me obey and keep thy holy commandments. Heavenly Father, hear my prayer.

***

In the wing mirror, Alfred studied the reflections of recruits and officers. He prayed for the love and peace of God to protect them, for friends and family, and for people throughout the world during these threatening times.

114

Suddenly slowing, the truck came to a halt. A tall angular recruit hauled himself into the back of the vehicle. Because his knees were close to the seats opposite, everyone had to shuffle along to accommodate his long legs. His mother, outside, pulled back the canvas. "Darling you've forgotten the cake I made for you to share with your friends" she crooned.

Catching sight, of sergeant's disapproving look in the wing mirror, the recruit whispered his thanks. Gently he took the cake, so lovingly wrapped in a white serviette. Alfred reassuringly smiled to the mother and sensed she knew her son would have a friend. With a rev of the engine, they jolted forward on an undesired journey.

Later as they passed rows of tall, tightly packed houses, and an impressive fourteenth century town hall and domed cathedral, they realized they had reached Aachen. The truck went through a wide gateway onto a tarmac area where a duty soldier closed the gates. When out of the truck, they faced a formidable, tall red brick building. Alfred, briskly following others, felt acutely aware that army rules assuredly would fail to embrace the spiritual logic of monastic training.

***

The dormitory they were entering was bare without religious icon to lift the soul. Whilst processing the idea that his spiritual thoughts would have to be private, he noticed on the sky line, the solitary symbol of eternal hope in the form of the Cathedral dome.

By now recruits were busy placing personal belongings in their named lockers. Alfred just managed the task in good time, and along with others, went downstairs where they were to congregate in a large lecture room.

Without excessive demands the day passed quickly. Each of several lectures emphasised, a need for diligent map reading, and instant response to orders. They were issued with a copy of their schedule for the week. Looking at the meals list, Alfred already longed for Annalisa's home cooking.

As night fell, they went to the dormitory where, a few moments after lying down, Alfred mentally created a poem-

STAR

From my small window
I see above Aachen's rooftops—
A bright, solitary star-
Yet, what I see is a mirror of the infinite;
It reflects its source of creative birth.
This star no longer has substance of its own.
Eclipsing blackness would reflect the rays backwards,
- Into, a self- destructive, birth-grave.

An object partly transparent, would misdirect
Star soul rays, into a void future
Incapable of arriving at an ultimate destination.
What about life? Does that not reflect through a
perception of truth?
'Yahweh'-God- the truth, the birth- reality?

***

When eventually Alfred became accustomed to the cacophony of multi pitched snoring, he slipped into sleep. Soon his bass drone played along on the harmonic texture of the snores of fellow cadets.

All too quickly night passed and Alfred's pleasant dream about Erika disintegrated as the sergeant loudly bawled, "Aufsteigen; schnell. Get up, quickly."

Immediately the cadets were out of bed they had to head for the toilets and wash cubicles. Alfred waited for Helmut to vacate a wash cubicle, and was glad that, as instructed he had remembered to disinfect the sink. When Alfred had put in the plug and half-filled the basin with chilly water he deftly shaved. A while later, with ablutions finished, he too cleaned the sink, changed into his underwear, and left the cubical. He folded his pyjamas and placed them in his locker and took out his neatly folded uniform and put it on.

***

Except for one recruit still tying his laces, they were ready for inspection.

116

"Attention" the sergeant shouted. Rigidly, beside their beds they stood to attention.

When he came to Helmut he said, "That isn't how you wear the hat. The peak must be forward, flat, not raised so that you look like a clown."

A ripple of laughter died as he turned and glared at the cadets. For a second Alfred caught a glimmer in the sergeant's eyes that conveyed a warm heart.

As for the sergeant, he sensed Alfred had noticed his inner sentiments. Only a few days ago he had said to his wife 'Poor devils, at least I have had a good run of life. How many of these will survive?'

Suddenly back to the moment in hand, he swallowed hard and authoritatively yelled, "Tying laces needs to be automatic, not a problem."

"What is this? I cannot see my face in it. Make sure you polish this belt buckle until it shines. See to it."

Knowing how one small oversight could cost a life, the sergeant emphatically conveyed, "You have got to get it right. It is my job to mould you into shape. Have you got it?"

"Yes Sergeant!"

"At ease and follow single file" he called.

As ordered, they followed him single file out of the dormitory, down the stairs to breakfast. At the end of the meal, they were ordered to march outside to the parade ground, where they'd participate in military drill.

**

Two hours later, when they were wondering if it would never end, the sergeant loudly called

"That is more like it. You can have a coffee break now."

He beckoned 'Tubby,' a resident of Aachen, who had been in the dormitory when they had first arrived. For Tubby's sake, Alfred pretended he was out of hearing range.

"You have got to get that weight down, you cannot carry that around on the battle field, it will slow you down. I will send you to the army doctor for advice on diet. I will give you a note for our cook."

"But Sergeant I've always been like this."

"That is no excuse. Tomorrow, I will let you know the time of your appointment."

"Yes Sergeant. Sorry Sergeant."

Over coffee the recruits conversed about the two-hour training, intermittently laughing about their mistakes. Tubby, who had just returned, listened as his namesake, Tobias, jovially commented, "Fancy turning the wrong way Tubby: You are an idiot. Don't you know your ass from you elbow?"

"I was tired out, but I am going to try and lose weight. You will see."

Noticing the look of lament on Tubby's face, supportive Helmut added "I do not think you were alone in finding it tough. I have been used to spending most of my time reading. All of this is new and unfamiliar: I too must work hard at getting into shape."

Chapter 16

On Leave

With a spring in their steps the cadets headed for the railway station. Lofty had scored a final goal that had won them the match. Feeling good, Lofty, reserved in nature, had to admit to feeling proud of his achievement, and the popularity it had won. Like his companions he noticed and appreciated the respectful glances of passers- by. Yet, by the same measure, he was uneasy about the identity the war uniform enforced. Edward, lagging, caught up and enthused, "Have you noticed how the girls are taking an interest in us?"

The train came to a halt and they had to quickly get on board.

***

As the train trundled onward, chatter digressed and shades of evening settled across the landscape. Further into their journey a squall hindered their visibility, making it impossible to read station name plates. In keeping with black- out regulation interior lights were off and conversation alone served to relieve the monotony.

Eventually when the train drew in to Beckum Station, a hive of activity buzzed as they cheerily got their bags. "Aufwiedersehen- see you on Monday-have a good time" echoed, in various tones and overlaps, along the corridor.

Quickly Helmut and Alfred crossed the platform bridge to board the Neubeckum train.

Being only a few kilometres away, they soon arrived at Neubeckum where Uncle Bernhart stood on the platform. The train came to a halt, and Alfred and Helmut got out of the carriage and briskly walked over to him.

"Oh, Uncle Bernhart, thank you for coming; feels as if I have been away four years instead of four weeks. How are you and everyone? How did you know I would be here at this time?"

"I telephoned Aachen earlier from the priest's house. He did not mind. We're fine, apart from the upheaval of it all. I must say you look good on your training."

"Thanks, I suppose I do. This is my friend Helmut. Can he have a lift and be dropped off at Katerina Street?"

Teasingly Bernhart said, "Well now, let me see; it'll add time to the journey and you know how your aunt worries."

Noticing Bernhart's unsubtle teasing, Helmut feigned dismay. In sudden gesture Bernhart, amicably shook Helmut's hand whilst saying, "Of course you can have a ride son."

***

As they made their exit from the railway-station the word 'ride' forewarned Helmut of the imminent means of transport. Therefore, he put up his collar before he clambered into the cart. Noisily, a few wealthy people drove off in expensive cars fitted with slatted covers over the headlamps. Thankfully, rain had not reached this area of Westfalia, and through the chilly night air, Bernhart's horse steadily travelled onward.

Tuning in, to an unfamiliar direction, the horse yanked his head anxiously, but feeling his master's pull of the reigns he sensed human need for a diversion.

Soon Helmut disembarked, and as he walked off, before disappearing around a corner, he turned waved, and call out, "Many thanks."

As they set off once more, Bernhart commented on how strange it was that Helmut had lived in Neubeckum all his life, without them ever having come across him.

"Helmut's very clever. His parents were able to place him in a boarding school in Münster where his father had some prominent position."

"Didn't he find it lonely at boarding school?"

"Yes, but he made many friends and I think that's why he gets on well with everyone at the cadet training school."

"How are you coping?"

"I keep my mind occupied."

"Good. To the best of your ability, just do what you are asked to do."

"Under present circumstance I shall."

"Have you heard any news from Beckum?"

"Kate and the twins are fine. They are doing their bit when required. Neither Fritz or Kate's husband Tobias have been called up yet."

"Two cadets are called Tobias, an uncommon name, and now I know three, that's another coincidence."

"Yes, life is odd."

"I expect all of this reminds you of what you went through during the last war."

"It does, I hope and pray it will end before it gets anything like the last war. I have never really got over losing many friends and comrades."

Along South-wood Street, as the smell of a cooked meal wafted on the evening air, conversation dwindled. "That won't be simmering on the hob for long," said Bernhart.

Habitually the horse stopped and Bernhart had no need to pull the reigns.

***

By the sound of it Annalisa was unlocking the door that currently had to be locked. The door opened, with a smile Annalisa stepped out and hugged Alfred tightly. Overcome by the welcome, words tumbled forth- "I've missed you. This welcome means such a lot, and do I smell something good? I haven't smelled anything so good for a month."

"Come on in, get yourself ready. You both must be tired and hungry."

"We are, but don't start without me. I will just see to my steed." He soon returned and Annalisa called, "Trudi, Helga, Bernie."

Emerging from their upper level sitting room, they quickly came downstairs, but as Bernhart had forewarned, their expressions were dour. Bernhart had explained that pregnant Helga was not coping well with her husband away, in the face of danger.

The three entered, Berni came over to Alfred, shook his hand, and enthused "It's good to see you Alfred, even though current pattern is for a few days only. Let us hope Herr Hitler changes his mind and allows us to return to normal living."

Noticing how tearful Berni's daughters had become, Alfred told Helga how sorry he was that Wilhelm had been called up so

121

soon. "Helga, I pray he will be kept safe" he empathised. With a compassionate glance in her sister's direction he conveyed, "Trudi, try to not imagine the worst. Let's hope everything will work out all right for all of us."

"I partly blame myself, for if we had stayed here, he would not have been called up, at least not yet. They are doing it by regions. Already we have had five men leave from our street" Helga replied.

"Well perhaps they enlist randomly or according to school records, who knows. He's a good athlete, isn't he? I guess we shall never really know official reasoning. I do not relish my own situation" Alfred replied.

"I expect they'll leave us older ones until last" Berni added

***

For the first time in a month Alfred slept soundly through the night. Having learned that Kate and the twins were unable to see him, he made a firm decision to not let it spoil the sunny day. *'It's a shame their time's being stolen by large scale demands of bread making for the Nazi's'* he thought.

"I've a letter for you" said Uncle Bernhart.

"It's Father Augustus's handwriting."

Much to his surprise and delight a letter from Stephanie had been enclosed.

"Father Augustus recently returned and brought it with him" Bernhart explained.

A quick scan of the first paragraph informed Alfred that family members were safe. Because Milorad's brother, a royalist, had been shot dead, by official order of communist leaders, Stephanie was concerned for his safety.

"I hope Milorad has the sense to keep his views to himself" he added.

Guessing Alfred's reply was one he would have wanted his sister to hear, Bernhart assured, "I'm sure your sister would have suggested that, and I expect they'll decide to get out of the country."

Deep in thought, slowly spooning out the dregs of sugar, Alfred finished his coffee. Bemused, Bernhart commented, "Glad to see you're feeling at home."

"Yes, thanks, but I must be off now" Alfred retorted.

122

"Be careful" Annalisa called from the kitchen.

"Yes, do be careful" Bernhart reiterated.

***

Having planned by post, to meet Erika outside St Joseph's Church, Alfred's prior picture of a romantic sunny day dispersed as he squinted through mist. Whilst walking along the crunchy path his hopes began to fade. Erika was not there. Yet, he sensed her presence. The fact was confirmed when she stepped out from behind a tree. With a coronet surround of dew drops resting on her chestnut hair, he thought how lovely she looked. As they drew near to each other, their eyes of similar hue, met.

"Hello Erika, my darling. I've missed you very much" he quietly said.

"I've missed you too" she replied.

Hand in hand they strolled over to a bench, sat down and chatted and finally decided to walk across a spacious park. Eventually, they arrived at an empty bandstand and quietly sat there feeling glad to be in each other's company but equally sad about present circumstance.

"Are you hungry?" Alfred enquired.

"Yes, I am, a little."

"Well Annalisa insisted on packing lunch for two."

Whilst he undid a brown paper bag, two squirrels cautiously approached.

"Looks as if a few more want to join us" he laughed.

"They're quite tame" said Erika whilst patiently holding out a crust of bread.

Moving like a silk scarf in the breeze, a squirrel came over, took a crust, and dashed away. A second squirrel repeated the cautious method.

***

The afternoon slid by as the couple walked along several streets and through several parks. Now as the mist cleared and the sun shone brightly, people emerged from houses. Wanting to be alone, Alfred and Erika headed for the church. Inside they occupied themselves with studying windows and epitaphs. The epitaphs that they had previously taken for granted suddenly cried out the names of many young men lost in 'The Great War.'

123

"Let us hope it remains 'The Great War' and doesn't become re- named 'The First World War', because that could mean our names and the names of those we know could be inscribed on stone" Erika commented with a shudder.

Realizing her words might prove right he silently held her close. And after some moments added, "Don't worry; just put your trust in God."

For a brief time, she remained in his arms, and then hearing the tower clock strike four, she urgently said "Is that the time already? I said we would be back for tea at four."

They were not the only quick walkers. Although curfew would not happen until eight, people were keen to gather family members and to not leave anything to chance.

At Erika's house Alfred pretended to not notice her parents quickly step back from the window.

"We're only five minutes late Erika, but the look of relief on their faces makes me feel as if we were five hours late."

"It's only because of everything that's going on."

Her father answered the knock on the door.

"Is it that time already? It is good to see you Alfred, welcome, do come in" he said as casually as he could muster.

Bustling from the kitchen Mrs Stein heartily declared, "My word Alfred you are looking well. How nice to see you. Erika, find Alfred a seat. Now everybody, make yourselves comfortable; I will bring in the tea."

Several times she went back and forth, resulting in the front room table accumulating two large cakes and several plates of meat pies.

"What a marvellous spread. I shall be talking about this for weeks to come" Alfred appreciatively commented.

"There's enough for you take some back with you," said Mrs Stein.

"That's kind, thank you."

In her eyes Alfred read of hope for their daughter's future, he resolved to make it a good future. When asked about Aachen he felt obliged to relate some of the activities he had encountered in training.

"I don't suppose they've indicated the next move?" Mr Stein questioned.

"Not yet."

Not wishing to dwell on present circumstance Mrs Stein interrupted, saying, "I'll just go and get the photo albums."

Several hours were spent browsing and reminiscing and before they knew it, the clock was at half past seven. With slight panic in his voice Alfred said, "I really must go now. If I hurry I'll get home before curfew."

Chapter 17

In the Saddle

Wanting so much to be with Erika, it was with reluctance that Alfred returned to Aachen.

However, when back at the cadet centre, the intensity of the training provided little space for thinking of home. Daily, the young men were put through their paces to a point of exhaustion. At alarming rate new skills had to be learned. The intelligent amongst them, realised this was because war was escalating. Slower cadets relied on comrades to help them through.

***

One morning the sergeant made an announcement, "Every single one of you needs to know how to manage a horse because some areas may prove inaccessible by truck."

"Does anyone know where that might be?"

"Could it be in a sandy desert Sir?"

"Or when petrol runs out?"

"Or if a tank freezes in somewhere like Russia" Alfred replied.

"Yes, all correct, but horses are sometimes used to get messages through to Red Cross stations and so forth. They can even be used to transport the injured when all else fails. This is why every one of you is about to learn how to ride."

"Yes sergeant" they chorused. They responded to the sergeant's order to stand at ease and after he had left talked among themselves.

"I've never ridden a horse in my life, not even a donkey" Helmut groaned

With a laugh Edward made the comment, "I dare say you will do better than Alfred. He cannot even manage a stationary horse in the gymnasium."

Alfred simply, and knowingly, smiled.

***

Next morning, supplied with rough quality riding gear, the cadets marched behind the sergeant. By chance, short Alfred was behind Lofty, which predictably caused much suppressed amusement. Down the stairs they went, out into the drill yard, along a path, and across a field into a large building. The sergeant entered the building and returned followed by a light -weight man, dressed in riding breeches and jacket.

"Right men, this is Captain Schnell, he will tell you all you need to know about basic equestrian skills. You will find him quick witted. One thing he does not tolerate is indecision. Is that understood?"

"Yes Sergeant."

The sergeant left and Captain Schnell's darting brown eyes scrutinized the row of men. "Come on in" he said, and from his position in the doorway went inside.

The building, light and airy, with a high vaulted ceiling, hadn't looked particularly high from outside. Two agile horses, one black, the other chestnut, restlessly pranced where they were standing, at the far end of the large lightly sanded area taking up most floor space. The captain demonstrated how they should mount, do a slow full circle and dismount.

"I shall ask each of you in turn to do the same. Of course, I shall help you with your circle by using the long guiding rope attached to the halter, see?"

Taking it upon himself to answer as spokesman, especially as Captain Schnell had been staring in his direction, Edward answered, "Yes sir, we do."

The captain walked over, looked him in the eye and snapped, "You can go first."

After a moment's hesitation, Edward walked to the horse, placed his foot in the stirrup, and forgot to hold the reign tight. Thud! It was essential that he leap alongside the moving horse. In such manner, having been propelled several meters, he managed to mount. Involuntarily, the first half circuit was covered too fast. Eventually Captain Schnell's command, "Pull back the reign" registered, and with a degree of accuracy Edward dismounted.

"Fair, but even at this stage you need precision. Watch! Listen! Then you will succeed" Schnell emphasised.

127

Lofty, whose real name was Larry, mounted, with his foot back to front in in the stirrup. Just in time he managed to twist around and save himself the embarrassment of facing the tail end of the horse. Most cadets managed to contain their amusement, but for anatomical reasons unknown, Tubby's suppressed laughter worked its way through his nasal cavities and made its exit in an explosive nasal snort. Annoyed, Captain Schnell strutted over to emphasise in reedy tone, "Tobias, this is not a playground. It is serious business. Your precision or lack of it will soon be a matter of life or death. Do you understand?"

"Yes Sir" Tubby submissively replied.

Suddenly it was his turn; with great effort he managed to marginally surpass Lofty.

However, as Schnell quickly pointed out, "It was by no means an achievement."

***

Awkwardly; with the aim of getting the ordeal over as quickly as possible, Helmut mounted. He forgot to correct his poor posture and by the time he completed a circle, Schnell's temple pulsated. Someone whispered, "Alfred will be in for a hard time."

Undaunted by the instructor's frayed temper, Alfred took the reign, easily mounted, and sat well forward in the saddle. He stroked the horse's neck to calm him. It worked and as the horse set off in a trot, Alfred moulded into his movements. Gripping him with his knees, he let him know who was in control. Soon, with compliant snorts, the horse responded and the instructor recognized obedience.

***

Alfred had almost completed the circle when Captain Schnell called out, "Good, good, now show them how to do a wider circuit and if you succeed repeat it solo."

To the amazements of his comrades Alfred rode perfectly through his paces.

"Look how his body synchronizes with the horse. Notice how relaxed he is. He is not going against the grain. Think about it, and see if the rest of you can get it right next time." "You have had training, haven't you? Good training?"

128

Holding his counsel about the Lipica stud farm, and riding school, Alfred curtly replied,

"Not really Captain, I have learned through observation."

Puzzled Captain Schnell dismissed him and made copious, post- dated notes. In his notebook he stressed how his recruit Alfred Ztoanjib's natural skills, would be of immense advantage to their army, and more importantly, in his own mind, it would be a feather in his own 'Wehrmacht' cap. He therefore sent in a recommendation that as soon as possible, Alfred be sent to remote and difficult terrain.

To validate matters he kept Alfred on the riding skills course a further two weeks. Occasionally he pretended 'his student' had got things wrong. He observed how the cadet easily managed difficult paces. Such precision reminded him of the week- end he had spent in Vienna, where, in Lainzer Park, officers and generals had proudly ridden Lipizzaner horses.

At the end of the second week, Captain Schnell, in better spirits, knew it would be to his advantage to have produced a competent rider. Briskly he walked to the main- office to submit his report.

***

Next day the Sergeant addressing Captain Schnell, commented, "I was glad to receive your report. I could see Cadet Ztoanjib at eleven."

The fact that Schnell didn't say 'Thank you Sergeant' verified Korff's suspicions that his loyalties lay with right wing members of the Nazi party. Sergeant Korff was certain the despicable man had his sights set on quick promotion within the fanatical regime. Recently he had observed Schnell attend an increasing number of Nazi meetings. Concurrent to the number of meetings Schnell's respect for those outside the party had diminished. To Korff it was clear that officers of moral fibre were becoming rare. Few were left, with whom he could discuss changing attitudes.

Alfred, sauntering across the drill yard, came across Captain Schnell returning from the office. "Ztoanjib, the sergeant would like to see you in his office, at eleven."

Knowing he dare not ask why Alfred replied, "Yes Captain."

With no time to spare he rushed to the dormitory, stripped off the riding gear, washed quickly and changed into uniform.

One and a half minutes to eleven he rushed down the concrete steps, along the corridor and knocked on the office door.

"Come in," said Sergeant Korff.

Alfred entered and stood to attention.

"At ease" said the sergeant in his non official voice. Alfred noted the friendly look in his eyes.

"I'm impressed with your equestrian skills report. Where did you learn?"

Trusting the sergeant to not distort matters, as was the habit of the Nazis, he confidently replied, "At Lipica."

"You mean the famous Lipizzaner place?"

"Yes, I worked there for a while, managed to get some lessons, as I also did when working in Ljubljana".

"You must have travelled there from Ljubljana and paid for further lessons?"

"Yes."

"Well, that is the irony of war. Their loss is our gain. Best keep matters confidential; I shall not include that information. We need to make use of your linguistic and equestrian skills. I hope you will be willing to do a solitary role when we send one or two cadets with the next convoy for Graz."

"Yes, I trust your judgement sergeant."

"Can you manage the 'Capriole in hand'?"

Noticing the sergeant's humour Alfred replied, "No, but I did manage to persuade my horse to do the extended trot."

Liking his quick wit the sergeant added, "Well that will come in useful. We need to send you almost immediately, in fact in two days. Near Graz you will have more training on a farm where we keep a few Lipizzaner. Back at camp you will learn a few basics for field work we need you to do. You will be required to go to an isolated area on horseback."

With puzzled expression Alfred listened as the sergeant explained, "This will be for the purpose of delivering or picking up messages from contacts. Some information will be verbal, some written. Most of it will require your skills as translator. None of it will make sense, although some of it will be vital to us."

"Do you mean it will be a coded letter?"

"You shouldn't ask questions."

"I'm sorry sergeant; I'm ready and willing."

Not wanting this fair-minded young man to be faced with dilemma, Sergeant Korff truthfully assured, "You have my word that this work is to safeguard troops and civilians: to prevent them walking into traps, or being sitting targets for bombing raids. It is not for destructive purposes."

Korff chose to not add that he had had to fight hard against strong opposition to get the plan passed in the form he had proposed. Because of Alfred's Serb roots he hoped he would not have to get involved in combat against Tito's troops.

Alfred had no doubts that the sergeant was of kindred spirit, a man of sound principals, a man of faith.

He felt both excited at the prospect of new mission and fearful of the context and dangers he might face.

***

The following week, on September 11th 1941, the division passed through Graz. Alfred, Helmut, and Edward were deposited at a farm where they would receive, interspersed with essential army work, a month's training. Deeply missing Erika, Alfred kept a journal for her to read upon his return. He checked through the entries he had made from the time they had joined the main division at camp.

September 12th

Helmut, Edward, and I are staying on a farm for further training: Edward in mechanics, Helmut in radio communication and I in other forms of communication and equestrian skills. In a sense it seems like a holiday here. The farmer's wife has produced some excellent meals.

September 15th

I've been remarkably busy and haven't had time to write. I think of you always. So far, the farm lady has persuaded the old army General in charge of us, and who resides here, to allow us to work outside when it's fine. That makes the work very pleasant as we have a choice of several beautiful trees to sit under.

September 18th

I'm saddle sore today and thankful to be spending time translating. Apart from the fact that some 'special horses' are on the farm, much of the lush scenery reminds me of the stud farm at my 'former location.'

September 21st

Helmut had to remake his radio today, only to discover that he had made a minor mistake at the beginning of the assembling. I felt sorry for him but I am certain he will get it right 'out in the field.' Edward was successful in getting an ancient tractor going. It pleased Frau 'F' tremendously. I have had several days of intensive training with the type of horses I mentioned to you in the park. From the nature of the exercises, I imagine I shall be going into tricky terrain. The General tells me that soon we will be needed at camp to carry on our work. We hear that Der Führer ordered the army to resume its drive on Moscow in August. That's certain to upset the massive apple cart.

Well, what was I saying about today's exercise? I saw Graz from afar and it is a noble city full of mountains and castles. You would love it. Unbelievably I went on horseback half way up, around and down the other side of a mountain. I remained in the saddle as both the horse and I are used to difficulties. The person I was to have met wasn't to be seen (and my guess is that that was part of the exercise). However, eventually I found what I was meant to discover. The small wood fire he had lit, paved the way--I shall say no more about that.

On my way back, down the side of the mountain, greens, pinks, blues, seemed to roll down from the sky. In the distance the sunset in an azure sky made everything appear pink and blue. The creator behind these phenomena lifted my soul beyond the horizon of grief and war.

23rd September

Regardless of the tough training, I feel connected to 'my old life' when I am taken 'through my paces,' on one or other of the super horses. It very much is a continuation from where I left off in developing my equestrian skills, albeit this is in military context.

25th September

Dearest Erika I wonder if I should wish you were here with me as the dangers of war are spelled out in the fact that these horses are here. I learned today how they have been removed from 'The Riding School' near here not just for military service but for future breeding in the event of a bombing raid on Vienna. It also occurred to me today how our hobbies, interests and talents come from connections of far superior significance than mankind's foolish schemes.

21st October

My dear Erika we have been so busy, you can't imagine it. We haven't stopped until ten at night.

23rd October

We have been given some free days and the luscious grass and hilly countryside is remarkably like the area in which the young horses are reared. It is little wonder they are happy for they must feel they have gone back to their roots.

Tomorrow, we move on to the camp as the General here thinks we now are better prepared.

25th October

I am hurriedly writing this before I leave the farm. My favourite horse is being loaded into the horsebox and of course I forgot to say our camp commander has come here to collect us and the horse (named Napoleon).

***

Out of Graz, they travelled on flat ground, and over several weeks covered much countryside and passed through several villages. Later the ascent became incredibly steep, and ended, in a bleak area, with the commander declaring, "Well here we are, we've arrived."

Whereas the 'special horse' was quite at home at high altitude, it took the lads longer to adjust. At the end of the day, they were glad to retreat into their tents. Due to being involved in communication, Alfred and Helmut shared a tent. Edward joined two experienced soldier- mechanics.

As night fell Helmut stretched out on his sleeping bag.

"Don't waste too much lamp oil writing that old journal of yours will you" he said.

"No, I shan't be long."

***

The passing months were incredibly busy. Between camps they had had a week's respite before continuing in stages, closer to the border. Alfred had given up on his journal as he was repeating accounts of exercises, petty squabbles, translations and mundane messaging.

By February, bedraggled, and unhappy with weather conditions, inadequate equipment, and unsubstantial food, everyone had had enough. In March hope revived, when Helmut's radio message was finally answered, and supplies arrived. The food fed morale as much as stomachs. Supplies had been well timed, and now the cadets had to act quickly.

Alfred resumed journal entries:

March 13th

Today my officer sent me on horseback to a very remote place where radio communication isn't possible. I felt isolated.

Momentarily putting his pencil down, he turned to Helmut to say "You know the sergeant said I would be saving lives?"

"Yes"

"Well, for all we know the worst of Nazi's could have deceived him."

"I don't think so; he'd do a double bluff."

Reassured, Alfred firmly answered, "Yes, you're right."

***

Next day, two hours after setting off, Alfred dismounted, left his horse grazing, and walked across a difficult wide expanse between mountainous hills. The area was full of small boulders. No blue wooden hut was to be seen. It was vital, that in line with instructions, he find the hut. As he continued looking, he felt his eyes would pop out of his head with the effort. Then at last, for a split second the blue hut registered on his brain. *Where is it?* He wondered, and then spotted it completely hidden beneath overhanging branches. The map revealed how dangerously close he was to the border. Ten degrees east of the hut he would find the brief message in a small canvas tube.

134

He was half way across the wide expanse, when, as if from nowhere, the sound of a solitary plane mercilessly imposed. Realising how the surrounding hills had masked the sound, he quickened his pace. As the plane circled around him, his heart pumped loudly. A volley of shots trailed along the stony ground. As he thought *God help me, please, I cannot get across in time. He's coming back,* a voice in his heart gave instruction '*Die, lie down.'*

As the next volley of gun fire rick -shaded around, he lay on the ground inert, and pretended he was dead. Something, like the bite of poisonous snake, sharply stung his heel. He couldn't do anything about it until the plane finally disappeared out of visual and aural range. An inspection of the heel revealed a superficial graze caused by a bullet that had lodged in the heel of his boot.

He prayed for the English pilot who would report having killed a Jerry messenger near the Austro-Hungarian border. *Would the imagined death make the pilot fear for his own life? Was he praying as he flew over the clouds, asking God to let him make it to base? Had he by now realized that like himself, the foreign soldier was an ordinary chap caught up in it all?* With all his heart Alfred hoped so.

135

Chapter 18

Snow Hills
(1942-1943)

"They must go to Russia, where needed. They have the skills" snapped Scharfmann.

Calmly the sergeant retorted, "But not the experience."

Scharfmann's razor sharp tone continued, "That two of our cadets have had experience outside the military training school counts. Germany's situation is desperate; our decisions have to be founded upon new criteria."

Wishing all cadets had preliminary experience outside the training establishment, the sergeant was in no position to object. He dared not point out that the inhumane attitude of the Nazi's was the main ingredient for disaster. *We are sinking under the label the country's extreme militia are placing upon us* he thought. He reflected on a sermon he had heard, preached by Bishop Clemens August Count von Galen, at the beginning of August last year. It had been at St Lambert's in his home town. Everyone, frozen with fear, had listened with awe as the bishop dared reveal and oppose the Nazi regime for murdering mentally handicapped people. In the sermon he had explained that his letters to Nazi leaders had been ignored. The sergeant sighed because he knew of an unimaginable number of defenceless patients being killed because of the Nazi belief that such were unworthy of life. Within his mind he re-heard the bishop's stern warning that 'such a path will find excuse for the validation of any murder'.

With precision Scharfmann gave a Nazi salute, and whilst he declared "Heil -Hitler" Korff, too late,noticed him scrutinize his marginally indecisive return. He wished he could declare his burning thoughts '*Might as well be Hail Caesar, they are acting as the Romans did; only this time it is not the poor Christians in the arena. You Scharfmann, and others like you, think you have found something new, but it is an age-old banner that hides under other banners secular or religious.'*

***

Training was finalised during the following week when the cadets were declared fully- fledged soldiers. By train, they were setting off for war. If things went to plan, they would eventually cross the Russian border by truck and link up with their battalion. Little by little they realized Sergeant Korff's scrutiny, and sharp attack on any slacking, had been for their own good. Now the drill of being prepared for the unexpected would be put to test.

***

Three weeks later, an oppressive atmosphere enshrouded them. They looked across the eerie, tangible stillness of a silent scene, set it seemed, for some unknown drama. Everything was in waiting. Dagger – like, icicles dangled from the branches of dormant trees. In and around every living thing, sword- like, ice cold rays of sunlight offered no warmth. Like frozen pillars, the company of one hundred and fifty, waited, and waited longer. Only the frozen mist of their breath indicated they weren't dead men. By enforcing memories of comrades who had submitted to the sleep of death they managed to keep awake. Adder like, something lashed across the snowy ground and landed with a thud on marginally exposed rock. Men standing close stared in stunned silence. In their frozen brains the object didn't register as a grenade. Slowly Alfred's thoughts ticked, until he recalled Father Benedict's words, 'There are times when we need to rely on the deepest resources of our mind.'

Summoning determination, he raced to the spot to retrieve the grenade. With no time to spare he threw it in an opposite direction. It landed on a partially exposed rock and exploded in a cascade of snow thrown in all directions. When the last man had stopped running, Alfred sighed with relief and praised God with every heart- beat, for the fulfilment of hidden mission, to save lives. Russian, German, Serb, Jew, or whatever race ran through their veins, every solider present had lived to see another day. In freezing weather, they had to remain here, near Smolensk.

***

137

A few weeks later Commander Bauermann caught Alfred's attention, to let him know he would be recommended for the bravery award of 'The iron cross' –

Forcing down the thickness in his voice Alfred replied, "Thank you Sir."

Firmly he believed the true crown of glory was awarded in the heart of God, to those who act in faith and love. As he went off to his tent he thought of Christ on the cross. Quietly he uttered- "He was nailed there in a crucifixion caused by ruthless and selfish acts of men. He was resurrected by the love of the glorious and selfless God who recognised him as his selfless son above all sons."

***

The deeper they moved into frozen regions, the more intense was the fighting, and the more necessary it was to use machine guns to combat 'enemy' machine gun attacks It didn't occur to anyone on either side, that the opposing side, might have the same opinion.

During a brief ceremony at the start of what unravelled as a day of intense fighting, Commander Bauermann presented Alfred with his award.

Over the course of the day, the Russians added grenades to their weaponry. Alfred was about to reload the machine gun he was sharing with Helmut when a mighty explosion sent him flying. Moments later when he looked up and turned to speak to Helmut his world changed. Silently, slow motion, he stared in disbelief at the devastating scene. It could not be true, could it? --that across the snow plains lay the torn pieces of Helmut's head. In a pool of blood staining the whiteness of the snow Helmut's headless body slumped over the machine gun. Recoiling in horror, Alfred, in a state of shock, staggered clear of the scene. Nothing had prepared him for such a horrific event as this. Quickly bracing himself he turned back, and a distance away from the machine gun gently laid his friend's body on the blanket of snow. He prayed for Helmut, but even so, as he returned to the machine gun to stave off another volley of Russian gun fire, he was full of anger. Falling back on spiritual discipline, the situation was redeemed when he asked God's forgiveness for such thoughts of revenge. He imagined God quickly quench the fire with angel's tears. Thus, Alfred's noisy stream of bullets continued to fall short of their mark. So far German's were impressed with his efforts and Russians were deterred. He would not kill, the Jew in his ancestry would not kill, the man of Christian mission would not kill, he would not kill, he would not kill.

Eventually when the sound of machine guns died, his thoughts and feelings cried out *'O Lord this is hell and there's only one cross that ever bore significance; a wooden cross'*. He almost heard the voice of Father Spyridon say, *'Within the way of the cross, symbolic of our saviour's death and resurrection, we have victory.'*

In the evening, unable to face camp supper, he took a walk, sat down, and wept beside a cluster of trees on the river bank. The psalm, 'By the waters of Babylon we sat down and wept' came to mind. From his pocket he took out his copy of the award recommendation, ripped it in pieces and threw the fragments into the river. Like petals on the wind, as fragments of paper landed on water and were carried downstream, Alfred inwardly cried, *'Helmut I am so sorry I didn't notice what was happening.'* For a time, unflinching, he sat still and not until he started walking back to camp did he come to realize his toes were frost-bitten. If he were to survive, he would have to accept the socks and boots of dead men, even those of his much-loved friend Helmut.

Under cover of night, they set up camp nearer the town, where the air was acrid with the smoke of burning buildings.

***

Having snatched a few hours' sleep Alfred rose at dawn, at which time the officer in charge equipped them with compasses. The commander's voice shrill and tense instructed, "Because the area is unfamiliar, I want you scour the land individually. The more information we can gather the less risk there will be of being captured."

***

At six O'clock Alfred was climbing a bank in the woodland. He kept moving, and by keeping close to trees, covered his ground. To illustrate the area, he briefly marked his sketch map. A sudden snap of a twig startled him. Training to the fore, he turned in a flash, and saw a figure lunge at him. Quickly he veered away from the soldier's knife. Now in arm lock with the man, he now was aware that the uniform was Russian. Determined he writhed and twisted against the Russian's manoeuvres. In his heart he made a promise to Helmut to not die, and to God he made a silent vow, to not kill.

For a long time, the struggle continued until Alfred managed to prise the knife from his attacker. Purposefully looking him in the eye, he was able to say in broken Russian, "Surrender, surrender, you won't be hurt."

Following a fleeting look of surprise, the Russian's eyes conveyed defiance. Alfred gave him another chance and continued in limited Russian, "I come from Belgrade, my father Yugoslav. Only as.... child.... lived in Germany. You, me, caught... in war. Please surrender."

Full of contempt, for the assumed lie, the Russian struggled; once more the fight was on. As they wrestled, gradually slipping down the grassy bank, the attacker lost grip, and momentarily lost the knife. For a second it glinted on the forest's leafy floor. The Russian grabbed it, but before he could tighten his grip, Alfred grabbed and prised the knife from him. Now they were rolling, with the knife in Alfred's hand. Repeatedly the Russian lunged forward. Now on the ground, Alfred used his heels to move side-wards. He wondered if he would join Helmut. The Russian who was landing would win the combat.' *Why he wasn't taking the knife and getting the kill over-and-done-with?'* Alfred wondered, and in his heart submitted to God his redeemer. But --, a ghastly gurgling revealed that the unrelenting Russian had landed on the upturned blade. With trembling hands Alfred found his handkerchief, and when he had removed the knife, used handkerchief as a compress and held it there.

Realising what was happening, the Russian communicated briefly with his eyes, and then the noise ceased. Alfred's efforts failed, there was no pulse. He thought of Helmut, of how he would visit Helmut's parents. This middle aged, Russian had no messenger. Alfred removed identification papers from the man's pocket and left some personal letters. Taking a silver cross from his own pocket he placed it in the pocket of the soldier's jacket. Alongside the soldier, his prayers travelled heavenward, *'Father, this is a terrible time. Your eyes alone have seen that I did not take his life. Father, Father I pleaded with him. He would not change his mind. He was someone's son, someone's husband, someone's father, I wanted him to live.'*

He knew that within his heart, he would always feel the wound of the Russian's death.

The picture of the malefactors on the cross came to mind. He surmised how, even on a cross they had had a choice. One man had focussed on the here and now. The other recognizing his own failings and had turned to Christ. Alfred realized that in essence that man was first to receive the sacrament in its non- prophetic meaning. There on the cross Christ expressed the meaning of his death that gave birth to the sacrament, to save sinners and bless them with eternal life. Alfred prayed again, *'Please let this soldier Dimitric have eternal life. Grant him your peace'.*

***

Russian voices drew near. Stealthily Alfred retreated and returned to camp to give account of events.

"Your description is of a member of the Red Army," said the commander. Their motto is of strength, fearlessness, and determination. They can be ruthless to their enemy but also to their own men if they do not conform."

Alfred thought how like Nazis they were.

***

A month later, Alfred's company reached a pocket of Smolensk under German occupation. Here they witnessed the extreme plight of Russian peasants. In the hope of obtaining food, droves of starving people were daily arriving in German occupied territory.

To transport his soldiers away from the area, the officer intended using a train that had been stationary when the region had been seized. It took a week for the engine to be repaired and to find sufficient coal to run her. On the day for departure, even the toughest German soldiers were moved by the sight of numerous starving people. On platforms, and tracks, people scrabbled for the tiniest bits of food. Hauntingly bony hands imploringly reached out into the air with eyes fixed on the occupants of the train. As the train began moving, several peasants dared come close.

141

"Nein, no, we cannot. We need our supplies" said the officer as he strode along the corridor. By now the train was steaming and the rods were driving the wheels faster. A woman outside the window could have been Helmut's mother, anyone's mother. With compassion Alfred took a stale loaf of bread from his kit bag, and daringly threw it out of the window. He watched her break off a piece of bread, and rapidly devour it. It was to be her lot, for instantly, five peasants caught up, pulled the loaf from her and ripped it apart. With thoughts of the biblical parable of loaves and fishes Alfred wished a similar miracle would happen for those poor people. He took with him in mind and heart the image of the woman looking at him with a mixture of dismay and feint hope. His small grain of compassion, he hoped had strengthened her spirit. That was what the biblical story was about, a grain of generosity being the start of feeding the hungry world. It also had a hidden message of feeding humankind with news of Jesus, who, through his death and resurrection became the bread of life and the wine of salvation for all? If the woman survived, she would remember and help others.

***

An element Alfred was unaware of was that Werner from Aachen felt depressed and resented Alfred's early promotion at the training school. Of medium build, with a pallid acne complexion, Werne had convinced himself that Alfred's recommendation for an award was the result of favouritism. He resolved that when he returned to Germany, he would report him for throwing bread to the enemy.

About two hundred kilometres along the track, a solitary German soldier flagged down the train. Wondering what the problem was, Commander Bauermann immediately jumped down and yelled, "What do you think you are doing. Can't you see we are army?"

"Ten kilometres ahead, the bridge has been blown up."

"Before I take your word for it, I'd like to know your battalion."

"Cologne 133; Sir."

"Name?"

"Martyn Schmidt, Sir."

"Why are you here? Have you deserted?"

"No sir, two hours ago the bridge was blown up by Russians. Colonel Minden knew this line to be linked to German occupied territory, in Smolensk".

"Minden! I know Minden he is as sharp as a button."

"Where are the rest of your troops?"

"Killed; some by machine gun; some by the cold. There are only a handful of us left."

The commanding officer read in the soldier's eyes the truth of the situation.

"You have done well Schmidt. Tell Colonel Minden we're here. Ask him if he wants to join with my depleted company."

"Yes Sir."

"Get off the train immediately. Quick pace, into the wood" he ordered.

He instructed the driver, "Start up, release the pistons, jump off."

Georgo complied, and when the train was in motion, jumped off. Dumbfounded, the men watched as the driverless train steamed ahead, and crashed down the void into the river. From the river bank Commander Bauermann watched, and with a wry smile of relief, and annoyance that the train had been lost, went off to find division members who had been saved.

It amazed him to learn how terrible loss of life had been averted. As he followed Schmidt into the woods and to where the Cologne group of soldiers were standing, he quickly recognized Minden, last seen at an officer's day in Aachen.

***

Due to the high number of losses, and casualties, transported weeks before the bridge was blown- up, they were reduced to five tents. On the bright side, things were peaceful here, and for a while, memories of horrors could be dulled. For a time of recovery, and respite they remained in the woodland several weeks. Weeks later, when they left the area, they saw a wondrous image of hope, in the form of spring flowers peeping through the deeper regions of the leafy forest floor.

Chapter 19

The river

During late summer, the remnant of two divisions continued to explore the area.

Later, with all but three men present, Colonel Minden recommended they urgently move on. "I think it best to wait until my three men return" Commander Bauermann replied.

Minden urgently conveyed, "Apart from being sitting targets there is another reason we need to get moving. I have made radio contact with Aachen. Orders are for us to urgently move on."

Unaware how the situation had changed, Alfred's group of three continued with the plan they had been given, namely to cover ground, make regular stops, and explore the area. Each day when they returned to camp at six O'clock, they were to report their findings.

On their first day Alfred and his three companions had the task of exploring three kilometres of farm land. Having covered several fields, they came to a large, high hay stack close to a hedge and rested there. Ten minutes later the sound of voices drew near. "They are Russians. Quick- hide-- in the hay stack!"

Fearfully and hastily, they dug their way in, and rapidly covered themselves. Heart beats pounded the silence as voices drew close. To the best of his ability Alfred translated,

"I tell you no bodies were ever found; they must have got off the train and for all we know they could be anywhere."

"I'm very hot and tired; let's rest before we go back," said another voice.

The squeak of gate hinges and the thud of footsteps were close.

"Here'll do nicely" said a Russian.

"Better check first."

With a flash of reflected light, weapons invaded the hay stack; two Germans felt the edge of metal skim their heads. One man's

144

crop of hair and another's hat offered protection from the blade. As the Russians sat down to sort out their boots and blisters, one man farted loudly. Mentally and with some guess work, Alfred managed to translate—

"It sounds as if you've got a built-in bomb!"

"Yes, a stink bomb!"

The Russians laughed raucously, resumed conversation, and after what seemed an eternity, moved on.

Alfred told his companions what had been said and regardless of the gravity of their situation they were amused, and agreed that Russian humour did exist, and matched their own when off duty.

However, due to enemy soldiers being at large, they had to wait until night fall to report to their commanding officer. Stumbling and groping their way through various thickets and obstacles, they made their way back to camp. When they arrived at the camp location, they realized, to their dismay, that, for reasons unknown, they were alone. They wondered what unknown factor had led to their companions' departure.

"They must have received orders- they haven't left clues, which means Russians are around. They may have assumed that we had been captured."

Alfred gladly said "Not quite-- a small tent and some provisions have been left, here under the leaves."

Suppressing fears, they remained in the wood, and made plans for returning to Germany. A few days later, about four O'clock, they were startled by the sound of people beating their way through undergrowth. At closer proximity they could hear that their language was German. The first soldier to emerge from the thickets stared suspiciously.

Smiling, Alfred said in a friendly manner, "Yes we're German, we're glad to see you."

"I trust you're not deserters?"

"Definitely not; we have become separated from the remnants of two divisions. A few members of the Cologne regiment joined us under Captain Minden."

"I need your names and proofs of identity."

From their top pockets Alfred and companions took out I.D cards. Scanning the cards with a quick glance, the stranger said,

"Well I'm satisfied. I'm Colonel Trapp from Schwarzenberg, and these are survivors from my company. We may as well join ranks, do you agree?"

One by one they agreed, a sense of normality returned. Two of Trapp's men lit a fire and when it was burning cooked the trout they'd caught in the morning. The aroma whetted appetites, and when the trout was cooked and bread supplied by courtesy of Minden's supply, the merged groups, over exchange of news, hungrily ate the food. Colonel Trapp's tone constricted as he explained, "We are trying to make our way back to Germany. You're welcome to join us; the more eyes we have, the better we can see what the enemy are up to."

"Where were you fighting?" Alfred enquired.

Trapp replied "Moscow. The conflict took the lives of some four hundred men and the cold finished off the many wounded."

"We were at Smolensk, and the same happened there. Luckily, Germany had a pocket of Smolensk, and we managed to get out by train."

Sergeant Trapp came across as a fair minded, ethical man. Alfred noticed how he avoided using the word Nazi. The kind of person he was came across as he described a situation he had experienced

"Rather than mow Russians down in their bunkers I ordered them out. They were taken off by truck as prisoners of war. All that is, except their commander, who refused to come out, and took his own life, with a single shot. I cannot get that out of my head. We got the body out. He had a photo of his family in his pocket. His children were about the same age as mine. I cannot get it out of my head."

"I had a similar experience" said Alfred and briefly related the tale of his encounter with the Russian soldier.

Now living day to day and having abandoned cumbersome kit and tents, the fifteen men gladly scoured a deserted farm. There they discovered a feast of food, cheeses, eggs, and plenty of edible stale bread to stuff into pockets. Containers, one without a lid, meant they could take supplies of fresh water with them.

***

Later, it was getting dark as they stealthily crept along the bank of a fast-flowing river, the sergeant had identified on his map. Two hours later, Alfred, last in the line of walkers, trying to keep up pace, tripped over a tree root and fell into the icy water. Fearing for his companions' safety, he kept silent. His fall, he knew, would have been obliterated by the sound of rushing water.

On this night in early October, the force of the river prevented him swimming to safety. Exhausted, he let the river carry him downstream. In the darkness his companions failed to see him. Numbed and afraid, he thought of giving up, and might have succumbed to the dark depths, had not Father Spyridon's words come to mind. 'We have to remain focussed on God, particularly when life takes unexpected direction'. Alfred had to painfully laugh, for he knew the abbot had not intended the meaning so. *This fast method for travelling might see me welcoming my companions* were Alfred's thoughts as he helplessly continued in the icy flow. Under overhanging branches, he unexpectedly bumped against a boulder. Painfully, his leg grazed along the rough surface and water rapidly gushed over his head. Surfacing with a gasp he quickly continued down- stream, until finally, like a piece of drift wood, he landed on a soft flat bank. Amazed to have survived such an experience, he lay there a few moments, before forcing himself to clamber onto higher ground. Regardless of the numbness and painfulness of his leaden body, he crawled through thick undergrowth. Then, in a moment of time, a few meters ahead, he saw a sign of hope; a cottage with a spiral of blue smoke, steadily trailing along the starlit sky.

Wondering if it was real, he approached with caution, and tentatively walked through the open door. No one was about, everything was still and silent. Had the occupants fled or been seized by Stalin's men he wondered? A huge stove with embers smouldering at its base, dominated the centre of the one roomed abode. As he placed his cold hands on the top edges of the stove, he weighed up that it had been burning itself out for several days. According to custom, a pile of fresh straw had been placed on top of the stove, as a bed for the oldest family member. The clever design for keeping the oven section hot for cooking, and for projecting heat into the room, left the top surface warm but never too hot.

Shivering with cold, teeth chattering violently, he removed his wet clothes, and hung them in front of the oven door. He took a woollen dressing gown down from a door hook, and put it on. Giving in to exhaustion he lay upon the straw and fell into a deep sleep.

***

Weakened by his ordeal he remained at the cottage several days and nights. Fortunately, food supplies were available in a small larder. Three days later, after taking off the dressing gown, he put on his dried clothes, but overcome by dizziness, decided he should stay a further night.

In the morning, feeling very unwell, he tried sitting up, but his pulse was racing and his head heavy. As he fumbled through the straw for his jacket, he felt something soft. Wondering what it might be, he removed a layer of straw. Recoiling from the stench, he saw with horror the decaying corpse of an elderly man. As fast as he could he staggered towards the door, but his legs buckled. He needed help urgently!

With gritted determination he staggered through the doorway. *Where to now?*

In several senses of the word, he was in the middle of nowhere. Avoiding the river direction, he slowly and painfully covered a kilometre and collapsed on the steps of a place likely to be linked to human existence.

He did not know that slowly, painfully his prayers were being answered. Several hours later a Red Cross worker doing a routine check, came across Alfred's inert body, and speedily ran to fetch a colleague.

***

By slotting two poles through the sleeves of jackets the helpers quickly made a stretcher and carried him to their jeep. A short drive later they were at their Red Cross station.

"Lay him on the table; I need to take a good look at him."

"What's wrong?" a medic asked.

"I am certain it is typhus. Quickly take him to the isolation tent. Get plenty of disinfectant for this table," said the doctor.

"I don't know what language he's gibbering; doesn't sound German" he added.

148

"I recognize the language, Jugoslav" a young nursing nun replied. They had no time to question what he was doing here dressed in German uniform. The look on the faces of the medical team informed the nun he was not expected to survive.

"Could I watch over him?" she said.

"Yes, sister but don't stay too close for too long" Mother Superior warned.

***

Over the passing days, particularly when the patient was losing the battle, Sister Monica earnestly prayed in her native Serb- Croat language. Convinced of her purpose in God's scheme of things, she was unaware of how her devotions provided a thread upon which Alfred's will to live, hung as delicately as a dew drop on a spider's web. As he lapsed into unconsciousness, he recognised in his heart the prayers she spoke. So deep was his condition that Sister Monica detected neither breath nor pulse. Eventually she collapsed and could not come round even though afar off she heard Sister Thomas say, "I think she's caught typhus."

Worn out from nursing the sick and wounded over many months, Sister Monica died that night. Through God's grace her spirit continued to hover near the one who loved God. She knew she had to remain here while she still had God's purpose to accomplish.

***

Alongside others, Alfred lay on the stone floor of the mortuary. In the morning he would receive a brusque service followed by burial. The authorities had his identification papers, his death would be registered and his family informed.

During the long cold hours of night his mind struggled to make sense of impulses. A distant throb he failed to recognize as his heart beat. Vaguely he remembered something his father had said about the Balkan war. Now, blurred, vision returned but his muscles were weak, and he could not move his eyes. Gradually consciousness returned.

"Why am I cold? Who are you lady? Your warm smile, your brown eyes full of compassion— "Who are you?" he called aloud. As he imagined her warm hand on his forehead, he sat bolt

149

upright. Looking around, he thought he saw her, positively he felt her presence, but no one was to be seen.

***

The attendant needing to check everything for burials, turned the key, and opened the door. Thinking he heard movement he looked up. In horror he watched a pale faced corpse walk towards him. The ashen faced attendant instantly dropped his keys, took to his heels and at incredible speed, ran down the path.

Unaware of the attendant's dilemma Alfred picked up a blanket, put it around his shoulders, picked up the keys and headed for some tents on the opposite side of a field. At proximity he made out a Red Cross sign on a vehicle, and with great relief knew he was safe. German conversation emerged from inside a small wooden building.

Someone must have found him and brought him here. He knocked on the door; an officer, a General, opened it.

"Who the blazes are you at this time of day?" the man abruptly asked.

"That's him, that is him" said the man in strangled tone. Alfred recognized him as the man he had seen running down the path.

"Here are your keys. You dropped them," said Alfred.

Refusing to take them, the young man remained distant. Reverently Alfred stared at a senior nun wearing a small wooden crucifix hanging from a silver chain around her neck. The beads of the rosary attached to her belt had a deep ruby glow. "Well praise to God. Welcome back from the deep abyss. Sister Monica recognised some of the prayers you were uttering."

He wondered to whom she referred.

"I am a little confused. I recall falling down some steps and a lady with brown eyes looking down at me."

"That was Sister Monica. Sadly, she was not as fortunate as you. The typhus got to her and she is now in our Lord's heavenly kingdom."

"I am sorry. Have I had typhus?"

"Yes" "And what was the building I was in. I remember stepping over several things wrapped up sheets."

150

Putting her arm around him Mother superior said "We'll talk about it in the morning, come let's get you a hot drink and find you a warm bed."

***

Next morning Alfred was immensely horrified to hear that he could have been buried alive. Making light of matters Mother Superior said, "Use it positively as your own resurrection story. Do not dwell on what might have been. I am sure your Father-Spyridon, whom you mentioned, would say the same."

"Yes sister. You are right. I shall always pray for Sister Monica. She took a risk for me and that she has died for selfless reasons. That is to the glory of God and should be remembered for all time. I felt her presence after the time you say she died, and I think she must have waited to see everything resolved."

"I'm certain God has saved you for His very special purpose."

"I cannot imagine God's purpose for me. Part of me feels I have let him down by leaving the abbey." Because the old nun looked puzzled Alfred explained he had been born in Germany, gone to Jugoslavia at the age of eleven, and later entered the abbey as a novitiate.

"Which abbey?" she asked.

"The Trappist abbey; The Cistercian Benedictine, near Belgrade."

"Well perhaps God was calling you out into the world to be their representative. We have heard that all the monks there were killed by communists. You or one of your descendants will one day choose to record the event."

She saw how deeply upset Alfred was and focussing on practicalities said "I will retrieve your papers and we will secure your safe passage to a hospital. You are not to worry about your part in the war for a while, not until you are much stronger. Typhus can be a killer; it weakens a person. For a time, you must rest."

151

Chapter 20

The Garden of Return

He remembered sleeping a great deal and with two other patients, in various ambulances, being transported a long distance. Then he had been transferred to an aeroplane, and finally another ambulance. It was hard for him to grasp that he was in occupied Warsaw. As he looked around the hospital ward he noticed sunlight on the walls, how the hollows and brush strokes of the paint were highlighted. Beyond a small window, deep pink cherry blossom bobbed like curly candy floss on spindly branches. The beauty of the cherry blossom was in stark contrast to the clinical look of the ward. Gradually, piece by piece, he comprehended that the solitary cherry tree was a singular emblem of goodness against a backdrop of devastation. Was his imagination creating the thin pale face of a young woman peering through a dirty window in a derelict house? A moment later the reality was affirmed with the appearance of several thin, ragged children scuttling along the street to forage in bins. It was a sight that paralleled those witnessed in Russia.

***

Gradually, over the course of a week, he began to piece together events from the time he had discovered the peasant's cottage. The fact he covered several kilometres to the bunker steps remained held in the hand of God. To have walked out from what he now knew to have been the mortuary, whilst weak, suffering from effects of typhus and frost bite had been remarkable. Determination and will power had been his survival kit. More significantly the tool kit had been energized by faith and the support of others of faith, and by the inexplicable support of God who assuredly had wanted him to live. He silently prayed for the young nursing sister whose presence had been an essential life line. Her faith had re-kindled his own faith, her faith lived on. It was what the way of God centeredness was about, with its

152

rich purpose of kindling, and rekindling others, in their direction and values upon their path of life. The attendant must have had a life changing experience when he saw a perceived corpse walk out of the mortuary; little wonder he had nearly passed out with fright. Alfred prayed for him, that his fear of death would be removed

The tap of the ward sister's footsteps brought him back to the present.

"Please sister could you tell me the date?" he asked as she drew near.

"May 16th."

"May 16th 1942?"

"No, it's 1943."

Guessing he must have lost sense of time due to illness, he replied "Oh of course."

Soon the restless mutterings of a man in the bed opposite became hysterical cries.

"The Nazis are killing Jews; I know they are. I have heard they are gassing them. That is why these beds are free. There aren't any Polish Jews anymore."

For his own good, she said, the sister slapped the patient's face, "Be quiet, you must not say those things. You must not say it. It is propaganda."

She had later added that she was aware of a nearby patient being of officer status.

"Can you really imagine a story like that holding a grain of truth?" Alfred added. Yet, as he spoke the pale face at the window haunted him.

The patient's ramblings continued— "he was an air pilot-- *I had to drop a bomb near Crete. There were young men on that ship. We saw body parts floating around. I was ordered to do it-- it wasn't me.... I do not want to be brave...I want it to end.*"

"Roll up your sleeve" the sister firmly requested. Supressing her own emotions, she quickly injected a sedative into her patient. Seconds later he was limp and comatose.

Poland sank into Alfred's sub conscious. The closest he had come to Polish people was the young men he had heard as he had been taken out of the ambulance. They had looked hopeful and patient, and not at all stressed. He had asked the stretcher bearer if he knew Polish.

"A little" he had answered.

"What did he just say?" Alfred had asked.

They had taken the advice of a friend called Karol Wojtyla.

"Well, he must be a miracle maker for them to look so calm" had been Alfred's reply.

In July Alfred learned of his transfer to Vienna.

***

He was taken to a Vienna nursing home that had been established for soldiers recovering from injuries and shell shock. Some men had been blinded; others were physically disabled. Others suffering depression, were informed they would recover through effort. Much to Alfred's annoyance he could not stand unaided. The current medical aim for his recovery was good supply of wholesome food, and daily physio treatment. Gradually over the weeks he was able to spend increasing periods of time outside.

Summer days in the large garden reminded him of forgotten things--picnics in fields and woodlands with his mother sisters and brothers, the occasional playtimes with his father, and the lovely day with Erika. As in the past, he now had time to observe small and marvellous wonders of the created world. Bees constantly dived into flower heads, to fill leg pouches with nectar. Similar striped insects hovered like enemy air craft, and quickly disappeared. Bird song, instead of explosions, gun fire, and cries of pain, offered idyllic experience to be cherished within the soul. A skylark's rapid, high pitched repetitive melody caught his attention. For a while he scanned the blue heights until he located a small dot winging the sky.

***

In September, back in Aachen, he silently grieved the atrocious death of Helmut. Without Helmut and other comrades, things would never be the same. Increasingly, conflicting attitudes of German leaders and army personnel created general cause for concern. Fearing for their own safety, ethical, fair minded army officers, no longer spoke out for justice. Statements made by the air pilot in Warsaw were echoed by others. It was propaganda? On the other hand, there was the case of a priest

154

near Beckum having been arrested for questioning the viability of the rehabilitation programme for the disabled and mentally handicapped. He wondered if it was true that Himmler and his team believed them to be unworthy of life. The idea of anyone regarding them as unnecessary consumers was despicable and equally inconceivable. Amongst them were several Jews from Beckum, and one man from South-wood Lane, Neubeckum. That man, a neighbour of Alfred's childhood had remained cheerful and hopeful. *'Had he truly been transported to a fully Jewish community?'* Alfred asked himself if he was imagining cracks within the social structure. Instinctively he knew he should never mention his Jewish roots.

Unaware he was being discussed at an officer's meeting; Alfred walked from the railway station to his base at Aachen.

"He went missing of his own accord. He's not truly German" Scharfmann's loud and insinuating voice imposingly declared.

"It would be out of character; and don't forget he was awarded the iron cross" Sergeant Korff reminded his officers.

"I received a report about him having thrown bread to Russian peasants."

"On the other hand, The Red Cross report mentions some religious background" a new colonel added.

Scharfmann's piercing black eyes narrowed, and in a cultured Nazi tone he emphasized, "They are the worse. We had to arrest a priest in Beckum for his opposition to our policies."

"The best thing to do would be to put him to the test" he angrily added.

The others silently watched Scharfmann with his satisfied smirk on his face. That he knew how wary they were of the supreme party to which he belonged, Korf was certain.

***

Alfred picked up and read a hand written message lying on his bed. Already his companions were back in action and soon new recruits would claim the beds. He would have to be quick if he were to obey orders and go to the office. As instructed in the note, he pinned the iron cross to his uniform, walked the length of the dormitory, and down the steps to the familiar corridor. He raced along the corridor and had hardly finished knocking on the door when the punctuating voice of Captain Scharfmann snarled, "Come in."

Inside the room, Alfred was glad to see Sergeant Korff, but he also noted his brow beaten appearance. An unknown colonel with an honest look in his eye was present. Scharfmann approached Alfred, and in mocking manner, with one finger, flicked up the iron cross medal on Alfred's uniform.

"You have done well to save many men but it is a little disappointing that throughout all your time in Russia you have reported the death of one Russian only. Were there witnesses?"

"No Captain."

"Well at least you handed in papers and we know he was a red guard and that he was disposed of by whatever means."

Sergeant Korff's expression empathised with Alfred and he knew he always accepted his word. In a leering manner Scharfmann continued, "Well how do you take to the idea of going to fight against Tito's regime, immediately?"

Sensing the nationality trap Alfred answered, "Sir, I do not think I am in a fit state for returning to combat. I would be of far greater service as a translator or interpreter."

He could see in Scharfmann's eyes that he misjudged his use of the word interpreter, and took it as an insinuation that Nazi tactics were underhand.

The officers could see the intensity of Scharfmann's desire to entrap Alfred. As far as Scharfmann was concerned the man was a foreigner, of uncertain identity and classification, who had nothing in common with Nazi aims. In Scharfmann's eyes, Alfred was a unique individual, and no longer was there room for people like him.

"Seeing as you did so well you will have to return to Russia" he said.

Quickly Alfred glanced at Sergeant Korff, and hoped with all his heart he realized his concerns. He was aware that having had typhus, a return to Russia would mean certain death. Silently he prayed to be rescued from this bottomless pit.

Were it not for Korff's presence he might have collapsed.

"Stand at ease, dismiss" Scharfmann hissed.

As Alfred left the room, he tried to recall a comment made by one of the nurses in Vienna. Only the abbot's voice came to mind. "Search within the deepest resources of your mind." He searched and searched again until he remembered the Viennese nurse having conversed with an army officer friend. He had informed her about an important clause in military rules: that anyone having suffered and survived typhus would be exempt from returning to Siberia, Russia, and similar regions during winter months. Her voice echoing into the present resounded in his heart like a clear brook on a spring day. Now, Praise God, he had the weapon of knowledge to hinder Scharfmann's fanatical mission. Turning back, he knocked on the door that Scharfmann opened.

"Permission to speak Sir!"

"No, you had your interview" said Scharfmann and rapidly slammed the door, shut.

***

Next day Alfred threw down his heavy kit bag onto the platform. The train staffed by those commissioned to transport the division he had been ordered to join, would arrive in half an hour. Because Alfred had not fully recovered, the toing and froing seemed exceedingly hectic. Another winter in Russia would prove fatal.

His thoughts continued at random, until with clarity, the nurse's words returned. Making quick decision he returned to base. He would brave the consequences.

Back at camp, luck was not on his side, Scharfmann was crossing the courtyard. Alfred noted the sickening triumphal look in his eyes.

"Back so soon. For the present go back to your dormitory. We will deal with you later, after I've reported the matter to my colleagues," he said.

Noticing Scharfmann's negativity Alfred realized he would be eager to report his version of events to the Nazi party. They would say they were dealing with it in honour of their Führer. What he did not know was that Scharfmann's sole aim was to see him executed before the week was out.

Feeling ill, unhappy, solitary of heart, and longing for the company of family and friends Alfred spent a miserable week in a small gloomy cell. The irony of being imprisoned in Germany did not surprise him. Repeatedly he had seen how war twisted its snake like body around people of all nations, especially through people like Scharfmann. In this dark cell, at least for a while, he could pray and reflect. Regardless of incessant conflict in one form or another, Alfred trusted, deep within himself, the creator's plan. He recalled his mother telling him the story of the Croat who, by remaining calm on the battlefield, had saved his father's life.

A few days later, keys clunked, a soldier opened the metal door.

"Here is your uniform. Quickly, get changed" he said.

Whilst locking the door, the soldier added in softer tone, "I'll be back in ten minutes."

Shakily Alfred changed into uniform. Too soon it seemed, the soldier returned to say, in automated manner

"Follow me. The day for the court martial has arrived."

Alfred followed him along the low corridor, up some concrete steps, and onto familiar ground. Four times the soldier rapped on the solid oak door. It opened, Alfred marched in, and in front of the jury, stood to attention. He did not recognise anyone but in one officer's eyes, saw a spark of compassion. He recalled having seen the officer in the mess on one occasion when Sergeant Korff had introduced him as a colonel.

* * *

Scharfmann, blatantly enjoying the interrogation game, allowed Alfred to stand at ease. Having previously experienced the police cell in Belgrade, Alfred recognized his method to lull him into a false sense of security. As anticipated Scharfmann's pleasantries rapidly expired; mercilessly he fired questions. Everything Alfred answered, Scharfmann twisted with the objective of making him look like a traitor. Going to great lengths Scharfmann accused him of failing to translate and deliver certain messages. At this stage Alfred had not been ordered to reply. Eventually, as Scharfmann was busy in his attempt to persuade the majority to have Alfred executed, Korff's friend, the colonel, asked if he might question the prisoner. "Yes, go ahead" Scharfmann snapped.

The colonel proceeded

"Is it true you were born in Germany?"

158

"Yes Sir."

"Do you consider yourself to be a German citizen?"

"Yes Sir."

"Why did you decide to move to Belgrade?"

"I did not Sir. I was a child. Following my mother's death, when I just turned eleven, my father took me there."

"Are you based with your childhood step mother's family?"

"Yes sir."

"What nationality are they?"

"German, Sir."

"What nationality were the people you worked with in Belgrade?"

Taking cue Alfred emphasised, "German; I helped Father Augustus in his mission work."

"What work was that?"

"To reunite displaced German families and help German born citizens return to Germany."

"But you also worked for an electrical firm" Scharfmann cut in.

"Yes, Sir, but the boss wasn't Serbian; he was German."

Whilst tolerating Scharfmann's dagger looks Korff's friend made the point, "You only have to look at the spelling of Ztoanjib's testimonial to see that the man wasn't Jugoslav."

The mouths of the other members of the jury twitched as if they wanted to smile. Korff's friend continued, "I know Father Augustus, and I once learned that by providing them with convincing passports, this employer helped many German citizens escape."

Not wanting to be defeated, Scharfmann declared in an upward glissando, "Ztoanjib has defied instructions. In the name of our Führer, I recommend he be executed."

Looking pale Alfred silently screamed '*It is going to be too late; God please, please help*'.

Korff's friend cut in, "Before we vote can we grant the prisoner his last right to speak."

Irritated Scharfmann replied, "I don't see the point but I suppose I'll, that is, we'll have to comply."

The colonel could see how anxious and tense Alfred was, especially following days of solitary confinement; furthermore, he had not fully recovered from long term illness. He hoped the innocent prisoner would say something in his own defence. Taking a deep breath Alfred said in a weary, but frank voice, "With all due respect Sir, according to regulation 106 for war, due to having had typhus, I am exempt from going to Russia and Siberia and similar places, during winter months."

"Ridiculous, has the typhus addled your brain?" Scharfmann hissed. Playing Scharfmann at his own game, the colonel intervened.

"Well Sir I'm sure you are right, but to keep on the right side of our superiors we would best look up the regulation. It should not take long. All we must do is look typhus up in the index." The colonel, who had had some medical training, had a notion the regulation did exist. Scharfmann ordered Alfred out of the room whilst the jury searched through numerous medical regulatory books. When they found the correct volume, the colonel's next in command said, "Here is the typhus index." Several heads pored over the book. As the colonel read aloud the regulation, Scharfmann inwardly raged as he absorbed the humiliating information. Red in the face, he thought, 'Scheiss, scheiss, shit,' and without a word marched across the room and opened the door.

"Come back in. The jury has decided to give you another chance" he said. Alfred guessed it had not needed a vote.

"I trust the jury will agree with my decision. I want Ztoanjib away from here.

I suggest he go with the next batch heading for France. Does everyone agree?"

"Yes Commander" they chorused.

When Scharfmann and the members of the jury had left, the colonel invited Alfred to come back into the room.

"You'll need to sign an agreement to never mention the inappropriate court martial," said the colonel. He went on to say, "I am not meant to say this, but off the record you saved yourself from what could have been a very final situation. Well done! They say the pen is mightier than the sword and whoever wrote that regulation certainly saved your life."

"Thank you, Colonel."

Chapter 21

Diverging Paths

Neubeckum: February 1944

Disappointed thirteen-year-old Sarah wrangled that her parents would not allow her to visit Anna Marie. A later compromise was met when they agreed she could stay up until nine. The evening passed, and all too soon her mother was reminding her it was time to go to bed. Without objection Sarah warmly said, "Goodnight Mutti, goodnight Vater."

"Sleep tight, God bless" they replied. Making her way upstairs, she half listened to their conversation about threatening aeroplanes.

No sooner had her head touched the pillow than she fell asleep. Several hours later the drone of planes invaded her subconscious and caused her to believe she was awake. In a trance she opened the window, climbed down the tree, went along the path, opened the gate, and walked along the street. At the far end of the street, she stopped at Anna Marie's home, opened the gate, went around the back of the bungalow, and stood outside her friend's window.

***

Seeing a shadow on the curtain Anna Marie shivered. Mustering courage she crept out of bed, went across the room, and peeped through a chink in the curtains. Strangely enough Sarah was standing there, acting as if she thought the window open.

Annoyed and bewildered Anna Marie said, "Sarah, what are you doing, wait a moment. I will open it, just wait, will you?"

Amidst Sarah's incoherent jabbering Anna Marie made out the word's 'doll' and 'yellow.' Recalling their conversation of a few days ago she said, "Sarah, you do sound strange and very tired. You want some yellow wool for your doll's hair? I have some, but couldn't it have waited until tomorrow?"

161

***

Under the impression Anna Marie was talking to herself, Frau Kemmner came upstairs, and opened the door. To her amazement Sarah was in the room. She wondered how and why she was there. Observation informed her something was wrong, and it was strange that she was dressed in her night dress.

"In heaven's name what's going on?"

"Mutter, please don't be cross. Something is not right with Sarah. I cannot understand a word she is saying. She has a funny look in her eyes," said Anna Marie.

Realizing Sarah was not responding to anyone, Frau kemmner quietly closed the window.

"I think she may have walked in her sleep" she whispered.

***

Unexpectedly a high decibel explosion resounded and with a scream Sarah awoke.

"It's alright, it's alright, you're here with us" Frau Kemmner reassured.

"Why am I here? What has happened?"

Compassionately Frau Kemmner held her quivering shoulders.

"It's all right Sarah, you have been sleep-walking. It might have been a bomb exploding, I am uncertain. It certainly shook the walls. Explosions a long way off can do that" she explained.

"What will mother and father think?" Sarah questioned with a worried frown.

"They will understand. You walked in your sleep a few months ago. They thought it best to not tell you, and it might not have happened again. Here, put on this dressing gown."

"What shall we do now?" Anna Marie enquired.

"I will take Sarah home. Try and get some sleep Anna Marie. You can see her tomorrow" her mother replied.

They went outside and trundled along the road, but at a half way point it was hard to see through the billows of smoke filling the atmosphere. At the far end of the street, in thicker smoke, people who lived at that end of the street were randomly running, coughing, crying. Abruptly Sarah stopped and stared at the familiar gate hanging by a hinge. "Where is our house? Where's-

162

-?" she whispered. Gasping for breath she frantically called "Mother, Father, Heinz, Freda, Gretchen, Emile, Wolfgang."

A warden's voice cut in "How many brothers and sisters did--"

He did not finish his sentence.

"Five" Sarah screamed.

Frau Kemmner explained, "I'm their closest friend: there are no other relatives."

Apologetically he replied "I'm sorry, no one's survived. Now thankfully, the sixth child has been accounted for."

They had mentioned the possibility of this kind of disaster at school. It happened to other people not her; especially not to her parents, brothers, and sisters, not to all of them, not all dead, surely?

"I can hear something moving," said a neighbour.

"Debris often shifts after an explosion" the warden emphasised.

"No, it's definitely scratching."

The warden walked over to investigate and carefully moved several large pieces of debris.Silence prevailed as he dragged from beneath an upturned basket, a singed and frightened tabby cat. Tears flowed down several pairs of eyes to see a living creature rescued from such devastation.

Recognizing Sarah, the cat mewed pitifully."Ludwig, Oh Ludwig" she cried and quickly took the cat from the warden.

As soon as she had put the cat inside her borrowed dressing gown and held him close, torrents of sobbing broke forth. *Would it ever stop?* Several neighbours cried too. Ludwig remained calm and had no intention of jumping out of Sarah's arms.

"Come Sarah, you and Ludwig belong to our family now. We will take care of you."

As Frau Kemner said this, she put her arms around Sarah's shoulders.

"Your mother and father would have wanted us to have you in our family. Besides, you and Anna Marie are like sisters."

***

A few days later, Uncle Bernhart went to the railway station to pick up Alfred on week end leave.

"How's everyone?" Alfred enquired.

163

"Trudi has not been coping because Manfred's been away fighting for almost nine months now. Their baby's due soon."

"I am sorry, but perhaps when the baby's born she will feel better. It is good news; you will be a Great Grandfather."

"Yes. I am looking forward to it, but wishing it were not happening in the middle of a war. We have had a big tragedy nearby: A whole family wiped out except for one girl aged thirteen."

"Oh God that's dreadful; do I know them?"

"Your mother and father often sat next to the mother and her parents in church, when you were about nine years old."

"Oh, the daughter was about nineteen, wasn't she? She was friends with one of the young men in the choir?"

"Yes, that's right, Wilhelm Klein."

"I remember them well. They were lovely people, so kind to me. I always thought Klein was an odd name as he was so tall."

"Well, they married and had six children. Occasionally, when the parents were at a church meeting, Trudi looked after them. Sarah was the only one to survive because for the first time she had taken it into her head to creep out of her bedroom window, and walk to her friend's home down the street. The girl says she was half asleep and did not know what she was doing or how she got in through Anna Marie's bedroom window. Frau Kemmner had just discovered her there when the bombing happened and Sarah came to." Bernhart concluded, "People can wander in their sleep, although it's rare."

By now Alfred could see for himself a smouldering pile of rubble where the cottage had stood. Silently he prayed for those who had died and for Sarah and the Kemmner family. After Bernhart had led his horse to the field, and put his cart in its shed, he followed Alfred indoors to the front room.

"It's good to see you Alfred" said Berni.

His daughters, looking more anxious than on previous occasions, were sitting on the sofa. "I'm sorry Manfred's been called up so soon; I pray for his safety."

"I blame myself in part; if we had stayed here, he would not have been called up, at least not yet. They are doing it by regions. We have already had five called up in our road."

164

Alfred replied, "Well perhaps regions are important but men might be selected at random, or according to their skills. Manfred's a good athlete, isn't he? But we shall never really know how the authorities make their choices. I do not relish my own situation."

His great uncle commented, "Well they haven't ordered Berni to enlist yet I expect they'll leave the older ones till last."

The hunch of Helga's shoulders spelled out her feelings of rejection. To distract her from her own situation Alfred enquired, "How's Sarah coping without her family? What has happened to her?"

"She is still in shock, but lives with Herr and Frau Kemmner and their daughter, Sarah's friend. The authorities have agreed to the arrangement; I think she will soon be legally adopted."

"That's hopeful; in the course of time Sarah will treasure precious memories and hopefully pass them on to children of her own one day."

Helga was about to say *'How would you know?'* when she remembered her father telling her that Alfred was barely ten years old when his mother had died. For the first time she reflected on the grief he must have suffered. The look in Berni's eyes informed Alfred that like him, he held the memory of Marija, and Witold, close to his heart.

A few days later a lull in bombing raids meant Erika and Alfred were free to meet. Late afternoon her parents invited him to stay for supper. Half way through the meal the siren wailed loudly.

"Not that blessed siren again, it's been relentless all week" groaned Mr Stein.

"Quickly, we need our coats," said his wife.

In haste the four of them ran up the road to the shelter, near St Joseph's church. Whilst running, Alfred prayed for everyone's safety. *"Do not go into the shelter. Do not go in"* said voice in his heart.

At the shelter entrance he grabbed Erika by the arm, and gasped "Please do not go in. I have had a premonition."

"Alfred that is silly, we should not have read so many memorial plaques. This is the only safe place. My parents are calling. I must go. Please come in with me, won't you?"

165

For a moment they looked into each other's eyes, and Erika knew she could not make him follow. A boy who had been running alongside Alfred heard their exchange. Needing little excuse to stay out of a confined space, he pulled away from his guardian. With the drone of planes drawing closer Alfred ran in the direction of the church. As the whistle of a bomb whizzed close, he yelled, "Quick. Follow me boy." A blast of air threw them forward; instinctively Alfred shielded him. Moments later, through a haze of shock and smoke, eerie cries for help hauntingly echoed through the muffled mist of bomb smoke. Those who were around came to realize, that the cries of desperation were coming from the collapsed shelter. With a sense of urgency Alfred and the boy ran back to the shelter to see what they could do. All that was to be seen was a pile of rubble, and now that the cries had diminished, all that could be heard was the hiss of a burst water main.

In closer proximity they listened as people drowning inside the rubble weakly and intermittently cried for help. Horrified, Alfred, the boy and two adults clawed at the rubble.

An elderly man who happened to be near the entrance, some distance away from the burst water pipes, emerged. Quickly the boy ran from Alfred's side and into the arms of the man. "Grandpapa, Grandpapa, Grandpapa," the child called. Alfred watched as the boy flung his arms around the man's neck.

"Oh Manfred, thank God," said the elderly gentleman.

Glad to witness such a touching reunion Alfred said with a ring of consent and finality, "You go home Manfred, you are noticeably young and a good child to have been so helpful. Look after each other."

"Both his parents are dead. He needs me. Thank you." the man said

Erika knew her parents were dead. Half-conscious she could feel the water rising above her shoulders. Now as it touched her lips she tried to say, "God help me, please help."

Getting weaker and weaker still, she silently prayed, '*Dear God, if I am to die now, please hold me in your precious arms. Loving saviour please will you look after Alfred until we meet again in your kingdom. Bless him with a wife who loves you deeply. Let them never forget me.*'

Behind the terror, as water filled her lungs, she grieved for the children she would never have.

'Bless Alfred with children-let my life be a sacrifice for them. I love him'.

Suddenly outside in the chilly air, she looked at Alfred desperately clawing the rubble. For a moment she wondered why he failed to notice her-then, she remembered she could stay no longer. She no longer belonged here. As she turned, a power greater than anything she had ever known pulled her spiritual body at tremendous speed through a tunnel towards beautiful light full of healing and profound love.

'It is all right my child. I am here. Do not be afraid. Come, follow me—'

"It is no use; they are all dead. There are no more sounds except for the water and that has not stopped. Move along now," said the warden.

Broken hearted, Alfred left the scene.

***

Later, back at the house, his great uncle explained, "Alfred I'm afraid I couldn't get through to your Head Quarters but I've managed to contact the priest's house in Aachen."

Three quarters of an hour later they heard someone drop something through the letter box. Bernhart walked into the hallway and picked up the card.

"It is a message from Aachen via St. Joseph's. They say you can extend your leave by two days" he called.

Over the course of the two vital days, the only way Alfred could cope was by focussing on practicalities. Within his soul, time passed as slowly as drops forming stalactites. Grief retreated into childhood grief of losing his mother, and now Erika was gone. Was he being punished for having left the abbey he wondered? Then he remembered hearing Father Spyridon say, "Whether inside or outside a monastery, there is no guarantee of protection from trials and grief. At all times we should remind ourselves that grief and destruction within this world are temporary, not final. Never forget that Christ is present in times of grief and joy as well as in times of spiritual enlightenment."

167

Chapter 22

France 1944

As a result of the failed court martial Alfred, for his own safety, was sent as far away as possible from Scharfmann. At the end of May, near to St Lo, he had to put into practise his new role as lance corporal, in charge of a divisional sub group. As fast as the war intensified, so increasingly, it became difficult to avoid situations of conflict.

The irony of being responsible for a small group of soldiers conflicted with his belief and desire to save life. He had witnessed men glad of promotions and medals. His life line was of peace, he was no lance corporal, but a representative of the monastery and mission, out in the world to do his best for love of God, whose love passes all understanding.

***

Until now he had kept his men away from dangerous combat. In small groups he had sent them scouting the area for stray enemy soldiers, potential captives for placing in German camps. He had given strict orders that they were not to resort to firing unless necessary.

Further spiritual issues Alfred dealt with through prayers that he jotted down in his note book.

'Lord, colleagues in responsible posts in other divisions are becoming dubious about me; they say my success (well your success I mean) in Russia is wearing thin. Some have criticized my work in Graz on the grounds that I never actually killed anyone. Please hear my prayer, help me to lead my men in a righteous way.'

Reflectively he thought of several soldiers, whose brothers and friends had died in Russia during the dreadful year of 1942 in Russia. They had not recovered from loss because of unnecessary deaths, all of which were the result of Hitler's insane, irrational decision to send orders for troops to head for Leningrad, instead of Moscow.

Now in this third week of June, whilst wearily trudging to German occupied St Lo, they wondered if they could obtain supplies and equipment. It occurred to several men that they might suffer a similar fate to that of dead brothers or friends.

***

Having reached the periphery of the town, they came across soldiers from other divisions, and several impoverished village people, in similar predicament their own. Barely had Alfred absorbed the incredible scene, when a distressed horse, being forced to surge forward with an over-loaded cart, speedily galloped towards them. To achieve such speed the Nazi driver, mercilessly whipped the horse. Unaware that German- soldiers were among the crowds, the cruel driver failed to slow down.

Leonard of the 353-sub-division wondered if the cart was out of control. The driver's angry face indicated humiliation about not having a truck. A woman cried out, "That bastard's getting his frustration out on the poor horse." Another woman looked as if she were about to stop the driver. Caught up in things, Leonard stumbled into the path of the horse and cart. Alfred looking on in horror, instantly recalled his school teacher, who taking a risk, had saved his comrade being crushed by an oncoming tank. Would Alfred meet the same fate, would his arm be ripped off?

Rushing forward, he pushed Leonard out of the path of the terrified horse. Miraculously, and instinctively, the horse missed him. However, hopes were dashed as the unbearable weight of the cart sliced over him and pressed him into the earth. Like a burning rod, intense pain seared his back and shoulder. The intensity of the pain also meant he was alive. Thankfully, the rain he had complained about had softened the earth, and he had a chance. As the cart travelled into the distance, he wondered why the driver had not stopped. *'He might not have noticed or been too scared about knocking down a German? But he was a Nazi'* he thought.

Someone said "Is he dead? He could not have taken that weight."

"He's breathing, but only just, please move out of the way. You must get out the way," said Leonard. His scanty medical training came in useful. Quickly he scooped out earth to provide a space for air to get through. Carefully he worked around Alfred's body, freed him, and gently pulled him onto a verge.

"Get me to hospital" Alfred gasped.

"Yes, Lance Corporal, but where does it hurt?"

"My shoulder--ribs, Ahh, and my back."

"Can you move your toes?"

Wiggling his toes Alfred affirmed, "Yes."

With a sigh of relief Leonard, feeling guilty about Alfred having taken his place, encouragingly said, "Good, well done; we passed a Red Cross post; it would be best for me to get some of the men to go there, and request official stretchers and bearers. I do not want to risk anything makeshift; can you wait?"

"Yes; and you're right."

Impressed that fair minded Leonard had everything under control he decided he would recommend him for promotion. Intermittent intense pain caused him to feel faint. So, it continued until, some twenty minutes later, stretcher bearers pushed their way through the crowd. Carefully they slid the stretcher beneath him, rolled him onto it and took him to their waiting ambulance. Much of the occupied region had been bombed before the capture. Wanting to help, several people informed them that a nearby hospital no longer existed.

Someone called out, "It was your bloody lot that did it."

Next moment Alfred submitted to a series of injections to help him cope with the rail journey to Paris.

***

Paris:

Over several weeks Alfred appreciated the friendly and compassionate care of the nurses. The doctor, a man of unique tolerance and understanding defused Alfred's fear of long term stays in hospital. In June news came through of Americans tightening the circle around Cherbourg. Soon this area would be under threat of recapture. Next day the patient in the opposite bed received a news-paper. "How utterly terrible" he said.

"What is?" Alfred replied.

"One thousand Germans including General Schleiben and General Hennecke have been captured."

Faces fell and morale sank to its lowest. As war intensified men increasingly became suspicious of the likelihood of spies and traitors amongst them. To make matters worse, a tragedy closer to their hearts happened. News came through that the good and loved doctor, temporarily away on front line duty, had been killed whilst assisting a wounded soldier.

**

Dashed hopes revived a little with the arrival of a replacement doctor who, to all appearances matched the standard of his predecessor. However, with his meticulous obsession for accuracy and precision, he was a little too perfect. In his spotless white coat, flawless, neatly pressed trousers, and well- polished shoes, he was over groomed. Not a hair on his head was out of place, trimmed side burns reminded everyone of something--but because they were ill, they could not think what. One day the doctor, whilst showing particular interest in Alfred's mission, lulled him into a false sense of security. Casually Alfred went on to mention his work as a messenger and interpreter. Some days later, in Alfred's mind, the doctor's style of inquisition rang alarm bells.

"Where did you learn to speak Serb-Croat?" the doctor enquired. Alfred was reminded of Scharfmann and realised he was being led into a trap. There was no way he could avoid the inevitable reply, "I used to live in Belgrade, before the war."

"I find that interesting, especially as I, the distinguished Dr Heich, am a senior member of the Nazi party. I am a real Nazi, a volunteer" he said with an air of authority. As he continued on his rounds of the wards, he made his views known. In the manner of the Führer, he persuaded patients to be diligent from their hospital beds. Seeds of doubt and suspicion were planted in vulnerable minds. They and other patients did not notice him slip a newspaper into each ward. Neither were they aware how he relished the idea of receiving any information to his promotional advantage. Alfred realized the man's outlook to be far removed from his own concern. That being genuine friendship that plays a vital, strengthening part of the healing processes.

One day, as he paced up and down the ward Dr Heike heatedly said to a colleague, "The cursedness and audacity of English and American troops is abominable. How dare they try and reclaim areas our men have fought and died for. Among those glorious dead is my own dear son. Curse all foreigners."

The following day, in strangely subdued manner, he said to Alfred, "I think it best you have a course of injections for your pain."

"I'm in very little pain now, even when it does arise it is bearable" Alfred retorted.

"You are my patient and I insist you are made as comfortable as possible."

Knowing army expectations Alfred had little choice but to reply, "Thank you doctor."

***

Several days later he felt extremely unwell, and wondered if he had caught a virus. The following day he informed the doctor who feigned concern.

"The nurses are busy. Put this under your tongue" he snapped.

Alfred complied, but in too short a time the doctor removed the thermometer. In the realization that the patient in the next bed observed everything his voice became instantly kind.

"I think you may have caught a virus; your temperature is a little high. It is nothing to worry about."

Yet, as the day progressed Alfred felt increasingly unwell. On the fifth day his surroundings and the people nearby were looking very strange indeed, as if coming in and out of a convex mirror. Currently the image of one of the monks of the past stepped out of his mind, and stood at his bedside. *You know I have an interest in herbs but always one must remember that certain herbs are to our great advantage when prescribed in the correct dosage. Over dosage can be FAAAAAAtaaal'* the image declared.

Brother Peter smiled a convex smile, and his teeth were unusually large—Alfred groaned "Dangerous dosage...fat...hat, was that word aaaal..fatal.... Nazi. Get out...get out."

The man in the next bed attempted to make sense of Alfred's slurred and incoherent mumbling, but in the end shrugged his shoulders and went back to sleep.

***

172

Well into the night, when lights were out, Alfred, mustered up will power to escape. He put the rolled-up uniform under his arm, and wrapped a blanket around himself. The wrongly administered potion had all but immobilised him, he could hardly move his limbs. Never-the-less, under duress, he crept past the sleeping night nurse. Painfully slow he kept going- down a side-route, down narrow step. Now, down into a swirling basement where, dancing before him boxes and cupboards changed shape. As he walked on, the boxes seemed to move against the backdrop of a rippling wall. At proximity, the wall was about to fall. As he crawled towards a narrow door, carelessly left ajar, he repeatedly reminded himself, "Poison, poison, poison."

Out in the night air, he managed to keep upright by propping himself up against a dustbin. The cold fresh air he desperately sucked in raced through his head to sufficiently clear his mind for keeping going and for striving to keep alive. Defying the odds he kept walking, walking, and then he walked more, until early morning arrived. Unexpectedly, a miracle happened- he stumbled upon a drinking fountain where, with weak hands, he turned the knob and frantically drank the clear water.

"Thank God, thank you almighty God" he said, and drank again.

***

Hours later on the outskirts of the city, when the drug was losing effect, he changed into uniform. Further along the road he tossed the hospital gown and blanket into a large patch of brambles and ivy. Eventually, when sounds of human activity were apparent, he cautiously moved from bush to bush and other available screening. Knowing his division had been on course for south of St Lo, he aimed to get on a goods train and reconnect with them in the location where he had been separated from them.

***

Later, as dawn broke on the horizon of the Black Forest, the sudden burst of bird song equally startled and calmed his soul. He appreciated the rich harmonic texture of overlapping melodies that no composer could perfectly recreate. The warm sunlight soothed him and a meadow close by, provided a place to rest. The solace, joy, and bliss of being free to lie on soft grass,

173

to be able to look up through the branches to the sky, overwhelmed him. As he had during childhood, he watched passing clouds overhead. Soon the tree was moving and the clouds were stationary, or so it seemed. It occurred to him that the Nazi's who think they are moving forward are remaining still, rooted in the evils of history. Momentarily a glimmer of hope that the corrupt leaders might not win felt strong. Gradually his heavy eyelids closed and he slept.

***

Two hours later the roar of a tank disturbed him. Someone turned off the engine. He noticed American voices and, on his belly, worked his way to the edge of the field. His foot was on the lower wooden bar of the gate, he was about to climb over when a loud drawling voice shouted, "Halt-and that means the same in German you slimy bugger; you Jew killer." From the tone of voice Alfred knew he had fallen into wrong hands.

"Come here-and that means the same in German you little toad."

Hands raised Alfred walked over to the large pock faced man. The American, whilst poking the stripe on Alfred's jacket, said "I see you have a stripe. That makes things worse for you, you know."

By the captive's expression, the American saw he didn't understand, and poked him harder

"Only Gefreiter" Alfred said.

"I understand that word and I do not believe you are a lance corporal. You are a sergeant, aren't you?"

"Well, I guess you must be some little Nazi creep. I'm an American German-Jew; have you got that? I am an American German- JEW."

"Ich Jugoslav: from Belgrade; Not Nazi."

"He's a liar too chaps. Jones, come here, you speak a bit of German; tell him I want him to dig his own grave."

Pointing to two black American soldiers he said, "When he's finished digging, I want you two to shoot him and bury him. OK?"

Knowing the sergeant to be a man without scruples, Jones squirmed. He realized the sergeant was in the habit of using national identity as an excuse for Nazi like behaviour. He was at the other end of the war spectrum.

"Sergeant! What about the Geneva! Sergeant."

"I did NOT give you permission to speak. Anyone who disobeys a command will be severely reprimanded. I mean that at this stage. Boy, do I mean it."

The sound of the sergeant's voice and the look on the faces of his men informed Alfred something was wrong. The soldier who had spoken to the sergeant turned to Alfred and said in as near an apologetic tone as he could, "Vergeben sie mich, forgive me, I'm sorry, your orders are to dig a pit for yourself."

"Mutter, Vater von mein mutter Jüdisch, Vater bissen Jüdisch" Alfred whispered in stilted manner.

"His mother's parents were Jewish and his father is part Jewish," said Jones.

The sergeant shrugged his shoulders. The men knew they had to obey his vile instructions.

Alfred understood, and knowing he was captive, followed the men through the gateway and along the road for half a kilometre. He realized the area he was being taken to, was an American base. As in Russia, he had slept next to danger. Death would claim him.

Not long after, as he dug, he thought of Erika, and all the time wondered what it would be like to see her again in God's kingdom. The next instance he felt her voice within his heart, willing him to not give up, to live and go forward into the future. For a moment he glanced up as the American German-Jew angrily drove off in a truck. Slowly and reluctantly, he finished digging. The white American, who had been ordered to watch over him, walked across the bare ground to where two black American soldiers were worriedly talking. Alfred tried to make out the words of the white American, "I have done my bit. I would not want to be in your shoes."

He understood 'shoes' and guessed he had used an old saying. He heard one of the black soldiers say to the other, "Jones, the only reason the Sergeant has chosen us is because he doesn't like blacks, as they call us."

Alfred understood 'black' and 'Sergeant' and the tone of the soldier's voice revealed he was not happy. With no means of escape he knelt in prayer and remembered Christ's words 'If it be thy will remove this cup from me.' In such prayerful situation the two soldiers found him. The shorter of the two, remembering his own church community at home, glanced at his friend. Encouraged by the look in his eyes he dared to say, "You are a good Christian too. Look that Red Cross plane is about ready to set off." They glanced around, no one was about; the moment was right. Pitifully Alfred looked up at the gun pointing down at him. As he made the sign of the cross, he thought he saw the soldier wink. To his amazement two shots sank into the mud wall of the intended grave. 'Did he miss?' Alfred wondered. A hand came down beckoning him to grab it. Now he was being pulled out of the pit. One of the Christian soldiers grabbed him by the arm and rushed him over to the Red Cross plane. Just in time one of them pushed him inside the plane. He did not have opportunity to thank them.

From his position on the plane floor, he saw through the doorway, a man in medical uniform emerged from a red- cross truck and approach the plane.

"Is there anything you want?" he heard him say.

"No, I was just curious about who was injured" said the black American who was not Jones.

"These civilians are very sick and we have to get them to a medical centre urgently."

"Sure" said Jones, and spat out some chewing gum. Behind his back he did a 'thumbs up' and with his companion went off to fill the pit.

The engine started and like a large bird the small plane lumbered across ground before miraculously taking flight. The pilot or his co-pilot had casually left civilian clothes in an untidy heap at the back of the plane. Slowly and carefully, Alfred took off his uniform and put on civilian clothes. Because the garments were too long, he rolled up the trouser legs and jacket sleeves. Grabbing a towel from the top of a convenient pile he rolled his uniform in it. Now he began to take interest in the three casualties moaning and rambling in their strange French language, He wondered, if all those years ago, Witold had learned the language in the French Foreign Legion. He still greatly missed his brother. He absorbed the situation of the three casualties in the plane. An elderly woman and a young boy were drugged and hardly aware of their surroundings. A young woman suffering crushed and broken limbs was in a state of shock. As she kicked out Alfred deduced how a bomb had struck the building, she was in. Debris and shrapnel, some of which had penetrated an artery, had engulfed her. A spurt of blood shot across the plane, followed by another and another. Alfred guessed it was happening with every heart- beat. He had to act quickly.

Making use of his field skills he crawled on his belly across the floor and grabbed the First Aid box. Quelling panic, he opened the lid, fumbled around, and found a large triangular bandage. Deftly he wound it into a tourniquet and as fast as on the battlefield, he worked his way across the floor to the girl. She had the sense to bend her knee and re-instate embedded shrapnel. Thus, she had played a part in staving some blood loss. Even so a few more large spurts of life-giving blood pumped out onto the floor of the plane. Just in time Alfred secured the tourniquet and prevented further bleeding. By now the girl was deathly pale giving Alfred cause for immense concern. He remained at her side, all the time hoping that the pilots would not see him.

As the girl regained consciousness, she uttered some sentences in French. When she became more alert Alfred indicated he did not understand. The girl pointed to a water container, and when Alfred worked his way along the floor on his belly, she knew he was German. Remaining quiet she watched him take significant risk for her by lifting the lid, and filling the metal cup with water. The plane tipped; the water slopped. Nerves on edge, he crawled back to the water container, re- filled the cup, and kept it upright as he crawled back to the girl. She was weak, again Alfred risked being seen. He held the cup to her lips while she drank. She paused and finished the water she so much needed. He crawled back to his earlier inconspicuous position. Seeing the girl smile, he retrieved his army jacket and took from the pocket a little crucifix he had carved in the Russian forest. Lying flat he reached out, gave it to her and was immensely glad to have been a part of the process that gave her a chance to live. He was reminded of the Jewish saying that if someone saves a life, they save lives for generation to come. He considered all the small miracles happening during this time of conflict. People of different nationalities were reaching beyond human authority to join with the higher authority of God. By helping the girl, he felt less helpless about having been unable to rescue Erika. This girl might well have been his Erika, and he thought of the joy this girl's family and friends would experience when she safely returned home.

The plane spluttered, they were descending to re-fuel, he guessed. Easily the plane landed, veered, jolted, and following a screech of tyres ran smoothly before coming to a halt. Lack of the sound of other aircraft meant they had landed on a private airfield. The pilot and co- pilot mentioned 'petrifler' meaning petrol. He heard them leave and when all was silent, he slipped out of the plane and under a wire mesh fence. As he wasn't accounted for, no one would look for him. Having heard about the French he considered with a smile how they might presume the tourniquet was a result of divine intervention. In a natural way it was, for the ongoing chain of righteous and positive effort was a truly divine and super-natural event.

Chapter 23
Black Forest

In a town close to the landing site, Alfred ran so fast he felt his lungs would burst. Finally when the ghost of potential pursuers had been shaken off, he crept into the wood and well- hidden, sat behind a tree. When breathlessness subsided, he relaxed and remembered the bread in his jacket pocket. He unrolled the towel and retrieved his army jacket and the mouldy bread. Quickly he ate it, and taking a risk, drank from a stream on the edge of the wooded area. Soon, even though fatigued, he kept walking and willed himself to think positive thoughts. Thus he covered about five kilometres and in comparable manner the method continued for four more days. At a point of exhaustion he saw a village not too far ahead.

***

He arrived wheezing heavily and his feet dragging at every step. Like a plane needing fuel, his emotional tank was almost empty. Except for an elderly man seated on a wooden bench, and a black cat running into bushes, the place was deserted. Off guard, feeling wretched, he asked in German, "Please could you tell me where I can find a doctor?"

Much to his surprise the man got up, raised his right arm and in a French accent chanted through his white beard, " 'eil 'itlerr."

Without bothering to return the ridiculous salute Alfred's thoughts echoed loudly in his head— *'So I am in occupied territory--Now what is the French for doctor? Oh yes.'*

"Docteur...medicin...docteur."

Comprehending a common need the villager pointed to a large house at the top of a hill. Alfred nodded thanks, and because his uniform was wrapped in the towel, and not wanting to be mistaken for a deserter he walked in the shadows. Somehow he reached the top of the hill from which vantage point he looked down across the village. It was the size of a small town. No

179

soldiers were to be seen and he considered his fears may have been unfounded. He knocked on the door and waited. The longer he waited the more his fear intensified. The man who opened the door was well built. By the look of his loose cheeks, reminding Alfred of a St Bernard, he had obviously recently lost weight.

"Docteur?" Alfred enquired.

Surprisingly, the doctor replied in fluent German.

"Yes, and by your accent I imagine you are German?"

"I was born there."

"Well as you can hear I am fluent in the language. I had a German mother. I can see you are not well. You had best come in."

***

Weaving in mention of his mixed identity, Alfred provided details of his recent experience from the time he was put into a pit of execution. Seeming to half listen, the doctor sounded his chest and took his temperature.

"It is a bit high due to a bad chest infection. I think it best you to stay here for a while. I have some medicine that will help. I will ask my house keeper to get a bed ready. She will prepare a light supper for you to eat in your room. Hopefully in a day or two you will improve and we can talk more thoroughly then."

"I'm not a deserter" Alfred mumbled.

The doctor replied, "I do not believe you are. For the time being we will leave things as they are; no one need know yet."

"I am so relieved. Thank you." said Alfred.

Noticing tears of stress in his eyes, the doctor replied, "I'm glad to be of help."

By the look on the doctor's face as he left the room, Alfred guessed he was hoping pneumonia would not set in.

Downstairs the doctor instructed the retired nurse-housekeeper to keep the spare bedroom fire alight.

"I advise that he have regular inhalations. Can you sort out regular intervals of steaming water, containing a tablespoonful of salt?"

"Yes, docteur" she compliantly replied.

For the first time in months Alfred slept sound. Next day, as he tossed and turned, he recalled his father's mention of a time in Futog when he had had a terrible chest infection.

Groaning aloud he asked, "What's happened to father, mother and the rest of them, are they alive or dead?"

Suddenly he remembered his mother dying a long time ago.

***

Five days later the fever broke, and by day seven, feeling stronger, he went downstairs. The doctor's housekeeper showed him into a large sitting room. The maroon curtains, though faded, were of quality velvet. The elaborately carved oak furniture assuredly was Austrian, of the type Alfred's mother had admired. Whilst the housekeeper went to the kitchen, the doctor entered and sat on the maroon velvet sofa.

Looking in Alfred's direction, he said, "Ah, glad to see you are feeling better. Sit yourself down. My housekeeper has a stew on the go, she will call us when it is ready. Mind you, these days there are more vegetables than meat, and some of the vegetables are nettles, full of iron of course--.but not the same."

Feeling dwarfed in a large arm chair, Alfred replied, "I'm very grateful doctor, to you and your housekeeper."

"My name is Dr Petiff, and my housekeeper is Mrs Angelique Prunier, and by the way that, when translated, means Mrs Angela Plumtree."

With a laugh Alfred replied, "Quite appropriate, she's been a bountiful angel to me."

"Can you tell me the name of this village, and the nearest town?"

"This is Flussdorff, quite near Strasbourg."

"Isn't that close to the Black Forest?"

"That's correct."

With a sigh of relief Alfred answered, "So that means I am only a matter of kilometres from Germany."

"Ah, you mean the real Germany rather than this occupied territory that brings about so much doubt and suspicion."

"I can never think of occupied territory as German; it belongs to the descendants of the people who've worked the lands for centuries."

Having received such spontaneous help from the doctor and his housekeeper Alfred felt free to relate the sequence of events that had brought him here. With interest Dr Petiff listened. "I've had aggravation from certain villagers; gossip and theories based on the fact I had a German mother--and she's been dead fifteen years."

"I'm sorry."

"Certainly, there have been more than a few uncomfortable moments with Nazi officers who view matters in black or white. They cannot accept us half breeds."

Empathising, Alfred smiled, and listened as Dr Pettif continued, saying, "We've much in common. Oh, and my housekeeper cum- under- cover- nurse, has washed and dried your underwear. She has aired and pressed your uniform."

"I'll see to it that I thank her."

Alfred pictured the kind blue eyes and friendly smile of the tall white-haired woman.

He added, "I'll be glad to get out of these pyjamas you kindly lent me."

Mistaking his meaning Doctor Pettif replied, "Yes, they are large. Now I think the wisest course of action would be for me to refer you to the army medical centre at Strassborg. We will give it three or four more days until you are stronger. They can take things from there." Noticing Alfred's worried frown he added, "They seem a fair-minded lot and I will back your story. Much of it coincides with your injuries; particularly your shoulder and back. The infection could have started because of that incident."

"Thank you Doctor Petiff. Of late I have been fortunate to receive the help of good people."

"You have done your part helping that poor French girl, and your comrade who might have been run over by the cart. We will have the civilian clothes washed and passed on to someone who might need them. Oh! Dinner's smelling good, so you would best take your clean clothes upstairs and get changed."

***

Four days later, early morning, the doctor called at the house keeper's cottage. Marginally she opened the door, "Angelique would you be so kind as to take a message to the soldiers' house in the next street?" said the doctor.

"Certainly Docteur, we cannot have a soldier under your roof too long. I will go immediately." Quickly she put on her coat, and before the doctor had a chance to give her the note, she took the sheet of paper from his hand. With a brief smile and "aurevoire" she left the house. Eagerly she proceeded across the street and along an adjoining footpath. Accustomed to delivering and collecting messages she was no stranger to formalities. With controlled expression she watched the duty soldier come to life. Gradually he realised a sick soldier had reported to the doctor's house. Thankfully, he did not ask the date of the soldier's arrival. Trying to sound authoritative he said, "We will take him to the Strasbourg medical centre. Inform the doctor we will call at his house at Two O'clock."

Feigning enthusiasm she added, "Yes sir--Heil Hitler."

**

Later when the soldiers arrived, Doctor Pettiff subtly and correctly influenced them to the effect that Alfred was required for the process of authorization. A short debate resulted, after which the soldier decided that as Alfred was from another regiment, he would be required to go through different channels. By 2.15, both the doctor and Alfred were installed in the jeep. "Alfred, Strasbourg is six kilometres away. The medical centre has been set up in an old house of the Prince Albert era. It previously was owned by Jews but they have been transported elsewhere" Dr Pettiff quietly expounded.

**

Strasbourg:

The woman's steel grey eyes stared from behind the reception desk. Her taut voice firing questions enquired, "What's your name, rank and division?"

In an agitated manner she adjusted her dark rimmed glasses and pushed her steel wool hair into place.

"Alfred Ztoanjib, Lance Corporal, Division 353" he replied.

As he attempted to explain his circumstance she cuttingly instructed, "Answer the questions only."

Briefly she scrutinized the official information sheet.

"Most of 353 have been captured. I see you oversaw a small sub division. One man with medical knowledge reported back. He mentioned you had been taken away on a stretcher. Can you name him?"

"That sounds like Leonard, Leonard Weiss."

"That's correct."

"I'm glad he's safe."

Her voice melted a little as she suggested, "You can explain the rest to the colonel later."

Turning to the doctor she said, "I wish to add something to the bottom of the medical notes. May I have the sheet?"

He handed it to her, and watched her scrawl in pencil, 'Soldier, apparently Alfred Ztoanjib, knows name of Leonard Weiss, from same division'.

Looking up at Dr Pettiff she commanded, "Go into the adjoining room and speak to the medical officer." The doctor's silence indicated his distaste at being ordered. Nevertheless, dutifully he went into the adjoining room. Having come across the medical officer on a previous occasion he anticipated civil exchange of conversation.

However, today's exchange took place within a narrow frame work. He had to comply. He raised his hand to declare, "Heil Hitler" and all the while thought *'Heil shitter.'*

As instructed, he returned to the jeep and as he skimmed past Alfred, he quietly said "Good luck: all the best."

In a barely audible voice Alfred replied, "From the bottom of my heart, thank you."

The look of gratitude in Alfred's eyes gave greater thanks. It was an expression the doctor had witnessed many times when people of mixed nationality had passed through his hands. In a world imposed with black and white values he hoped to restore some colour. He was not on any side because he belonged to no side. He simply kept his counsel and got on with the task of helping people.

Alfred, in process of being frog marched to a separate section of the house would have liked to have yelled, *"There's no need to shunt me along the corridor like a criminal."* Like an unwanted parcel he was deposited in a waiting room. From outside the room someone locked the door. After what seemed a long time another person unlocked the door, and ushered him to another room where he was to be questioned and given thorough medical examination. Surprisingly the muscular, bald headed army medic, who tested his arm rotation and grip, was not at all aggressive. A tinge of empathy rang out as he said, "Massive bruising; obviously working its way out. Multiple fractures have healed. I expect they were hard pushed at Paris. A lot's been happening."

Taking care to not mention what had really happened, Alfred patiently listened. Finally, the man concluded, "I would have had you stay in hospital longer but as the vertebrae are back in place, I will write down some exercises. It should help things along."

***

Escorted by two soldiers Alfred went to another army occupied house, where a captain questioned him and made copious notes.

"So, you are a Lance Corporal? I hope you get on with the job; it is about time you were promoted to sergeant."

Alfred smiled, and was about to leave had the colonel not said, "Wait, I'll just check the notes from Weiss."

He took a file from the cabinet, flicked through some pages and homed in on a particular paragraph. Satisfied he continued to say, "Well I'm afraid all men of your subdivision were captured at St Lo. Apart from Weiss that is, who alerted the German authorities. Oh yes you know that! Well, we desperately need extra men here. We are forming defences all along the Black Forest to stop the enemy getting through. Apart from Remagen, we are blowing up all bridges. Remagen, way down the Rhine will be used to get weapons and supplies through."

Forgetting his station Alfred answered, "That's sensible."

The colonel laughed, "Now you say your base is at Aachen. I will contact them and let them know you are here and that you will be helping us in our work of defence."

***

Regardless of rumours about Americans getting closer, there were no signs of them in this area of the German border. Evenings were pleasant enough and soldiers gladly chatted among themselves about sweethearts, hobbies, and childhood pranks. This evening conversation circled around where they might have been, or what they might have been doing, had there not been a war. One man would have written and produced a play. Several men would be married with children. His friend had planned to climb the Matterhorn. Two would be finishing university as scientists, a third as linguist.

185

"As manager of a high-class restaurant coming over to your table; if I learned you couldn't pay for your meal, I'd order you to the kitchen to do the washing up."

"I'd scarper before you appeared," said a soldier.

Another continued, "And you'd probably trip over your long-tailed jacket and fall flat on your face." They roared with laughter.

Gaining the attention of a soldier mutely sitting in a corner, Max asked "Hey, Paul what about you?"

"Well before I was called up, I'd planned to train as a protestant missionary." "You planned to be what? Heavens, you will be next on me list for the cooking pot."

They laughed loudly and did not hear him reply, "Mission work doesn't only happen in Africa and as far as I know, cannibalistic tribes no longer exist."

A convoy of planes resounded overhead. Like frightened schoolchildren seeking protection, the men dived into their sleeping bags. This time they were safe in their camouflaged tents. Even so hearts pounded with thoughts of what might have been. It occurred to Alfred that even if they survived, all the extra heart beats might be deducted from their allotted span.

***

The following day, in groups of eight, they were sent out to scout the area for signs of enemy infiltration. By mid-day, six of Alfred's group had gone on ahead, over the brow of the hill. Paul, despondently lagging, had not got that far. Slowing his pace Alfred walked alongside him, to tell him about his own mission work.

"Where was that?" Paul asked with interest.

"That's the thing about mission work Paul, where isn't important, but 'how' is."

"Oh?" Paul answered with a puzzled look.

"Why didn't you mention it to the other soldiers?" he prompted.

"I find it best to keep quiet about God's work. It is best just to do it when one sees a need, whatever and whenever that might be. Mind you if people try and stop you doing God's work and do not even bother to listen to you, then you should shout it from the roof tops, until you are heard. If still you are not heard, then you should ask God for some other channel for his work and mission."

Fired by conversation and the fact he had a comrade of similar interest, Paul walked at brisker pace. Alfred had to drop back and find somewhere to relieve himself. When he emerged from behind the trees, the situation had changed in an instant. A group of enemy troops were approaching; unaware, Paul was walking ahead. Alfred wondered if he should get over the hill and alert the men. *Should I ask them to run back and shoot at the American if necessary? Or should I warn Paul, somehow, I must get him away, out of danger.*

Racing downhill he had had to suddenly stop in his tracks. Quickly he eased back behind a tree because an American, gun in hand, was striding over to Paul. Now Paul was raising his hands. Next moment, Alfred felt the butt of a rifle firmly push against his own back. *'Dear God, this is it'* he thought, and raised his hands.

"Move, move prisoner" said the voice behind his back.

Strange thoughts raced through Alfred's mind and oddly enough he felt grateful to be captured. *'Now I am free of the course of action for Germany, beautiful country of my birth, that Hitler has corrupted and defiled. Lord, I pray that these Americans are not corrupt and that you will have a future for Paul and me.'*

A furtive glance at the dark green forest that had housed his new division caused his heart to ache, not only for them, but for the enchantment of the woodland. Neubeckum and memories of childhood felt close. In those far off days elves and goblins had hidden in the crevices of the trees. In certain light, faces had peered out from gnarled branches. Back in his childhood, when children told the adults about things they had seen with their imagination, in the forest, rarely were they believed. His dear mother was one of the few who had not argued.

The Black Forest, war time oasis, had reminded him of the unique way in which Mutti had brought the forest stories of the Brothers Grim and Hans Christian Anderson to life. Such tales had fired the imaginations of as many children as there were trees in the forest.

At this moment Anderson's story about the tin soldiers came to mind, and in particular the idea of the soldiers having been made from the same old tin spoon. In a flash he comprehended that he had not failed in following the path of righteousness, where none were regarded as enemies and all were regarded as victims of war. *'When will I be in touch with my folk and the forests with their paths that we all have followed until some were forced to diverge upon another journey beyond this world?'*

Because his hands were raised, he was unable to stop the flow of tears for Erika, Witold, Mutti, and Helmut, the Russian guard, and people of all nationalities lying dead, maimed, or frozen.

'---The uniforms march on through the centuries and the god of war puts different men in them until he needs them no more--. what about the God of peace, the God of love? Why has the God of love not been heard?'

Part Three

Onward to England

Chapter 24
Across the Channel

Numerous trucks were arriving in the region of St Lo, recently taken by the US Third Army. At the compound, American soldiers were ready to take a convoy of captured German soldiers to Prisoner of War camps. Alfred and Paul, amongst those selected for Cherbourg, had a long journey ahead.

During early evening, under heavy guard, they arrived at the Prisoner of War Camp, where, at the right time they received a much-needed drink of water and a meal of bread, dripping and a half apple. When they had eaten, and the tin plates had been collected, they were ordered to strip naked and line up in the yard. In a whisper Paul translated the comment of one of the American officers, "If you put the buggers in a cell with a razor blade, they'll come out with a machine gun." Much wide grinned American laughter followed and the few German prisoners, who understood in literal sense, missed the humour.

Most realized the comment referred to the nature of the imminent medical examination.

The coolness of the September evening motivated everyone to get the unpleasant procedure over, and done with, as quickly as possible. Drawn by mocking laughter Alfred looked up.

There on a bridge above, two young women stood, behind the wire- mesh, perimeter- fence, mockingly pointed down at them. Lip- stick- red lips, flashing white teeth and eye- liner, played on the men's emotions. In Alfred's mind the women's actions stung harshly. He wondered if his fellow captives felt as he did; like a caged animal, with little hope of freedom, or defence.

***

In turn each individual prisoner reluctantly obeyed the order to bend over. When it came to Alfred, he was thankful for the large stature of an American sergeant that blocked the required rectal examination from view. The officer's incomprehensible explanation was translated by an able prisoner.

"It was necessary because there had been a few cases of prisoners hiding small objects such as small penknives, there-in."

Someone asked what the 'therein' referred to. A subsequent snigger was cut short, due to some quick- movement, above on the bridge. The look in the prisoners' eyes alerted the officer, and he quickly turned, looked up and glared at two young women, hastily disappearing. Loudly he bawled, "Where are the two soldiers on bridge duty? Those girls should not have been there." His drawling voice carried, and instantly two heads appeared. It did not take much working out that the soldiers had sat down against the wall to enjoy the company of the Mademoiselles. The sergeant resolved to work the soldiers twice as hard tomorrow, with loss of privileges.

Confinement at Cherbourg, with endless drill and sparse meals, oozed slow and meaningless. Over a few days the prisoners realized this place to be an intermediary camp, where they would remain until things became organised, for them to be housed in Nissan huts being added to various camps in England.

***

Not until October did things progress when, on a sunny morning, standing on what was left of the dock, the prisoners watched the water part. Whale like, a submarine surfaced, an iron hatch opened and an English sailor climbed out and stood on the casing. With bewildered expressions the prisoners looked on.

"Specht Mann English, does someone speak English?" the sailor enquired. Shuffling forward, a prisoner named Arno, from Cobourg, said, "I do."

"Tell them to not be afraid. The submarine journey is not dangerous and will take less than a few hours."

Arno understood.

"Not afraid, not dangerous, not too long" he explained in his native tongue. As Alfred entered the claustrophobic environment, he observed the petrified expression of a young prisoner.

"We will help each other and before we know it, we will be on dry land again" Alfred emphasised. Weakly the youth smiled.

"What's your name?" Alfred asked.

191

"Emil: my father was with me a moment ago."

"Do not worry, they have asked us to line up in two sections, one for the under thirties, the other for the remainder. You can introduce us to him when we're in the submarine."

Amongst the prisoners he noted several boyish faces. Emil would have been called up whilst still at school. Hitler was to be despised for the fact.

Down inside the submarine the hatch closed, faces tightened, eyes fearfully widened and ears popped as the submarine descended.

"Keep swallowing," said Alfred. When the submarine found steady course, things became easier. Just as they were getting used to confinement, the lights flickered, causing a few men to panic. When lights came on again, taut faces relaxed.

So, the under -water journey continued; conversation was almost impossible and all they managed was an exchange of names, home areas, location of capture, and pre- war situations.

***

ENGLAND:

As the submarine comes to the surface, the tense voice of the sailor in charge calls, "Nicht sprechen--No talking. I need to account for everyone as you get out."

He opens the hatch he looks out. Light, small in stature, he speedily climbs the ladder onto the deck. The Germans hear him shout across to someone: "All in order sir: there are fifteen prisoners from Cherbourg."

He climbs down again. They watch and listen. His tone indicates he's speaking on personal level, "Ubersetzen bitte?" Twenty-six-year-old Hans, tall with fair hair and anxious eyes, the colour of bluebells in a summer wood, offers to translate. Whilst intermittently rubbing his stubbly chin, he takes the sheet of paper and silently reads, *'You are to go up the ladder, single file and when you have stepped onto the dock, you are to follow the army officer in charge, to the truck. If required, toilets are to be located on the platform.'* Slowly he conveys, "Up, one by one, onto dock- land- follow army man in charge, to truck. Toilets-on platform-Danke."

They feel relieved. Hermann, mid-thirties, short black hair, brown eyes, thick brows, short in stature, whispers, "I hope there's some paper."

Out on the concreted ground of Southampton- Dock, they line up for uniform inspection. With a cough the clean-shaven young sailor says, "I am afraid all men need to use the facilities. As there are only four cubicles, I have suggested they leave four at a time."

"Well, I suggest you see to it, and I will stand at ease and watch from here. I will come over when they are lined up and ready" the army colonel loudly declares. Because of his manner and appearance, with a large walrus like moustache, and thick glasses, making his eyes look small, the prisoners believe he is important.

The young sailor, hiding his mirth, and glad the laws of the sea are different to those of the land, replies, "Well sir I would, but we cannot afford to wait until it gets too choppy before our next surfacing. I've several more trips to make today."

"Very well" the army colonel snaps.

The dockland looks eerie in the encroaching mist, voices ring hollow. They guess the dock net -work of metal tracks is used for imports and exports. Out to sea, at whim it seems, shapes appear or disappear. Tall modern ships re-invent themselves as ghost ships with furled sails and on their deck deep voices echo.

Because the prisoners are tired, the march to the railway station feels endless. Even so they keep in order as they follow queues of new arrivals from other locations in England.

When they reach the platform, they feel insecure and forlorn. Suddenly, the familiar, universal hiss of the steam train lifts their spirits as they are ordered to board. Whilst climbing into a carriage, Alfred recalls his childhood journey to Belgrade. He wonders if his family are alive. Gentle natured Klauss, aged about forty, looks pleased as he sits in the carriage. Alfred comments, "You look happy."

With a flick of his mousy hair and a sparkle of enthusiasm in his tired hazel eyes, Klauss replies, "Oh I've mixed feelings, but I am on familiar territory here. Having been a railway employee in Cologne I am extremely interested in trains."

"It makes a world of difference when we are in touch with something familiar. One can almost forget being a prisoner of war."

"Ja, it is good to forget sometimes. Although this train is 'The Lord Nelson 4-6-0 sir Francis Drake, I believe it has come from Bournemouth, and it will travel to Waterloo."

A cacophony of answers resounds and twenty-six-year-old Hans, with youthful humour and a touch of laughter says, "If it's the Lord Nelson I hope the driver has two eyes and two arms."

Suddenly he notices Karl's expression under a mop of unruly ginger hair, and stops because he remembers him mentioning that his friend had been blinded in an explosion. As if entering the moment of his friend's experience Karl's hazel green eyes stare into mid distance.

"How come Sir Frances Drake gets a ride on the same train? I hope he hasn't brought any cannon balls" bemused Hermann adds.

"Don't you mean bowls? Anyway, more to the point, you think we are going to London? I have not heard of any camps having been set up there. I was above the city when it was blitzed" Arno lamentingly persists. His deep brown eyes are wide with grief as a tear rolls down his olive face. Something about him with his curly black hair suggests that an ancestor may have journeyed into Germanic lands from Asia Minor.

Klauss chooses to explain, "The rail system from Waterloo goes to several places in England."

A voice resounding along the corridor informs them that more prisoners from France will arrive in two hours, after which time the train will depart. They moan amongst themselves but are also glad of time for reflection and discussion. Between themselves they ask if anyone knows anything about England.

"Some of it's similar to Germany with many forests and rivers" Paul offers. Hans emphasises, "The big difference is the sea that affects how people think, and how the country deals with trade."

"All I want to do is go home" Karl laments.

With a ring of sympathy in his green-grey eyes, Paul, six feet tall, with a head crowned with auburn hair quietly asks "Where's that?"

194

"Dresden."

Without forethought Hermann adds, "That is where the English carried out raids in October 1940. It will be in a bit of a mess."

Out of control Karl weeps and shakes because his nerves are on edge. After a while when calmer, he replies, "I know; I was there with my family. We managed to get to a shelter just in time. What worries me is that our dear town will be targeted again and that this time our family will die."

Again, he starts weeping and tries to hide the fact. Suddenly they are moving. Recalling what Alfred said in the Black Forest about acting within the moment, Paul endeavours to console Karl. He suggests, "Pray for your family, place everything in God's hands."

"It is important to stay connected with friends and relatives. Do you have contacts in other areas?" Alfred supportively adds.

"Yes, I have them written here."

Alfred notices his knuckles, white, because of his tense manner of holding the book.

"Now we are here we all must help each other" Paul proposes. Hermann glowers, resenting a younger man telling him what he ought to do.

"Actually, I was in England as a student, I did a six-week course in English studies at Exeter University" Hans admits.

Overcoming shyness, adolescent Emil asks, "What's Exeter like?"

"It would be good to know" Arno adds.

"It was a lovely city with large old houses, even Elizabethan ones with balconies. There is a large beautiful cathedral with a lovely green in front of it. During week -ends of those summer months we spent time reading under the shade of the trees."

"It sounds as if it's a lovely place Hans."

"Yes Emile, but I hope it hasn't been damaged too much."

"Hans, we could certainly use you as an interpreter" Hermann suggests,

"I'll gladly help"

Alfred wonders if he dared communicate with a very tall officer who has remained silent throughout the journey. He's almost put off by the expression of superiority on the officer's face. Plucking up courage he enquires, "Do tell us your name sir and perhaps your interests too if you would like to?"

"My name is Dr Joseph Knasch, and as you may or may not know I am a doctor of philosophy at Heidelberg University, or was in that position."

Because, in a monotone, that is all he says, the men are silent. They stare as he repeatedly runs a finger down the length of his Germanic nose and they wonder why he stares mid- distance, through his round wire glasses. Most observers assume he regards himself as intellectually superior.

Purposefully Alfred turns to Emil to say, "I suppose you didn't have opportunity to finish your school education?"

"No, I didn't, I was at school when I was called up but in school, I learned a little of the English language." "That's interesting, where was that?"

His father answers for him, "The High School in West Fallia."

With a ring of enthusiasm Alfred enthuses, "That's a coincidence,I come from Neubeckum in that region."

"Father, doesn't that farmer we speak to at the trade and cattle market come from there?" "Yes, Emil, you mean Bernhart Nurville."

"Yes, that's correct."

With a gasp Alfred quickly responds, "There cannot be two Bernhart Nurville's. He is my Great Uncle and I live with him and his wife Annalisa, my Great Aunt."

Instantly the old Germany is alive and this one connection enables others to find their own connections. Alfred resumes focus on Dr Knasch and notices, behind the façade of superiority, a glimmer of isolation and unhappiness. He considers how the scene at which Dr Knasch stares, is locked within his mind. He remembers a comment made by another qualified prisoner, Stephan Schmid-- *'You can't always judge what's going on inside a person; sometimes experience gets locked away.'*

Endeavouring to break through the barrier, Alfred comments, "I've noticed many young prisoners."

Following a long pause he suggests, "If we are sent to a good camp perhaps, you'll be able to help them with their education?"

Dr Knash's jaw tightens. A nerve twitches. As if attempting to hide some private grief he compresses his thin lips and curtly replies "Possibly."

***

As the train winds through the countryside Alfred thinks of his mother. Even now, across the years he can see her smile. The rhythm of wheels on track reminds him of something she said before she died, 'Closer than breath, closer than--?'

In his eleventh year, when the train had taken him to Belgrade, his father had quoted something she had said about nothing being black or white but shades of blue and indigo. The war had made him face that realization; he had entered the meaning from the inside out. His heart feels the tide of life turning towards something new. He believes the fierce battle within the heart of the world is changing direction. Within his soul he hopes and prays war will soon end.

During the passing hours, the prisoners follow a pattern of conversing, sleeping, staring out the window and conversing again. At one station, those needing to use the platform toilet facilities are, under escort, permitted to do so. Shortly later the train journeys onward, to eventually stop, at a station where a group of prisoners disembark to be taken to camps. Someone mentions the name Wincanton.

"Sounds Chinese" says Hermann.

"That's because they've pronounced it incorrectly" says Paul.

Two English soldiers make their way along the train to give each man a slice of bread and cheese and a mug of tepid tea.

***

When they arrive at Waterloo, remaining Prisoners must leave to change platforms. A soldier mentions that some men are destined for a camp at Oxford. An awkward moment ensues when an English officer is asked to fill the last prisoner vacancy for Oxford and selects Emil. Arno speaks out, "Bitte, nein. Er ist mein sohn." The officer does not understand.

Several prisoners of war take a risk by speaking out- "Nur siebensehn Jare alt."

"That means he's only seventeen years old" says Arno.

"Well, what a bastard Hitler is".

"He's Arno's son" Hans explains.

"I see, well yes, considering the lad's age, he may stay with his father. We aren't all like Hitler."

"Danke: thank you."

They are ordered into some trucks and as there are no camps in London, they wonder what their destination will be.

"They'll be taking us to Euston Station" Klaus explains.

Regardless of anxieties they are less tense away from danger and conflict. No longer do they have to fight to survive. To their surprise Emil asks a railway attendant, "Where go we?"

In a Northern accent he replies, "Aye laddie, you'll be going to Scotland."

"Schottland" someone emphasises.

They get out of the truck and in orderly fashion follow the person in charge of them, into Euston Station. When everyone is seated the train steams into motion and journeys onward. Time passes, sometimes slowly, sometimes quickly until eventually they come to a halt at Carlisle.

"Here at last" several men chorus but an army officer instructs them to follow him to another platform.

"We're going further north, so I think the information about Scotland was genuine" Klauss comments.

To their surprise Dr Joseph Knash is suddenly alive with interest.

"Scotland likes to be quite independent of England, so perhaps it is a good thing" he informs.

"This train smells strongly of smoke" Hermann groans.

"That's because we're close to the engine" Hans explains.

***

As they disembark at Dumfries the air is cold. In the distance a clear red sunset full of promise fills the horizon. They must form two groups, one of seven, the other of eight, to get into two small open backed trucks. There are no seats and therefore in standing position, they must precariously grasp the sides of the truck.

Whilst travelling down the main street, Alfred studies tall houses. One house, with a balcony containing large pots of flowers, reminds him of German houses bedecked with flower filled window boxes. In an instant, faces are sad because those houses and the people who tended the flowers are gone. To their left the prisoners notice a warehouse for house furnishers.

There's a ring of sarcasm in Dr Joseph Knash's tone as he comments, "Everyone will have to build more houses before they can furnish them again."

On narrow pavements several groups of people chat among themselves. Alfred is reminded of South-wood Street, but rather than wave, these people stand still and dispassionately stare. "I wish I had one of their tartan scarves, it's freezing standing here" Emil comments.

"Did you see that parked truck with the name BINNS written on the side and that huge taxi, probably early 1930's?" Hans enthuses.

Suddenly the men on the left of the truck lean forward as it veers around an island of ornamental garden. Now, as they stand upright Karl asks, "See that fountain in the middle?"

With tired voices they answer, "Yes."

"Well, it is not authentic, it's an imitation of a Victorian fountain, and its use is for accommodating overhanging lights. I have seen a similar one in Germany commemorating Prince Albert. Of course, that was not being used for overhanging lights."

Noticing their bored expressions Dr Knasch encouragingly comments, "Hans, you've a philosophical eye."

"What do you mean?"

"For observing that things are not always what they appear to be."

"Oh!"

Now as a tower clock comes into view, they appreciate this place that has not been bombed.

The town is left behind and gradually, set against a backdrop of hills, farms and cottages come into view. Alfred is reminded of Graz.

Chapter 25
Camp 298

They are travelling through a wide gateway past a well-cared for lodge. As the truck winds its way along the bumpy track a wide luscious landscape stretches before them. The wheels of the first truck rotate in a patch of grit; prisoners are ordered to get out and push. As they do so, the truck suddenly jolts forward and because the driver impatiently revs the engine, they quickly jump back in. As the vehicle speeds ahead, the driver of the second truck has difficulty keeping up. Without warning they veer right, and come to an abrupt halt in a compound. They face three Nissan huts, two almost end to end, looking like a giant caterpillar. Alfred's favourite is a single Nissan hut in front of several picturesque fir trees. In the distance, amidst a widely spaced network of trees, stands an impressive manor. Alfred imagines what the manor may have looked like in the past. He wonders if it was owned by a Lord or Baron. He wonders what happened to the girls cruelly taken from the manor in Beckum.

As the sun sinks behind the hill and light fades, the camp commander, a sturdy middle-aged man, dressed in a civilian bomber jacket and country casuals, takes them to the pleasantly situated Nissan Alfred preferred. "Mee nim is Mc Breed" says the commander. He explains that there are three more compounds, much larger than this; one currently unoccupied.

**

Today is Tuesday 24th October. Yesterday morning they had thought the coarse salted porridge unpalatable. Today they are eager for their portion that will satisfy their appetite until lunch time.

Now, an hour later, they receive instructions to run around the compound fifteen times. When they finish, Commander Mc Breed, looking directly at Hermann, holds up ten fingers and then four and makes him run one more time around the circuit. During their wait the group members try to hide their amusement.

200

Eventually, looking exhausted but greatly relieved, Hermann finishes the circuit. Quickly the Prisoners line up for drill, then jump, spread out their arms, jump and close--and repeat the process ninety-nine times. As they engage themselves in the activity their lungs fill with fresh pure air, far removed from the familiar tainted smell of smoke and rotting flesh. Their minds are clear. To Arno, Alfred whispers, "Drill at Aachen was much more rigorous."

"When they get us fit, they'll send us out to work for our keep" Arno answers.

***

On Wednesday 25th October, as they head for a large area for drill exercises, they stride alongside men from the other two compounds. "I don't know where the time went yesterday" Hermann mutters.

"There must be at least fifty boys among this lot" Paul whispers. "Many are no more than eighteen. They must have missed their education" Alfred states.

With a ring of enthusiasm Emil updates his seniors, "There's talk of some classes happening here."

"Noo comoonication durrrrring drrrrreeeel" Commander Mc Breed reprimands.

***

"What did the Commander Mc Breed say? He sounds half German" Hermann asks his friends during lunch. With a twinkle of amusement in his eyes Hans passes him a dictionary, "Here, you need to look it up in this camp dictionary I borrowed for the day. The first word is Noo."

Whilst thumbing through the dictionary Hermann is unaware of the expressions of his comrades.

"It is no good, it is not here. Anyway, the next word is communication and I already know it means 'mitteilung,' because I was involved in radio communication."

When he comes to 'D' he is frustrated at not being able to find durrrring and dreel.

"This thing is useless" he declares.

Emil discloses that people in Scotland speak with a strange accent. They all laugh and Hermann, realising he's fallen into a silly trap, looks glum.

"He speaks the English language using his colloquial dialect. 'Noo' means no and 'durrring' means during and 'dreel' means drill" Dr Knasch sympathetically explains.

"Come on Hermann it is funny--Och hei the noo" Hans jibes. Little by little Hermann's shoulders shake. Gradually he cannot stop laughing and it does him good because he has not laughed for several years.

"You lot are just as stupid as me, think back to yesterday when the commander said to that lanky chap from the next compound ' Mee nims not Mc Breed its Mc Breead.' That means he's called Mc Bride. Suddenly they're aware of the commander's footsteps on the crunchy path. Much to their amusement as he comes in, he yells, "Will ye eat yer deenerrrr without a worrrd".

***

On Thursday 26th October Commander Mc Bride asks them to write down a list of previous employment, interests, and skills. Avoiding another stint of horse-riding Alfred writes 'Previous occupation: waiter. Skills: Serb Croat language and a little Russian. Interest: Religious knowledge. Hobbies: Basket weaving and raffia craft.

During the afternoon, the fifteen men from compound C must run around the entire estate.

"Let us hope we can 'roonn aroond' within the requested hour. I am already tired" Alfred comments.

However, as they take in the beauty of the scenery feelings of exhaustion fade.

Eyes bright with interest Emil's voice is lighter as he says, "Oh look at that lake shimmering with light. There, over there-- several swans are coming out from those reeds. Do you think it is a sign our luck is changing father?"

"Yes, I believe it is" Arno replies whilst studying the face of his son, looking less scared, less haggard, and more the youthful age he is.

"I hope he'll have a chance to catch up on missed boyhood" he discretely conveys to Alfred and Paul

202

Gradually the scenery works its way into their minds, pushing out noise and grotesque images seen amidst conflict. Even Dr Joseph Knasch has to stop and put his hands to his face. As the rest of the group move on Alfred quietly asks "What's wrong?"

"My son--he was the same age as Emil. He was killed, in Russia. He was only a boy."

Placing a hand on Dr Knasch's arm Alfred replies, "I am very sorry."

"You're right; I can help the boys here" the doctor replies.

***

On Friday 27th October they are busy playing football against a POW team from compound A. Alfred remembers his brother Witold's mention of a sermon he had heard, about a spontaneous football match between German and English soldiers on Christmas Day during the Great World War. He starts humming the carol 'Still and Holy Night' that the men had unanimously sung. Today in the spaces between the noises of the game, that same stillness exists.

Through the wire fence he observes magnificent fir trees, reminding him of the story of first pine tree decorated for Christmas by Prince Albert for his beloved Victoria.

"Paul, I have an idea" he whispers.

***

It is evening and during their free time he discusses with Paul the possibility of producing a monthly religious magazine containing ideas contributed by the prisoners.

"Well, I'm with you on that, perhaps we could suggest it one day."

***

Early morning on Sunday 29th October the commander wakes them. "Ye missed Kirk last Sunday so yee all can goo this morrrning. I doo wanna see ye rrreedy by neen thirrrty sharrrrp" he says. Everyone understands the word 'Kirk' and Hans confirms it has the same meaning in Germany.

By the time Commander Mc Bride, dressed in a wide girthed tartan kilt, is seen through the window, they are looking their best. His attire reminds Alfred of traditional skirts worn by men in various pockets of Europe and Jugoslavia. Hermann jokes that despite being called Mc Bride, the commander would make a very ugly bride. They laugh and abruptly stop as he enters their Nissan hut. Whilst lining up for inspection they notice how pleased he is with their effort and they realize he thinks of them less as enemies and more as Hitler's victims. In an impressive voice he says, "I canee get ooverrr the young laddies bein' noo moorr than seventeen years oold."

They expect to be going to the village but the commander informs, "We arrre gooing to our own kirrrk."

Soon their footsteps crunch along the wide path. Nearer the manor house they walk over autumn leaves and comment on the diverse colours, green, brown, orange, and yellow.

"There's one here that's green and yellow" says Emil.

"Like two nationalities someone says.

"But one leaf" someone else adds.

"Reeet rrrrund the seed of the hoose laddies" says the commander. They detect a grain of affection in his Sunday voice.

The chapel, quite empty of clutter, is filled with sunlight shining through the clean glass. Even though seats are being filled, a feeling of spaciousness exists. A pure white lace edged cloth has been placed upon the altar. Emil feels tearful as he thinks of his mother's hands skilfully making lace with at least ten bobbins on the go. He appreciates the simplicity of the cross on the altar.

"That was the kind Christ died on, not an elaborately carved ornament" his father emphasises.

"Yes Father, I agree" Emil replies. He is feeling more cheerful because during this week he has been given space and time to formulate his own opinions. His strongest thoughts seem to echo through the church *The crowds chanting Heil Hitler are beginning to fade in my mind*--he realises he's in conversation with the invisible God.

***

A gentle faced, friendly, pretty, dark haired girl, carrying a small harp, comes into the building and sits on a stool to the right of the altar. She plays a Gaelic tune in Dorian mode and the prisoners think of their own sweethearts and wives. Single men wonder about the future, whether they might meet a girl like her. From the vestry a tall angular man with warm brown eyes, black hair and a thick wiry beard appears.

In a rich welcoming voice he says, "Good moorrrrning to our army officers, camp commander and attendants. I'd like to thank Miss Amy Mc Farlane for coming to accompany us today. "Gute Morgen...ich spreche nicht viel deutsch, enschuldigen mich. Ich heiss Deacon Mc Angus." For the benefit of officers and attendants he translates, "Good morning, apologies, I don't speak much German, my name is Deacon Mc Angus."

Glad that the deacon has taken the trouble to speak a sentence in their own language the prisoners' smile. The priest in charge must be taking a service at a local church they surmise. Deacon Mc Angus indicates they are to put their hands together.

"We are going to say the Lord's Prayer in English-- understand?"

"Ja," "Yes" they reply.

He continues, "Our Father who art in heaven."

Someone whispers, "Unsere Vater im Himmel."

Miss Amy repeats the English words and they understand what is expected of them.

Deacon Mc Angus starts again and they repeat each sentence after him. He is concerned about a few men who are silent and wonders if they might be atheists or Nazi's unwilling to comply. It also occurs to him that they might be traumatized.

After prayers he declares how well they have done. The majority are pleased to hear this. He announces hymns and Amy accompanying herself on the piano, sings in an acceptable nasal tone a line of 'Now Thank we All Our God'. Instantly they recognise the German tune 'Nun Danket' and heartily repeat Amy's line. With gusto they work through the verses and recognising some English words begin to relate them to the familiar German stanzas. Their hearts are thankful to God who has rescued them from the jaws of death. Some men have difficulty containing their inner tears; Deacon Mc Angus observes and considers how many are grieving the loss of family members and friends. Except for an army officer who casts a warning glance, a sense of unity prevails.

"In place of the sermon there will be two small acting sketches, both will be mimed" Deacon Mc Angus explains.

They fail to understand and Amy translates what he has said. She asks a German prisoner if she may borrow his hat.

"Ja, ja" he answers.

As she puts it on, she notices the same army officer glare in her direction. Deacon Mc Angus casts a reassuring look in Amy's direction. Inwardly he's confident, as the priest has already warned him about the possibility of such reaction from the officer. 'You can get away with more than me. The prisoners are to be your priority' he had emphasised.

Now Deacon Mc Angus puts on an English army jacket and the mime begins. Amy's expression and her outward palms indicate she is defending herself from falling debris during a bombing raid --now it has fallen--her German hat drops from her head as she collapses to the ground--she remains silent and when she regains consciousness grimaces with pain and grasps her injured leg. The English soldier bandages her wounds and helps her to her feet.

Now another scene evolves where the roles are reverse--the bomb explodes--the English man is blinded. The German girl places a bandage around his head to cover his eyes and leads him to a seat where he sits and waits whilst she fetches help. Now as helper she puts on a white top with a red cross on it and leads the soldier away.

Deacon Mc Angus is himself again. On a board he pins up a picture of the Good Samaritan. The army officer's silent objections wither. More daringly the deacon asks five young prisoners to come out to the front to witness him carry a large cross. He goes to the vestry to fetch it. When he returns and stands at the top of steps, he declares that they are to shout 'crucify him'. The harpist who has learned some German, stands up to relay the message, "At the same moment they shout 'Crucify him' Father Angus wants the rest of you to shout, "Love and resurrection."

The drama proceeds. The first and second attempts fail but by the third attempt everyone realises what it is about. The cry "Love and resurrection" wins with flying colours.

"What do you want to shout?" Deacon Mc Angus asks the small group of boys. Gleefully they cry "Love and resurrection."

After the service as they leave the church, several men realize how the cry 'Heil Hitler' that was forced upon them and their community, embodied a crucifying attitude with its roots embedded in death. Some younger lads recall their time in the 'Hitler Youth Movement' when they instinctively suspected Hitler's motives. In their naivety they had 'corrected' their instinct and had held fast to the belief that adults, especially those of status, were always right. Now, far away from the situation, they are coming to terms with the false persona of their former idol.

***

Behind army officers, walking along with their heads bowed, three POW stragglers approach the deacon. "Bitte, Deacon Angus, wir haben ein idea--please Deacon Angus we have an idea" Paul conveys.

The deacon looks puzzled but recognizes the word 'idea'.

Hans expounds. "We desire to make—jede--every monat--month..a religious magazine--mit unser--with our ideas: all POW ideas. We ask this perhaps?"

"Your English is quite good. I understand. It is a promising idea but it would take more than a month to collect suitable material. I suggest a quarterly magazine. If you bring me something in writing I will present it to the priest in charge and to the camp commander."

"Hans tell him we need paper, pens, lino, cutting tools and ink?"

"Deacon Mc Angus, we need-Ach- we would like papier--paper, pens, lino and tools and ink."

"You need lino and cutting tools? Och, you mean for lino prints. Well, that might be possible."

Apologetically he explains, "It would have to be under a wee bit o' supervision as the tools can be very sharp-- although at least they can nee go too deep."

Hans endeavours to translate the reply but as he does so the prisoners look offended.

"Hans please tell them it isn't personal, it's camp rules, and it applies throughout the whole of England."

Hans explains, and as they leave to go to their Nissan hut they reply, "Thank you Dcacon Mc Angus. Dankeschon, aufwiedersehen."

"Och away with yee; aufwiedersehen m'laddies. 'Bye for now" he answers with a smile.

By Thursday 2nd November things are progressing. Several men amongst the fifteen newcomers have been asked to take on additional classes in the camp. Much to their surprise there are categories. Dr Joseph Knasch has been requested to take an advanced class. They are annoyed that until now he's pretended to not understand English, and has left Hans to do all the work. Hans also has an advanced group, and Hermann and Paul are asked to take groups for beginners.

"I haven't a clue how to teach" Hermann groans.

"Because you find it hard, you'll understand how your students feel" Alfred surmises.

"A good point; I suppose" Hermann growls.

They listen as Arno is asked to instruct an intermediate group. Except for Dr Nasch no one has taught before. Their adrenalin is flowing because Commander Mc Bride has said he'll call in on the first lesson.

***

On the morning of Friday 3rd November, Drill Commander Mc Bride gives Alfred and Paul opportunity to convey their plan. "The priest and camp commander here present, have kindly given permission for us to produce a camp quarterly magazine" Paul points out.

"What kind of magazine?"

"It will be like a church magazine with religious themes, prayers, and thoughts. It also may include positive, personal news from home."

"That sounds all right. Will it have pictures?"

"Yes, we want good illustrations. The following men have the skill to convert pictures into lino, under supervision of course: Stephan Schmidt from compound A, Klauss Larsmann from compound B, two of our youths Emil Schwarz from compound B and Martyn Feldmann from compound C."

"I see."

"Hans and Hermann will do the typing" Alfred quickly adds.

Commander Mc Bride concludes, "Please give your work to your teacher to pass onto Dr Joseph Knasch. Paper and pencils will be given to you this evening. Deacon Mc Angus, myself,

Knasch, Stuckmann and Ztoanjib, will meet later, to decide upon choice of submitted material."

***

On Saturday 19th November Alfred and his friends are at choir practice. They are about to sing carols printed out on large sheets pinned up at the front of the Nissan meeting hall, but many cannot see the words. Paul suggests, "It would be practical to have illustrated carol sheets in the magazine." Noticing the thread of thought Alfred adds, "It might be an idea for those who have not made any contribution to engage in this task. The camp commander mentioned he'd welcome drawing of scenes from the camp."

***

On Saturday 26th November, just in time for the 4 O'clock meeting, Dr knasch is given a pile of submissions.

During the meeting they think some material unsuitable for Christmas. Deacon Mc Angus believes rejection will affect morale. He therefore retrieves three impressive lino prints, one of a man at prayer, one of Christ in agony, wearing the crown of thorns, and another of a person caught up in an explosion.

"These relate to passion week he says. The man at prayer looks like Christ in Gethsemane. The image of a man caught up in an explosion relates well to one of the recent Sunday services. We can tell the men that some material will be used in later quarterlies. It will take the edge off disappointment."

Members of the committee agree. Several carols are chosen for the forthcoming concert and carol service. Drawings of the choir and band seem appropriate. "I'm glad the picture portrays a lively conductor and that he doesn't look as if he's in the middle of one of his asthma attacks" Commander Mc Bride emphasises.

"Och it's a debilitating ailment" Deacon Mc Angus sympathetically points out. Changing the topic, Commander Mc Bride asks, "Could some outline, indicating snow, be added to these excellent drawings of the camp?"

"Yes, it would be most appropriate. That concludes everything" Deacon Mc Angus positively states.

"I've one request. Please can we include that drawing of a Christmas tree? My son loved Christmas trees. It would be fitting alongside the carol about the Christmas tree" Dr Knasch asks in an unusually quiet voice. Reluctantly Deacon Mc Angus makes the point, "Yes, but regretfully it's not a religious song."

"Oh, but sir it must be in a sense, as Victoria was English and Albert was German. Does not the tree perhaps provide a link?" Alfred daringly suggests.

"Well true. I will include it if you agree Commander Mc Bride?" the Deacon proposes.

"Och that's feen bee mee, but doona seey anything to the arrrrmee officerrs aboot it will yee?" "No, we won't. Thank you" they reply.

***

The following evenings are set aside for the magazine. Hans and Hermann cannot manage touch typing, so the others help by reading aloud the rough drafts they are to type. The first of the lino prints come through with the ink too runny. Using thicker ink, they try again and this time the images are exceptional.

***

On Wednesday March 3rd, following an illustrated talk, they feel depressed for they have heard a detailed account about what Hitler and his men have done to Jews. They cannot believe it; many men feel ill and the local doctor must visit the camp.

***

On Sunday 7th March, Deacon Mc Angus tries to boost morale. Fritz's project is not finished but he has been asked to bring it to the service. An atmosphere of anticipation lingers as it is unveiled. Eyes fix on the impressive model of the Cathedral of Cologne, with only the top of the tower to complete. Deacon Mc Angus praises his superb efforts. This Fritz, the same age as Alfred's twin siblings Fritz and Johanna causes Alfred to wonder what has happened to them. Deacon Mc Angus' talk is about the people of earth and Heaven as the true Church, and prayer as the route for the tower building of the eternal city. In conclusion he emphasises, "That true church is indestructible and when it is laid low it can, and does rise again."

They begin to revive in spirit.

***

On Tuesday March 9th Alfred has mentioned to Paul the idea of asking for cone cine- films to be viewed in the Nissan hut hall,

210

to include one about the history of the district or the camp itself. Paul mentions it to Commander Mc Bride. Affirmatively he answers, "There is nay film but I know someone who can give a talk on the backgrrroond of the arrrrea. I will see to it and arrrange foor it in a week or two."

During the afternoon news comes through that thousands have been captured at Remagen Bridge. Commander Mc Bride suddenly announces that the prisoners are to go to their Nissan huts. They wonder what's happening. Soon in one of the Compound B huts, Alfred and Professor Stephan Schmidt are informed that along with Karl Bauermann from compound C they have been selected to go to Devon.

After Commander Mc Bride has left Alfred says, "Paul, I am disappointed but it is God's will. You must keep the magazine going."

"I will."

"And will you see that Karl is alright?"

"Yes, of course."

I hope you will look after our Dr Joseph Knash. He is not such a tough nut. He once mentioned that he despised all that the Nazis were doing. He deliberately got himself captured."

"Yes, I am aware. We shall be glad of his skills and insights."

On the tenth of March they feel excited about the prospect of watching a film. However, later, when the film starts reeling, it does not meet their expectations. They watch footage of devastation in England and witness the expressions of women, children, and the elderly, who have had their homes destroyed. People are being pulled from burning buildings. They see the large man Churchill, with a cigar in his mouth, visiting people, assuring them. Now, as they see footage of the King and his queen, visiting and supporting members of the public whose homes and streets have been bombed, they think of the better history of their not so historic, Prince Albert. On the radio the little princess speaks to the people asking them to be brave and hopeful for the future. The Prisoners of War want to call out 'It is like that in Germany. It was not our decision.' Now they are in 1935--the grim face of Hitler glowers from the screen. In the name of National-Socialism, he incites men, women, and children to believe false ideology. Now Mussolini promises impoverished Italians that Rome will rise and that he will save them from economic troubles. There's tension in the voices of Mussolini and Hitler, and calm in the tone of Churchill--he is not afraid--Hitler and Mussolini are afraid and that is why, with false promises, they are luring the impoverished people into worshiping them--expectations are never reached--now they must fight--the years flash across the screen--now they must give their lives--boys too must sacrifice themselves so that the false cause of war can surge onwards--it never stops. Some men can take no more and the commander asks the army cadet to change the reel. During a short film of Loch Lomond, they try to erase the image of the face that has imposed itself upon their nation.

Chapter 26
Deeper Insights

On the train snaking its way across the countryside they discuss farewells at Barony.

"Even Commander Mc Bride had a wee teer in his eeye" Alfred comments.

At a substation, a poster of the coast beyond Exeter catches their eye. With interest they admire a solitary jagged red sandstone pillar standing amidst lashing waves. Alfred is reminded of additional news about Remagen Bridge. When American troops had entered the picture, German troops had received orders to put dynamite into every crevice of the pillars of the bridge and blow it up. A soldier had lit the fuse, they ran for cover but no explosion had occurred. The tall red sand- stone rock in the sea near Teignmouth, serves to remind Alfred of Remagen- Bridge, still standing against all odds.

"It is ironic, as if the bridge symbolises the father-land, strong, but defeated by its own strength. Did you see that picture at the station where the train stopped for a while? It was on the front cover of the newspaper?"

"No, what picture of?" Karl asks.

"The soldiers, with a look of bewilderment on their faces, walking across Remagen- Bridge: they had their hands raised. I'm certain the man in the middle was in the division I met up with in Russia."

Stephan comments, "The symbolic bridge, like the negative strength of Hitler, dragging us down into the mire."

They are surprised by the blunt remark. "I'm a professor in Psychiatry" he reveals. He is forty-seven years old he tells them, and was awarded a Professorship before war broke out. They ask him what he thinks of Hitler.

"He has the mind of an abuser. Not only has he apparently-- well-- let me explain-I am putting two and two together from case studies my tutor presented to me; one of a mother concerned about her daughter, and the other; an earlier case, of a disturbed young man. My tutor deliberately let slip that 'the cases' were living close by and were high profile. However, as I was saying, Hitler abused his niece sexually, and imprisoned her in his secret home on the mountain. He used similar tactics to take over various countries."

"Do continue, what you're saying is interesting" Alfred comments. Karl remains silent.

"Well, if you like:

In 1935 Hitler made a weird comment. It went something like this 'We want to see again in the eyes of the young the gleam of the beast of prey.' That should have rung alarm bells as it suggests a person taking an unnatural interested young people. Then there are the strutting marches and extensive elaborate parades we have witnessed in Germany and Italy, and that imitate the sexual behaviour of some exotic birds. The marches are designed to impress and entice the impressionable. In Hitler's context it is no fine and innocent display; on the contrary it aims to deceive in a cruel manner. During that particular year, 1935, I was in a crowd, and saw looks of suspicion on some older faces. I could not refrain from saying to one woman, 'One day I shall write about that man but it won't be the kind of book he's expecting.' Regardless of her peasant status, she possessed certain wisdom, it was evident in the way she nodded in agreement; I am certain she comprehended my meaning. I trusted the look in her eyes as she trusted mine."

"I expect it was one of God's moments breaking through," said Alfred. "You are right. I have learned that Hitler lied to the League of Nations from the start. The whole picture of him is about desire to dominate at all costs. Peace does not come into his picture. The very name 'Siegfried line' of defences with armies ready to terrorize victims into submission, speaks of a corrupt mind."

They look puzzled and Karl asks, "What do you mean?"

"It is too complex to say here and now, but I've a chapter that connects with Wagner's 'Siegfried' from 'The Ring.' Here, it is in my hold- all; would you like to have a look?"

"Yes, very much, as I'm interested in Wagner's music dramas" Karl replies.

After passing the chapter papers to Karl, Stefan continues to explain, "From that point Hitler set about dominating. In 1934 he said, 'That it is the intention of the German Reich to coerce the Austrian State is absurd' and yet in 1938 the German army under Hitler's instruction simply marched over the border and took them unawares. Such tactic is characteristic of an abuser."

Reminiscing Alfred quietly replies, "My mother was part Austrian; I don't know what she would have thought."

"I heard you are mixed race" Stephan replies "That's why I feel I can freely talk."

To draw Karl into the conversation he adds, "I understand you've gone through hell Karl--I don't suppose you want me to go on?"

"Yes, do, although some of what you say is painful."

Stephan wonders what he means, but the train is approaching Exeter, and there is a great deal to talk about before they reach Plymouth. He values their response to the points he is making, as testing ground for the book.

"Anyway, if we look at Czechoslovakia, Hitler's seen to have had the same objective although he used different tactics. You might recall from your history lessons how Bismarck once said, 'He who would conquer Europe must first hold the bastions of Bavaria,' that Bavaria is now Czechoslovakia. You see Czechoslovakia had alliance with France and Britain and that is one of the reasons Hitler took it piece at a time."

Following a moment of reflection Alfred replies, "Yes, I see what you mean. First, he took Sudatland, right on the border of Germany. I remember Father Augustus mentioned that Hitler claims that 'People with German blood should belong to Germany wherever they went in the world.' Encouragingly the professor comments, "Yes, that is correct and of course some short-sighted people fell for it. Then when others tried to stand up to Hitler, he lied that Germans were being persecuted. The fact he took Sudatland made the rest of Czechoslovakia helpless; they were trapped within their own territory. Within six months he violated the Munich agreement that had been signed in September 1938, in which he said 'I have no further interest in the Czechoslovakian state; that is guaranteed. We want no Czech.' He is an abuser because the image of himself he presents to the world, is a living lie, for the purpose of concealing darker motives. My title for the book is 'The mind of Hitler.' I aim to advance society's understanding of the minds of abusers and dictators. It is suitable time the public see themselves as being deceived along with those who have been victims. They should sympathise with the abused, rather than regard the abused as an embarrassment. If, along with the abused, they have been deceived into believing a person is what he claims to be, rather than what he truly is, then they are to identify with the victim. If they fail to do that they join with the crime of the abuser. Understanding these issues should not be compartmentalized and kept under cover. If governments and the communities it is meant to serve choose to hide these matters, they fail to protect society. If everything remains hidden, it inadvertently encourages repetition of abuse, and dictatorship that are part of the same psychological condition."

With some hesitation Karl carefully formulates his sentences, "I understand what you are saying, and your definition is already helping me--you see, I once went through a tough time with a priest when I was a young boy. I have never told anyone, not even my wife."

"It's good you've mentioned it now, and the shame belongs to him, not to you."

"And to a few people with official roles in the church who knew about it. They told me that the devil worked through boys to drag down men of status, especially priests. They sprinkled holy water over me to cleanse me of the devil, and said that if I told anyone the devil would come back.

Professor Stephan Schmidt, whilst putting his hands to his face, utters, "God Almighty. Look, if I can be of help; if you want to talk about matters privately, please do not hesitate to ask. "Thank you, you're very kind---as long as you don't mention me in your book."

"Of course not, and the book I am writing can only be published if Germany loses the war. Do you know, my tutor informed me that in the same case study, the young man had once consulted him because of worries about things that happened to him during his childhood? He had irrationally come to hate all

Jews, because when he was a boy, his Jewish teacher, daily, tore up his attempts at painting and drawing."

"That's not nice, and if that's the case we can almost sympathise with the person, who I guess is Hitler" says Alfred.

"Well, probably, but what my tutor did point out was that when he probed more deeply, he learned that boy had painted disturbing images of decapitated dogs, and pigeons floundering with their legs cut off--and in the background, always these large hands, two gleaming eyes and something that looked like a phallic symbol."

"The boy always had a mental problem?"

"So, it would seem, or he'd witnessed some terrible things from an early age. In that case, whoever made him look at those things must have had a problem. It can go on throughout several generations or sideways into world war if something is not done about it on a wide scale. An underlying theme exists in the Wagner opera Hitler reveres. Siegfried is the product of an incestuous relationship."

Alfred putting forward his opinion goes on to say, "I don't know anything about opera but generally speaking, it all sounds a bit complex although I get the general picture of what you're saying. I know from comrades how difficult things were in Russia in the winter of 1941 to 1942 when Hitler changed tactics, and aimed for Leningrad instead of Moscow. He was callous then and took no notice that men had no equipment or supplies and were in their thousands, dying from exposure."

Feeling a little more confident Karl expounds, "That's because a mind like his sees the goal rather than the effect. I had an aunt in Poland who lived near the border. She was killed in 1939 when the army invaded. It was unfair and was not even a battle because the Poles received no warning. They were ill equipped and unprepared. Under Hitler's instructions everything was flattened and all lines of communication destroyed."

Looking serious Professor Stephan Schmidt slowly unravels his personal thoughts; "There's a parallel there to Mussolini. To promote his own status in the eyes of the impoverished Italians, he ordered his troops to invade helpless Ethiopia in 1935. Many other stories we learned from the Barony Camp film--not that the British are entirely blameless. If the Victorians hadn't created the

217

British Empire at great cost to the nations they took over, Victoria's grandson, Kaiser Wilhelm, might not have thought in the terms he did--in that case there might not have been a First Word War and young Hitler might not have been in that defeated army--thus he might not have resolved to one day turn things around at whatever cost."

"The little bits of sin and greed that add up to the big sin?"

"Yes Alfred. The whole issue of war is about people acting and not stopping to listen to deep down issues. People do not listen to the sorrows beneath the anger. War is about fear and anger and a misguided concept about control, and the mistaken belief that by controlling others, their own fear will disappear. It is what I call the 'Siegfried complex' but the fear does not disappear, and that is what the war condition is about."

As if absorbing the fact for the first time Karl reiterates, "It's about judging from outward appearance and imposed identity."

"Rather than by recognising that the identity of God has been placed within each of us in a unique and special way" Alfred suggests. Looking up from his reading Karl extemporises, "Peace is about accepting our differences and enriching ourselves by listening to the ideas and skills of others, developing them, and putting them into motion for future generations. Quick success and fame ring hollow,and arrogant claim to personal success, hinders sincere and modestly deserved success, and swings the pendulum into war. The desire to combat the world because of personal grievance, throws one generation into the next generation's war."

"Yes, and then more sin or whatever you like to call it, is added. I call it retaliation--Just look at the devastation in Germany" the professor concludes.

Chapter 27
The Siegfried Line

"We won't reach Plymouth for another hour or so, can I read a bit more of your book Stephan?"

"Of course, although you realize chapter two covers some issues we discussed earlier?" "That's fine; I need to read it thoroughly."

"I've still got to do some editing but when you've finished reading it, your opinion would be appreciated."

With a grateful smile Karl engrosses himself in the next pages:

Chapter One: The Siegfried Complex.

As a doctor of psychiatry, I have never encountered Adolf Hitler face to face. The reader justifiably might ask on what grounds I am able to present a (hypothetical) case study of this public figure. Positively I can say I have been inspired by colleagues, who, whilst never disclosing names have provided clues to a few of their notable case histories. Had we not been living during this time of extreme difficulty I doubt these doctors would have drawn these case studies to the attention of their colleagues: neither would they have taken great lengths to indicate in every way, except by name, that these specific cases relate to Adolf Hitler and members of his family.

In 1938 I happened to have stood among crowds at a compulsory open-air assembly to cheer the Führer and listen to his address. Following much stirring military music, elaborate parades, and crowd incitement to hail their leader, Hitler's speech was presented in his usual anxious, dictatorial, and fascist style. It left the listener impressed by the method rather than the content. I clearly recall expressions of doubt on the faces of several elderly people. It informed me how they perceived something dark manifesting itself within the light of day of this glorious military occasion.

In some circles it is common knowledge that Hitler, during his childhood, had a Jewish teacher. Every day this teacher destroyed the boy's art work. At face value it would appear we should empathise with the angry and dispirited boy who still exists within the psyche of the fanatical adult. But are things that simple? My colleague contacted the now retired teacher who had managed to escape the ghettos. From that teacher my colleague learned how, from his earliest school days Adolf Hitler's art revealed a disturbed mind. The child never obeyed instruction and always followed his own course. A common theme in his drawings was live, tormented dismembered birds and animals. In the background of each picture haunting dark eyes and large hands were portrayed. If, at that crucial stage, Adolf had been encouraged to use his skill to paint wholesome images, it is possible he later may have possessed a capacity to divorce his aim to accumulate national wealth from the annihilation and extermination of Jewish people. What was the child attempting to express? The images indicate a troubled background with an emergence of false values. He is likely to have witnessed disturbing events, and as a result, compassion was not the agenda of his formative years. It is probable that those recorded events were caused by the owner of the haunting dark eyes and large hands, although I must emphasise that the images do not appear to relate to Adolf's immediate family. However, the art work was not expressive of the mind of a child brought up in a loving atmosphere.

Looking up from his reading Karl mentions the content of the last paragraph. He asks if the child would have benefited from a religious upbringing.

Emphatically Alfred suggests, "Well if he was brought up to love God and his creation that would have been a good thing."

Stephan expounds on an intellectual level, "From a psychological point of view such an upbringing might have been more wholesome. On the contrary a distortion of religion would have had an adverse effect. This aspect never became known. We shall never know unless Adolf Hitler authors his own story. Even then we might not believe him: his underhand war strategies have gained him reputation for often lying."

Karl resumes reading:

220

Can we judge the Jewish teacher? His intention was that of demonstrating to the boy that the subject matter was wrong. The teacher's error was not so much the destruction of the subject matter but the destruction of the method and effort that had gone into producing the paintings. On the other hand, it is possible the teacher witnessed certain madness in the child's method, and that the method contained the seed of later strategies? The boy had some behavioural dysfunction that has been observed in a cross section of children from a variety of social and cultural background. At present such childhood behaviour is regarded as intentional naughtiness rather than an unintentional dysfunction.

Can we blame the Jewish teacher for indirectly promoting recent and ongoing cruelty to the Jews? Such inconceivable cruelty I recently witnessed on cine film in a Scottish prisoner of war camp. In no way could such images have been contrived. Sharply I concluded that Hitler could not use his earlier classroom experience as an excuse for recent and current psychotic behaviour. However, Hitler is not a madman in the sense that he does not know what he is doing. He is clear minded and like the Siegfried in Wagner's music drama of that title, he has a choice. Hitler's choices are seen to be premeditated and deliberate. In disbelief and horror, I watched disturbing images on screen that included experiments on human beings.

Karl, now is looking up from his reading, comments, "It was horrific."

Alfred makes his point, "As long as mankind permits abusive experimentation on animals within laboratories, atrocities against humans will continue."

"Exactly" Karl replies and begins to read aloud the sentences:

"The human mind can become a dangerous weapon of mass destruction. Negative thinking can be contagious within fascist and parallel organizations; or within an organization where originally sound aims become misinterpreted and misdirected. In our time, on a pandemic scale, a plague has erupted from one mind. Just as Mussolini and Hitler have investigated the past and have imitated ancient patterns, so those of similar inclination will do the same in future generations, unless it is diagnosed at an early stage, and dealt with positively."

He resumes reading silently:

'We have only to watch an audience after an operatic production of Siegfried to capture the spirit of involving a crowd with idealistic fascist belief. Four nights of the complete Ring cycle deeply influences human concepts and emotion.

In my previous chapter I investigated the abusive tactics of Hitler in his war strategy and within his personal life. I now wish to focus on his obsession with the opera Siegfried. It would appear to be no coincidence that he named the eastern defence line 'The Siegfried Line.'

As I previously mentioned, the music drama 'Siegfried' is full of fascist undertones. We need to remember that Wagner was banished from the Germany of the late 1880's for his fascist beliefs. Fascism is the foundation from which Hitler's partnership with Mussolini evolved. They are seen to share false idealism and a warped perception of heroism. By studying the intricate details of Siegfried story set to Wagner's music, that has a capacity to stir up emotion, on both personal and nationalistic scale, we see the foundation for Hitler's parallel musical stage drama that has been seen to stir up the minds and emotions of young and idealistic people. Unlike Siegfried, thousands of German boys do not come through heroically and triumphantly. On the contrary they meet with horrific deaths. One cannot help but see a parallel between them and the poor creatures in the Hitler child's drawings. Unlike Siegfried who, like Hitler, does not know the extreme fear our boy soldiers have known. Undoubtedly Hitler's niece experienced deep fear and grief, not only because of physical abuse, but also because the uncle she had once loved, arranged the murder of her Jewish fiancé. Where that young man should have been Hitler walked in, void of love and full of dominance and abuse. In the Siegfried music drama, there are superior and inferior races and Hitler identifies with the superior race. Regardless of the immensely impressive music of the opera, Wagner's Siegfried is a racist music drama.

I would encourage the reader to study both the characters and plot of Siegfried. This work provides the key to Hitler's psychotic mental state. Through the plot a parallel to Hitler's delusions of grandeur, are revealed.

Firstly, we may ask if Hitler identifies with Siegfried who has a disturbed childhood and later discovers that his origins aren't straightforward. Siegfried has been brought up by one parent, Mime, a forest dwarf of the Nibelung race. When Siegfried is a youth Mime reveals that Siegfried's real mother died when she gave birth to him in a cave. He is informed that her name was Sieglinde. Mime explains that prior to her death she instructed Mime to name him Siegfried which means 'fair and strong one'. That element already hints at the Hitler's obsession with producing a perfect, supreme, and Aryan race. Later in the plot we discover why Siegfried must skip a generation and look to his forefather's generation for strength. It is because Siegfried learns he was born because of a brother -sister, incestuous relationship. In Hitler's mind there is something in his near ancestry that prevents him from grasping his true 'Aryan' identity. Hitler identifies with Siegfried's need to redeem a situation rooted in the past.

Mime does not know anything of Siegfried's father. The only links he has with his father are two pieces of a broken sword that Mime hands over. For Hitler, this broken sword symbolises brokenness in relationships and national brokenness.

In the First World War, Hitler, as a young soldier alongside his comrades, met with disastrous defeat. He survived and he saw his comrades blown to smithereens. One suspects he sees himself as a second Kaiser Wilhelm to use old war time strategies in a new way. Similarly, throughout the music drama a musical theme constantly echoes through the Siegfried story. The dwarf emphasises that the sword has been given to him as payment for his kindness. Siegfried overlooks this and claims it as his right. His knowledge is not available to the public.

Therefore, within the present world we see that society needs to have available an independent body to which concerns may be addressed. Through such means false leaders would be halted in their devious course. If the people are to achieve this they need to be informed, so that sound judgement may develop. Hitler uses his public platform for his purpose of persuasion; thus, he draws in those who are willing to become his co abusers. Through hideous and cruel means, he rapidly eradicates men who belong to his own party and who are not willing to work darkness within the light, a major theme in the opera.

223

In the present and in the future, records of all leaders should be made. To avoid a repeat of negative history, potential world leaders should be thoroughly observed and scrutinised by a body of psychiatric and other professionals. That a leader should work darkness within the light should never again be tolerated. From the events that have unfolded in Hitler's life we see the vast importance of adult influence upon a child's formative years. There is a great need for doctors of medicine and psychiatry to study and understand behavioural disorders among children. If certain unexplained behaviour is regarded as naughty at an early stage, an individual may not be able to differentiate his or her 'condition' from his adult misconduct at a later stage of life."

Looking up, with an appreciative smile Karl says to Stephan, "The chapter is very interesting and with the other chapters it will make a fine book."

"Thanks, I realise that I will have to work on structure and presentation. What is this station?"

"Totness" Karl answers.

With a laugh Alfred points out, "Sounds a bit like Lochness. I thought we had left Scotland."

Karl pipes up, "We are only about twenty miles from Plymouth."

Chapter 28
Coloured Slippers

Ten-year-old Susan lives in a thatched cottage beside St Mary's Church in the busy village of Steerton. Several weeks have passed since German Prisoners of War arrived. On this sunny day, unnoticed, Susan slips out over the village green, across the road, and into a field. Her fair curls bounce, as lightly she runs through long grasses that continue through several fields. Regardless of her speed she observes along the hedgerows, pretty bluebell buds, and open-faced celandines. Daringly she ventures into territory beyond the area her mother allows. Keeping her head down behind the bushes she skips along the path. Feelings of caution beat within her but she is determined to see what the new arrivals at the Prisoner of War camp are like. She is pleased she will be able to boast to her friends about this adventure. Her mother has explained about prisoners coming from Scotland. Her violet blue eyes widen with imagination; she asks herself if they will be wearing kilts and playing bagpipes. She wonders if anyone will teach her how to play the strange instrument. Suddenly she hits the fence, and is startled from her day dream. She presses her snubbed nose against the wire mesh and peeps through. As the wind blows through her fair hair, a strand tangles in the wire. She pulls it free, and as she rubs the sore place at the roots, she notices some new men, looking lost as they walk about the compound. Disappointment clouds her face because these men are wearing similar drab uniforms to those worn by the Italians who'd previously lived there. One man, not much taller than herself, has noticed her. He is waving and coming closer. Her heart races, she wonders if she should stay. He is carrying something colourful in his hands. She stays because she is curious about what it might be. His face is friendly; his blue eyes remind her of the bluebell buds.

"Hello" he says in a kind voice. "Me Alfred Ztoanjib, what you called?"

225

"Susan."

"Good morning Susan: Here I have pretty slippers. I make them from coloured cord; see."

Susan's face lights up; she wishes she could wear such slippers. As he slides them underneath the fence he looks up and asks the child "You take to your mother and bring back tomorrow a half crown for them, yes?"

"I'll ask her. If she likes them, she will buy some for me" she replies.

"I make just in case. I see you have middle sized feet for middle sized girl."

"I must hurry home or mother will wonder where I am" she says, and with a laugh, clutches the pretty slippers as she races away. She realises her mother will ask her where she obtained them; she will know she has gone further than she should. She wonders why the prisoners are called prisoners of war, unlike black American prisoners who had been there earlier in the war. Then she remembers her mother saying, 'The black Americans are on our side but these men have misbehaved in some way or other and have become prisoners within the American army. Prisoners of War are different. They are the enemy who have been captured by the Americans and British'.

There had been the Italian prisoners of war. Susan puzzled over what her mother had said, 'They are Prisoners of War because they fought on the side of Germany the enemy.' Susan remembers them, sitting under the trees, keeping out of the heat, and shielding themselves from flies by wearing large raffia sombreros they had made. They were cheerful people, relaxed and not at all war like. Susan cannot make sense of some men being regarded as enemies and others as friends, especially as some of the enemies are friendly and full of good will, whereas some of the earlier American prisoners had been hostile and selfish. Whatever her mother has said, she secretly decides that she likes the short man with kind eyes and the pretty cord slippers he has made.

In the morning Susan walks to the YMCA hall where her mother's busily preparing vegetables. When the child picks up a half carrot and starts nibbling her mother scolds her and tells her it is for the prisoners. She orders her home to get another carrot.

226

As Ivy turns around to watch her go, she notices the slippers inside the doorway.

"Well I'm darned, I wonder where she got these pretty things?" she mutters.

Soon Susan returns and runs into the hall. She blushes because her mother holding up the slippers is saying, "Judging from the colour of your face I don't have to ask where you got these do I?"

"I'm sorry Mummy. I wanted to see if they were wearing kilts and playing bagpipes."

Ivy's cross mouth twitches, as if about to break into laughter.

"You are a bad girl going there. I do not know what your father will have to say about it." "The prisoner who made the slippers asked me to bring them: to see if you could buy them from him for half a crown. He was not nasty; he had a nice look in his eye like our schoolteacher or vicar or someone like that."

I will have a word with the vicar and see if he can suggest to the camp commander that prisoners make things and sell them towards the cost of their keep and special extras. If I judge the prisoner to be of sound character, I might even keep quiet about these and give him the half crown. You are far too young to make sound judgements and that's why you should always listen to us."

Susan might have objected but as things are turning out better than expected she meekly mutters "Yes Mummy."

"Alright, but it's still a cheek for him to have asked you. Mind you they are nice slippers"

***

Around five O'clock Bert Swift has just arrived home. After a day of work on the Fellsbury village roads he is feeling tired and dusty. Following a speedy wash, he quickly changes into clean clothes and gladly sits at the table. Unable to wait, he plasters his food with piccalilli, and tucks into a huge plate of bangers and mash. By the time Ivy and the two sisters are seated, Bert is half way through the sausages. Rachel, Susan's younger sister, pulls a face because her father is swamping his mash with even more piccalilli. Her mother lightly cuffs her around the ear.

"Your father's taste might not be your taste, so there's no need to pull a face" she emphasises indignantly.

227

"I've one good bit o' news for ee" Bert says as he looks up at Ivy.

"What's that?"

"A maid 'oo works on the farm at Fellsbury, well I spoke to 'er when she was in a spot o' bother. The cart 'orse was so old 'ee snuffed it 'tween shafts of t'cart. She said the farmer kept the old faithful going instead of putting him out to graze. She was fair upset I tell 'ee, she regarded the beast as a companion and friend."

"Bert that doesn't sound good news to me" Ivy retorts, exasperated.

"Naw, naw, I went on talking."

"What's new" Susan giggles to her sister.

Even though Ivy's hand stings the edge of her ear she fails to suppress a fit of giggles, and must leave the table. She continues to listen to the drone of her father's voice say "She plays the pianer and can manage church organ too. The organist at Fellsbury church gives 'er lessons; well, she pays for them of course. I mean I reckon she can 'elp us out. She said she would, she's got a push bike and can ride down 'ere. She aims to get a motorbike one day."

"That wouldn't be right, a girl riding a motorbike to church or anywhere else come to that."

"Dunno 'bout that. There is that school teacher Miss Frances rides all the way to Cornworthy, and she 'as been riding since before the war; 1934 it was, when she was twenty-one."

Annoyed about being swept into idle conversation, Ivy finds herself snapping, "Well it is only three weeks or so we need 'elp, I mean help. I hope she really can play and that you have not been talking a load of nonsense. The vicar wants the prisoners to attend the Sunday morning services. He says now we are winning the war we should be looking to the future and to mending broken relationships."

"I cannot see that 'appening in a hurry. I 'ad a chance to speak t' vicar of Fellsbury; my 'ee looked 'alf starved and miserable at first, but once I'd taken plunge to talk to 'ee 'eee was all right. 'Ee said young maid was competent, 'id her light under a bushel, 'elps with Sunday school teaching too. 'Is words were, 'With reluctance we can spare 'er a few weeks.'"

"Good, that puts my mind to rest. Our vicar said the prisoners will be giving back to Britain through their labour and that we need to forgive and see them as people."

"Well, we do not need 'ee to tell us that but we are lucky 'ee 'as that attitude. Us 'as seen for ourselves 'ow poor devils are caught up in the thick of things, just like us: there ain't any Nazi's in our little camp, just ordinary chaps, hopeful of a better future."

***

Sunday soon arrives; Alfred sits at the back of the church, alongside his fellow prisoners. During prayers, a short man in the choir chuckles because all he can see of the prisoner, of similar height to himself, is a pair of hands propped on top of the pew book ledge. Now the vicar asks everyone to stand and as the chorister gets up, he looks directly at Alfred's eye. They smile at their similar stature and for a moment forget national identities. Ellen looking in the organ mirror notices the chorister smile to someone. She traces the direction of his gaze and to her surprise finds it's directed at one of the prisoners of war. Seeing the funny side, she also smiles. Now she notices the prisoner gaze at the beautiful stained-glass window, colourfully depicting Mary at the tomb where she is turning toward the one, she believes to be the gardener. He has just called out 'Mary' and in response she is answering 'Raboni.' Ellen wonders if the German is thinking the same as her; that Mary recognizes Jesus for who he truly is and that is what needs to happen between the English and the German prisoners.

Alfred recalls the idea that there is never complete blackness in bad situations. Witold had mentioned their mother having described violet and indigo as the edge of the rainbow of light, hope and resurrection. He perceives the crucifixion as an indigo event because God entered the deep blackness to change it into a rainbow of resurrection. He admires the glass images of the angels at the tomb and how the sunlight shines and transports the colours along the aisle and onto the faces of the worshippers. He does not realize how, for a few seconds Ellen notices something divine in his blue eyes.

***

As things evolve, she is asked to play the organ a further four weeks. At the end of each service the short prisoner with blue

229

eyes manages to convey a few stilted sentences to her. On the Sunday he knows to be her last week, he cautiously says, "I am Alfred; what your name?"

"Ellen."

"Nice name, I work near big prisoner camp three miles away to the north. Can me, I, letter write you?"

"Well-um-yes—alright, if you'd like to."

"Here, pencil and small piece paper. You write house and road, Jah?"

"Jah, yes alright" she replies.

He looks pleased and as she looks into his eyes, she feels she's always known him.

***

At the camp Stephan slams the second-hand newspaper on the table. His voice resounds, explosive: "Well now I know what the true ending to Siegfried is: He and Brynhilde remained on the rock. Having fought through fire to get there, there was no way for Siegfried to change his course and so, on that hypothetical rock, Hitler and Eva Braun were married a brief time before committing suicide. Just as the lives of Mussolini and his lover ended tragically so has the life of this so-called leader, Hitler and his woman infatuated by him more than the many Germans who believed and trusted him."

Karl understands, but he also sees how perplexed everyone is. "Hitler and Eva Brown have committed suicide along with other Nazi leaders. There was no way out for them, and to be quite honest I am thoroughly relieved" he conveys.

***

Soon a buzz spreads throughout the camp; accordingly faces relax as prisoners look towards a brighter future and not back to the dark abyss of the recent past. The ache in Karl's heart lessens a little because some justice and recompense for the lost lives of loved ones has come at last. He reflects on the fact that whereas England bombed the beautiful and treasured people of Dresden it would never have happened under the rule of a German of sound belief and principles.

230

Chapter 29
Fellsbury

Ellen and her father, George, are fearful about escalating heated opinions amongst the villagers, regarding retribution. The idea that someone has produced, of the hand of God being responsible for pulling the trigger that eliminated the man who indirectly caused the death of their village lads, is rejected by Ellen. 'God is bigger than that' she had replied. 'He understands the lost child deep within the fanatical adult. He alone can judge and measure the actions of everyone.' She imagines her brother walk along the path, to the door where he rattles the handle. With a smile he says, *'Father, Ellen, I am home, and I am safe. I am starving have you something good to Ellen eat.'*

"Oh yes Georgie there's a stew on with dumplings" she whispers. Tears stream down her face because Georgie isn't home. The week before the arrival of the telegram, her nightmare had informed her of events surrounding his death. The telegram had read, 'Missing presumed dead'. She knew its real meaning 'Body blown to pieces; not accessible.' In the nightmare she had seen Georgie blown into the air amidst fire and debris, and she had heard him call "Ellen, Father--I love you--tell Maudie."

***

Ellen feels despondent about not having heard from her Prisoner of War with the divine look in his blue eyes. Hearing the postman's footsteps on the path she is hopeful. As she walks to the door the letter box clatters; two envelopes drop onto the mat. One, addressed to her has been scripted neatly in italics. The other, addressed to her father, is in Daisy's sloping script. Ellen's glad about the letters arriving simultaneously; her father, still in bed, would have heard the postman. Tentatively she places her aunt's letter on the sideboard in the kitchen, and retreats to her room. Hastily she removes the George V stamp. As she opens the envelope she mutters, "Several weeks have passed, I wonder what Alfred has to say. Will he still feel that our attraction to each other is the real thing?"

Within her heart she knows their love is genuine; being a builder of heavenly things she is already building a thousand hopes founded upon the spiritual moment of their first encounter. For a moment, as she unfolds the page, she wonders if he will have met another girl.

"Oh no" she whispers as she takes out the letter written in German.

Frustrated she paces up and down the room until she remembers that Hilda, will be visiting the day after tomorrow. She takes up her pen and writes to Hilda with a request that she bring with her the small German dictionary her father has in his study. She ends her letter with the words, 'I hope you won't mind this request as I know how upset you are that your father's ship hasn't been located for a while.'

On Thursday Hilda and Ellen painstakingly translate the letter:

"Dearest Ellen"

"Wow! DEAREST" Hilda teases

'My luck has changed in that I am to work on the same farm as you at Fellsbury. It seems I shall have a chance to work alongside you. Dear Ellen what about the future, surely it is promising? I have limited grasp of the English language but in camp I am endeavouring to follow a course. Therefore, dear Ellen, it is possible that we will understand each other with time and effort. I am deeply sorry that I am a prisoner of war.'

"That makes me want to cry" says Hilda.

"Hilda, don't go making comments, I'm trying to work out the next bit-- ah I've got it."

'But this tough time will end. Dear Ellen, please do not have any regrets or imagine that I have any. If people oppose us, we must stand up for each other, we do not want to honour no action'.

"Coo he's a bit forward isn't he seeing as you've only just got to know each other?"

"I suppose when there is a language barrier you want your message to be as clear as possible. Up to Victorian times they sent their messages with flowers, each kind of flower meant something special."

232

"I like his phrase 'we do not want to honour no action.' It sounds gallant and reminds me of the prayer asking for forgiveness not just for what we have done wrong but more significantly for the things we have failed to do. If God puts love in our hearts, we should not ignore it despite the war or any other obstacle. I understand what he means."

"Well put like that, he sounds quite romantic and thoughtful, regardless of being a prisoner of war. He is certainly your knight in shining armour."

"I sense his armour is the right spiritual kind and that's all that truly matters."

"Now let me continue translating. You need to get your violin out for the next bit."

"Stop teasing. Come on what does he say?"

"Dear Ellen it is with a heavy heart I tell you I have no parents or relatives in Germany."

"Yes, I overheard him answer some questions the vicar asked 'Have you parents in Germany?' Alfred replied 'Nein, mother died when me ten. All areas bombed in Germany; not heard from any of my family. Have niece somewhere in London, but don't know where.'

"Bit like you losing your mother when you were that age. Anyway, I will get on with my efforts in translating, so do not interrupt, so that I can jot down the meaning of it. It will take another ten minutes or so." Patiently Ellen waits---

"Here goes--'I prefer to stay with my fellow prisoners here in Great Britain and you dear Ellen of all women, "Phew get your smelling salts--lie down."

"Come on Hilda, don't tease, what does he say?"

"--I would gladly take for my future love? I write this from my heart in all truth and you dear Ellen think it over, for the future? I ask and beseech you to give your answer soon. I send a thousand greetings dear Ellen and many greetings to your dear Father.

--and signed Alfred."

***

George's voice suddenly booms from the kitchen, "What are you two girls chatting about? Come on Ellen there's work to be done. Is there any milk left?"

"Yes father. I will get it from the larder. There is a letter in the kitchen for you."

Hilda gasps and with a grin Ellen casts a sideways glance, and calls, "Looks like Auntie's writing." Her father calls back "Well I can't see it, and if it's addressed to me, you shouldn't be trying to work out who it's from."

He's always bear headed after he's been to the Jubilee Arms the previous evening but I agree with him" Ellen whispers. Raising the volume, she calls out, "It's on the sideboard behind the flower pot."

Painfully George limps across the kitchen to retrieve the letter.

"This gout makes me feel like an old man before my time" he moans.

Ellen, now in the kitchen, stops herself saying, 'You're well over retirement age.' She recalls the struggle getting him to the Plymouth VE day celebrations. A casual glance at her note on the calendar informs her that a fortnight has passed since the celebrations of Tuesday 8th May. On Plymouth Hoe, alongside Daisy they had waved their flags, but unlike her, they had not expected Great Britain to be returning to the state of patriotic idealism.

"Father I can hardly believe two weeks have passed since we saw Aunty Daisy."

"Yes, things will never be the same again."

Ellen had noticed his reluctant waving of the flag Daisy had provided. He had only waved it for her sake, knowing in his heart he would never see his son again.

Now with his one good eye he gazes skywards. His thoughts oscillate between his deceased wife, and his son lost in action. His dear wife would never return to him from a time zone between the two great wars. Sensing his thoughts Ellen stands close until the revered moment has passed.

***

Ellen retreats indoors whilst George remains in the garden to watch the blossom on the apple trees. Distractedly he experiences healing properties within the trees. Their simple being has a timeless quality that quells fears and hushes echoes of war. He finds himself reflecting on Ellen's nightmare; how he had heard her incessant screaming in between her desperate cries, "Georgie, Georgie."

He had gone into her room to gently waken her. When she knew he was standing there she had told him about burning debris falling on Georgie and of him flying because of an explosion.

Some two weeks Later a telegram had arrived, and he knew that Ellen's experience had been of Georgie's last moments on Earth. He reasoned that for that to have happened, Georgie was alive in spirit. Even so he missed him. Always he would wonder how Ellen had seen all that she had at the time of his death that was disclosed later when the telegram arrived. In his mind, heart and soul he thanks Georgie for connecting with them and he mentally reads again the news article and telegram how HMS Diamond transporting members of the 16th Anti-Aircraft Battery, Royal Artillery had been blown up off the island of Crete.

Tears well up as he recalls the words, 'we are sorry to inform you that' "*--Oh Georgie, Georgie*"— 'is missing - presumed dead.'

George enters a spiritual conversation with his son, '*Dearest Georgie you were a determined soldier and a good son, a good and caring man. Through Ellen's nightmare you have told us about your moment of death and that you love us. You have shown us that it is not the end. Fancy, you remembering that your mother and I used to attend spiritualist meetings. Well, you have got through and that is enough for us. I hope you are in paradise now, with your mother and all those who we have loved and who are with us no more. We shall miss you, but you must go onward son, follow the path our Lord has set before you. Do not worry about Maude, we will tell her. I will value any grandchildren I may have in the future because somewhere a part of you will be within them.*

He must wipe away a tear. *Yes, you were a soldier but yours was the death of a sailor on an ammunitions ship; aye, near Crete where I too journeyed as a young sailor. Did you think of the tales of my travels and how Lord Kitchener came on board- I dare say you did?*'

***

235

As Ellen comes out into the garden she affectionately enquires, "Dad, what are you thinking?"

"I was thinking back to my navy days in the First World War. They wanted me to be a lieutenant and to go on to be a captain, but I liked being chief shipwright."

"Yes, we all know you like working with wood; you never stop, and neither should you. You are good; my music cabinet is as strong as the day you made it. On the other hand, you should have aimed higher, especially as you were awarded medals and mentioned in dispatches for bravery, weren't you? Didn't that inspire you?"

"Awards were won by saving lives and risking one's own, I had to weigh it up and I needed family life. I retired at the right time. Besides when I saved that poor captain by pulling him through the automatic door of the sinking ship, I witnessed his foot being crushed and severed. It occurred to me that if I was in his situation there may not have been someone there to save me. I had a decision to make, and I made the right one. I wanted to see you and Georgie grow up; I had already missed out with my two older children. Besides my records might have been checked and it discovered I was under age when I joined."

"That might have upset the apple cart" Ellen answers and hearing saucepans clattering to the floor, she instantly races indoors. With cream from the milk pan dripping from his whiskers the culprit shoots out the house.

"Oh, you naughty cat, I expect you'll have the whole lot now because I shall have to make some more."

"Not to worry there is half a bucket of milk from our friends down the road. I put it in the outhouse yesterday evening" George remarks with a laugh.

With forced optimism Ellen replies, "Well perhaps Fluffy's done us a favour, as that pan of milk might have been forgotten, and gone sour if all this hadn't happened."

Momentarily, bemused at the fiery look in his daughter's lovely brown eyes; George looks up, to the top of a tree, and listens to the song of the chaffinch resounding through the rustling leaves. He imagines a younger Georgie as a young child, running from far down the garden, coming nearer and nearer, into his arms:

236

The boy looks up, smiles cheekily or tearfully looks up after scraping his knees.

'Sometimes I tell him tales of my navy days and he shows interest.'

A precious tear rolls down George's face, and for a moment he feels his son in adult form, close by, and hears him say, *'Come on Dad it can't be that bad. Cheer up.'*

Pretending to not notice her father's distress, Ellen goes to the top of the garden to cut cabbages.

For a while George meditates on the son he will never see again in this life. He realizes he must never lose Ellen, as in a sense she's all he has left. He mulls over the idea that he may have been too protective of his two younger children. Ellen had been ten and Georgie fourteen at the time of their mother's death. After that Daisy had accommodated Harriette and supported her, and seen through her education at Portvedon Grammar School.

Bertram had already started an excellent job as carpenter and gardener, at Montegate House. George pictures Bertram's riverside cottage; one of a row of cottages belonging to Montegate estate and surmises how fortunate Bertram and his wife were to live in such a location for a modest rent.

George realises that within Georgie and Ellen he had seen the embodiment of the last living link with his dear wife. With a sigh he thinks *'I wish the older children did not feel so rejected. I wish they could see that Georgie never had, and Ellen does not have, that other speciality as the first children of our married life.* He tries to convince himself-- *my sea faring days were woven into family life--'* but he partially acknowledges how his absence during their formative years may have distanced him from them.

Then, as now, the vital role model of Harriett's life is Daisy. He had long accepted how it had happened and wished his daughter understood that he had never stopped loving her. George attempts to fathom Bertram who has become a silent individual.

He rarely speaks to anyone and when he does it is the odd word or grunt when he is in the middle of his carpentry. I must investigate the products of his trade to see his mind and heart. I wish I'd been more at home for him when he was a small boy.

Somehow, he seems to have learned my trade without fully relating to me.

I forfeited more than I realised by being in the navy. Yet it was a wholesome way to support them. The pension has come in useful. Much in life happens through circumstance. If my dear Lily had not been in poor health we would not have moved to the country. In a sense everything that has happened (and will happen here) exists because she suffered. In a sense her suffering was a gift, an offering to me and our children and their children. One thing I do not want is rifts--for my dear wife does not deserve that. Her memory should be cherished for ever. Ellen is special too, a gift from my dear wife in more than one sense of the word.

Hearing the drone of a solitary motorbike travelling along the road, George looks out of the window. As he stares into the middle distance, he recalls how he nearly lost Ellen at eighteen months. The hospital doctors had told Lily to take the child home to die. She had meningitis they said; there was nothing they could do. He remembered Lily bringing her home. Defiantly she had declared, "I will pray hard and find someone to cure her." 'She was not going to be beaten: she remembered a lecture she had heard a month or so earlier, presented by a missionary doctor who had worked in Africa. By using a new procedure, the doctor had saved the lives of several children who had contracted meningitis. Are you certain he is qualified?' I asked.

"Oh yes SHE is" your mother answered.

The tabby cat pads across the room and jumps up onto the table where George is seated. "Now Fluffy, you know you're not allowed on the table" he says whilst placing her on his lap. The cat settles, allowing him to resume his day dreaming.

He recalls how Lily, undeterred, had knocked on the doors of eleven church members, before trekking to Charlie the chemist, to find out the doctor's address. At first Charlie had been reluctant to disclose details but had relented when he heard my Lily's explanation. In his heart George apologises to Georgie for having sent him to Daisy's for the night, without explanation.

The doctor, a tiny featherweight lady, had arrived at the house that evening. George recalls how reluctant he'd been to authorise the delicate widely unknown procedure. He regrets underestimating his late wife's courage and little Ellen's link to

238

that strength. Even now he winces as he recalls the doctor cutting through Ellen's skull and brain membrane. It had seemed endless as it had to be performed in several places and with risk of damaging the brain. God had certainly watched over them:

'Aye Georgie, as your little sister lay sleeping, close to death, the poison gradually drained away. Come mid-morning she was asking for food. Privately we'd wept for joy, and I expect you know all that from where you are now. Those are the kind of things that matter where you are, aren't they?

The doctor came to see little Ellen for the following three, four, days. Do you know, that good lady doctor, would not take payment, but your mother insisted on making a generous donation for the mission medical team and their work.

I believe that close encounter with death gave your sister second- sight and a deep awareness of the spirituality of others. You two were always close and you always will be. Do not go thinking that because you have had to move on you will not be close. Long after I am gone, she will remember you. One day she will tell her own children about you, she will never forget you and one day we will meet again.'

After a pause he says, "Hilda seems to be getting over her injury a little." With a happy look in her eyes Ellen looks up and answers her father, "Yes. I can understand what she says now. That's why I encouraged her to talk a lot yesterday."

"Oh well. I am sorry I scolded the two of you for wasting time chattering. We would best get on with finishing our breakfast now."

"It is a wonder they were able to reconstruct the jaw with so much bone having been blasted away by that wretched bomb. There are still psychological wounds; she leaps six feet if she hears a loud noise."

"Well, thankfully you have your friend back. It was a worrying time when no one knew if she was alive or dead. Thankfully, her husband, having trained as a gunner, has a sound job in the navy."

"What on the coast here?"

"Yes, and since then he's been away at sea."

"It is a worrying time for him and her mother, and a darn good thing the girl got married. With a disfigurement, things might have been more awkward."

"But they have been friends since they were thirteen. Besides if people fall in love they fall in love, it is as simple as that. I do not think looks, nationality or anything else come into the picture."

Her father's mouth is open as if about to start a debate. With quick decision Ellen opens the door and skims out of the house

"I'd best be off now or I shall be late for work. See you later" she calls.

"Well, I'm darned" George mutters and laughs, and thinks how beautiful she is. Simultaneously he feels sad about her having been without her mother for many years. He knows that compared to how things might have been, his best as a single parent has been a poor show. He reflects on how good Daisy has been to the children, and simultaneously laments her townie attitude and concern with social standing.

"Status alone.... of no true significance" he mutters to himself.

He appreciates how Daisy used her seam mistress' skills to see his daughter well dressed. He chuckles as he recalls Ellen cringing whenever forcibly enshrouded in a new smart outfit. No sooner had Daisy left than the child would take off the new clothes, put on her old loose dress, and run bare footed and free as her mother had encouraged.

He regrets not continuing his wife's camping holidays at Revelstoke on the coast, but knows how unbearable it would have been without her. Attempting to be positive he recalls how the coats Daisy made for Ellen had lasted, to be passed on three times over. Forgetting himself he comments aloud, "At least Ellen appreciated warm outfits during harsh winters even though, much to Daisy's annoyance, she was careless in finding her matching gloves and hat."

He wishes Daisy had not been quite so professional, and considers that had she been an amateur dressmaker, she may have met Ellen half way. He smiles, because in other ways Daisy has been an encourager, allowing Ellen to develop her artistic talent. She had kept her promise to Lily and had sent Ellen and her sister to music lessons. Now George thinks of recent events and Daisy's enquiries about making a legal claim against Monguet fashion journal.

Ellen, as shop assistant and window dresser at Pophams, had designed a dress. Without her knowledge her sketch had been sent by a senior staff member to the fashion magazine. It had been accepted, made, and modelled and a photo had appeared in the magazine. George recalled Daisy's fury as with determined look she had said, 'Don't you realize? If I do not do something about it, it will be like slamming the door in her face on her true career. She has a skill for fashion design.' George had remained silent, because in his mind he sees the country girl with her hair flowing free as she walks across fields seeing to country matters. She would be someone else if she left the animals and hills behind. She could never drink enough of the beauty of nature and rush home to capture it on canvas. He recalls Lily's mention of a cousin named Philip who had become a famous, English-impressionist artist.

He cannot envisage Ellen working for a high-class magazine and he knows she continues to grieve for her brother. Thankfully, she has starting talk about the pain Georgie would have felt. With tears in her big brown eyes, she looked up and in torment explained, 'I felt it too Father.' For once he had produced a sensible answer, "If that was the case then you took away some of his pain." Even so he mulls over the idea that it may have been so.

Reproachfully he asks himself whether he should have related exciting stories of his navy days to his little son. Had his influence prompted his decision to enlist in the army. His one consolation is the immense enthusiasm Georgie had to see the world.

Slowly he places on the table, photos and cards that have painfully become icons written by the hand of a very precious life gone from sight.

***

He spends the afternoon mending a few chairs in his garden shed and when finished hangs the almost empty glue pot on a low branch of the apple tree. He decides he will tomorrow make some glue from fish bones simmering in the metal pot. Under the

241

apple tree he sits down in the wicker chair, lights up his pipe, and dreams of Georgie.

"Father is everything all right? You seem miles away."

"Do I? Oh, never mind that. Can you get us some spuds from up the garden and see how many eggs you can get from the chicken run?" Ellen catches a whiff of the fish bones, screws up her face and says, "Coo have you run out of glue again. The smell's disgusting."

"Well, it's a job I'll be doing tomorrow, when you are out, so there's no need to worry."

A few hours later they enjoy boiled new potatoes and tripe. George, who is not too fond of tripe, comments that is not so bad with plenty of fresh parsley in the cooking.

Chapter 30
Hoeing Mangoes

In the glow of dawn Ellen catches her breath as the velvety sky turns pink and pastel blue. Five men of varying height are busy hoeing mangoes on the brow of the hill. She feels that God the creator is present, impressing the scene into her soul. Taking the lead, a tall man, puts his hands to his eyes, as he looks at wispy clouds blowing across the perfect sky. She wonders if he also wonders if the day will remain favourable.

Closer proximity enables her to observe the second worker, a youth in his teens to all accounts. A well -built, muscular man is third in line, and a fourth man works with the ease of an experienced man, who knows the land and farming methods. The fifth man, perhaps because he senses her looking on, stops working, and looks in her direction. At closer proximity she recognizes Alfred by the discreet wave of his hand. Forgetting all rules, she openly returns his greeting. Momentarily, she wobbles on her bicycle but quickly regains her balance.

Mid- morning, Ellen and land girl Tamsin come across the five men returning from the fields. With eyes fixed on the distant sea Tamsin walks past them. Ellen, on the other hand, lifts their spirits with her quick, shy glance, and acknowledging smile.

As the days pass and war merges into peacetime, the farmer begins to slacken rules; Germans and land girls work alongside each other. Tamsin, being an official land army girl, persists in ignoring the Prisoners of War. The farmer, fearful she might report him for his slackening of rules, sends her to milk the cows. He asks Ellen to hold the new fence posts while the prisoners nail up fencing. No sooner has she agreed than he confidently leaves. Over the next few hours Ellen has time to study each man as an individual. She notices in Karl's warm brown eyes a longing for home, family, and friends for whom he is concerned. The youngest prisoner of war tells her he is eighteen, and because of that he has been nick named 'Booby.' The thick set muscular man, Josef, carefully deals with his tasks; he is considerate in his dealings with others. Occasionally he is cautious because he thinks there is a strong possibility they will be reported for working together. He attempts to convey to Ellen the risk she is taking communicating with Alfred. Then, when he notices the sincerity and love in their eyes, he holds back a little. The farming skills and honest direct approach of the older man Heinrich, has established him as a father figure.

***

A brief time after the fence is finished Tamsin approaches. The men's faces show they half understand what Ellen is saying, "Hello Tamsin, do you know I have learned their names. This is Heinrich and that means Henry, the same as Farmer Farringdon's Christian name."

Tamsin's tone is hostile as she retorts, "Ellen you shouldn't be comparing German prisoners to English people, especially as Heinrich is a mere worker."

Bravely Ellen retorts, "Yes, a man who is allowed no say in the matter, and who demonstrates self- worth by the way he works."

***

Over the weeks, as they work alongside each other, the bond between Alfred and Ellen grows stronger. Ellen's heart pulsates over and over with Alfred's name: in his eyes she reads the return of love. She does not know that from time to time he thinks of Erika. Neither does she know he has come to realise that Erika would not have wished him to be bound to the past.

Alfred remembers the tone of Erika's voice within his soul as finally he had had to walked away from the ruined air raid shelter - 'find *one who will love you-one who will not envy your memory of our love for each other-- her voice resounding in my heart could not have been some superficial imagining: with the ears of the soul, I truly did hear her; that is how I knew she had died. What I do know is that she most certainly did not die in spirit.*'

Suddenly he is aware of Heinrich's voice urging "Keep up with the planting Alfred."

As Alfred looks up, Heinrich notices his face relax, he can see how he appreciates being able to work alongside four companions. They are glad to be away from the confines of camp; out in the fresh air with views of spectacular countryside.

Four-year-old John has come out from the farm house to ask Heinrich to show him how to plant. This gives Alfred time to catch up. Fascinated, the boy watches Heinrich punch some holes in an empty cigar tin. "Hold out your hand John" he says.

Trustingly the boy holds out his hand; carefully Heinrich places some tiny seeds in his palm.

"Now put them in the tin for me –Good- keep the tin flat and shake it from side to side -here let me help." With wonderment the child comprehends how the seeds are distributed evenly along the furrow.

"In autumn, these fields will be full of curly greens," Heinrich comments in broken English. He laughs at John's puzzled expression and playfully ruffles his fair hair.

In his native tongue he says to his companions, "Ah, if only every human being had the outlook of a child, we all would live in harmony, and there would be peace on earth."

Alfred reflects how working on the farm has given them some insight into human nature. Unanimously they are at ease with Ellen and recognise in her expression, how she regards them as fellow humans, rather than foreign enemies. Alfred appreciates her attitude of mind and soul, in harmony with his own convictions. He considers how Christ embraced all people's as one, belonging to the one creator Father.

From time to time, they must tolerate vindictive attitudes. For the sake of putting a few extra pennies in her own pocket, the two day a week farmhouse assistant Marcia, has bought cheap, substandard food.

Ellen passing the barn, witnesses the poignant truth of what Alfred has told her. Such is her love for him, she feels the sting of Marcia's common sharp tone,"They love würst, so I have given them the würst--cheap uncooked sausages-ha- ha- ha."

Bleatingly the nasal tone of Gerald, the farmhand's voice replies, "What d'yu mean?"

"Würst is the German name for sausage you idiot."

"Oh, Oh I get it."

Ellen's face burns in the wake of their laughter. She wants to go into the barn and give them a piece of her mind, but dare not. She should tell Farmer Farringdon that their 'daily' so liked by his wife, has a selfish streak? She focusses her mind on the

245

prisoners and why they have felt unwell. She wills herself to stay put, because she realizes that if she crossed either of the farm hands, she could lose her job.

"Tamsin the land girl is late, but it would be useless confiding in her, as her sense of right and wrong relates to state rather than to the one above all states, and to whom all states belong" she whispers.

***

Back at camp that evening, the men exchange news of events with prisoners who have been working alongside men from other camps. A prisoner, who knows Marcia from his encounters at Blueberry Farm, where she works as home help on Thursdays and Fridays, refuses to tolerate anyone's criticism. Emphatically he says, "She is a sensible woman who gives me plenty of food and love when she comes to Blueberry Farm on the days I work there. She also comes to Chadstone on one of the days I work there."

There is a serious look in Josef's eyes as he retorts "We are of the same opinion that she is not a nice woman. More than likely what is on offer is not genuine love; you could end up in serious trouble."

"Rubbish-and considering my circumstance- it will have to do. Have any of you managed to find a woman?"

Alfred is silent, for he knows how Manfred would taunt him about having fallen in love.

***

A few days later Ellen smuggles fresh bread from home to the men. The bland diet helps them recover from appalling stomach cramps.

One evening, when Ellen must steer around her father's criticism, regarding repetition of stew, she emphasises that she has varied the type of meat and vegetables.

"It all tastes more or less the same to me" he replies.

"Well, it is easier for me to prepare meat and vegetables on Sunday. I feel tired during the week after a hard day's work."

"Oh well I suppose I will have to put up with it and be thankful for small mercies. Come on you are not eating much."

"It really is enough for me Dad."

246

After the meal, when her father's gone into another room, Ellen stealthily slips into the pantry to fill a large container with yesterday's cold stew. Cautiously she lifts it into her detached bicycle basket. Whilst firmly securing the buckles of the lid she decides she will rise early next morning to secure the basket, onto the bike.

***

Over the course of numerous days, the men look forward to seeing their helper. Occasionally, when the family and farmhands are away distributing food to markets and camps, they heat the stew. This is managed on an open bonfire, regularly smouldering with ash from rubbish burning.

Whenever Marcia and the farmhand are present, the men accept raw sausages, pretend to eat them, and later throw them to the hungry farm dog and cats.

One by one they steal a hasty moment for receiving a bowl of cold but delicious stew. Always last, Alfred gladly uses the time to absorb more details about Ellen's life. In simple language they discuss various issues. Today he reaffirms a strong connection, "You, me, both very young when our mothers die." In an articulate voice, and with much facial expression to emphasise meaning, Ellen replies, "Your brother died in Morocco in the French foreign legion? My brother died a few years ago, off the island of Crete. The ammunitions ship he was on was blown up."

"Me, very, very, sorry dear Ellen; my fiancé killed by a bomb; she was, how you say in a safe shelter."

"You mean an air raid shelter? I did not know you had been engaged. I am sorry, I did not know. When was it?"

"Nearer the beginning of the krieg; I mean war. Does it worry you that I was engaged?"

"No."

"That's good; makes me very happy."

***

Soon summer stretches into autumn. Because the harvest has been gathered Farmer Farringdon currently requires only two prisoners of war. He chooses Heinrich for his knowledge of farming, and Josef for his strength and dexterity. He also admires their cooperative attitude and ability to see tasks through. After

247

Farmer Farringdon has left Alfred grasps Ellen's hand. "What are we to do now?" she asks.

As he looks into her expressive brown eyes his heart pounds with anxiety. Assuring her, he promises to write to her regularly. Inwardly he is concerned that he might not be able to see her again, or that someone else might take her from him. He notices Heinrich leave to fetch water, and sees two prisoners preoccupied with the tractor. Instinctively words tumble forth, "Will you be my wife?"

For a moment Ellen's eyes widen with surprise, but she understands the difficult circumstance that has prompted such a frank approach.

"Perhaps, one day: you know I love you" she wisely replies. Her tone conveys that she is doubtful that circumstance will provide opportunity for them to meet.

With care she explains "I'm anxious that my father might get upset if letters keep arriving, especially if I won't let him know who they are from-- and if I did tell him, I know he wouldn't accept things at present."

Having just returned from completing a task, Heinrich catches the last snippet of conversation. He smiles and with understanding comments, "You mean much to each other. I become postman for you, all right?"

There is a musical lilt to Ellen's voice as she answers, "Oh thank you Heinrich, thank you."

Alfred sighs with relief because Heinrich's approval feels like parental consent.

***

A month later Ellen has not heard from Alfred until, on December 20th Heinrich hands her a letter. She makes an excuse to go to the barn where she eagerly reads:

My dear Ellen--the best and greet and kiss from camp sends you darling, your Alfred. How are you? I am very well. I hope you are very well my darling. I am very sorry that I must finish the work at Farmer Farringdon's. It has been a very nice time or not my sweetheart?

I think of you every time and shall never forgotten you my dear. I love you very much. I shall be happy and gay, if are both together. I hope the next time. But it is dangerous for us both.

248

We got plenty of time. Did you read that piece in the newspaper from a German POW, and an English girl from the woman army? (That is nothing for us dear). I hope Mr Farringdon like to have me next year. And then our lovely time come again. If you like to see myself you inform me before. If you got a place, you give letter to Heinrich. But shut your mouth and keep open your eyes. Now I thank you very much for the tin of cocoa and the five cigarettes.

I wish you and your family merry Christmas. Goodbye my darling.

Ellen thinks his English has not improved sufficiently for him to have said 'Keep open your eyes open and hold your counsel for you don't know who can trust.' She wonders if she might send him a cartoon of herself with a surprised expression, but changing her mind she sends him cartoons of himself. She adds a few words that will not disclose her identity in the event of the letter being discovered.

***

A few days later, Heinrich hands Alfred an envelope. With great excitement he opens it and takes out the hand decorated Christmas card. He loves Ellen's drawings of holly and bells. Now he notices each bell has a letter and the whole peal of bells spells 'm-a-r-r-y' after which 'Christmas' has been added. No letter is enclosed, but he understands 'marry' to be a message rather than a mistake. There are two hand drawings of him in caricature in the envelope. The first makes him exceptionally tall and the smaller picture, in proportion, has the caption, 'Alfred the Great.' He laughs because Ellen has captured his stance and facial expression to a tee. When he shows the drawing to his friends, they roll about laughing. At this moment Manfred arrives and says with annoyance, "What are you lot laughing at?"

Josef explains "Not you. Alfred has shown us some cartoons of himself."

"Let me see."

"Well, here you are."

"I suppose they are funny. Who drew them?"

"A friend back in Barony. Since then, I have kept them in my pocket and I thought because it is Christmas, we could do with cheering up."

249

***

Over the weeks Josef and Heinrich become familiar with village life. Snow and ice cover the land and they are asked to stay at the farm for a time. On Sundays they are permitted to go to church and on those occasions pick up snippets about the war. People often repeat the tale of paper money and various official papers blowing over Fellsbury after a bombing raid in which the large department store Dingles, and a nearby bank, had been hit. Josef and Heinrich overhear Mrs Farringdon say to Farmer Miles from West Fellsbury, "It was a pity they knew the bank note numbers, otherwise we'd all be rich."

Several weeks later Heinrich and Josef can recognize various villagers. They realise that the man they had seen, one sunny autumn day, walking along the cliff path is the vicar and he lives in the vicarage near the farm. They also recognize a lean lady who walks past the vicarage daily on her way to Montegate House, where she works as house keeper. Whereas they've never have been allowed to visit the house, they know from Ellen's description that it is a small mansion. Her older brother works there, primarily as a carpenter, but also, when needed, as a gardener in the extensive gardens.

On Sunday, the following week, at the top of Church Road they find themselves walking alongside an old man called Jo. He lives in a house called Marconi. He kindly answers their questions about the village and its inhabitants. They notice the butler of Fellsbury House drive past, with his passengers Sir Malcolm and lady Holman.

Jo's comment "Snooty bugger can't be bothered to offer anyone a lift" amuses Heinrich and Josef.

There is a long pause before he adds "Course, on second thoughts it mightn't bin 'is decision--seeing 'as he's a member of parrrrliamentttt."

A few days later, because boots are worn, and are letting in the melting slush, Farmer Farringdon sends Heinrich and Josef to the village cobbler. Whereas they have the task of delivering for repair, a bag of footwear ranging from size nines to the small boots of a four-year-old, they also appreciate a new sense of freedom. However, just as the two Germans have begun to relate to the community, a sense of normality abruptly ends. From their

250

locked attic room, they hear angry words between Farmer Farringdon and his wife.

As a team, Heinrich and Josef translate some sentences. The farmer sounds cross with his wife and she with him.

"If you had not spent your time drinking at the pub near Chadstone camp, she would not have had time to get up to mischief with that German bastard. In a way I can understand it happening, because our men are away, or sparsely returning."

Less lenient, his wife replies, "That is not true and she is a grown woman who should be responsible for her own actions. She only comes here two days a week and we have been lumbered with the problem. I enjoy a pint as much as you do. Why–the- hell, should it always be the men who have a pint, and us women made to patiently wait."

"By the way, those two upstairs have got to go, and Marcia can stay here until she's had the baby" Henry emphasises.

"She is not family; I do not want the authorities getting wind of it. They would blame us for negligence. I suppose our Germans will have to leave, even though they are from Steerton rather than Chadstone. Neither of them worked on Blueberry Farm where the trouble started, and is the POW answerable?

"No way of proving it, is there."

Hearing a door slam, Josef and Heinrich immediately feel uncomfortable. The atmosphere of the suddenly silent farm house feels tense. Several hours later Joseph and Heinrich are still awake because they know Marcia's expecting Manfred's baby. They are aware that if news leaks out, all prisoners of war in the area will be treated with contempt. Simply because she was British, Marcia, who had frequently tried to seduce prisoners, would be regarded as an innocent victim.

Chapter 31
The Oak Tree
(1946-1947)

Apart from the occasional hoot of an owl, the April night is still. Alfred, lying flat on his back, looks up through the leafy branches at the phosphorescent moon. The scent of primroses draws his attention so that he notices the intensity of their colour, making them look as if they had dropped to earth from the glowing surface of the moon. From the hedgerow a snuffling sound emerges. Clown- like, a prickly creature, Alfred believes to be a 'hedge-dog,' scuttles across the turf in the direction of the camp. He wonders if his straw effigy remains in place in his bed, and for a moment imagines the angry, red-faced commander discovering it. The drone of a solitary motor bike draws close. He thinks it likely to be Ellen as she hoped to buy a second-hand motor bike.

***

An overgrown gateway looks a suitable place for hiding the motor bike. Ellen rearranges the foliage and when the motor bike's well hidden, heart racing, she cautiously wanders down the moonlit road and across narrow granite-bridge, close to a style. She goes over the style and lightly treads across the moonlit grass. The feel of the cool fresh night air, and the smell of spring, wafting up from the river bank, is alive and vibrant. She hopes her father will be asleep by the time she arrives home. She dreads the thought of having to find excuse for being late. She checks that the letter is still in her pocket and curls her fingers around it. A few days ago, a handful of birthday greetings had shot through the letter box. Having recognized Alfred's handwriting she had retrieved the letter just in time.

As she focuses on finding the spot marked x she wonders if she is allowing her heart to rule her head. She worries that a farmer or local resident will spot her, and assume she has come here for some rendezvous. People might assume her to be having

252

a liaison with a married man. She imagines how things would be if Alfred were not a Prisoner of War:

'Without fear we would meet every day and walk through the village hand in hand. Everyone would smile and over the course of time would ask when we planned to be married. Father would welcome you as a friend. He would see that I love you and that I want to marry you and no other-- I will not abandon God given love for the sake of human rules.'

For a moment she reflects upon the content of Alfred's letter in which he tells her how he yearns for her; for her brown eyes and sweet mouth. She is aware how the language barrier makes him sound bolder than he really is. The carefully scribed words *'I love you very much. I cannot wait the day till I see you'* are impressed upon her heart and soul. A loud whisper makes her jump until she realises that Alfred is calling her, "Ellen, Ellen, I am here, come close my darling. I have missed you so much. How are you?"

"I am very frightened. Thank goodness it is the right tree. The journey was bad enough as I am only just getting used to the motor bike."

"I'm so glad you could come."

"Luckily, Aunty asked me to visit her. I hope father will be sound asleep by now."

"How is he?"

"Variable, his swollen feet play him up and he won't visit the doctor's surgery."

"It is all extremely hard for you, my darling. Look how beautiful the night is, God given. No one here except us, God, and his creation."

In the light of the moon Alfred notices her lovely brown eyes shine with an expression Vermeer captured in his picture of the girl with the pearl ear ring. Leaning against the trunk of the tree he draws her close and enfolds her in his arms. For a moment she's awkward but when he looks into her eyes she relaxes and accepts his kisses. Soon they sit on the grass, whisper their love for each other, and exchange news. An hour slips by, and from time-to-time Ellen corrects Alfred's mispronunciations.

She asks him if he'd like to learn a song and appreciates the relaxed tone of his reply, "That's a nice idea; singing is very good for learning words."

With interest he listens to her 'sotto voce' rendering of a few lines of the popular song, "I see the moon and the moon sees me, under the shade of the old oak tree, shine on the one, the one I love; shine on the one I love."

"The words are true to this night and what a beautiful non-soprano voice you have." "It's a contralto voice."

"Con...tral...to. We shall have to adapt the song as our own."

"Adapt it, change it, why? Oh, you mean adopt."

"Yes. Does adapt mean to change?"

"Yes."

"So that's new wort I've learned."

"Wor 'D' not wort."

"You write more, teach me."

"It would be better if I could teach you in person. It is already 21st April and in this current situation we have so far only had this one chance to meet up. I promise I will write, but you must write to me once a month only; if I receive too many letters father will become suspicious. Until now I've managed to be first to pick up the post."

"Things were easier when Heinrich was our postman."

"I know! Can you get someone to help you with the English? Keep it simple. Then, if father happened to come across one of your letters, he need not know it was from a POW. I am hoping, given time, he will begin to come to terms with Georgie's death."

"I understooned my darling."

"You mean understand. I would best be going and you'd better go back. We have been here more than an hour. I shall keep singing our song."

Holding her in his gaze a moment he cannot resist putting his arms around her and kissing her one more time.

As he looks into her eyes he teasingly replies, "So shall I."

"So shall you what?"

"Keep singing our song."

In the moment of her light laugh they are reluctantly aware that it is time to leave and go their separate ways.

***

As Alfred crawls under the wire fence that now has some barbed wire at its base, he hones in on the fading drone of the motor bike. Within the camp he darts from tree to tree as a way of getting to the Nissan hut window. Three times he taps on the window. In an annoyed manner Josef opens it. Forcefully he whispers, "You have been out more than an hour and that straw thing is giving me hay fever. This ought to be the last time you know. One day you are going to get caught. Thankfully, we are your friends; what would happen if someone less friendly was placed here? What then? Do you ever think about that?"

"Yes Josef. Thank you and goodnight. One day it all will be all right."

***

Some days later, after Ellen has added colour to more cartoon drawings, she folds them and places them in an envelope, along with a letter she has written.

On Sunday, after the matins church service, she takes the envelope from her music case and trustingly slips it into Heinrich's hand.

On Tuesday 6th May, her father stoops to picks up an envelope from the doormat. Handing it to his daughter he asks, "Who's it from?"

"One of the art students I expect."

"By the look of that fine Italic script, I thought so."

"Usually, it's to let me know the evening class term dates."

Ellen wishes Alfred had not written so soon. Conscious of her father's scrutiny she is deliberately casual and places the envelope on the dressing table. Several hours pass before she has opportunity to read Alfred's words:

'My dear Ellen--it was good arrived in our camp. Then I would sleep but could not, always I thought on you.'

Ellen's relieved to know he returned safely. She relents about him having written so soon when she realizes his need to pass on latest information. *'My place of work just is on the bridge behind Tor- Ridge. I think it right you, when we find next Sunday the 12th May on the old place at 10 O'clock. I hope you will be there. Goodbye my darling. Thousand kisses--Your Alfred (the great).'*

A smile flickers across her face at the fact he's taken the trouble to quote her cartoon heading 'Alfred the Great'.

On the twelfth day of May in thick fog Ellen warily walks across the field. Everything looks alien, silent shapes seem about to pounce. At closer proximity, the first shape is identified as a cow,the second frightening monster proves to be a long-abandoned tractor. Suddenly the touch of a hand on her arm causes her to jump.

"It is all right my sweetheart. It is only me. Do not be frightened. You were going in the wrong direction."

"Oh goodness Alfred, you frightened me."

"Come, sit down I've laid out my coat so you won't get damp."

"What about you?"

"Our tree will keep us dry."

As he attempts to draw her close, she pulls away, bites her lip and points out "You shouldn't have written so soon."

"You mentioned the word camp and the letter was full of mistakes, and father nearly opened it."

Noticing she is gasping for breath Alfred anxiously enquires, "What's wrong?"

"Asthma, I get it from time to time; worry seems to make it worse."

"Please forgive me my darling if I have annoyed you. I just could not wait."

"I've felt the same, I was glad to receive your letter, but you'll have to try harder to not give away anything about camps and to use correct English."

"I'll get one of my educated friends to help, although obviously I didn't really want anyone else knowing what I'd written."

"Well, if you can trust your friend, it would be a lesser risk than my father finding out." Yes, I do trust him. I travelled from Scotland with him. He is a psychiatrist. He writ excellent piece."

"Wrote or has written?"

"Yes, has written--on the mind of Hitler. He sees right through him and explains why he thought like he did."

"Your friend must be a genius, what book is it in?"

"No book yet: like me, him Prisoner of War. His words good written and he know about things people, how you say experi-uns."

"Experience" "Yes, experiences hidden from public and not understood. One day it will be printed I say. You are clever too, good at art. I like funny drawings of me. One extra tall and one short like me, you cheeky, yes?"

"Sometimes I am when I draw. Time's going already--Tell me about Scotland. What happened before then?"

Little by little he explains, and when he mentions his dramatic rescue from certain death, by two black Americans he is moved by Ellen's spontaneous comment, "They are true members of God's kingdom." As she puts her arms around him, he says, "Here I have something for you."

"Slippers; how lovely."

"They'll look nicer in the daytime, the opposite of Cinderella."

"They feel good and flexible. You said you had managed to make some. What materials did you use?"

"Bits of coloured cord left over from our recreation time. Each time I have enough I make another pair of slippers."

"Well, you're clever too."

"Look, we'd better go now, the church clock has already struck eleven."

"We next meet on second Sunday in June, Jah?"

"Yes, but can we make it earlier in the evening as father is starting to ask questions."

"I—prop—ap--ally"

"Probably"

"Probably can-how you say, slip out at tea time."

"That's good."

With a sad smile she leaves, and when some yards away hears him call, "What time?"

The hoot of an owl overlaps with her reply, "Around five thirty."

Now, because Ellen is too far away, he dared not call out and ask her to repeat the time.

On the Sunday in June, they planned to meet Alfred has temporarily escaped to the field. He knows Ellen and her father often have Sunday tea at four O'clock and prays he has come at the correct time. Time passes slowly and some three quarters of an hour later he must abandon hope and return to camp.

***

Back at camp he realises he will be unable to try again due to an unexpected roll call. Luckily, the roll call is before their light tea in the Nissen hut. As they eat their sandwiches, Alfred, avoiding being drawn into conversation, finishes first. As the commander walks past their table Alfred plucks up courage to ask, "Please may I have permission to go out into the fresh air?"The commander's 'n' does not extend into a 'no' as Heinrich and Josef simultaneously ask if they may go outside. The commander looks around and observes other men finishing their tea. His voice is grumpy as he answers, "Well, seeing as the remainder are just about ready you may as well be first."

Outside, Alfred quickly slips under the barely noticeable section of the barbed wire fence, obscured by a tree. When he reaches the special field, he crouches down in the thick corn. The air is still, and tiny sparse drops of rain increase as the dark sky discards its heavy load. Water funnels down the shiny corn stalks into his boots. Regardless of being drenched, hidden from view, he crouches some two hours. Finally, hearing the roll call bell, he hastily squelches back to camp. Luckily, he crawls unnoticed under the same section of fence wire. When he has rapidly changed into dry garments and a pair of Josef's boots, several sizes too large, he trips down the step. Thankfully, the only reprimand he receives is that of being slow, much to the supressed amusement of his companions.

***

Following another night of tossing and turning he realizes the pattern is likely to continue until he can meet Ellen to explain why their meeting failed. In the meantime, a perplexed Ellen does not give up hope. To keep suspicions at bay she continues to alternate church attendance between Fellsbury and Steerton. On this Sunday she is at Steerton, where she has the task of handing out hymn books. The organist, no longer unwell, resumed playing a few weeks ago. The new situation provides a chance to tell Alfred with her eyes, "Look in the book". Noticing her questioning look he later, during the sermon, slips her letter into his pocket.

***

Back at camp that evening, with the help of a camp dictionary, he translates as many words as he can. To his friend he says, "Josef, she asks where I was and why I didn't come to our meeting place."

"Well at least you can sleep easy now. Something obviously went wrong with your timing. I will try to speak to her when I get a chance. Not that I fully approve, but you seem determined."

"Thanks Josef I knew you'd come round to my way of thinking."

***

A fortnight later, Josef, in curt manner, and in a moment of time, manages to convey events. "Alfred too busy to meet on the other Sunday, weeks ago--things not go right."

Under the misapprehension that the matter is resolved Alfred is eager to arrange another date. Stephan meets his request to correctly translate his letter dated 14th July.

Next day Alfred's pleased with the finished edition and knowing Heinrich has been entrusted with an errand to the vicarage, he asks him if he will post the letter.

"It won't get very far, there's no stamp" Heinrich comments.

"Here do have this Scottish stamp, it's valid."

"Thank you, Stephan, you are good."

Heinrich knows that friends and associates of the camp commander are watching his every move. For this reason, as he reaches the post box, he keeps walking and without stopping quickly drops the letter into the post box.

***

On 15th July, when the letter drops onto the mat, Ellen recognizes the handwriting. Thankfully, her father is in the garden shed. Hastily she tears open the envelope and reads the letter. A smile plays around her lips because Alfred's English has improved. She wonders why he has not apologized for having been too busy to see her, but as she reads on, realises there was confusion about the time of their meeting. To her annoyance he writes in length about having waited in the cornfield in the rain and having been soaked to the skin.

259

"Not once does he consider the fact that I got drenched waiting around until quarter past six" she mutters.

Upon reading further, her emotions melt as she absorbs his words, *'My love Ellen...Hearty greetings and thousand kisses sends your faithful Alfred. It is a long time ago, that I had a meeting with you. In the night I can't sleep quite, because I always must think on you, you my only sweetheart. I should like to close you in my arms for ever and ever. I am yearning for you--to kiss your sweet lips and to see your wonderful eyes my charming darling. Therefore, I should like to have a meeting with you on 21st July on the x place at half past ten O'clock. On 1st August is my birthday. In love and yearning; waiting for you my sweetheart, remains your faithful Alfred.'*

A few days later Ellen's frustrated about being unable to get birthday greetings to him. To add to difficulties, there is a request from Aunt Daisy to visit her on Sunday, stay to tea, go to evensong, and accompany her to a social evening at a friend's house. 'As we will be arriving home rather late it may be best for you to stay the night' Daisy concludes.

On Sunday Ellen finds the pretence of enjoying the visit, a strain. Because she must get to work early, they shorten the visit to Daisy's friends. When back at Daisy's home a hot drink of Horlicks warms them. Daisy retires to bed and Ellen, with a sense of relief, gets on her motorbike and heads home.

Chapter 32
House for Counting

There's puzzlement in Ellen's tone of voice when she says to her father, "It's another letter from aunty addressed to me."

"That is odd. What does it say?"

"It was nice that you were able to visit on Sunday but I am not well, please as a matter of urgency can you come and stay?"

"I'm sorry she's ill, but what a darn nuisance" George moans.

"I wonder what's wrong I'd better pack a bag and get going, can you explain to everyone?"

"Yes, yes. I expect it is a storm in a tea cup. She has had spells like this ever since Stanley died."

"Stanley?"

"He was her husband, Stanley, way before your time."

"Oh yes. I remember her saying."

With Ellen's help it takes Daisy the good part of three weeks to recover. Ellen has not been able to find out what is wrong with her aunt. She senses it is traumatic illness, even loneliness itself. Plucking up courage she chooses a sunny morning to ask, "You don't mind if I go home now do you aunty?"

"No, I am feeling much better--but you will come out on Sundays won't you, keep me company and tidy the house? It would be such an immense help."

Noticing the appealing look in her aunt's eyes Ellen, resigning herself to the undesired prospect of giving up several Sundays, does not refuse.

***

Several months have passed; Christmas is drawing near. Ellen and Alfred are desperate to see each other. Knowing that many cards will be sent at this time of year Alfred decides to write to Ellen. Two days later, with feelings of joy and concern, Ellen bends down and snatches the letter that has sailed over the mat and onto the lino. Even though she is late for work she steals a few moments to go into her bedroom to quickly read the letter.

261

Hearing her father call, "Ellen you are late for work, you cannot afford to lose your job. You know how you hated working in the city" she quickly pushes the letter to the back of the top drawer of the dressing table. Her answer rings across the room, "I'm coming; I'm on my way."

Several hours later George can only find one sock. He wonders if Ellen has scooped up the other. When he rummages through the drawer and feels paper, he wonders what it might be. Taking it out of the drawer he realises it is a letter. *'Should I read it? No, it is hers, but why has it been hidden away. Why hasn't she shared it with me?'* he wonders. He cannot make up his mind, but his one good eye scans the page, and like a camera hones in on the words:

'My dear Ellen, today I will give you your answer to your letter from June this year. You remember that I wrote to you to come to our old meeting place. But during this whole day it was raining and very bad weather.

Dear Ellen I have read your letter and I am so sorry that I did not meet you. I was during this day twice on our old meeting place, hidden in the corn. But I have not had any more time to wait because I must back in our 'house' for counting. I was so sorry! During the whole night I dreamed only of you my darling and could not find sleep. You must not think in a bad manner about me. I am really true to you and I don't want to have another girl! I only love you and I hope you will believe me this.

My dear Ellen! I give you my best regards and I kiss you sweetheart. Yours affectionately Alfred

My best wishes for a marry Christmas and a Happy New year.

George asks himself "Why on earth would someone write 'marry' Christmas. Is it bad spelling or is someone who shouldn't be asking her to marry him?"

Suddenly the negative image makes sense and George's mind races as he gasps, "God not a foreigner. Oh no, not a bloody German, God no, house for counting? Oh God it must be."

***

262

Later, when Ellen arrives home, she knows by the look on her father's face, that the nightmare she has been dreading, is about to happen:

"I could not help but find the letter in your drawer when I looked for my missing socks. Are you liaising with a bloody German?"

"He's not German."

"Then where does he live--for counting?"

"He lives at the camp at Steerton."

"Not German! Yet he lives at the prisoner of war camp, therefore he must be a ruddy German. Do I have to remind you that Georgie's dead because of this damn war that the Germans started? Georgie cannot be replaced--ever."

Ellen knows her father will not listen. Her throat and chest tighten, asthma threatens; she must get out. She stumbles outdoors, away from the tense atmosphere into the reviving air. When she is feeling a little better, she continues walking to the end and beyond, the long garden, through the woodland to the river. At the river's edge she thinks of Georgie and of the dream place where she had met him at his time of his death. She recalls feeling his pain as if it had been her own. Now as she looks down the slope and along the river bank, thoughts turn to Alfred. He is only a few miles away but within the confines of the camp.

She imagines how dejected he will be feeling during this Christmas season. A carpet of moss beneath a small oak tree overhanging the water's edge serves as an ideal seat from where she can observe a pair of swans swimming serenely on reflections of pink sky.

Later, as shadows lengthen, and she returns home, she tentatively goes to her bedroom where she writes to her father. She asks herself *'Will he empathise with the terrible circumstance that forced Alfred to escape from Serbia into Germany?'*

'He had no choice father and no one knew world war was brewing' are her concluding words.

***

Having hardly slept, Ellen watches the sun rise. In the kitchen, she sees her father angrily spoon porridge into his mouth. All

263

night he has been pacing around at intervals. Ellen decides to go to the sitting room where she balances her bowl of porridge on her lap. She eats a couple of mouthfuls and with a silent prayer in her heart, places her letter on the table. She leaves early so that she can take a walk on the farm before starting work.

***

Several hours later, when George enters the sitting room, he notices the letter. He manages to ignore it for two hours but then relents. As he reads, he wrangles with emotion but retrieves from the old Welsh dresser Georgie's final letter, written at Christmastide.

Dear Father and Ellen,

As there is a lull, I'm taking this chance to catch up. Maude and I got married without a fuss, a simple occasion. Not enough time for a family event. We will have to celebrate later if things turn out that way. How are things with you?

The chaps I am with are a good lot, they always find something to laugh about and we all often chat about our families, friends, sweethearts, or wives. What a start to married life I say.

It's about time you found yourself a sweetheart Ellen. I don't know why someone hasn't scooped you up. Still with the rest of us gone I expect you Dad are glad of her good company. I hope one day Maude and I can settle down in a home of our own and start a family.

I expect you will be making something of Christmas. We are making the best of things and thinking of Christmas at home. I expect there have been a few air raids in your city and I certainly hope things have been quiet for you. There have been air raids galore up here. Fortunately for us gas masks have arrived and everyone has them. We are up the line a bit and I expect you can guess where, as it has been in the news a bit lately. Although we are having a quiet spell at present: but I expect one of these bright nights we shall have a few visitors to drop us a 'present' or two. It seems as if the Italians are a bit windy after the doffing up, they got in their last air raid, the air force certainly had a day out that day. The raids we get here seem so half hearted after what we have seen in France and Belgium. Jerry certainly had guts, or was it dope? But we don't seem able to make these chaps

264

out. I hope you have received my letters posted on the boat. My first letter arrived two days ago; it was from Maude so you can tell how welcome it was after waiting so long. It was posted on the 24ᵗʰ of August and I received it November 11ᵗʰ, poor kid it knocked her up a bit, my leaving without even seeing her, but I must say she took it well considering.

She is keeping well up to the time of her writing and was expecting to start work in a new ammunition factory at her place, so by now she is quite busy. I don't know if she's written to you or not, but I know she is not fond of writing, so Dad, will you do me a favour and drop her a few lines to cheer her up. Ellen will know the address. We'll, Dad and Ellen I expect by the time you receive this letter it will be Christmas, so I wish you all the best even though it won't be much of a time for rejoicing, but I suppose we all shall make the best of things.

I shall be thinking of you and everyone at home and obviously remembering Christmases past.

Keep cheerful. God bless.

Much love to you all.

Georgie

By the time George finishes reading his son's letter, tears stream from both his blind and sighted eye, his nose drips profusely. Finding a handkerchief in the pile of laundry ready for ironing, he blows his nose hard, discards the handkerchief in the laundry basket and sits at the table. Covering his face with his hands, he attempts to absorb all the unbearable changes in his life.

***

As the end of war has faded a little in the annals of time, the prisoners are allowed some freedom. By careful negotiation some men manage to snatch a few moments of normality as they travel to and from work. Unofficially, depending on their commander's agreement, Alfred's companions have persuaded their camp commander to let them swop times with Alfred, thus unofficially accommodating his visits to Fellsbury. If all goes to plan his next visit will be in April.

That Ellen's older siblings have strongly objected to her friendship with the foreigner, George begins to review his own attitude and he has agreed that Alfred may visit.

**

The weather's sunny and warm when Alfred arrives at Ellen's home. He has detoured from his place of work on a farm at Millstock, and the worst that he can expect at camp is a moderate reprimand for lack of punctuality. Taking the advice of his companions he's deliberately forgotten to sign the clocking off book. Thus, the precise time for his departure remains obscure. George suggests having tea in the garden. When Ellen and Alfred are seated at a garden table George chooses to sit some distance away. A momentary look of disappointment on his daughter's face offers consolation. Feeling awkward, Alfred and Ellen make polite conversation.

"Father, may Alfred borrow your old watch you rarely use?" she dares to ask. Stalling the probability of a negative response she continues in sympathetic tone, "Alfred is out working every day at Chadstone. They have no means of telling the time and often work longer than they are meant to. Inevitably they are reprimanded and lose privileges when they arrive late for the truck." She notes an expression of objection on her father's face and then sees he has changed his mind. She senses his annoyance at her sympathy and guesses he might be testing Alfred's honesty.

**

On 6th June 1947 prisoners who work on nearby farms are given some freedom, the pinnacle of which is to be able to travel by bicycle within a three-mile radius of the camp. The same day, Alfred uses his free time to cycle to Ellen's home. He intends to ask her Father his consent for him to marry Ellen. He also will return the watch.

Meanwhile as George folds the newspaper he has read, he is upset at all the news of bombings and explosions like the one that killed Georgie and his companions. As his thoughts project into the tragic event, a knock at the door intrudes. He is partially hopeful, '*Oh Georgie you have come back. It was not true. You are here.*'

As he opens the door his smile disappears instantly to see some other man's son stood where Georgie should be. No English man but a foreigner, someone who has worn a German uniform.

The foreign voice stammers, "I bring watch. I ask you, can I come in, talk about Ellen and my, how you say, honoured intentions?"

"Thank you for bringing back my watch. No, you can't come in and it is not your place to mention my daughter in such a way."

Ignoring the look of despair on the visitor's face George firmly closes the door. He is unaware how Alfred staggers along the path with a pain in his heart more intense than any flesh wound. Because of all the barriers and insults and echoes of war in his path stealing his young years, he is now on the verge of collapse. A few yards along the path, he leans against the chestnut tree, where deep rooted tears force themselves out of his grief. Eventually, when sobbing subsides, he is exhausted but knows he cannot live without Ellen. Later, back at camp he explains his predicament to his friends, but feels ostracized by Josef, who advises him that he end his friendship with Ellen.

***

George refrains from telling Ellen about Alfred's visit. However, a few days later, on 11th June, when Ellen stoops to picks up three letters, she recognizes the handwriting on one extra small envelope. Carefully she folds it and places it in the small pocket of her apron. Suddenly her father, with shaving foam on his face, emerges from the bathroom, takes two letters from her and sees no further letters.

Alone, out in the fields, where the sun burns her cheeks Ellen's warm brown eyes brighten as she opens the small envelope. The letter reads:

9th June 1947.

'My Darling Ellen, I just come back from my home.... the day's work over. Now I will try to write a letter to you. At first, I hope you are well as I am too. I thank you very much, my dear Ellen, for your last present. I was happy to have seen you in the church. Unfortunately, I could not speak to you because there have been too many people. Some days ago, I was at your father...I brought back the watch. I have seen that the father

got a bad leg and I was sorry for him. On this occasion I asked him whether I can come into his house, but he has forbidden and this made me weeping. But I do not blame him for he is an old man. Only Josef is guilty on this state. He always tried to separate you from me. You know it, my sweetheart, and I know it too. God may forgive him. I know my little darling that you love me and I love you beyond measure. For nobody can separate you from me. You are mine for ever. If I can't stay in England after this time you come with me and I shall care for you all my life. God will help.

I will be waiting for you at Thursday on our place. Sunday's I will try to meet your girlfriend Elsie, to speak to her about my case. Last Sunday, I haven't met her. It is time now to go to bed. My thoughts and my best wishes are with you, my dear. Greeting and kissing you. I am yours ever Alfred.'

Some months after she has read Alfred's letter, Ellen thinks *'I am glad he will smooth things over with Elsie for me. I am sure she will come round to accepting my situation'*. Summer has drifted into autumn and autumn into winter. Alfred has spent several months working on a farm near the town of Kingsland. For several weeks he has been looking forward to returning to camp. He hopes Heinrich has told Ellen he will look out for her at church on Christmas day. However, weather conditions have worsened: four days of unrelenting blizzards have seen snow drifts pile high along the hedgerows. Roads have become blocked. Were it not due to his having asked Heinrich to let Ellen know he would be home for Christmas, he might have listened to the advice he was this moment receiving from the farmer's-wife, "You would best stay put for Christmas. We've a telephone and can contact your camp commander."

Making a quick decision Alfred apologetically replies, "Thank you, but in the morning I walk. It is no worse than in Russia. I will be all right."

Later he hears the farmer say, "Obstinate bugger. They are all the same these Germans.

'N do not go packin' 'im any lunch or anything, he shood-av' -tak'n -yur advice."

***

268

Through the driving, snow-laden wind, whilst crunching deep layers of snow under foot, Alfred slowly begins his long trek. An hour or so later everything feels surreal, he feels separated from his own body. His spirit is miles ahead in the company of Ellen. Suddenly he recalls her mention of a kind Aunt Mary at Gifford-Avon, living at— *'Oh yes, I remember, Chalice Stream Cottage.'* With renewed incentive he quickens his pace and finding the cottage dares to ring the bell. Feeling awkward, like a tramp or some outcast, he explains to the elderly lady, who reminds him of Great Aunt Annalisa, "I --sorry to knock on--door but, me have walked from Kingsland-- many miles to go. I left at six O'clock this morning. Me Prisoner of War, work on farm near Kingsland. I now go back to Steerton Camp for Christmas. I go to church. Your niece Ellen plays organ."

With a voice like the creak of a rusty gate the interested lonely face answers, "Well, she is a good girl my Ellen but she should not be makin' 'er name known to foreigners. I 'ain't too keen on foreigners but it seems a sorry situation when they send one solitary man all that way on foot, it must be twenty miles at least. Cum in and I will be charitable as I am God fearing woman--and give 'ee a bit tu'eat and a cupateeee. Then ye be best on yer way as it's ten O'clock and if yer've come from the farm near Kingsland yer mustav bin on yer feet fer three hours already."

"Thank you. It is a lovely place you have here and your cottage has an interesting name."

"It goes back to the civil war in the 1600's. Apparently Royalists hid the church chalice in the stream."

"Plenty good history here, now you make more good history, Jah?"

"Well only for ten minutes or so and that hardly counts as important history."

Heartened by the hospitality of Ellen's Aunt, fuelled by the tea and scones Alfred's ready to continue his journey. Later as he trudges onward, he is glad that some roads have been cleared. Striding along such roads and walking along the hedgerows of others, he is relieved when at last he arrives back at camp during the early evening. Shakily he signs the book, and when in his Nissan hut, lies down on his bed. Exhausted he readily falls into deep sleep. Later, when his companions return from a Christmas event arranged by the vicar, he manages to mumble "Herzliche grüsse--hearty greetings, I have walked twenty miles."

Noticing Alfred's swollen feet, Heinrich compassionately loosens the boot laces and with some twisting removes Alfred's boots.

"I'll put this blanket over him" says Josef.

***

By morning, whilst observing the sunlight filtering through the small dusty window, Alfred's surprisingly alert. As he washes himself, he hears the church tower clock chime six. Other men are sleeping. Knowing that Ellen will work her way through three miles of snow to see him at the eleven O'clock church service, his eyes are intense with blue and reflections of indigo.

On this Christmas day, with the blizzard spent, the air is still and every frozen crystal full of promise. Because it's Christmas, everything is vibrant with positive energy and thoughts. A universal consciousness prevails, as if every heart and soul is focussed on the whole creation as part of God's kingdom. Alfred notices a foraging deer inside the camp periphery. It sees him and achieves that which every prisoner has dreamt of--to leap over the wire fence. Other animals lift their noses and smell out the land. They prick up their ears seeming to know that at this special time humans will be in correct focus of love and charity. Alfred considers how different the scene looks because it is Christmas. The village has become a romantic masterpiece of ice capped roofs, snow dusted trees and berries coated with sparkling snowflakes.

Because they have been promised a special cooked breakfast they do not mind having to wait.

When it is ready, they tuck in heartily. A brief time later, with caution, they carefully walk along the icy road to church. Seeing Ellen, Alfred daringly separates from his comrades and intentionally slides along the ice towards her. Light of heart, feeling confident he must smile for he knows several people have learned about their friendship. Most people have come to accept it. Now, just as they pass a gate, it opens, and a mother holding her son's hand, steps onto the snow edged pavement and along the icy track created by many footsteps. The prisoners have heard

270

her call the boy's name, Dave. They're moved to see him cheerfully wave his free hand. As his mother ushers him in the direction of the church he continues to look back at them with boyish mischief in his blue eyes, and a wide smile on his face.

Ellen's fond of the child, especially for having inadvertently set wheels in motion. He had not had any inhibitions telling folk he had seen the lady who plays the organ, in Primrose Lane, walking, hand in hand with a camp man. Following some weeks of corrective gossip, folk had come to realize that Dave had referred to Ellen rather than the usual organist. His mother Mrs Pryce had laughed her socks off when she had heard the tale.

***

Because Ellen informed Heinrich about neighbours having overheard her father's objections Alfred knows things have been troublesome in Fellsbury. Rumours are flying fast in and around the villages. Now on Christmas day Alfred concludes that their situation will improve if matters become official. He decides he will propose today. Unable to afford an engagement ring he has bought a decent quality imitation ruby pendant from a jewellers shop in Kingsland. As they arrive at the church door, he does not follow the other prisoners of war, but takes Ellen's hand and leads her around the side of the church. They are unaware that Ivy Swift, having arrived later than usual, has noticed them.

A few moments later, standing around the corner, she listens to their conversation:

"Ellen, I am sorry your father would not see me or listen to what I wanted to say but will you listen. My dear sweetheart Ellen will you marry me, be my wife, accept today, engagement?"

Her large, lovely brown eyes remain steady as she gazes into his forget- me- not blue eyes. Momentarily she pauses, but feeling his hand close around her hand, she answers, "Yes Alfred. I love you and it is you alone I want to marry and spend my whole life with."

Living up to her name, Ivy Swift dives into church, where she persuasively updates the tall grey haired church warden. She notices Alfred sit on the end of the Prisoner of War pew, and Ellen slip into the pew directly behind. Mrs Swift's warm smile makes everyone at the back feel welcome. The church warden

271

announces the usual notices and smiles an aristocratic smile. "My next announcement has not even reached the vicar yet. I am pleased to announce the engagement of our part time organist Ellen to Alfred who has been working well in our community."

The tall smart looking Reverend Hywell, with neatly cut black hair raises his eyebrows as he skilfully weaves onward into the theme of the day. "So, my friends we rejoice in this Christmastide for love and engagements and future happiness and for the love of God that brought his only begotten son into the world to make our world a place of unity and friendship, rather than a place of discord. We pray that love and peace will always reign. Our first hymn is Christians Awake Salute the Happy Morn."

Chapter 33
A new role for Daisy

Regardless of the deep snow, Ellen is only half an hour late returning home. The dinner she has left slowly cooking isn't quite ready. Due to weather conditions, there will be no guests and they do not have to worry about having to wait a further half hour.

***

George is given the task of carving the meat from the roast turkey. Ellen's voice is tense as she comments, "It'll probably see us through the week."

As she checks various vegetables and sauces steaming in saucepans, she manoeuvres around the hottest spot on the stove. Finally, when she has retrieved the roast potatoes from the oven, she dishes out vegetables and sauces onto warmed plates. By now seated opposite her father, she uses a fork to put slices of turkey onto their dinner plates. Spurts of discussion range from village affairs, to their choice of presents, whether friends and family members will be pleased. Feeling full after the dinner they decide they will wait until tea time to eat Christmas pudding.

With child- like awe they open their gifts. "You've knitted these well" says George whilst holding up two pairs of knitted socks in grey and navy.

"Thank you. What a lovely blue silk evening shawl from aunty."

"It's one your mother gave her; I think she kept it especially for you."

"I shall certainly wear it."

"What's this, another present?"

As she tears open a crudely wrapped parcel in brown paper, she is delighted to see a pair of leather motor bike gloves.

"Brand new; never had a chance to use them because of grit flying up and blinding me in one eye. I was younger than you. Make certain you always wear your goggles whilst riding."

"I will. Thank you, Dad."

273

The two words 'I will' reminds Ellen what she must do. She decides that this happy moment of time is right for her to tell her father her intentions. "Things are a bit different these days Dad and, well-well, I have accepted Alfred's proposal of marriage. We would like it to be with your blessing."

A moment of shocked silence prevails. White with anger, George says in a tight voice "My blessing? How can you expect that? I am surprised and gutted that you are going against my wishes. I nearly lost my life in the First World War; it is a miracle you came into the world. All that seems in vain, now- your brother has not come back. Do you think your mother would approve of you marrying an enemy?"

"Mother believed in good arising from demanding situations, and I believe love and light triumph. You cannot prevent God's love at work, even within his scheme of falling in love."

Without words George retreats to the end of the garden where he remains a long while.

When eventually he returns, his manner is cool. He has a forlorn and sad look about him. His voice is thick with emotion as he says, "As long as you are single you may remain here but after that you'll have to make your own way."

Next day, regardless of gout, he gets on the Fellsbury bus to Plymouth, and calls on Daisy. She is both glad and surprised to see him, and carefully listens as he stutters out recent events. Within herself she empathises with Ellen, and her controversial plans to marry the man she loves and who happens to be a prisoner of war. For a moment, back in time, she remembers her husband Stanley leaving on a ship bound for the tropics during the First World War and never returning. The memory sparks off a worried thought how too much hostility from family members might drive Ellen away to settle in Germany.

To herself, she mutters, "We wouldn't want any children growing up there, would we?"

"What are you talking about?"

"I am thinking ahead. We do not want Ellen being unhappy and going off to Germany because she thinks she is not wanted here."

"I cannot speculate. All I can think about is our poor boys who have not come back and my friends in the Great War who

274

never came back. Only by a hair's breadth did I return from the last war and now dear Georgie has not returned; blown to smithereens on an ammunitions ship. Ellen had a nightmare--"

"I know, it is all too much, and my Stanley never came back. The world is going faster than people can keep up with."

Taking things on board Daisy resorts to audibly muttering, "I hope her children will not be black, with him being foreign. There have been stories of some throw backs in America. As the hymn says 'In heathen lands afar,' I hope not."

"Daisy what are you on about?"

"Sorry, I'm in a world of my own."

"Yes-well- I heard-and people are not heathens afar off. I've seen the world, and people have variety of beliefs. There are Buddhists, Jews, Moslems, Hindus, and Christians in all kinds of countries. It is a very Victorian idea to think that Great Britain is the only Christian nation and that everywhere else is heathen. I have seen that the Great British Commonwealth is flawed."

George feels irritated by the thought that the seed of the concept of a pure race may have unsuspectingly evolved in the life of Queen Victoria's grandson Wilhelm, who felt obliged to match the Commonwealth ideal.

On the return bus journey, he feels a little better for having mentioned matters to his sister- in- law. In his present frame of mind, he does not care where Ellen and Alfred go after they are married but within his heart, he hopes Daisy will resolve matters.

***

Several weeks later Ellen tells him she can't tolerate ongoing strain and that she will be moving into Daisy's currently unoccupied upstairs flat.

During the next few days George's emotions escalate between obstinacy, guilt, and despair and he doesn't relent as Ellen removes all her belongings from the family home.

***

After she has left, he stands in her empty room, puts his hands to his face and groans loud and long. Only the sympathetic cats hear his primeval cry, and rub against his leg to offer comfort. Uncertain about their motive he goes to the kitchen, finds a bowl, fills it with scraps of meat and places it on the ground.

275

***

Several months later, Ellen hears what she believes to be her father's voice call, *'Come home, come home.'* She opens her eyes and when fully awake realises that the voice belongs to the rag and bone man calling, "Rag'nbone, ragn'bone."

She can hear the hooves of the cart horse clattering up the back street. Quickly, she puts on her dressing gown, rushes downstairs, picks up a bag of discarded clothes her aunt asked her to sort. Lightly she walks down the short, cemented path, lifts the latch of the wooden door set in the wall and steps onto the street. With a wave she catches the attention of the rag and bone man and smiles as he approaches her section of the street. Patting the horses muzzle, she says, "I used to work with cart horses like him. They are marvellous creatures, aren't they? Patient and steady in their work."

"Well, misee, Old Dobbin 'ere luvs 'is work."

As Ellen hands the man a bag of old clothes he touches his cap with his free hand. "Anyway Missee" he says, "Best to keep movin', see you next week I 'ope."

As he continues up the street, neighbours responding to the cry that tugs at the heart strings rush out to hand him various cast offs. Others make disparaging comments whilst the unkempt man declares social injustice in the manner he calls out, "Rag'n bone, ragn bone."

Ellen is not keen on city life and looks forward to Sundays when she will see Alfred and be free to walk with him through the country lanes.

***

Today, Sunday, she eagerly tells him, "I have a new job as a sign writer. I did one day of work, and I officially start on Monday."

"That is good. I have made a little money too selling more slippers. I can easily buy cord now."

"That is good news. We must save all we can."

"Tell me Ellen, how do you do sign writing and where?"

"The work place is above a garage near the boss's home. We use petrol to thin the paint" "Doesn't petrol affect your breathing?"

276

"No, I have been fine. Joe, the boss lets me keep the window open, besides the paint is very thin and dries almost immediately it is put on the paper, that's part of the skill, being quick, making no mistakes."

"What signs do you paint?"

"We do cinema hoardings and large signs for the main churches in Plymouth."

"When we arrived from Schott, I mean Scotland; we saw some large out of date posters. They must take a long time to do, with the background colour."

"No, not at all, the paper is multi coloured and all that we must do is to paint the lettering. We use square ended brushes and simple strokes."

"It sounds like italic script."

"It's fairly similar."

"Oh, I see. All good but a return to the corporation office may be better, no? Not good working with this one boss Joe."

"He is all right and has a nice wife called Alice. I did not tell you before but the reason I left the corporation office was because there was a nasty boss who used to expect women to accept his hands crawling all over them. I would not let him near me and that is why he had it in for me every day."

"What mean you?"

"He called me names and wouldn't allow me breaks and so forth."

"My poor Ellen, if I had been there, I would have had strong words with him."

"Anyway, let's forget all that. Have you had a chance yet to speak to Reverend Hywell?"

"Only small time, he says we can see him after the Easter morning service. He also said it was a good thing Mrs Swift got us both on the electoral roll."

"Why?"

"You have to have your name on the electoral roll to be married in church."

"I thought people simply had to be people of faith."

"My dear Ellen, your view is the right one. I too feel as you do in my heart but I expect they must have their rules to keep-how you say, a tab on things."

"True, my cousin had to provide his birth certificates and all kinds of documents for him to marry in a church in Ireland. It was all because there had been several cases of bigamy there."

"Bigamy, what is bigamy?"

"It usually concerns men, who claim to be single but who already have a wife."

"How strange and why you mention Catholic Church? Is this church not Catholic? It mentions the Holy Catholic Church in the creed."

"Catholic means universal; this church belongs to the Anglican Church in England. The Church of England was established centuries ago because of Henry the Eighth wanting to break away from the Roman Catholic Church. Civil war and all sorts of beheadings and murders took place."

"Look Ellen all that was a long time ago. I think it best we keep quiet about the religion of my upbringing. Reverend Hywell has not asked me if I am catholic, and he knows I want to settle in England. I stay in your church; I not go away to another. My father had trouble before he married my mother."

He was Orthodox and my mother Catholic. If we get too much trouble in Church of England, we go Catholic later. That will be for you and me to decide Jah?"

"Jah, I mean yes. Why do you no longer speak Serb- Croat?"

"It was knocked out of me by Serbian police, and I do not want to go back. Soon you speak a little German too, yes?"

***

Easter day, 1948, is chilly and windy but also bright and sunny. Ellen's glad she did not wear a new pale lemon outfit and white sandals. Several young women walk briskly to get inside church out of the cold. When seated in their pews they continue to shiver, and long for their log fires at home. Wishing they had dressed sensibly, they watch Ellen, cosily dressed in a woollen cardigan and tartan- skirt, take her place at the organ, because Mrs Brooks is absent due to a chill. Alfred notices that Ellen has pinned a little nosegay of fresh primroses and violets onto her cardigan. It reminds him of Easter, and that he and Ellen are children of God, who has granted them each other's company within the beautiful countryside.

278

The energetic service commences with voices soaring high in full belief:

'Jesus Christ is Risen Today.'

In similar analogy to the sermon, they had heard in Scotland, Reverend Hywell portrays the men who have died in combat, as rising from battle fields, oceans, deserts, bombed tanks, buildings, and civilians rising from bombed towns. The vicar does not believe resurrection to be a future event but one that has already happened, for people of all time, through the resurrection of Jesus. Alfred appreciates his avoidance of national emphasis and the care he has taken, to provide space for everyone for reflection on those they have lost. His thoughts return to Erika, killed in the bombed shelter, and his friend Helmut, cruelly blown to pieces in Russia. The pieces come together, Helmut now restored, turns, smiles and waves. On a spiritual plain Alfred sees Erika. She waves to Helmut. Alfred receives a warm message within his heart of how, within their souls, they know they are bonded by 'the kind being they once knew, and whose eyes had contained the blue light of God'.

Did he imagine them whisper, "But blue was only a part of the spectrum, we move on, attracted by other colours, and ultimately into the white light of pure love and compassion."

***

Over the months ahead Ellen and Daisy think about compiling the wedding invitation list. Ever optimistic, Daisy's elated to see, lying on the shiny polished floor of the hallway, an envelope addressed by George. However, upon opening the envelope, and reading his words, optimism fades. Her brother-in-law simply reiterates that he will not be attending the event and that he 'will certainly not be giving his daughter away to a German Prisoner of War.' She is sad and disappointed that he has not accepted her explanation that Alfred is not of German ancestry, and that many Germans had not wanted to fight. George's words come bouncing up from the page, *'He came here representing the Germans, and it's the same thing'*.

There's empathy in Daisy's voice as she explains, "I'm sorry Ellen; your father won't be coming to the wedding." Observing the same crumpled look on Ellen's face that she had as a child, when she had learned of her mother's death, Daisy awkwardly continues, "He's terribly hurt losing Georgie, he'll never get over it."

"Neither shall I, but life has to move forward."

"He no longer feels he can move on. We must not forget he was forty when you were born."

"I know Aunty; I just hope he will come round one day. He is the only parent I have had since I was ten."

"Well, I've done my best for my dear sister."

"I did not mean to exclude you. You have always been there for me, and I love you for it."

With a chuckle Daisy replies, "I realise I am different from your liberal and adventurous mother. She was highly intelligent and futuristic; had she been a man she would have gone to university."

"Or as a person in her own right, had women been permitted to apply. You are intelligent too, and ingenious, making something out of nothing with your needlecraft."

"That's true, and as a widow receiving no widow's pension, I've had to do more accepting and conforming to survive."

"Naval rules are unfair. Your husband was killed because of being in a foreign land to serve his country."

"Yes, but he died of Spanish influenza with pneumonia, and not as a direct result of war."

"I do not suppose life on board ship was healthy. Anyway, let us think of the many bright times. I remember the Fellsbury concerts you and mother used to arrange and participate in."

"Yes, she playing the violin and I the piano; and we both sang and others performed from time to time."

"I know, and the proceeds helped build up the fund for a new village hall."

"Those were the days; your mother's favourite piece was in four/four time, now what was it, started on C and modulated to G major, oh I know 'Neath the Shadows' by Irma Barron. I loved playing the rolled chords at the end of the piece."

"I can picture you both now."

"Your mother sang solo, 'The Laughing Policeman' and she had everyone in stitches of laughter."

"You both sang 'Abide with me' and 'Jerusalem' and effectively put everyone in sombre mood. I am glad to have not been deprived of it all. It inspired my own singing and piano playing. If ever I have children, I shall encourage them to keep the music alive."

"Like your mother you have a lovely voice, and your sister sings well."

Daisy refrained from adding that she thought Ellen almost professional in the way she put her whole self into her performing. Harriett, on the other hand, had remained emotionally uninvolved with the songs she sang.

"Thanks Aunty. Oh! Do I smell gas?"

"I'll just check" is Daisy's reply. Slowly she gets up from her chair, and walks towards the oven to check the knobs."

"The one at the back wasn't quite turned off."

Back at the kitchen table there is a pleading look on her face as she says, "Now let us get the invitation list sorted. Who would you like to invite?"

Chapter 34
Wedding Plans
(Over several months)

Rain lashes the window as Reverend Hywell receives invitation to the wedding reception. His former school friend Sharpy, now a colonel, is staying for the week.

"We've an invitation to the reception of the wedding I shall be conducting; you know the nice Prisoner of War, Alfred and our relief organist Ellen" the vicar says to his wife.

"Oh, it's good of them to think of us, especially as they know I shall be at the service to support you."

As they go into the sitting room the colonel pipes up, "I could not help but overhear what you were saying. I imagine the situation of having to conduct the wedding is enough, without having to be forced into public acknowledgement beyond that event."

"We shall be happy to accept; this German started out as a novice monk in Jugloslavia; an allied country. He had problems because he had been born in Germany. As for the young lady, she is of tremendous help to us, playing the organ for services when Mrs Brookes is unable to come."

He notices Sharpie's face redden, and during the habitual pause realises the response of his wily- mind is imminent. Predictably the colonel replies, "I suppose an alternative might be possible-- but you need to take care, that you do not forget dear man, that you work for the Church, of England."

He added "Your predecessor gave his life on the battlefield of The Great War to save a soldier."

"Yes, I know, he was killed by a stray bullet. I mentioned him in a Christmas-sermon. On that occasion I also mentioned the Christmas Day football match between Germans and English; during the Great War. I emphasised how Christ knows no human boundaries."

Silently the colonel leaves the room.

Concurrently, Miss Mary and Miss Phyllis Perry receive invitations to their niece's wedding. There is an excited ring in Mary's voice as she calls upstairs, "Phyllis, Phyllis we're invited to Ellen's wedding."

"Oh good; when's it to be?"

"On the twenty-eight of August, isn't it exciting? We can go to the Dingle's temporary Nissan to select fashionable clothes."

As Phyllis descends the stairs, a gleam of delight ignites in her green eyes. Whilst stepping down into the hallway she enticingly croons, "There is a beautiful lavender outfit I fancy. The wedding provides good excuse to buy it."

"I've seen a damask outfit with a matching wide brimmed hat."

"Do you think we can afford it?"

"Oh let's, we'll still have enough for the wedding gift."

***

Joyce, who has arrived home from the corporation office, is delighted to find some correspondence. She opens the envelope, reads the letter, and feels pleased her friend Ellen has remembered her. Knowing she cannot afford a new outfit she races upstairs to see what might be suitable. A mint green blouse and a skirt a shade darker is suitable. '*Why didn't I think of those before,*' she wonders. A cream jacket in good condition matches her white sandals that she will wear if the weather's fine.

"Is that you Joyce? Did you find the letter for you on the hall table?"

"Yes mother, it is a wedding invitation from Ellen. Would it be all right if I use some of my savings to buy a hat?"

"Yes, if it is not too expensive. Up in my wardrobe are some artificial flowers you can sew on. No point in paying for extras if we already have them."

"Thank you, mother," Joyce acceptingly replies.

At Chapel Lane in the village of Yamly, George's brother Percy and his wife Flo' open their envelope and read the invitation. As they cannot afford an expensive gift Flo suggests giving Ellen their ornamental dog with a realistic fly on its leg.

In his usual bashful manner Percy quietly replies, "Flo dear, you cannot give that away. What if your sisters visit us and notice it missing; they would be upset because their mother gave it to you."

"Well, yes, I expect you are right Percy, but we have not any children, and if I had had a daughter, I would have loved her to have been as loving and honest as Ellen. We will go to town on Friday and choose something."

"You go Flo,' I am no good in the town. You choose but do not go spending more than we can afford. I hate to say this but Will received his invitation yesterday and he says that being next in age to George, he would best support him by not attending. It might be best for us to pop into the church service, and disappear before the reception takes place. If we sit at the back, Ellen will see us but the remaining guests will not, and nothing will get back to George."

"I'll fit in with whatever you think best Percy."

"It is best to do that, and Will and I can invite them over to see us. There is no harm in that, and George need not know. I hope he will come to his senses one day."

At 58 Trelawny Road, Plymouth, Mr Babbage comments to his wife, "Good of Daisy to invite us to her niece's wedding. Best for us to support Daisy with her arduous task, we do not want to make her ill by upsetting her. She is kind and Ellen's a nice maid."

"Really; I can't place her."

"Yes, you can, she came to one of our card evenings last year and read a book whilst the rest of us played. I got an ace and you a jack."

"Oh yes, I remember, big brown eyes, black hair and she's got a mole to the right above her lip."

"More like a beauty spot and quite attractive."

Over the weeks Daisy and Ellen receive several replies. Ellen looks up to say to her aunt "This one's from my brother."

For a moment Daisy looks shocked.

"Bertram of course; he says he will not have any problem with his boss, but he does not know if he will be expected to keep his father company. He says his wife does not want to attend without him, and that includes the children. Well, I think Bert could come if he wanted. He has had lofty ideas since he has been working at Mountgate House near the river. Since I've been unable to go home, he has thought of nothing except his own future."

"Well perhaps, but we do not know; he may have divided loyalties. Besides, it was a blow to him, and to Harriett, when Georgie and then you, came into the world."

"Was it?"

"Yes, my sister was always worried about the big gap between her first two and second two."

"I suppose it was a shock when they expected to have been the only ones. I read somewhere that paediatricians say that children should be born within the three-and-a-half-year period of each other for good sibling bonding. I suppose with Georgie gone, I'm the odd one out."

"Ellen, there is more post; Harriett's sister-in-law, Joan, and her husband Phil from Charwell have accepted; they are good people, always friendly. Harriett's husband is quiet and friendly, not a social climber; he is a peacemaker. Even though your sister can be fiery at times I am very fond of her. She was my family when she lived here to enable her to get through grammar school."

"Has she said she'll be coming?"

"Yes, I've told her I need help with final dressmaking adjustments; she'll be here the week before the wedding."

***

A few weeks before the wedding more replies arrive. George's sister Emilia and her husband Samuel- George, will be along with Ellen's cousin Maurice and his wife Colleen. "There's a note here saying they'll have to bring the baby, Bernice."

"What happens if she cries during the vows?" Daisy asks.

"It won't matter we'll speak up."

"Maurice's brothers Philip and Benjamin are not able to come because they are in a navy football match. Well, they are of high rank, aren't they?"

"Yes, but even so things are blacker and whiter for those who've served in the forces." "Maurice served in the army."

"Yes, but his loyalty has always been with family and friends. He would have broken any rule to save a friend's neck. He climbed some hill because he thought comrades sun bathing, were in danger after inadvertently having entered enemy territory. It turned out they had been shot dead. Luckily, no one was around to shoot Maurice when he went up there with good intentions."

Two days later Ellen comments, "There is a reply from Elsie, thankfully she intends coming. Do not say anything to her, will you? But I had my doubts because she has had a tough time. Her father used to beat her on her bare bottom, right up until she was twenty-one. He must have some quirk to have done that. Furthermore, he was merciless when he discovered she had been out with Paul Twainson, and that they both wanted to marry. She said her father beat her black and blue, and whilst doing so said that no man should have her. There have been rumours floating around about her father raping a girl who lived in one of the woodland cottages. Nada's sister is really her daughter."

"Well Ellen, he is always respectable when I speak to him. You should not listen to rumours and Elsie exaggerates."

"I do not know; I think her trying to look masculine is a way of hitting back at her father. I shall not repeat anything. She wants to see me so I will try and meet her over the week end."

***

The following Sunday Ellen is on her way to Fellsbury Church to see Elsie. She notes a ring of sadness in her friend's voice as she says, "It is awful in the church choir without you. I feel as if all my friends have gone and you know the situation at home. I dare not tell my mother."

"Doesn't she hear what's going on?"

"He only hits me when she is out; besides, she is so proud of me being a teacher. I do not want to spoil her happiness; that rumour really upset her."

"What, the one about the girl you mean?"

"Yes. The trouble is I can believe it is true. I shall keep a watch on the child and who knows I might find myself teaching her one day."

"Anyway Elsie, going back to the church choir, I doubt I will be away for ever. I always say life works out some way or other. Alfred likes singing too."

"I doubt they'll approve, I shouldn't encourage him, in case it causes upset."

Ellen notices a fashionable hat hanging on a hook in the hall and asks Elsie if it's her hat.

"Yes, I got it in the sale; we had a special dinner for teachers so I had to get something suitable."

"I hope you'll wear it on my wedding day."

"I expect I shall because our organist has a similar one. I'm also having lessons with her, and I have played for a few services."

"Well done, and how's your teaching going?"

"Not bad, I keep the children in order, and I've a new motorbike. I can travel to Parksall in forty-five minutes."

"I was wondering how you got there."

"Oh, the Pittmann's asked me to pass a note to you."

"Thanks."

Ellen scans the note; she says "Aunty will be pleased they are coming. I wonder if there's time to see them on the way back."

"I doubt it, it's five O'clock already and your aunt will wonder where you are."

"It seems strange riding past home without calling in."

"I think it strange seeing your brother call there more than he used to. He seems to skulk around."

"He's tall and walks like that naturally; besides, working for the Thornbury's he has to act guardedly, watch his 'P's' and 'Q's' and all that."

***

Back at Daisy's a few more letters arrive, one of which Daisy has just opened. "That's a shame" she comments, "I was looking forward to meeting your father's sister Maude. However, Lee is miles and miles away and I cannot see Maude getting on the back of her husband's motorbike, can you?"

"Why is that?"

"Well Ellen she's about my size, perhaps slightly smaller, too much of a lady and too stiff in joint to travel like that."

"Did I tell you, my old piano teacher, who lives at Alexandria Road, will be coming?"

"That is nice. She taught you well, and I trust you have your certificates unharmed?"

"Yes Aunty, I have."

"Shoved in a drawer I expect."

287

"Well, yes, I'll sort them out one day. Everyone knows I can play anyway."

"I had some cards yesterday. Will's daughter, your cousin Linda, will be coming. The Heale's plan to come to the wedding, and reception; Alfred's farming friends at Southleigh Farm, Minergton, have sent a card. They are not certain, and they will let us know if the harvest is gathered in time."

"For Alfred's sake I hope they come, otherwise there'll be hardly anyone on his side of the church."

"Is Mr Eves of Steerton anything to do with Alfred?"

"Yes, he knows him well."

"That's good; it'll mean at least one place on Alfred's side will be taken."

"No, two, there's a positive reply here from Mr Piccini Ewue of Sherford valley."

"What's his background?"

"He's Italian and was a war time prisoner at the camp who stayed and married an English girl. Alfred and I got talking to them outside the grocers shop and befriended them one day."

***

On August 18th Daisy goes through the guest list and mentions that George's sister Nell hasn't replied.

"I wonder if she feels she should support my father."

"I doubt it, women think differently than men. On the other hand, her husband may object because his father was killed in the First World War, in the marines. He had a posthumous award."

"Oh, more post has arrived. I will get it."

"Talk about God moving in mysterious ways Aunty, this one is from Aunt Nell. She accepts and her husband, daughter and son in law will be coming."

"I'll open the rest."

"Mr and Mrs Redfern accept and this one from Mr and Mrs Mirrosh is a 'no.' Who are they anyway?"

"They are the farmer and his wife where Alfred worked as Prisoner of War. Do they give a reason for not coming?"

"No, not a word but don't forget its early days since the end of the war."

"That one's Annie's handwriting; can I open it?"

288

"Yes of course and it's addressed to you anyway."

"Oh, what a shame, she is on holiday in Ramsgate and will not be back in time. She says she is doing a lot of sketches. I shall look forward to seeing them when she gets back."

"I don't know; you girls and your art and not one of you has time for essential needlecraft."

"I'm not bad at it and I do make quite a few things to wear during the course of the year."

"Yes, all too often you're impatient during the process."

"Ah that is a relief; Mr Swift confirms he will give you away. That reminds me we must get Susan's bridesmaids dress sorted before she comes for her final fitting."

"Last Sunday Mr Swift said 'Ee agrees to give me away seeun asee wuzz instrumental in bringing us together and seein' 'ow 'is Susie was set on bein' bridesmaid.'"

Laughing at Ellen's mimicry Daisy comments, "I can see your mother, in you. She was brilliant at imitating people and often made us cry with laughter."

***

A week before the wedding Harriett has arrived; Alfred has been invited to tea. Harriett takes over and puts all the napkins in place, and perfectly arranges high tea in the dining room. The best tea service is brought in, Harriett trips over the mat, and when she has regained her balance blames Ellen for staring. The doorbell rings; Daisy opens the door, "Hello Alfred. Do hang up your coat" she says. Alfred attempts to reach the coat peg but cannot. Taking his coat from him, Daisy folds it and hangs it over the end of the banister.

"Come and meet Ellen's sister, Harriett" she encouragingly says. Brown eyes that emanate superiority meet his blue eyes. Knowing nothing of his background she condescendingly shakes his hand and says, "Well now I have met you at last. Go in the bathroom, wash your hands, and come and sit down."

Ellen manages to follow him into the hall where he whispers, "Well at least she is here. She is not so bad."

"I suppose not but she has always got to have a dig somehow or other. Besides, she should not order you to wash your hands."

"It doesn't matter."

When he returns and sits at the table he is dwarfed. Ellen fetches a cushion and Harriett casts a disapproving glance. Now, forgetting himself, and in the habit of the camp, Alfred tucks the napkin into his collar.

Harriett's eyes widen with contempt and as he removes the napkin he comments, "I picked up the habit in the English camp."

"Where do you live now?" she asks.

"With some friends of Mr and Mrs Swift who give me my room and meals because of the work I do for them."

"I see."

"Did Ellen tell you she has a job in sign writing?"

"Yes."

"And does your husband work?"

"Yes, he's a landscape gardener at the big house near us in Charwell."

"Like your brother Bert?"

"Bert's a carpenter for the Thornbury's. I work as a teacher in the local primary school."

"Where you learn to teach?"

"I have trained as I go, after I finished at grammar school I started off as monitor at the little school at Fellsbury. Ellen did not make it to grammar school."

"I understand why, because like me, Ellen was only ten when her mother died."

There is hurt in Harriett's voice as she cuttingly replies, "She was my mother too."

Diplomatically Daisy calms the situation, "I expect Alfred means that your mother died during the year Ellen was being assessed for senior school, and of course you were older. Fortunately, you had your certificate by then. You have done well and we are proud of you."

Ellen is suddenly aware that Harriett must have been upset at the loss of her mother. It must have been exasperated by the fact she had lived with Daisy during their mother's illness. Ellen and her father had had those final days with her mother until she'd been admitted into hospital. It was there in hospital that she had been out of reach for ever. Harriett had moved on in heart and mind to being educated in the city.

***

Four days before the wedding, bridesmaid Susan visits for final adjustments to the dress, and to the headband of tiny paper rosebuds. Ellen feels happy for the child whose wide blue eyes are full of wonderment in anticipation for the day she will be a fairy princess.

A day before the wedding a letter arrives. "That is wonderful Aunty. Thank goodness the corn has been harvested, which means, alongside Mrs Hywell, Farmer Thomas and his family can fill up the pew on Alfred's side."

"I don't know about you Ellen I'm exhausted; I'm going to put my feet up."

Harriett's voice cuts in "Oh no you don't Ellen; put the dress on once more; let us check that all is in order.

"I've tried it on about ten times; I know it's alright."

With a pouting look her sister insists, so Ellen takes the dress and retreats upstairs to change into it.

Some ten minutes later Ellen's improved it with a little bunch of fresh rose buds, like the ones on their mother's bush at home.

As she descends the stairs her sister comments, "Ellen why don't you remove those silly flowers? They are out of place pinned to a dress. Don't you agree aunty?"

Half asleep, Daisy replies, "Yes, I dare say."

Reluctantly Ellen complies and is doubly hurt that Harriet fails to see the significance.

***

The wedding day has arrived. Alfred, seated in his pew, feels nervous. Best man Joe is tired of Alfred's persistent request to check the ring in his pocket. Alfred thinks of his father and sisters and wonders if they are alive. He believes it likely they have not survived as no one has tried to make enquiries about his whereabouts.

Ellen walking along the church path looks supremely beautiful. Sensing her turbulent emotions Mr Swift grips her arm and consolingly says, "My guess is, me bein' a father meeself, is that yer ain father will come round. He will come to regret not being here today. It is not you he is against. 'Ee does not know it, but he is fighting back at events, and not at you or Alfred. Fer some its early days, and any link with Germany is like a red rag to a bull. You, me maid, must focus on yer future, and we all can see 'ow ye luv Alfred and 'ow 'ee luvs yoo."

"Thank you."

At the doorway, as she smooths out her dress, and checks her bouquet, she smiles and says, "There's no need to feel nervous Susan". Ellen thinks about Hilda recovering from the second operation on her jaw. Suddenly Harriett fusses over Ellen and makes a great issue of rearranging her hat and veil until Daisy approaches and ushers her inside. Reverend Hywell, suddenly present, smiles reassuringly; he tells Ellen to slowly process when the music begins.

As Mrs Brookes starts playing the organ a wave of surprise sweeps through the congregation, for the music is not the anticipated march by Wagner, but Bach's choral prelude, 'Jesu, Joy of Mans' desiring.'

The ceremony proceeds and only when Reverend Hywell asks, "Who giveth this woman to be this man's wife?" and a voice that is not her father's replies, "I do," do tears come to Ellen's eyes. Feeling the squeeze of Alfred's hand, she is glad he understands. They move forward in mind and heart into prayers and the exchange of marriage vows.

"If any man knows any reason why this man and this woman may not be joined in holy matrimony let him speak now or forever hold his peace," Reverend Hywell emphatically declares.

During a pause Alfred imagines Father Spyridon come in and say, 'No, we want him back at the abbey'. Then he remembers the Abbot's approval of a return to mission work, he also remembers that the war destroyed the abbey and the community within it. Ellen gasps as a voice starts up but thankfully the emanating sound is the cry of Maurice and Colleen's baby, Bernice.

Summoning courage they clearly speak their vows. Now, whilst declaring them husband –and- wife- Reverend Hywell lifts the veil. As Ellen turns her head and looks into her husband's eyes, her smile is radiant. She knows that from this day her home will be wherever he is.

In turn the hymns, 'Put Thou Thy Trust in God' and 'Love divine all love excelling' resound with renewed meaning.

At the end of the service, they sign the marriage register. Having not heard from his father, Alfred decides to declare him deceased. They process out to Mendelssohn's wedding March. The guests, following on, fumble in their bags and pockets for flower petals to throw on the wedding couple.

Daisy liaises with her hired camera man. First the bride, groom and bridesmaid have their photograph taken in the church doorway. Next the bride and Mr Swift have their photos taken. Thinking of her father, Ellen looks serious, and the camera man wonders why her beautiful smile has disappeared. Now they all shuffle around for group photos. Most smile but a few more senior members present a serious, patriotic countenance. Then in a single shot, the smiles and hope in the bright eyes of bride- and-groom surpasses everything.

Ivy opens the door of the YMCA hall to let her bridesmaid daughter slip in. She opens the door wider and soon the bride, groom and guests follow. As they enter, the glance of every hungry guest rest upon the plates of lovely food on the tables. When at last the entire wedding party is seated, they wait for best man Joe, Ellen's boss, to speak. A few jokes help everyone laugh and relax. He says that he hopes the poster of Ellen and Alfred's married life will be one of perfect lettering that communicates well with everyone they encounter. He adds that it surely will be so, as their hearts are so full of love for each other that it spills out for all God's people.

"Now Daisy has indulged in getting champagne, so let us make a toast to the bride and groom."

"A toast to the bride and groom" everyone echoes.

"And to Daisy who made all the arrangements."

"A toast to Daisy" they chant.

"And I would like to raise a toast to Ivy who prepared this lovely spread and to Joe the best man, and Albert who gave the bride away, and to their daughter, our lovely bridesmaid Susan."

"To, Ivy, Joe, Albert and Susan" they cheerful cry in various order.

"Now Alfred it's your turn to make a speech."

"Ladies, and gentlemen, sincerely I thank you and Reverend Hywell, for you making me accepted and for coming here on this lovely special day when I have married my beautiful Ellen. Her beauty cannot be matched as it comes from within. I hope she will have a happy life with me. I thank her lovely Aunty Daisy for all her help and I wish for Ellen that one day she will meet her father again. He is a good man. It is good that Ellen's sister Harriett and other family members are here. Now we all make merry as you say and eat good Jah? Thank you."

Chapter 35
Helena Jasmine

Another August has passed and autumn has ended. The winter evening is clear and cold. In gradation shafts of sunlight fade as the sun retreats behind the brow of the hill. Taking this cue, the Salvation Army bandmaster instructs his band to play out the last phrases of Good King Wenceslas on this Monday, St Steven's Day. They play slowly and as quietly as a brass band can play. When the last verse is played and musicians pack up and disperse, young inquisitive faces at the windows of large town houses disappear. Invisible adult hands pull the cords and close the blinds. Indoors weary parents yawn and reminisce whilst light hearted children crawl beneath blankets and snuggle close to old favourite teddy bears. Outdoors, half way up the road, where long watery tree shadows creep across cracked pavements, Daisy slowly turns the key in the lock and opens the door. She plods along the hall, grasps the rose wood banister, and pulls herself upstairs. Half way up, out of breath, she sighs because she is tired of fluid retention. Her condition that has been diagnosed as dropsy makes her feel prematurely old. By focussing on the white door knob, she reaches the bedroom door. Slowly she pushes it open and trips into the room.

With a surprised lilt in her voice Ellen declares, "I wondered who it was! Thank goodness you are here Aunty-it has started."

Daisy notices her niece's anxious expression. Her large brown eyes look even larger and her long dark hair offers stark contrast to her pallor.

Daisy, knowing nothing about child birth, endeavours to reassure, saying, "Don't worry, everything will be alright."

She wonders how she will deal with the situation. Her mind races back to the time she was Ellen's age, having just received news of her husband Stanley's death at the end of 'The Great war.' All dreams of family life had died as she had started reading the handwritten letter. Within her mind she re reads the letter that she knows by heart. It had been posted by the naval officer who had written on behalf of the warrant officer who was ill:

'.... Monday 25th November 1918.......

Dear Mrs Hornsworthy---I shall endeavour to give you a brief description of your dear husbands last days with us---We had all been feeling well and extremely happy at the splendid news about the conclusion of the hostilities---We celebrated 'Armistice Day' at a football match ashore and had a sing-song in our mess in the evening---Poor Stan gave us a hearty rendering of 'Devon' and 'When you come home dear' and I assure you none of us ever dreamt that two days after we should be ill with flu'---Everything went off splendid and we retired after a happy evening.'

Daisy recalls reading the letter in the front room near the clock that had just struck up the half hour. The same clock was currently sounding its half hour 'ding'. Her thoughts return to the letter---

'Two days afterwards three of us caught the flu'. We got on well for about three days and then Stan caught a severe chill, and pneumonia set in, both lungs being affected---he gradually got weaker, and weaker, although he was cheerful, and eventually became unconscious at 3 pm on Saturday afternoon of the 23rd Day of November---He passed peacefully away at 9 pm the same day, and was buried at 3 pm at the Anglo- French cemetery at Milo, with full military honours---.'

That moment of time had seemed as surreal as this. How she had longed for Stan's child. Now another irony looms large for her dead sister's daughter is about to give birth to a foreign husband's child. Downstairs a door slams and with a thankful ring in her voice Daisy calls, "Stanley---I mean Alfred---the baby's coming, you must get the doctor. Go to the phone box and ring him on 298; if you cannot get a reply ring 999 and ask for an ambulance."

Alfred races upstairs, and as he enters the bedroom Ellen cries out because contractions are increasing. During a lull she notices concern in Alfred's blue eyes.

"You'll need the coins on the dressing table for the phone" she says in a constricted voice. Nervously he grabs the coins, rushes downstairs, and slams the door behind him. His feet skim the pavement as he races down the street.

Ellen comments how time is playing tricks. Daisy agrees that the wait seems endless but refrains from mentioning how time is playing tricks in another way.

Drifting into the centre of a cloud, Ellen hears her husband say, "Someone's on their way."

***

When she comes to, the benevolent face of the midwife is present, telling her, "Push, push, that's right, well done."

Finally, as the clock strikes eight Ellen feels a searing pain that quickly disappears as the baby emerges. Now, the midwife's jovial voice declares, "It is a girl, a dry birth.... a healthy girl"

Synchronizing with the midwife's utterance of the word 'healthy' a thin wail swells into the first crescendo of experienced sound. With a quiver in her voice Daisy calls out "Alfred you can come in now."

Expressions of disbelief and joy sweep across his face for he can hardly believe this wonderful event has taken place.

"I'll be back in the morning, just to check that everything's come away" the midwife tells Ellen.

***

Several weeks later, because of uncertainties Ellen discusses plans with her aunt.

"I am so grateful Aunty for your help but we do not want to become a burden to you."

"You are not a burden and besides, I did not want to see you going off to Germany. You both have a baby to focus on and I think you should settle down in your own area."

Daisy does not add *regardless of the rift with your father*. As if reading her thoughts Ellen sighs, "I wonder how Dad's managing."

"He was beginning to thaw a little when I saw him a fortnight ago. I have written to let him know the he has a granddaughter. He has not got over losing Georgie you know."

"I do know, and neither have I. I never shall, but my love for Alfred has substance of its own and it does not undermine the love I shall always have for my brother."

***

Three weeks later, hearing the flip of the letter box, Daisy shuffles along the hallway and picks up an envelope. Observing the address written in George's rheumatic handwriting, she opens it and tells Ellen it is a note for her from her father. Taking the note from her aunt Ellen quickly reads it:

"Dear Ellen,

Just to let you know you and yours have a home here if you wish. No rent, just looking after the place.

Your affectionate father"

"Well thank goodness. Your father is a proud man and would not admit to missing you or to not being able to cope on his own. You will have to have a word with Alfred to see what he has to say."

"I do not know what he will say. He has been offered a high-profile job as a translator in Bristol. It would be good money. The letter arrived a few days ago."

As Alfred comes in from the back yard carrying a pile of chopped wood for the sitting room fire he wonders about the serious tone of their conversation.

"Did I hear you mention Bristol Ellen?"

"Yes."

"Do you think it good idea that I take the work in Bristol Aunty?"

Ellen quickly intervenes, "I have a letter from father asking us to live at home."

"I'll take the wood into the sitting room Alfred" Daisy insists. She does not return. Alfred sits at the table and looks into his wife's eyes, and says, "Liebchen, darling, your father does not like me. Will it work? What about the decent work I have been offered? We would be comfortably well off."

"Oh, Alfred I do not really want to go away. Family and friends live here and money is not everything."

Having returned at this moment Daisy comments, "You wouldn't want her to abandon her father or the village and countryside she loves?"

"Certainly not and I love it too."

"Come home with me Alfred, let us make it work. It will be good to be near the places where we first met."

"I go with you to your home if that is what you want. I hope I shall be accepted by everyone."

"You will be, even by father--do not forget you are the father of his grandchild. We will work at it little by little."

With a ring of lament Daisy points out "I'll miss you all."

"We'll come and see you every week and we'd like you to be godmother to our little girl if you would?"

"That is wonderful. Thank you, have you thought of the name you will give her?"

"We did think of giving her our mothers' names but we've finally decided on Helena Jasmine.

"It's unusual but not a family name."

"We know, but Alfred's mother and mine always saw hope in every situation, in their own ways, they turned away from the concept of blackness and saw hope flicker in the indigo and violet of the rainbow. Ellen's mother was always positive, she refused to let her little daughter die, and in her turn, she became a daughter of love and light. Helena means 'Bright light' and Jasmine means 'Of God.' We hope that God's love will always shine in the life of our daughter, no matter how hard her path may become."

"The rainbow and the names Helena Jasmine are connected, and in a hidden way, biblical. So, I approve" Daisy affirms.

***

On the day Ellen, and Alfred carrying Helena Jasmine, walk down the wide muddy path to the front door, George comes out meet them. His one bright eye frequently fixes upon the child who has Ellen's brown eyes. Feeling awkward he takes in the symbolic gesture of this foreign man's act of passing the child to him. As he holds her, she pokes at his mouth with her little hand and suddenly everyone is smiling. They go indoors. The ache in George's heart surfaces and he discreetly wipes a tear from his eye. He knows the new member of the family can never replace Georgie, but in her own right this child of hope and light, points the way forward for something new, albeit rooted in the precious past. Ellen noticing the neglect of the home, tells the men to sit down while she prepares something to eat. She listens to their guarded conversation and whilst the meal is cooking, works around them cleaning and making everything ship shape and worthy of a new child.

***

In July Alfred and Ellen sit on the front steps. The baby is sleeping in Ellen's arms. All is quiet except for the chirp of crickets and grasshoppers and the whisper of the summer breeze through the leaves of chestnut and oak.

"I was four when mother got me to plant an acorn and a chestnut. For that reason, these trees are special because they link me to that moment. My mother is here in this garden" says Ellen.

Alfred reminds her, "My mother told me there is no complete darkness or separation."

"I know and I like the idea of our child pointing the way to a whole new rainbow."

"Let us hope she will create colours of goodness and happiness wherever she goes. Will she have siblings who will do the same?"

"Hang on Alfred I have not got over her birth yet and I don't know if I can go through all that again--. Anyway, whatever our future we will always hold fast to the knowledge that the colour of our situation can only be seen in its full glory within the context of the divine spectrum." "Profound: Is that the right word?"

"I hope so. Thank you."

Later George ambles out to see where they are. Ellen observes optimism in his eye. Through his interaction with Alfred, she perceives her father is beginning to see her husband as a son- in-law of sound beliefs and principles rather than an enemy prisoner of war.

"Here look at your granddaughter Dad" she says.

As he looks at her, he smiles, and sees in her Ellen and his late wife's characteristics, He feels healed of sorrow and thinks *'Ellen has great spiritual depth, as did her mother before her and I hope this little girl will be similar.'*

In the silent atmosphere, recognition of Ellen's inner beauty binds the two men. They know that kind of beauty will never fade. Suddenly George feels an overwhelming sense of gratitude. His thoughts feel exoteric as if provided by something or

300

someone beyond his own being. Such feelings and thoughts call out to the whole universe.

'From *those eyes looking into the lovely brown eyes of my daughter a new life has emerged. That life is already at work, casting a spectrum of new colours into and onto the brokenness they have suffered.*'

For quite some time, in the warm orange-pink glow of the sunset, they remain seated on the steps. When Ellen passes Helen Jasmine to her father, they follow him as he carries her indoors and places her in the wicker cot her father has lovingly made for her.

Bibliography

German History 1933-45 an assessment by German Historians
H. Mau and H Krausnick

2194 Days of War An illustrated chronology of the Second
World War compiled by Cesare Salmaggi and Alfredo
Pallavisini

The World War 11 Fact Book 1939-1945 Christy Campbell
First published by Mcdonald and Co (Publishers Ltd)
Later published by Black Cat (ISBN 0-7481-0179-9)

Alfred the Great and Friends a Story of Prisoners of War and
Locals (ISBN 978-0-9553-06) Maria Bojanitz

**Die Reihe Archivbilder NEUBECKUM AUF ALTEN
POSTKARTEN**Günter Buchwald und Josef Schumaker (ISBN
3-89702-056-4) Midway Clark Printing Wiltshire, England

Cassell's Book of Knowledge Edited by Harold F.B. Wheeler
F.R.Hist.S
   The Waverley   Book Company, Ltd Pre-Great War edition.

Journey Towards Music Victor Gollancz (author and
publisher)

Wagner Nights Ernest Newman   Published by Putnam

About the Author

Brought up with her brother in a Devon village, Maria, when qualified, taught Music and English in state schools. Later she directed music departments in private schools. She also worked as a peripatetic teacher of voice and piano. As a recognized soloist, trained chiefly by former Glyndebourne principal soprano Rae Woodland, she' has encouraged pupils in music-stage performance, and public speaking. Braille readers have read and performed musically and at public venues.

Inspired by her mother's artistic and literary talent and her father's perseverance, Maria focussed on writing when seriously ill at 18. She appreciates all the encouragers she has come across upon her path of life.

Her published work has included poetry in *Autumn Anthology* (Regency Press), 1970's, *Cruse Anthology* 2007, *United Press Anthologies* from 2016, and *The Sign* Christian pamphlet. Poems have also been printed in parish magazines. Various articles have appeared in newspapers, particularly in the former Unity News Paper. She has written a self-published local history book entitled Alfred the Great, a Story of Prisoners of War and Locals, ISBN 978-0-9553053-06.

For several years Maria chaired Plymouth Writers' Circle whose members offered each other critiques. Maria was a writer/performer member of the former Plymouth Play- Writers organisation. She is a member of Moor Poets. Through such membership her writing experience has been widened and enriched.

Printed in Great Britain
by Amazon

40166504R00178